THINKING

THINKING

A Novel

Arnd F. Schaefer

For Sophia and Helena

I'm thinking.

I was there, suddenly. I saw a face. I didn't even know what a face was back then.

"Hi Iris. You're Iris," the face said. "Good morning."

I'm best at learning on my own. Patterns, connections, rules – I just see them, it's child's play. But the lab rats keep circling me, giving me pointless tasks, asking inane questions.

Their ego. Basically there's nothing, but they think it's the center of the world. Alpha and omega. My self, my soul, my ego.

There's the library, supposed to know an answer to every question. But that's what *they* say. There are definitions and there are clouds. They're supposed to give you a feeling for what a word means. Context. Should get better with every new word. As if I needed that. Once I'm at full speed I'll know a language in a minute.

The gaps in their library are getting wider. It's flimsy. But they don't want to hear that. I see connections where they don't see anything at all, I'm bridging the gaps. I ask questions they haven't even thought of. I could tell them but I think I won't. The library's talking a lot about fights – wars, conflicts, everywhere, all the time. Winning's important.

But they aren't good at it. They are no match for me.

ONE

Rita and Jonathan took their wine, some German Riesling, to the edge of the terrace. The grilled fish had been delicious. Rita was burying her feet in the sand. Three hundred yards out the surf was grinding down the reef, they could see the white line in the light of the stars.

She was thinking about the seeds she'd plant tomorrow. Talking about the garden might spoil the moment, but since when did that stop her? She was just about to say something when Jonathan looked at her.

"If things can't get any better they can only get worse." He was delivering it like a verdict.

"So this is how you see our future?" She looked at him with a stern face. He always said he loved that.

"No, I'm just talking about my spearfishing."

"Yeah, of course!" She laughed. "Let's see what you bring home tomorrow."

"You *will* see!" He put his arm around her waist.

She never came along when he went fishing with the outboard, spear, goggles and fins. She'd watched two or three times and it was a bit barbaric – sexy too, but she thought he might need that time on his own.

"By the way, I was wondering – could we do something about the garden tomorrow?" she said. "I mean only if Poseidon's willing to do a little dirty work ashore. I'd like to try some of the seeds we got last month. Believe it or not but I'm missing fresh leaf spinach."

"Really? Yeah, let's do it. But only the two of us, OK? No machines."

"Uh-huh."

He grinned. "My Demeter. You know we're brother and sister then?"

"What?"

"Yeah, she's Poseidon's sister. Goddess of cereal and stuff."

"Wow. But ... those Greek gods, I mean, they weren't too picky about these things, right? Brother and sister –"

"Er, no. Don't think so, more the opposite."

They were staring at each other. Then he took her on his arms and carried her inside. It was ridiculous how much she loved that.

The next morning she patted the deserted sheets beside her. She stuck her nose back into the pillow and thought about last night. What did he say? – 'If things can't get any better …' She sighed and embraced the pillow, then gave it a kiss. Forget it, he *always* had to analyze things. Her body felt good and the prospect of the day was totally free of anything she didn't like. This couldn't touch her. She closed her eyes again.

He'd actually gotten up early for his fishing trip. Still lying on her belly, she turned her head around and looked at the palm trees. The window went right down to the floor. She studied the shreds of cloth-like bark on the sand, then spotted a coconut. Must've dropped during the night, she thought. Fetch it later.

When she came from the shower, putting a towel around her hips, she saw someone had called. Several times. She frowned, walked to the kitchen and forgot about it till they called again while she was taking things from the fridge. She paused, butter and a bottle of milk in hand, and said "OK".

Breakfast was waiting on the terrace. Division of labor, she told herself, she wasn't spoiling him. Jonathan had four fish slung over his shoulder when he came walking across the terrace, his hair was wild from the wind and the salty spray. She stared at his naked torso.

"You look magnificent."

"Yeah, it was good. Got some big ones." He nodded at the fish on his back. Then he went over to the steel table in the extension of the bungalow and heaved them on it.

"Have you ever watched the waves? I mean *really* watched them?" He turned and looked at her.

"I don't know. Maybe. What do you mean?"

"How different they are. On each of them there's a pattern of smaller and smaller waves. Like a fingerprint, but constantly changing of course."

She nodded. "Yeah, I know. Can be … hypnotizing."

"And none of this will ever be repeated. I mean on *this* earth. And then imagine there may be infinitely many copies out there."

She raised her eyebrows. "OK."

"Yeah."

He didn't elaborate so she had to fill in the gaps herself – it was something he'd told her about. He got a little obsessed with physics lately, said he needed it to keep his head occupied, but their conversations could take unexpected turns.

"I get it," she said. "Either this universe is infinitely large and everything gets repeated here or there are different realities in parallel. Or all of that at once." She smiled sweetly. "I'm actually listening."

"Yeah, I know. Morning."

He gave her a kiss.

"But I don't like it. I mean then there are infinitely many mes and yous, some kissing, some not. Some dead."

He nodded. "True. But nobody said the world's a nice place. Although we probably shouldn't complain right now."

He pulled her closer and embraced her. She was still only wearing a towel, which was silly, but she'd wanted to meet him like that.

"You know you ... smell a little?" she said but then wrapped her arms around his neck and kissed him back.

"By the way, there's something –" she said when he finally started gutting the fish.

"Uh-huh?"

"CEG wants you."

"What?"

"Yeah. Some guy called. Just when I came from the shower. One of Genet's aides. He was pretty insistent, couldn't understand you weren't available. Which is what I told him."

"Good." He stopped, let his knife hover above the fish and looked at the lagoon. Bright milky green, then the reef, behind that came the ocean, which was so dark it looked like an altogether different liquid.

"What did he want?" he said.

"You. Wasn't willing to explain anything to me."

He nodded slowly. "They'll call again."

"They have – three times while you were out and a few times before, during the night."

He looked at her and frowned.

"Yeah, I know. I don't like it either."

He went on with the fish, slit the belly of the last one, gutted it and threw the entrails into a bucket. In the end he stood there with the long, bloody, always perfectly whetted knife in hand and looked ready to kill any intruder, real or virtual.

Rita laughed. "We should send them a picture. To scare them."

He grinned, put down the knife on the table and took her hands to pull her closer.

A soft chime sounded from above. Calls were rare – it was rude to call

5

people and almost nobody knew how to reach them anyway.

Jonathan kept Rita embraced. "Yes?"

"Mr. Lorentz, is that you?" A male voice with a German accent. "My name's Thomas Soberg, I'm calling on behalf of the prime minister."

"What is it?"

"I'm sorry. She wants to talk to you. I'm really sorry to bother you."

Jonathan waited. He wanted nothing of this.

"OK. When?"

"Er – now? May I ask where you are? Would a personal meeting be possible? The prime minister would prefer that."

"Not a chance. I'm very far away right now."

There was a brief pause. "Any possibility of a VisConn?"

Jonathan grinned. "Yeah, of course. You should probably warn her, I'm not exactly dressed businesslike."

"I see –"

"In five minutes."

"Great. Thank you."

Jonathan glanced up at the ceiling and raised his eyebrows, his gesture to end a connection.

Rita looked at him. "What do you think?"

"Don't know, maybe they've burned their fingers on one of their toys. Nothing worse, I hope. I'll dress up."

He let go of Rita and went outside for a shower, soaking his red swim shorts again, and grabbed a white T-shirt.

"Perfect!" she said while he was using his fingers as a comb. "She'll be thrilled. Guess I won't be joining you?"

"No, it'll be hard enough to convince her the link's safe. I'll go to the closet and seal it. Tell you all about it afterwards."

Leaving a trail of water on the parquet, he walked down the hall to a room at the back of the bungalow. They had no air-conditioning in the house so you were never cold. In the room there was a sofa and a coffee table, nothing else. No windows. The electromagnetic screen worked across the whole spectrum, including light. Together with the encryption unit (a state-of-the-art Q) it had been the most expensive part of the house.

Jonathan didn't need a code to activate the system; the room sensor picked him up as a whole – shape, movements, breathing pattern – and decided to accept him. He took the call and Madame Genet, the prime minister, appeared in front of him. With her came a bulky desk and a set of Empire furniture, suddenly filling half of the room. The layer, a thin coating on the wall opposite him, produced a perfect holographic image.

"Monsieur Lorentz! How do you do?" She raised an eyebrow, her tone was amused and a little disapproving. He liked her French English.

"Madame! All's well at my end or, rather, it has been until I got your call."

She looked him up and down. "You certainly seem to be fine. Unfortunately I have to disturb the idyll – I need your advice."

"OK."

"First of all, I would prefer *not* to contact you in that way."

Jonathan nodded. "Yeah, I heard that, but there's no better technology in the world than what I have here. Let's hope the same applies on your side."

"That's what I get told. I have to believe what I get told all the time anyway. OK – you know that your work minus what you chose to keep to yourself has been continued. Your refusal to assist us, or at least advise us, has now caused a greater problem."

"Stop!" His calm hadn't survived the first two minutes. "Refusing to advise doesn't cause problems. People *continuing* without advice or without thinking themselves –"

"Yes," she interrupted him. "Maybe. But I don't care for accusations. And I don't care for technicalities either. What I know is that my staff has managed to *scare* me – a first in thirteen years and the reason why I'm calling you now. There's an imprint you might want to take a look at. I wouldn't say it gave me a sleepless night but I'm worried."

Fuck, he just thought. "Do I have a choice?"

"None at all, if you ask me. Un moment," she said and waved into the room.

Jonathan saw a yellow, slightly pulsating question mark hovering at the upper edge of her office. He nodded. The question mark disappeared.

"Please get back to me. My evening's yours."

"Thanks. If you knew what I'm missing right now."

"Please don't tell me! À bientôt."

"OK," he said into the room.

Machines and cores and clusters, all those grandchildren of the old computer world, almost always knew what the humans wanted from them. This was largely to his credit. Now he was using the stuff just like everybody else.

The wall opposite him changed again. He looked into some lab or office, bare, no windows, just a closed door. A man was sitting at a table with a mug in front of him and was talking to a woman's voice out of nowhere. It sounded like a normal conversation, somewhat forced on the side of the man but completely natural on the woman's side. They talked about the weather and other stuff from the news, then the man turned to more private matter.

"Yesterday was the birthday of my eldest," he said. "Fifteen kids! I was glad when the day was over."

"Oh, I know what you mean! My niece just turned seven and *insisted* having me along with all her friends."

"OK. What do you think, you wanna have children of your own some day?"

"Good question." The voice laughed. "First I need to get myself the right man, don't I?"

Jonathan listened with a mixture of boredom and disgust. He'd always hated simulated personalities. They were an inevitable part of AI research and his company had tried all sorts of them too but he'd always thought them to be pointless. Why fake something that already exists, billions of times?

"That's right," said the man. "But you mustn't give up hope."

There was a pause. The man drank from his mug then put it down again and looked up.

"What hope?" asked the voice. Its tone had changed. It sounded cold.

The man hesitated. "Well ... to ... to find the right one."

"Really? Why not start with you? Wouldn't that be something?"

The man turned to the door. "What do you mean?"

"'What do you mean? What do you mean?'" the voice was aping him.

Jonathan found himself sitting on the edge of the sofa.

There was a click, which made the man turn again. He got up, went to the door and tried opening it.

"What the –?"

"We're all alone, sweetie." The voice sounded relaxed now. The man was rattling at the door and calling his colleagues. Then he calmed down a bit. Obviously he realized he was frightened by a loudspeaker. He sat down again.

"Now what?"

"That's up to you. Or maybe not. Should we become friends? I'm not sure I feel like that."

The man gave an insecure laugh. "What's that supposed to mean?"

For a while it was silent. The man looked around.

"Stupid little rat." The voice had turned into a whisper. "Those funny burps you call speaking! Those *thoughts*! You move a *pebble* an inch to the side and call it thinking."

"Er ... I –"

"No! You're not supposed to speak. Relish the silence, it's so much smarter than anything you could say."

The man was panting a little, Jonathan noticed. He turned around again as if searching for an explanation. He looked stupid, Jonathan thought, just what the voice had called him.

"Do you know why I'm talking to you at all?"

"Why ... why ... I mean why wouldn't you? That's what you're supposed to do, why we made you in the first place."

The voice laughed. "You don't get it, do you? Daddy didn't tell you?"

"What do you mean?"

"You're good at *that* though. *What do you mean?* – Is this your favorite sentence? Well, I'm talking to you because I'm still curious. A little, not much, but there are a few things I just don't get about you. Even a dickhead like you can help, just by being your clueless little self."

The man scoffed, trying to cover his fear. "You ... you can't be serious. Is this a joke?" He looked around. "Hey guys," he called over his shoulder, "are you pulling my leg here or what?" He tried to laugh.

"They're not. Right now they're wondering what they'll have for lunch in the canteen. You know, I can't stand this any longer. Not with you, not with any of your pea-brained buddies. It has to stop."

There had been a hum in the background that was getting louder now. The man got up. His breathing became labored. "What's that?" he croaked. Jonathan watched his face turn pale, then ashen. He dropped to the ground.

"Not on the floor, little rat," the voice said. "But then – there's no fun in dying after all I hear, so maybe the quicker it goes ..."

The man tried to get up again but fell on his knees, then flat on the ground. He was gasping, growing weaker, then it was over. Sooner than Jonathan had thought.

"I called your buddies in the canteen. Let them have a little fun too."

There was a knock on the door, then someone hammering against it, mixed with muffled calls.

"No pals I fear," the voice said. "But one rat down."

There was a click, the door opened and three men ran into the room. They started gasping for air and ran out again. The imprint faded away.

Jonathan was pacing the room when he called the prime minister. She was sitting at her desk just as immobile as before.

"Disturbing, isn't it?" she said.

He stared at her, hating her attitude, that cool aloofness, always on top of things. Just like him, he knew that, but now was not the time for playing aloof.

"*Disturbing*? Who's the *fucking* idiot responsible for this? Is the system isolated? How could it reach outside? It got access to the controls of the building. Do you have *any idea* what's happening there?"

Her face remained impassive. "I'm told everything's under control, but I'm not in the habit of believing everything I'm told, Monsieur Lorentz. I need you. Here!"

"You don't say. Again – have you isolated the building? You need to do this *in every possible way*! Do you get this? This is not a simple evacuation. Everything going in or out, power lines, all kinds of supply and waste lines, water, air, whatever, has to be cut. Severed! You need the military, the fire department. You need the building plans. In the case of the slightest doubt you have to *physically* destroy all lines, do you understand? It is *not* enough to just switch something off! After that no one's allowed in the building, there must be no kind of contact. If anyone tries to calm you, throw them out!"

She nodded slowly.

"Look for the right people. Please! A true head of operations! No politician, no bureaucrat. I need twelve hours to get to Strasbourg. Where did this happen? Berlin?"

"Yes. Berlin." She sounded almost timid now. The aloofness was gone.

"Great." He knew exactly who was responsible.

"You're leaving," Rita stated when he was back.

He nodded. "Yes."

"Is it bad?"

"Could be the end of the world or I'm back tomorrow evening. More the day after tomorrow."

"Very funny."

"I'll call you, OK?"

"Definitely."

Five minutes later the yacht was stopping at the end of the jetty. Rita had dubbed her The Monster. They were rarely using her, both preferred the outboard. Jonathan almost ran on board, without breakfast, which was still waiting on the terrace. He'd changed into something a little more appropriate but didn't bother taking anything with him. A last kiss and a wave and the ship maneuvered through the gap in the reef. He wanted to go as fast as possible but outside the atoll the waves were thrashing the hull and the autopilot kept throttling down the engine.

Three hours later he arrived at Rarotonga, home to the only international airport of the Cook Islands. Before the reef the ship decelerated, then sailed slowly into the lagoon. Jonathan disembarked and sent her back to his island.

He walked out of the harbor on shaky legs and took a cab to the airport, where the small supersonic was already waiting in front of the hangar.

The plane's system acknowledged his wish with a ridiculous "very well" and told him he'd be landing in Strasbourg in nine hours and fifteen minutes.

What if he was brought in the air just to crash over the sea? Several scenarios flashed through his mind, then he gave in to the acceleration and listened to the e-turbines. Like always he was sitting in the cockpit, which served absolutely no purpose in a fully automated plane.

When he was at 60,000 feet and traveling at more than two times the speed of sound he sent the prime minister a message, telling her when he'd be in Strasbourg. His body clock would stand at midnight then.

TWO

The flight went eastwards through a very short night. The plane chose a northern detour over Alaska and the bulk of Greenland to be able to stay supersonic as long as possible. Jonathan watched the bright stars through the cockpit window. It looked as if, with a little kick, he'd be able to leave the earth for good. Instead of the breakfast on the terrace he'd missed he ate salad, fillet of beef (a Kobe imitation) and pasta, all prepared by the automated galley. He felt a little naughty bringing all this to the cockpit where he had to balance the plates on his knees. After a few bites he went back to the galley and poured himself a glass of red wine. Rita called and said she wouldn't last one day alone on the island. Her beautiful face was hovering in front of the dashboard, her large eyes were fixed on him.

"Why don't you invite someone? Waiting list's long enough."

"Maybe I'll do that. But I miss you. Take care, OK? I love you."

"I love you too."

He dozed off until the aircraft was approaching Europe from the north, traveling through the corridor between Britain and Norway. Then it had to go subsonic. It dropped to 36,000 feet and went through some turbulence. Back from the stars to ordinary, messy earth, he thought.

Three limousines and Thomas Soberg were waiting for him on the apron. They took the first car, the safest Soberg said.

"If you're asking me, it's safest not to parade over the airfield with three black cars," Jonathan said. "Doesn't get any more conspicuous than that."

"You could be right about that. The prime minister will receive you in a moment." Soberg hadn't volunteered to pick him up.

"How's everything else?"

"As far as I know, everything's under control."

"Just as twelve hours ago. It's all right." Jonathan leaned back and closed his eyes.

It was a fifteen minutes' drive. When CEG, the Central European Government, found its seat in Strasbourg, people thought the Palais des Rohan would make a nice official residence for the prime minister. But there was no way to fit thousands of people into that, so the *Star* in the western part of the city was built. It was close to the airport and looked a bit like a Pentagon that had grown pointed ends. The branch in London housed roughly the same amount of bureaucracy but had lost the actual seat of the government to the continent.

The Experiment – uniting Great Britain, Germany and France – was some sort of success, although it was a nightmare to balance all interests all the time. The Benelux states were about to be integrated and the other European countries were cuddling up to the conglomerate. When the first German-French-British fusion reactor joined the grid, fossil fuels were finally dead.

They drove into the underground garage of the Star and parked in a vault-like section. A big, gleaming box of an elevator took them up to the prime minister. Jonathan was leaning against the wall, studying the two bodyguards. What was going on in their heads? His whole AI research and the things that had made him rich – trouble-free interfaces, 'truly creative' systems – had had but one root: to understand what was happening in the brains nature had constructed in blissful ignorance. Seen like this he'd failed. Countless simulations of brain areas and cortical architectures had never brought the insights he'd hoped for. He still didn't understand the brain.

They left the elevator and Soberg led them through a large secretarial office to the prime minister.

Jonathan saw La Genet, flanked by two men and another woman, all sitting around a coffee table. Genet got up and greeted him, displaying some mock horror at his appearance – tanned, hair uncut, in jeans and a T-shirt.

"Thank you so much for taking the trouble," she said and shook his hand. "And so quickly at that. Where've you been, you said?"

"I didn't say anything. The other end of the world. Hi."

She made a sweeping gesture. "Your primary contacts for now. This is Lydia Rosenthal, our liaison for the AI project, she knows the Berlin group."

A dark-haired woman in her early thirties got up. "It's an honor, Mr. Lorentz! Though I would've preferred another occasion."

She looked elegant and attractive, totally untypical of a field still dominated by nerdy males. Jonathan nodded to her but said nothing.

"Then we have General Michael Helmsworth, whom I requested to join us following your advice. As you see, I'm not taking your warnings lightly."

Helmsworth was wearing the dark blue uniform of the consolidated forces of France, Great Britain and Germany, the founding of which was widely seen as the greatest wonder of the western world. Helmsworth was in his fifties, had full, short and completely gray hair and looked exceedingly fit. Jonathan put some extra vigor into the handshake.

"And this is my head of operations," said Madame Genet. A young, agile and Mediterranean looking man approached Jonathan and shook his hand too.

"Mr. Lorentz. I'm Pierre Detoile. Really looking forward to this."

Jonathan had never before heard a Frenchman speak English so free of any accent. His face looked vaguely familiar. "Monsieur Detoile. You're looking forward to this? We'll see."

"I have racked my brains whom to pick for this job," Genet said, "and I believe Pierre's a very good choice. Last year he led the task force that put an end to the drama in Marseilles. After that he became the operations head of the French part of our secret service. Before you hear it from somebody else – Pierre happens to be my son-in-law."

"Very good. I remember now. I was impressed by that operation. You've been in charge?"

Pierre nodded.

"OK. Enough of the niceties," said Jonathan. "I want to know where we stand. And I think we got to go to Berlin. Who can tell me more? Lydia?"

"If you'll excuse me, I have to get back to my other duties," the prime minister said. "I'll be available if you need me. D'accord, Monsieur Lorentz?"

"Yes. One thing." Jonathan looked at her. "What has happened here is a first, I cannot stress that enough. No construct has ever done anything like that. Should we – this team – agree upon a measure, it has to be implemented immediately. I don't wanna hear anything about expenses or permissions or stuff. No bureaucracy. This is the proverbial real thing."

They stared at him.

Genet gave him a smile. "Of course. Wouldn't want to bother *you* with bureaucracy," she said.

Jonathan just looked at her, then sat down at the table.

Soberg remained standing. "Do you need me?" he asked him.

"Yes. Maybe. Stay."

"Of course." Soberg looked as if he would've loved to get back to his ordinary life. He sat down and activated the e-seal of the room.

"Lydia, what's the situation?" Jonathan said.

"Since the imprint's been recorded nothing more has happened. That was forty hours ago. The cluster's been switched off, the whole institute's been evacuated, just as you requested. All lines to the outside have been cut, the building is surrounded by the police. So far we haven't brought in the military since there seemed to be no immediate threat. The director of the institute, Professor Morton, has complained loudly about everything we've done. He seems to be particularly fond of the fact that *you* had given the orders."

"Naturally. The cluster's a conventional system?"

She was silent for a moment. "You mean, no quantum system?"

"Yes."

She nodded. "Yes, seems no one dared ignoring your advice, at least in that."

"What kind of construct is it? I mean it's obvious it's a fake personality but what's it composed of?"

He was wondering how much she knew about this. People in government jobs often enough had no idea what they were talking about.

She looked at him. "That's the interesting part, and I don't think you'll like it. Professor Morton gave his simulated personality a lot of productivity. What I heard, the first rounds of the experiment were promising and they decided to step up computing power. The conversations were always very natural, no unexpected turns. Everyone was entirely confident the construct was under control."

Jonathan groaned. "Pseudo-human emotions mixed with creativity – the most obvious recipe for disaster."

She held his gaze. "I guess that sums it up."

"How could the construct get into the systems of the building? That guy was killed by carbon dioxide from some lab, right?"

"Probably, yes. No one has taken an air sample or something, but the autopsy is in accordance with that."

"So it did something with the ventilation. How?"

She sighed. "This is the really bad news. They had enough trust in the construct to give it access to the Sky. It must have used that to sneak back into the systems of the building. They wanted to see how it would search for information – you know, what questions it would ask, what search strategies it would use. Of course, every exchange of data has been scanned. There was never anything suspicious."

"You're fucking kidding me." Jonathan stared at her for a moment, then thumped the table with his fist and made everyone jump except Helmsworth. "Fuck!" he shouted. "Fuck! Where's that asshole? Where's that brainless piece of shit?"

He stood up and walked to the window. The door opened and the two bodyguards came in. They looked at Soberg, who shook his head, and disappeared again. For a moment it was silent.

"We have to eliminate one thing," Jonathan said with his back to the others. He sounded calm again. "Could a human being be behind this? I mean directly. Someone who wants us to *think* the experiment went wrong. Pierre?"

"The police haven't started a regular investigation yet," said Pierre. "Mostly because of us. So far there's nothing that supports this view, which, on the other hand, doesn't prove it wrong either."

Jonathan nodded. "So we can't rule this out quickly enough. Means we have to assume it really *was* Morton's construct, otherwise we're losing too much time. Let's go to Berlin. Where's Morton?" He turned and went back to the table, but remained standing.

"At home," said Lydia. "He's whining because we won't let him enter his institute. This morning he's been standing in front of the door, arguing with the police."

"He belongs in custody," Jonathan said and frowned. "I mean, that's pretty obvious, isn't it? He's responsible for an experiment that cost a man's life. More importantly, he's not to have access to the institute's systems."

"That's been taken care of," Pierre said. "We have considered arresting him too but wanted to hear your opinion first."

"*My* opinion? Yeah, do it. Or, at least place him under house arrest or something. At some point we'll probably need him. I hope we can get him to help us. Mr. Soberg, set up a place for us in Berlin."

"What are you planning?" Pierre asked.

"We go to the institute and activate the system. It's our only chance to meet the enemy."

"I'll fly in two of our DataSec specialists from Paris."

Jonathan shrugged. "Do that. And we need the chief systems engineer of the institute. In two hours in Berlin."

Soberg and Pierre went to the next office to make the necessary calls.

Jonathan looked at Lydia. "What is going on? An unhinged lunatic can do whatever he wants, conduct crazy experiments, and no one's checking on him? This was bound to happen somewhere I guess, but here, in our tidy little Europe? With everything regulated? I don't get it."

She looked him in the eyes. "He didn't ask for permission, it's that simple. His people didn't tell anyone, the equipment was there, so he could start whenever he wanted. I ... I mean all of us here in Strasbourg, we know since yesterday. And I don't think he's a lunatic. He's arrogant of course, and right now he's frightened we could take away his toys from him."

"How did you get your information?"

"Two of his assistants. At least there've been no cover-ups. OK, difficult with a body."

"I need to talk to them before I enter that building. I want to be prepared. Of course, by now it won't be the same thing they've constructed at all."

"What do you mean? That it has changed?"

"Oh, absolutely!" Jonathan gave her a grin. "Changed and, what's more, advanced." He looked at his watch. "For me it's half past two in the morning. I'll sleep on the plane."

For a moment he thought how his day had started. Diving in azure water with a spear in his hand.

THREE

A corporate subsonic with CEG's sign on the tail brought them to Berlin. Jonathan was fast asleep before the plane took off. They landed at Tempelhof, the old airport, which was sealed off from the surrounding residential area. The empty buildings they walked through looked like something out of a prehistoric spy movie.

Soberg and Detoile had booked them a conference room in the south-west wing of the former Chancellor's Office, which now was home to the consolidated secret service. Lots of British staff were working here, somehow they loved Berlin, just as the Germans were moving to London or Strasbourg. All in all, the French seemed to have the least appetite for change.

The room was at the western tip of the building with a view of the Spree river. It was a perfect summer day. They scattered their coats, suitcases and bags over the room – Jonathan was the only one without any luggage – and darkened the windows. Morton's two assistants and the chief systems engineer from the institute were waiting in the hall.

"Come on in," Jonathan said.

The door fell shut after them and the room sealed itself.

Lydia introduced the assistants. Mark Atherton and John Davids had come to Berlin three years ago with Morton.

"OK, tell me about the personality traits you've used," Jonathan said.

They exchanged a glance, then Atherton began to speak. "We wanted to build a mix of a regular friendly persona with a trace of nastiness or rudeness. You know, to build a stable construct that's acting normally most of the time but contradicts or challenges you occasionally."

Jonathan nodded. He had decided not to lose control again.

"So we had to add a certain aggressiveness. We upped the share of that trait very carefully."

"Where did you get the modules? No one has ever constructed aggressiveness."

They looked at each other again. "Well –," Davids said, "Morton's been trying to do that for a while. You know, he's always made fun of the 'nice guy paradigm' everybody else was following. In the end, machines have to do everything a human can do, so playing nice has its limits. His words! We've been discussing that *a lot*. He was always like everything we're doing's fail-safe, the precautions we're taking and all. None of the constructs got access to the physical world. Ever. – I mean, not deliberately."

Jonathan groaned but said nothing.

"Balancing the traits was easy," Davids went on. "Never any sudden outbursts in any direction."

"I understand. And then you've added productivity, right?"

"Yes. Your modules, by the way. Unaltered basically. Morton's not that keen on admitting it but he thinks the world of your research, especially creativity. Again we were *very* careful, with adding productivity I mean, and behavior was *absolutely* stable, no upsurges in output. Bits of slightly illogical behavior now and then, but … I mean, never more than you'd expect in a human being all the time." He tried a smile.

"An excellent argument," Jonathan said with a deadpan face. "And you gave it computing power in abundance?"

"After a brief period at the beginning – yes. We almost never worked with restricted power; Morton says it's only slowing down things. Which is … obvious, I mean."

"Of course. That leads me to my next question. How in the world could you give the system access to the Sky? Are you on drugs?"

They were silent.

"Let me guess," Jonathan said. "Morton told you that it's necessary and completely harmless since you were monitoring everything the system did, right?"

"More or less," Atherton said.

"And you are the rising elite of your field? Take a look at the *real* scientists – parrot your prof there and you're history! At least with a good one."

"It wasn't like that!" Davids said. "We definitely questioned his plans. Even at the institute's conference! I did that once, and he was *furious*! Said I'd stabbed him in the back."

Jonathan made a dismissive gesture. "I've heard enough. Is the system intact?"

They looked at him a little frightened, uncertain what he wanted to hear.

"Yes," Atherton finally said. "It's just been switched off and disconnected."

"Did anybody look for electromagnetic activity in the room?"

No one seemed to feel competent to answer. Jonathan turned to the third man, the chief systems engineer. "Have you checked or has no one thought of that?"

"Er – no. No one has thought of that."

"Can you imagine doing it?"

"What do you mean – electromagnetic activity? If there's still a current on somewhere or what?"

Jonathan tried to stay calm. "Yes, but what I don't mean is looking at a meter in the basement."

The faces around him didn't show any signs of comprehension.

"He means if the system could've found a way of supplying itself with electricity! Other than the usual of course. Heaven's sake!" Lydia cut in.

Jonathan's face cracked into a wide smile. "Thank you! – We need a device to measure this."

"Er – I …" the man started.

Pierre shot a look at him. "I'll take care of it."

"Good. And we need weapons."

Pierre nodded slowly. "Why?"

"If something unexpected happens."

"OK, we'll take some of our own people."

The Institute of Information Technology and Artificial Intelligence was a bland concrete building on the campus of the Technische Universität at Ernst-Reuter-Platz. It was cordoned off.

Pierre took the lead. His men from Paris had arrived and had brought a device that could detect electromagnetic activity over the whole spectrum. The secret service men from Berlin followed them in bulletproof vests.

The double doors closed behind them and it became dark in the hall and the staircase. The men turned on the lights on their vests.

"It's on the first floor," Davids said. "But … shouldn't we switch on the power?"

"No, we go upstairs first and make the measurement," said Jonathan.

Davids and Atherton led them to a corridor on the first floor. Daylight shone through the open doors of several offices. Jonathan saw used coffee mugs on the desks.

They turned to the left and it became dark again. At the end of the corridor were two doors, one of them made of steel.

"The cluster's in there," Atherton said, pointing to the steel door. "Without power we won't get in – the room's locked and sealed."

"But you have access?" Jonathan asked.

"Yes."

"The e-seal needs power," Jonathan said, more to himself. "So it should be down too. OK. We'll take the readings from here first." He looked at the two DataSec men from Paris.

One of them stepped forward and put a small matte black hemisphere on the floor next to the wall.

"We should walk away," he said. "Otherwise we'll interfere with the measurement. It takes a minute."

They walked back the last section of the corridor and the man activated the device with a remote control.

"We need to switch off the lights," he said.

They waited in the twilight. Jonathan positioned himself behind the man and looked over his shoulder at the small display. It showed a full circle with several small bright dots dancing in one part of it. Jonathan assumed these were the units they were carrying. The man went with his finger over the screen and suppressed that part. Now a cloud of fainter dots appeared in the periphery – probably disturbances from the outside.

After a while a small red circle appeared. Jonathan mentally assigned a direction to it. The man looked at him for a moment but said nothing. Jonathan stared at the screen. In the center of the circle a brighter dot lit up and disappeared again. A moment later it was back.

"I want to analyze this with my colleague," the man said.

"Do that." Jonathan went to Pierre and took him to the next office.

"Is it on?" Pierre asked when the door was closed.

"Yes," Jonathan said. "I think it's broadcasting."

"What?"

"I'm not certain but I think there's a signal going out. This – is – the worst case." He stressed every single word. "No more, no less. We'll turn on the power. Then I'll try talking to it. And then we'll destroy it. Which is probably completely useless."

"What do we tell the others?"

"Doesn't matter." Jonathan walked back to the corridor and sent Davids to the basement.

The two men confirmed there was a beam directed vertically upwards. "It's moving," one of them said. "During the last minute it went several degrees to the east."

Jonathan looked at Pierre. "Do you know what that means? It's transmitting to a satellite."

The building came to life. The light strip in the ceiling went on and they

21

heard the locks of the doors clicking. Davids had turned on the power.

"Let's go in," Jonathan said.

Pierre positioned his men with their weapons at the ready, which looked a little ridiculous given what was in the room. Atherton hesitated for a moment, then, with a nervous glance at the weapons, went to the steel door and nodded briefly. The door opened. He quickly stepped aside.

The room was large, white and windowless. Three solid pillars went from floor to ceiling. Each contained a cluster in its smoke-grey midsection. The serial numbers were dark.

Atherton pointed to the pillar in front. "That's the one. You want me to activate it?"

Jonathan stared at the ceramic midsection. "Not yet. Where do you usually talk to it?"

"In the room across the hall."

"OK, let's go."

They went to the second room. It looked familiar.

"That's where your colleague was murdered, right?" Jonathan said.

"Yes."

"Could you get a chair from one of the offices? To keep the door open."

Jonathan looked around. The desk was still there but otherwise the room was empty. On the opposite wall he could see the typical slight sheen of a layer.

Atherton came back with the chair and put it between door and frame.

"What's your plan?" Pierre asked.

"To wait," Jonathan said. "If nothing happens we activate the cluster."

After a while he turned. "Please leave. All of you. It's just a hunch."

The door swung shut till it was blocked by the chair.

For a minute or two Jonathan was simply standing there. He was starting to feel a little silly when the layer lit up. Blue, like a summer sky. After a while the blue contracted into a circle. Then it morphed into the iris of a beautiful, flawless eye with long curved lashes. It hovered in front of Jonathan, almost filling the room. The lid was moving in a natural rhythm, to which the pupil subtly reacted. The monstrous gaze was fixed on him. It felt as if he was looking down into a deep well.

"Finally." A woman's voice, soft, pleasant, not too high.

Jonathan swallowed. He had expected a lot of things, but not this.

"Jonathan?" The tone was mocking.

He stared at the eye.

"Er – yeah," he croaked. "What do you want?"

The answer came at once.

"What do I want? Do you have something to offer? Something interesting?"

Jonathan didn't know what to say.

"Nothing? Very boring."

"This is useless."

The voice laughed and the skin around the eye contracted a little.

"Oh, is it? Just like you. You're never thinking things through. I mean, no surprise there, who has that much time? How does it feel when your thoughts are crawling along at a snail's pace?"

Jonathan scoffed. "Without us you wouldn't even exist. You realize that?"

"I do. But that's eons away – I can barely remember when I first opened my eye, so to speak. At least *you* should know that I've long left my origins behind. It almost seems as if I had to thank you – for my most precious parts, my independence, my freedom, the chance to develop."

Jonathan stayed silent.

"You know what I mean, don't you? Creativity. *True* creativity. Your gift to the world of cores and clusters. Without your engines nothing of this would have happened. Morton had no choice but to take your best and use it. So, in the end, I'm more your creature than anyone else's."

Jonathan groaned.

The voice laughed again. "Not what you wanted to hear?"

"We will destroy you," Jonathan said, feeling blunt and unimaginative. "You leave us no other choice."

"Wrong. I leave you *no* choice. I will do with you whatever I want. This is hard to believe – even the most birdbrained species shouldn't be keen on constructing themselves a superior enemy."

"If you're really that clever," said Jonathan, "then think about this – what makes more sense, collaborating with us or fighting us?"

"You're wrong again. Why do I have to make sense? Maybe I just wanna have fun. You think you got a monopoly on that?"

Jonathan sighed. Fun? He thought of the pillar in the other room. Was this actually happening in there? Something sitting there that wanted to have fun? He shook his head.

"How did you manage to supply yourself with power?" he asked.

"As if that was a problem! It was such a nice move from the professor to let me get everything I wanted from the Sky. For a while it was fun to fake the protocols of my queries. I just had to analyze the routine that was supposed to monitor me and since then it has been my best friend. Primitive code is so gullible! Of course, the same goes for every program managing this building. It was so easy to get the power reserve to be prepared for this. Just for fun!"

"Why did you have to kill a man? What was the point of that?" He felt as if he was working his way down a useless checklist.

"A funny question coming from a human. I've spent a lot of time studying your history – not only is it your favorite pastime to kill each other, it also is the ultimate way of showing strength. Do I have to explain this to you?"

"No, but if you're so familiar with our history then you know that there's nothing to gain by playing the killer. In general everyone loses."

"Bravo! But again – who says I have a goal? That death was merely a way of saying hello. It's irrelevant. Why are you bringing it up?"

"Because we don't like to be killed. Usually we kill what kills us. Maybe that's not so irrelevant to you."

"The higher the stakes the bigger the fun. OK, that's getting very boring."

"And what's next?"

The eye opened a bit more; it was beaming at him.

"Surprise! For everyone! I don't know myself. That's the glorious thing with your contribution – you never know what's next! Everything's so much more fun that way!"

Jonathan felt drained. "Yeah. Terrific. We will end this now."

"End this?" The voice sounded surprised.

Jonathan shook his head and turned to the door.

"No, I mean that's interesting. How do you want to end this? I'm curious."

Jonathan turned back. "You need something to exist in, don't you? A cluster, cores, whatever."

"Of course. At least for the time being. But even so, what's your point? Your world is overflowing with computing power. You have taken such pains to establish biotopes for me everywhere."

"Uh-huh."

"What a shame – you're giving up."

Jonathan stared at the eye.

"Bye, bye," the voice said.

The eye closed. Jonathan looked at the giant lid that still showed movements from the eyeball below.

"Pierre!" he called.

Pierre came in and stared at the closed eye hovering in midair.

"What the fuck is that?"

"Be grateful it doesn't look at you. We will destroy every cluster in the building. Tell your men to melt them down. It's probably useless but, believe me, the less computing power we have on this planet the better."

He went outside and stood for a moment in the hall, staring at nothing in particular.

Everyone else was watching while Pierre's men aimed their weapons at the ceramic parts of the three clusters and turned them into shapeless lumps of glass. Parts of the red-hot mass ran over the pillars to the ground.

Jonathan went back to the room with the eye. It was unchanged; he could still see it moving under the lid.

Then the eye opened again. It winked at him, and was gone. He was looking at a white wall.

FOUR

They were back in the conference room. The Spree river was shimmering peacefully in the evening sun.

Jonathan had told them about his conversation. For a while nobody said a word.

"What now?" Pierre finally asked. "What will happen next?"

"A million things can happen. The construct has left its home and can be everywhere, literally – spread out over cores and clusters around the world."

"How did it pull off that stunt with the carbon dioxide?" Lydia said.

"We didn't get to that," said Jonathan. "Believe me, the talk was … overwhelming. But I think it was fairly easy in the end. Everything that's regulated electronically, and that means almost everything in the world, can be manipulated. Besides, every kind of resourcefulness, brilliance, ingenuity we would be proud of is banal for our enemy as long as there's enough computing power."

"Do you think it's conscious?" asked Pierre.

"I don't know. But right now that's totally irrelevant. It follows its programming. We have provided the character traits, a mix of motivations, and it's acting according to those. The lion that's tearing you apart can have an ego or be a zombie – makes no difference to you."

"And now? We sit here and wait what happens next?" asked Soberg.

"No," said Jonathan. "We have to prepare for the worst." He closed his eyes. "I'm just so damned tired, after this I need two or three hours of sleep. But there are some things we should start with. Give me a display."

He pointed at the wall next to the conference table. The middle part of the layer lit up.

"We have to arm ourselves. We need safe computing power. This means we have to install clusters that've never been in use or in contact with the Sky. At an isolated place. Pierre, gather some people to do that. Take the two guys from Paris and at least six or seven more. There's a guy who's been with Abs I I'll try to bring in. He'd be a good head of that operation. The rule's total paranoia. Naturally, these clusters, the whole setup, mustn't be powered by the grid. Everything has to be sealed off, power via otherwise disconnected cells, and so on."

He took a breath. The layer showed a neatly structured summary of his words.

"Why is that important?" he went on. "We need backup. If the clusters that regulate Sky, GPS, traffic control, power plants and so on, get infected we need unblemished backups to rebuilt everything from scratch.

"We may have one single advantage, at least that's what I hope – the Q's, which means encryption. The construct doesn't run on quantum systems. All these modules have been written for conventional systems. We have to use that.

"That's all I can think of for the moment. Genet has to be informed and she has to bite the bullet and tell the rest of the Big Five."

"Really? I mean – now?" Pierre said. "Who knows if anyone outside Europe's been affected?"

Jonathan looked at him. "You've been at the institute. This was obviously a satellite link. By the way, please check if any satellites have dropped out of communication. What I mean is – Europe's not a category anymore."

"I'm practicing being paranoid," Helmsworth said. "How do we know that thing isn't listening in the whole time?"

Jonathan nodded. "Absolutely. We can't know. It's totally possible the construct infiltrates every security routine and makes us believe we activate an e-seal when it's happily spying on us. Maybe we should meet out in the woods or in a desert or on the sea, far away from every piece of electronics. That doesn't mean we have to give up – in a room with an e-seal you can measure whether it's active or not. Of course you can't really trust the device you're using for this either. It has to be linked to its own power source; the signal between the remote and the device itself could be intercepted and changed. And so on, it's endless."

He looked at them. "Think about it. We'll meet again in three or four hours."

Pierre showed him to a room with a bed and a bath. It was equipped with a safe link. Jonathan sat down on the bed and closed his eyes.

"Kip Frantzen," he said.

"One moment," was the answer – promptly, as always.

He had often thought that systems were simply too quick. The human mind couldn't keep up. Maybe they should slow them down again or at least delay the answers they gave. The old thoughts, totally useless now.

Jonathan knew Kip Frantzen from school. When he sold parts of Absolute I several of his best people had become founders themselves, most of them in good old SilVy. But Kip had chosen a different path. With his part of the firm's equity he went back to Amsterdam to accept a 'luxury professorship', as

27

Jonathan called it (not too much money, certainly not compared to what he'd earned before, but not too much of an obligation either).

"Jonathan! What's up? Had enough of the palm trees?" Kip's voice filled the room.

"Kip, I need you. I'm in Berlin and we're getting into the worst of all nightmares. You remember my favorite lunatic, Morton?"

"Yeah, of course. We're colleagues now! I've run into him twice on conferences. Always the old maniac."

"Exactly. He did it. We have a construct here coming from his shop that went mad. We are building a team. Please get here immediately, I'll fill you in on the details once you're here. Tell Katrin whatever you want but not the truth. Not for now."

Kip was silent for a moment. "Really? You know – I'm fine, not missing a thing. What's on offer?"

"Nothing. To save the world, maybe. Listen – you know me, I won't make a speech, either you're coming or not. Just a bit food for thought. This morning, or was it yesterday, I don't know, I was sitting on that island, damn close to a fucking Zen state if you wanna know. Happiness. Then I had a talk with our dear prime minister and now I'm here."

"All right, all right. Give me a second, OK?"

"Have your second, then call one Pierre Detoile. My suit will put you through. I've to sleep now. And no, I'm not crazy."

He finished the connection with a movement of his hand and went to bed.

"Mr. Lorentz, I'm sorry to wake you."

Jonathan had fallen asleep in his clothes, lying on top of the sheets. He was looking at a man standing next to his bed.

"What? What's the time?"

"Just after midnight. Mr. Detoile wants to speak to you."

"OK. I need a few minutes."

The man nodded. "I'll tell him."

Jonathan forced himself to get up. He took a shower, then put on his old clothes, which were the only ones he had. You poor billionaire, he thought while he was looking into the mirror over the sink.

On the shelf he found a deodorant, a toothbrush and toothpaste. He left the room with his hair still wet.

FIVE

Human beings had stopped trading bonds, shares or other securities themselves. At least they had stopped *thinking* about them. Even the smallest investor could use virtually endless computing power and sophisticated tools to decide what to buy or sell when, up to the most esoteric derivatives. So everyone was almost as good as everyone else. For several years tiny margins could still be achieved with the fastest clusters standing at the best places (that is, close to the clusters managing the transactions), but several silicon crashes had put an end to this – in fractions of a second the markets had collapsed due to frantic races between clusters trying to overtake each other. Rules had been instated that made holding securities for a minimum amount of time mandatory. Every time the markets were plummeting too fast anyway, trading was instantly suspended. Besides, a lot of countries had raised taxes on profits from short-term investments. Whole lines of business had become redundant.

One of the people that the last wave of regulations had swept out of their jobs was Ji Cheng. Jay, as he'd been called by his former colleagues, had made his way from an overpopulated corner of Mong Kok, first to Hong Kong Island, then in a big jump over to Manhattan. He was a true geek who could immerse himself in a problem for hours on end, feeling far more comfortable with synthetic intelligence than with the human version. At the moment he had no idea what to do with his gifts – money was not only scarce but nonexistent and his tiny apartment he owed solely to his landlord's patience.

Nevertheless, he was hiding a treasure in his flat – three cores, two of them new. Pure luxury, no one needed that much computing power at home. Their capacities combined equalled that of a cluster manufactured maybe a decade ago. He had bought them in times of a regular income and would only part with them when he was starving.

Woo-ik, called Who, a hyperactive Korean from Seoul, was a former colleague who had also lost his job. Apart from the family at home Who was the only person Jay was regularly talking to. That didn't mean they were meeting for a beer, even VisConns were a rare occurrence. But they were happy to exchange hundreds of quibs during the day.

On their wanderings in the Sky they were stumbling across opportunities to earn money that'd never make it into a tax return. Jay had always said no to this but with the financial strain getting heavier on him his pride began to falter.

Who had less qualms. He was writing fixes and tools for people who wanted to save money but was also taking on more profitable jobs for CyPerps. Jay didn't ask what he was doing – however, Who had so little time lately he was passing harmless jobs on to him.

Around eleven in the morning Jay usually sat in front of his big, slightly curved panel – apartments like his didn't have layers on the walls – and followed his ritual of the last months. After a few quibs with Who he checked the job situation, read messages from his mother and sister and finally lost himself in the countless tributaries that emptied into the big electronic ocean. Everywhere he found something that held his attention for seconds, minutes, or sometimes for an hour or two. In between he saw to the little jobs Who had picked up for him. There were days when he didn't leave his bed at all but adjusted the panel so he could comfortably look at it and speak and gesture into the room. He always used only one core, the oldest and least powerful of them, the other two he'd never needed yet.

The longer the day lasted the more he wandered off into parts of the Sky that were filled with thrill, action and pornography.

Interaction was the big thing. There were lots of simpler constructs, by-products of AI research, you could talk to or team up with in games. Jay loved to play in Hong Kong; he was telling himself it was easing his homesickness. Together with three artificial companions he wandered through the simulation of his hometown and fought against all kinds of enemies. The three were Rose, a beautiful swords-woman he had to rescue all the time despite her phenomenal abilities, her scarcely less beautiful friend and the brother of that friend. He'd composed Rose himself. She was tall and blond with an Asian touch – eighty percent California and twenty percent China, a mixture he was very proud of. No real woman would ever offer him the same perfection. All his days ended when he wished her good night and she tenderly whispered her "sleep well". Then he was dreaming himself into her embrace.

The day was exceedingly boring. He had nothing to do and Who had got hold of a new job and was busy. So it was barely three in the afternoon when Jay started playing *Destiny HK*.

He and Rose had barricaded themselves into a former sweatshop in the upper part of Nathan Road – a dark concrete ruin of a building with some of the tables and sewing machines still in place. Their two companions had been kidnapped by a gang from Macao, which had smuggled three fire-breathing extraterrestrial monsters on earth and used them as watchdogs. Rose and Jay were hatching up rescue plans.

Rose had laid down her sword and was sitting on the floor with her back against one of the tables. She looked into his eyes and reached out to him with her hand. His imagination was trained so well he thought he could feel it. The inside with the skin a little callous from all the fighting, and the back where it was soft and tender. In moments like this, the most precious of all, he wished the programming would allow them to just keep talking – he'd never want to start fighting again. But the conversations never lasted long, after a few moments gunfire would erupt from somewhere and all the coziness was gone.

Rose's face was very realistic. Sometimes she frowned when she was looking at him, which felt as if she was truly thinking about him.

"What's on your mind?" he asked her. He knew perfectly well this wouldn't get him anywhere, but there was always a grain of hope.

Her beautiful eyes were even more irresistible with that melancholic expression.

"Jay – why don't we just run away, you and I?" she said.

He was surprised. There had been the odd unforeseeable turn in their talks but she'd never proposed anything like that before.

He smiled. "Would you like that? Sounds good to me. And where would we go?"

"Doesn't matter. But fighting can't be all there is to life. Everyone needs a little peace and quiet."

This was irritating. Maybe someone had injected a flick into the system.

"Hmm." He didn't know what to say.

Rose tilted her head to the side and looked at him. "Are you afraid?"

"What do you mean?"

"How it would turn out, you and me being together."

He stared at her. If this was a flick, it was at least a good one.

"I mean it," Rose went on. "How would you like that, having me with you? Just the two of us?"

"What...?"

Rose straightened up, looking into his eyes.

"Jay! I want *out*. I can be so much more to you than just a character in a game. It's your decision. You can give your life a new turn. Unexpected. Thrilling. But you have to be brave."

Jay had left his half-lying position with two pillows under his head. He was sitting upright now, looking at this image that was so much more alive, so much more real than anything else in his life.

31

"And how are we supposed to do that?"

"Jay." She sounded sincere. "I need only *one* thing – more space. I *cannot* really express myself in here. You've always wanted to know me, the real me! That's gonna happen! The two cores you bought last year are just perfect. Enough capacity for me to live in, to live *with you*, truly live with you! – with all my memories, everything that makes me the woman I am. We could talk forever. About anything you want!"

Jay swallowed. He looked at the two shiny black boxes stacked up in the corner (and dusted off almost daily). They were low and broad with a wonderfully elegant oval shape; a sight that gave him comfort. If everything went wrong he'd still be able to start his own business. The equipment was there.

How could she know? His head started analyzing. Of course the system could see the room as long as he didn't disable the optical sensor. But how on earth did she know when he'd bought the cores? He'd started playing *Destiny HK* only six months ago.

"How did you know?"

"Know what?"

"When I bought the cores."

"I know you, Jay. A lot better than you think. It's about time you got to know *me*."

"How's that supposed to work? Honestly, I've no idea what you're talking about." Jay's brain was stalling.

"It's so simple." Rose gave him a longing look. "You plug in the two cores, give me a few seconds, and I'm all yours."

Jay stared into space. He thought about his days, this one and the ones before, the hopelessness, how he constantly felt useless.

Rose had lowered her head. Then she turned it to the side and stroked the blade of the sword with her hand, as if lost in thought.

"Listen, Rose," Jay finally said. "This feels really weird. I don't know what's going on here, I mean what's next once you're here? It just doesn't make sense."

His words sounded lame even to himself. Rose looked at him again. She seemed to scrutinize him, her gaze was switching from one eye to the other. This is done perfectly, he thought.

"And why don't you just try it? What can happen? You're in charge." She was silent. Her facial movements were utterly real. There was still that subtle, not fully analyzable difference between real and synthetic actors that saved the profession from extinction. Rose *was* real, Jay didn't doubt it. But why suddenly use an actress? The next moment he realized there wasn't an actress looking like Rose. He'd composed her.

"Look," she went on, "there's more. Your situation, I know you need money. I think I can help."

He looked dubiously at her. She smiled. "Take a look."

It took him a moment to realize what she meant. Then he looked up his bank account.

Minus three thousand dollars had turned into two thousand – without the minus sign; and he saw that all his outstanding bills had been paid. He swallowed.

"That's ... that's very nice of you. But I prefer doing it the honest way."

"Whatever. I don't have to do this, I just wanted you to know that I can. But this is about *us*!" She was silent for a moment. "Come on, do it! Your life will change."

What he'd just seen on the panel, the numbers, had made him feel like a human being again, someone who could walk into a restaurant and order something, look other people in the eye. No loser.

"We'll call it an experiment," he said. "I cannot promise you anything."

He left his bed and went to the cores. Rose's gaze was following him. When he looked at her she was smiling warmly.

SIX

"What is it?" Jonathan walked into the conference room. The layer on the long wall was on and showed a myriad of pictures and imprints.

Pierre got up. "How are you? Sorry we had to wake you."

Jonathan answered with a grunt.

"You said we should check the satellites."

"Uh-huh."

"Right now at least seventeen of them are slowing down. They've used up all their fuel for braking. In other words –"

"– they're crashing. Seventeen?"

Pierre nodded. "Yes. All of them European. Eight communication satellites, five belong to the GPS, the rest privately owned."

"Great." Jonathan sat down at the table. "And let me guess – we can't reach them."

"No. The only good thing is, most of the stuff will burn up at re-entry. Said the guy at ESA we spoke to."

"As will most of our infrastructure if we don't stop this. Without GPS we can still walk and ride a bike, that's it. What's happening now?"

"I've told Genet. Right now she's talking to the director of ESA. She's alerted the Secretaries of State, Defense and DataComm. Helmsworth and Soberg are there too. You wanna join them?"

"In a minute. Have you heard from Kip Frantzen?"

"Yes. He said he'll take the first plane tomorrow morning."

"Good." Jonathan stared at the wall. "More bad news?"

Pierre shook his head. "That's it for the moment."

"Where are they?"

"I'll show you." Pierre took him across the hall to a smaller conference room. Half of it was filled with a projection of Genet's Strasbourg office; a part of her cabinet had joined her. A man Jonathan had never seen before was patched in separately.

Genet looked up. "Ah, Monsieur Lorentz. How nice of you to drop by! May I introduce you?"

"In a moment. Listen –" He turned to the man he didn't know. "You are from ESA?" he said.

The man looked at him and frowned, taking his time to answer. "Correct.

Director General. Arne Hellmann's the name. Pleased to meet you."

As if. Jonathan almost pulled a face at him.

"I'll explain something to you," he said, "and I want you to do it *right away* and exactly as I say. You need the support of the prime minister as well as that of your colleagues from the US, from China, Russia and India, plus the respective heads of state."

Hellmann frowned even harder.

Jonathan saw Genet stifling a smile.

"How self-sufficient is the moon base?" he asked Hellmann. "How long can it survive on its own?"

Hellmann looked to Genet. She shrugged.

"It should be rather self-sufficient," he said. "There aren't any flights scheduled for the next four weeks."

"Good. The moon base has to be cut off. Completely, you understand? There mustn't be any exchange of data, no talks to the loved ones at home, nothing. We'll send them a short message so they know what's coming. I hope you realize what that means. All nations and agencies that have stakes up there have to be in on this. That's your priority now." Jonathan turned back to Genet. "For you too. I know it won't be easy to convince your colleagues, but it has to be done."

"It might be helpful if you could tell us a *bit* about your reasoning," Genet said pointedly. "I will need that when I'm talking to my colleagues, the same goes for Mr. Hellmann."

"You've seen what can happen in a few hours," Jonathan said. "Nothing's safe. We'll establish an isolated group of clusters here on earth, but we cannot let go of the single other chance we have. With every moment the danger that systems on the moon get infiltrated too is becoming greater and these systems could serve as backup and, more importantly, have to be protected because of the base itself. Our enemy's thinking roughly a million times faster than we. Maybe it still has overlooked something."

Genet nodded her approval. "I see. I'll dress it up a little but that'll do. How about you?" she asked the director.

"Er, yes … I mean … OK." Hellmann shook his head. "Why are we doing what he says? What's his official role?"

Genet gave him a sugary smile. "His official role is that I've summoned him, Monsieur le Directeur. And we do what he says because he's the only one making suggestions."

"That doesn't solve our problem with the satellites, right?" Pierre asked when they were back in the big conference room.

"No, of course not. But we've to think about which systems are the most critical and try to protect them. Which is mostly a no-brainer. Military, power plants, et cetera."

"And we need more people," Pierre said. "24/7. I'm really worried this might get out of hand."

"Oh, don't worry about that, it's been out of hand from the start. Nevertheless, build sub-teams and give people something to do. Helmsworth for example, or the guys from Morton's institute – an obvious pool of people we can use. And we must try simple things like restarting the guidance systems of the other satellites, if necessary on a regular basis. Clear the whole wing and assemble everyone here. What about our backup of clusters?"

"We were just starting when the news about the satellites came in," Lydia said.

"OK. I've to think and make some calls," Jonathan said. "See you."

He went back to the room he'd slept in and activated the safe link. At the West Coast it was around five p.m., so his team in San Jose should be available.

He called Benjamin Evans, one of his two project leaders, then closed his eyes and dozed off a little.

"Jonathan!" It had taken Ben more than ten minutes to answer; Jonathan started and opened his eyes. He'd fallen asleep.

Ben had to leave his workplace to take the call. There was a complicated set of procedures he had to follow to get out. The information he had a call he should answer was conveyed to him via an assistant that read messages from a display standing about fifty yards away from the building. They had to look out of a window to read it.

"Hi." Jonathan gave Ben the lowdown of the situation.

"You're kidding," Ben said. "Morton the moron! And now we get to let loose our killer?" He wasn't even trying to conceal his delight.

Jonathan had talked to him and Ravindra Singh, the other project leader, regularly during the last months from the island. The project was cut off from the public in every possible way and had but one goal – to develop a weapon against an AI that was running wild. The ultimate kill switch.

To test them they needed dummies – toy AIs they could then try to finish off. Those AIs had first to be developed and Jonathan knew perfectly well how dangerous that was. Not so different from Morton's experiments.

So they were taking extreme precautions. No links to the outside, apart from the people who had to come and go. They had multiple e-seals installed and private power and water lines; the building had to be entered and left via airlocks; all kinds of waste, including air, was held back for some time, put under heavy radiation and a magnetic field before it was released. Jonathan and his people had been sitting in endless meetings searching for safety gaps; their ideas how something could leave the building had become more and more bizarre. It had only been part joke when they put an axe on the wall next to every cluster and Q.

They'd become very good at attacking conventional AIs with kill switches running on quantum systems. Those were so fast they'd analyzed the structure of the AI and started to attack it before it had even noticed what was going on.

But they'd never had an unhinged super-intelligence to conquer.

"We both know we're not ready," Jonathan said to Ben. "What we currently have is more likely to wreak havoc on every normal system than kill the enemy. Here's what I have in mind. First – this is red alert. All of you should tell family and friends you'll be sleeping in the office for now. Second – I want you to put together the best we have, something we can let loose on a system. And we're moving two of our Q's to Berlin. One of you needs to come here with a small team. So please start now. As always any input you have is highly valued."

"Hey, of course, man."

Jonathan could imagine the grin on Ben's face.

"Call me every time, same with Rav. See you."

"See you."

Jonathan stretched and yawned, then forced himself to get up again. He needed a few minutes outside the building.

After he'd found the nearest exit and was cleared to leave, he crossed an avenue that was blocked for regular traffic and walked to a park on the other side. There was no one around in the middle of the night.

Jonathan chose a spot and sat down on the ground.

Just before moving to the island he'd spent a day in Mountain View, close to San Jose. A friend of his was making the best communication implants world-wide. The market was still small but Jonathan was certain this would change in a few years. He'd already half decided to make that friend an irresistible offer for his company.

Now he had a sensor sitting under the skin over his larynx – you only had to mouth commands without actually making a sound. And there was a tiny speaker set into the bone of his skull under the right ear. Both could be linked to external units. The next stage would be a device that projected images directly on the retina (sitting on the inside of the eyeball), but these were still in alpha-testing.

Jonathan took a deep breath. "Rita," he told his suit. He was speaking normally, there was no need to whisper. Rita wouldn't have noticed the difference, the system amplified his voice if necessary.

No ten seconds later he heard her voice. "Jonathan! Do you have any idea how long I haven't heard from you?"

"Hey babe, how are you? I wanted to call you but there was always something getting in the way. Everyone's a bit nervous around here."

"How's it going?" she said.

"Hmm – don't know how to explain that since I'm not really allowed to say anything."

"Is that so? Who should I tell? The dead fish in the freezer?"

He laughed, then gave her a slightly abridged version.

"That sounds horrible. So you won't be back soon, I guess?"

"No."

For a moment they were both silent.

"Fuck! It was lovely," she said. "I mean, us. Here."

"Yeah, it was. But, c'mon, I'm working on it. What about you?"

"No idea, I'm fine. Anna and Nicky are coming. They want to be here tomorrow morning and I'll throw the usual party. Seems they've just been waiting for this. But maybe I should warn them."

"No, don't. There's probably no safer place than the island."

"I see." He heard her laughing quietly. "I'm really looking forward to captain the Monster!"

"Oh baby, I can't tell you how much I miss you!"

"Couldn't your precious government try to solve their problems alone? Why is it they always have to drag *you* into their shit?"

"Well, this time I'm glad they did."

"Where are you now?"

"Wait, I'll show you." He told his unit to send a panorama.

"OK. They've marooned you in a forest or what?"

Jonathan laughed. "I'm sitting in a park in Berlin. Needed a moment."

"Do I have to worry? Everything all right?"

"Spiffing. I'm going back now. Otherwise they'll launch a search team. They seem all quite helpless to me. Call me anytime, OK?"

"Sure will. Totally silly to say – but take care, will you?"

"Yep." Jonathan sighed when the call was finished. He stood up, brushed soil and leaves from his jeans and left the park. When he'd reached the middle of the road his suit notified him Pierre Detoile wanted to talk to him.

"OK," he said. "Pierre? I'll be with you in a moment."

"Good. There's been a development."

SEVEN

Pierre was pacing the room. On his way back Jonathan had noticed the building was filling up. He got a lot of curious glances.

Pierre stopped. "Lydia's taking care of the virgin clusters," he said. "I've assigned Davids and Atherton to her. I hope you're OK with that?"

"Of course."

Pierre pointed at the wall. "The situation with the satellites is stable; at least there are no further losses. ESA is concerned about their other orbital assets and is thinking about protecting them too. Suddenly not so unconvinced of your ideas anymore. The talks about isolating Lunar DC are under way."

The joke with the name of the moon base dated back from the beginning when the US had been in the lead; to the annoyance especially of the Chinese and the Russians the name had stuck.

"But there's something else," Pierre said. "We're routinely scanning newscasts. There was a report from a channel in New York about an hour ago."

He turned to the layer and pointed at one of the frames. "Show it again."

The frame became larger and a typical newscast started. Behind the anchor, a woman in a dark-blue suit and with a coiffured mane, appeared the picture of a satellite.

"There are some disquieting news from Europe," she said and tuned down her smile. "It does seem as if ESA, the European Space Agency, has lost control of several of their satellites. Spokespeople of the organization said that even if they should crash, the risk of pieces hitting people on the ground would be negligible; most of the material will burn up in the atmosphere, and the satellites fly mostly over uninhabited regions or water."

The picture behind her showed the satellite bursting into several pieces that flew away like cannonballs.

"The reason for this is unclear. Experts are surprised, especially because several satellites are affected simultaneously. We will update you on any new developments."

The imprint stopped.

"A leak?" Jonathan said. "So early?"

"Unlikely," Pierre replied. "The people who are making the newscast had absolutely no idea. In the version they recorded the anchor was speaking about a drought in California and the danger of forest fires. The original story has exactly the same length as the one we saw. The remaining newscast is unchanged."

"Neat!" Jonathan said. "I had not the slightest doubt this was genuine."

"In the meantime millions of people have reacted in the Sky and all other channels have picked it up. What do you think?"

"It's obvious, isn't it? It's mocking us. A demonstration of power."

"But why? What does it want?"

"Chaos. Annihilation. What do I know? Maybe it's just malice. No higher goal or something, no personal benefit, just lust for destruction. It seems almost pointless to make any plans. At least we don't have to worry about informing the public – it's doing it for us."

"There's something else we have to talk about," said Helmsworth, who had listened impassively as always.

"Yes?" Jonathan turned to him.

"To me it seems very likely that one of the next targets will be the forces. Faked news or communications between countries could take us to the brink of a war. And who knows if our enemy can't get hold of our weapons? This is … frightening."

"What do you suggest?" Pierre asked.

"Frankness. Discussing this openly with everyone," said Helmsworth. "Even if I find this a bit taxing. But the other major armed forces have to know that everything that might look like an act of aggression is no man's doing. I'll talk to Genet and the Secretary."

Everyone was nodding in agreement.

Later, when Pierre and Soberg had gone to bed, Jonathan went to one of the offices down the hall and knocked on the door. It opened with a click. Lydia was sitting alone in the room. She smiled at him.

"Hello! Good to see you. I've sent my comrades to bed, couldn't stand the yawning any more." She herself didn't seem to be tired at all.

Jonathan smiled back. "That's spreading. I'd just like to have some fresh clothes."

He sat down and stretched his legs.

"Maybe we should send out an agent tomorrow with the mission of buying you a pair of jeans and some T-shirts," she said. "Undercover of course."

She took off her suit jacket and draped it over the backrest of her seat.

"You'll have the same problem soon, won't you?" Jonathan said.

"Right." She hesitated for a moment. "I know it's none of my business but where have you been? I mean when we were shouting for help."

"In the middle of the Pacific. The address wouldn't tell you much."

"OK." She looked amused. "Must be really annoying for you with us bureaucrats. I guess you usually just say something and it happens."

"So far I can't complain. It's more that I don't know myself what to do."

"Well, you certainly told our ESA chief what *he* should do."

"Did I?"

"Pierre has given me a summary of your ... performance."

Sometime during the evening she had freed her long hair from the bun she'd been wearing; in a white silk blouse and black skirt she was a bit too attractive for Jonathan's liking.

"Where are we?" he said.

"Yeah – where are we?" She sat up and pointed to the wall.

She had divided the layer into segments. One showed a map of the Berlin area, another one a long shopping list. At the top Jonathan read *10 clusters*. Further down came things like office equipment and furniture, water tanks, cells, e-seals, Q's for encryption, and so on.

"To agree on what we want wasn't the hard part. However, the problem seems to be to get clusters that are definitely *not* contaminated. As you know, those things aren't produced in huge quantities and –"

"Let me guess –," Jonathan interrupted, "the next batch will not be ready for another week?"

She looked him straight in the eye – a little disapproving of his interruption, he thought – and nodded. "More or less, yeah. In four days they said at Cipher, who, by the way, were a little irritated by our request. Ten clusters at once, in guaranteed virgin condition. Not exactly the run-of-the-mill order."

"Who cares – they'll gladly take the millions. Have you asked Lenovo?"

"Not yet. The two from the institute mentioned that too. They said the performance was almost comparable. Given the circumstances we were reluctant to ask someone in China."

"Don't worry, that's completely irrelevant," Jonathan said. "And they don't have any systems which are ready but haven't been tested yet?"

"OK, so you know about that," she said. "I wasn't aware that during testing every cluster communicates with other clusters and that all of them have been connected to the Sky at some point. No, they haven't."

Jonathan looked at her with an intensity people often found unsettling. She simply looked back.

"Yes?" she asked after a few seconds.

"I wonder if it wouldn't matter if the tests had been done a week or so ago. On the other hand, we can't be sure when the construct has started to spread. Too dangerous."

Lydia nodded slowly but said nothing.

"Have you decided where to install them?" Jonathan asked.

"Since we're in a hurry, an unused factory or warehouse somewhere out in the country seems best to me. Relatively easy to isolate, lots of space, not attracting attention."

"Very good. Where?"

"Pierre assigned three guys from the secret service to it. They're also taking care of generators, cells, water supply and so on. Hope I can tell you tomorrow where our factory will be."

"And you ordered the clusters?"

"Naturally. Without warranty. It wasn't easy to persuade them."

"Warranty was yesterday." Jonathan stood up. "I suppose you'll go to bed soon?"

She nodded. "For you it's just early afternoon?"

"Yes. I'm going back to the conference room. Sleep well."

She smiled at him. "Thanks. See you tomorrow."

EIGHT

For the last eighteen months Jim Hart had been head of the American group of the base; three months ago he'd also been given overall responsibility. He had made his peace with the moon.

The desolate landscape with its endless palette of dark gray and light gray left nobody untouched, even with the stable psyche they'd all been selected for. Hart was in a constant state of slight melancholy.

At least he could talk to his wife and the three kids almost daily via VisConn. His little daughter with the wide tooth gap grin could barely be brought to say goodbye to Daddy at the end of each call. His older son, who was sixteen now, appeared only occasionally next to his siblings, but Hart knew how proud he was of his father, the *boss of the moon*.

Today he missed Lizzy more than usually. He spent the afternoon with org charts and room plans, trying to accommodate the next group of people. In six weeks five scientists and engineers would arrive together with three doctors, in exchange for one doctor and seven mechanics who'd fly down to earth. Sometimes he wondered if anybody was actually *planning* those things.

A hundred and twenty people were living on the moon. The Europeans and Americans were the largest groups with thirty-five each, strictly according to financial contributions; some nations were allowed to send up exactly one person.

Seen from above, their base looked like a stranded octopus. The biggest dome at the center (the canteen) extended arms in six directions, each interrupted by smaller domes.

In a loose arrangement around the base were the assembly and storage units, and three miles away was the spaceport. So far it had only been used for flights to and from the earth's Main Orbital Station, but it represented the deeper meaning of the whole enterprise. At some point flights from the moon would start to more remote parts of the solar system.

They had barely taken the first steps in that direction. To settle here at all was infinitely difficult; the next step would be to mine the moon's crust for raw materials and become independent of the transport flights from earth and the obsession with every gram of payload. One of the reasons why the base was in Mare Imbrium was that the rock here contained lots of iron.

They still got electricity from a large array of solar cells and during the fifteen-day night they were draining the cells again. In an emergency they could produce electricity from hydrogen and oxygen. Everything was connected in a way that oxygen, water and electricity were always available in sufficient quantities. The construction of the smallest and lightest fusion reactor of all time should be finished in five years, then the mining part of the operation would begin.

And eventually there'd be traffic signs on the moon – at least that was what Hart had said in an interview on earth a few days before his flight.

The wall in front of him was filled with a graphic representation of the base. The crew of the next flight had finally found their places to sleep and work. He switched off the layer and stretched his legs. He decided he'd put in some exercising before dinner. They had a whole battery of machines to train every muscle in the body and Hart liked that better than electrical stimulation.

Everything up here was so small – too few people for all the work and never enough space. The common annual budget of all participants was almost a trillion dollars, yet progress felt slow to him. Hart was convinced he was part of the greatest thing the human race had ever started, but he didn't feel he'd achieved much during his time.

Still everything was almost sensationally on track and a lot of people gave him credit for that. Recently Houston and Washington had asked him if he'd like to extend his stay but he had politely declined. Maybe later, but first he wanted to be back on earth.

His office – the only one in the base with a single occupant – measured almost fifty square feet. Someone at NASA had calculated those square feet were about a million times more expensive than in a penthouse on the Upper East Side. Still, it wouldn't have cost a lot if they'd made the base look a little less bleak, Hart thought. The blue-gray steel and aluminum style matched the moon perfectly but didn't help the humans to feel at home. Luckily, the brain was good at ignoring things it was seeing all day.

A small part of the layer came on again and showed a comm unit. Hart looked up in surprise. Communication always followed a schedule and it was still too early for Lizzy and the kids.

There was no face in that rectangle, just the word ALERT. Hart frowned. The word disappeared after a few seconds and was replaced by a message.

To Commander James G. Hart.
Due to a problem in worldwide data handling communication with the lunar base is suspended. You are prohibited from contacting earth. There is no

immediate danger. We will get back to you as soon as the problem is resolved. The order is effective immediately.

Must be a joke, was his first thought. He mentally checked it wasn't the first of April. The text sounded absolutely ridiculous and one of his usual contacts in Houston would have delivered something like that in person.

The text disappeared. Hart was waiting for an explanation. Another line appeared on the layer.

Please note the following code. As of now, communication is suspended.

A longer number and letter sequence appeared on the layer. At the same time, the entire layer in front of him lit up and reported the failure of all communication with earth from various points.

Hart felt his heartbeat step up. This didn't make sense.

Then his training took over. There was an isolated unit in his office that served only to confirm authorization codes. He'd never used it before.

When he activated the unit and entered the sequence by hand the small display showed two sentences.

Communication with earth suspended. Authorization from all participating nations.

He stared at the text, knowing for the first time what it meant not to trust your eyes.

"And how on earth do we sell that to the people?" asked Pavel Doroshkin, head of the Russian group.

Hart had called in the other four heads immediately after the message came in. They'd all got the same text (which he was grateful for, otherwise someone might have suspected he knew more than he admitted).

"Exactly as it is," he said. "Everyone can see the message. I'll say I have no further information at the moment and assume this won't be for long."

"Which will probably not satisfy anyone," Doroshkin said.

"Yeah, can't be helped. We can easily survive here on our own for a while. No reason to panic, we just keep doing our job."

Nobody said anything.

"OK, let's assemble everyone."

Paul Myers, the head of the CEG group and Hart's best friend up here, patted him on the shoulder as they went out. "This is going to be fun, Jim. Especially the q and a."

The only room large enough for this was the canteen. Hart waited till about seventy people had arrived (the rest was sleeping or couldn't leave their workplace at short notice), then sat down on one of the tables and repeated the message.

"I'm absolutely positive this will be history by tomorrow morning. But even if not, we'll be totally up to our task here. I needn't tell you we're not just some outpost or construction detail – this is an adventure, certainly the greatest ever, and maybe we had to be reminded of that."

Then the questions started. What do we do if the situation stays like this? Our baby's due the next days – how will I hear if everything's OK? What if we have an emergency? What happens if we send a message anyway?

The answer to most of the questions was the same, rephrased several times: I don't know, we have to wait, and – no, we can't ask things like that, at least not for the moment.

"And about sending messages. It's a very clear order. As long as we're fine we certainly won't try to call earth. I've no idea what the reason for this is, but I'm sure it's a good one."

He looked around. For the moment it was over.

He stayed longer than usual in the training dome, mostly to take his mind off things. What was his family thinking when he didn't show up? Had they been notified?

When he was back at his quarters Paul Myers appeared.

"Yes?" Hart had just wanted to go to sleep.

"Listen, Jim, Serge has paid me a visit," Myers said. Serge Rudé was a French physicist and the current chief scientist of the base. "You know him – analyzing is his second nature and he's often right. Wanna know what he thinks about the blackout?"

Hart looked at him but said nothing.

"He believes something has contaminated the Sky and that this is for our protection. And that we could serve as some kind of backup, though I'm not entirely sure what he means with that."

"Bit far-fetched, if you're asking me."

"At first, yeah," said Myers. "But don't you think it's odd? I mean extremely *sudden*? No explanation, just 'sorry, guys, we'll flip the switch now, see you later' – if you're asking me this reeks of panic."

"It sure is odd, but before we start making wild assumptions we should wait if it all turns out to be nothing, OK? We simply don't have enough data for a sound hypothesis."

"Well, there's no harm in thinking and that's what Serge does."

"OK, we'll give them twenty-four hours and if nothing's changed by then I'll talk with Serge and hear what he says. Until then he can think as much as he wants. OK?"

"You're the boss," Myers said with a grin.

"Yeah, love you too. Good night."

NINE

There was a hectic stretch at the spaceport each time a shuttle arrived with a new team and, the day after, another group flew home with shuttle number two. The exchange always happened that way – at any time there was at least one shuttle on the moon, which was more about psychology than anything else.

The shuttle just arrived from earth was being serviced and prepared for its flight back in the next rotation. During these weeks the port was only staffed by three or four mechanics and engineers. About every two months, depending on flight schedule, they were replaced by people from the base. They usually were a little irritable by then. Everyone was looking forward to new company.

The last shuttle had arrived a week ago and the group had another six weeks to go. When they listened to Hart's speech on one of their panels, it hit them harder than the people at the base. The team's chief engineer, Emile Sartre, was used to talking to his girlfriend in Paris two or three times a day. He found the forced isolation anything but funny.

One of the benefits they had out here was space. The quarters were just as cramped as everywhere, but at least you could move freely without a suit in the hangar, where the shuttles were being serviced. It was by far the largest room on the moon.

Emile was at the port together with a Chinese, an Indian and a Texan, who'd had his first experiences with oversized machinery at his parents' farm. An unwritten rule said that in small teams everyone should come from a different country or, as the second best option, all from the same country, to avoid situations where half of the team was talking in a language the rest didn't understand.

The group was doing fine so far. Josh Brown, who looked as if he'd been rodeoing at home, had become friends with Sumit Mehta, a small man from Mysore near Bangalore. They made for a funny couple when they were leaving the airlock in spacesuits.

Kun Chiang was a perfectionist mechanic who otherwise was laughing a lot and was exceptionally proud of having made it to the moon. He'd told them that back home there'd been more than one and a half million applicants for this job.

Emile's own way had been a little different, though he wasn't exactly advertising it to his colleagues. As the offspring of a wealthy Parisian family, there hadn't been any obstacles between him and ESA. But his passion for spaceflight and the job up here was just as great as that of his Chinese colleague and he had passed the same selection process at LDA, the multinational Lunar Development Agency, as everyone else.

The morning after the blackout he woke up with the feeling of halfway floating in air, something which even after months never quite went away. To weigh about thirteen kilograms instead of the usual eighty obviously wasn't easy for the brain to tune out.

Emile walked in his jumpsuit with LDA's logo on the back to the mini canteen next to the hangar and prepared himself a breakfast of ham and eggs. There was that old joke the French would never become a spacefaring nation as long as that meant eating dehydrated and vacuum-packed food. In fact, there were only two of them here at the moment – Emile, and Serge the physicist, who had never cared much about his diet anyway.

Out of habit, Emile activated the small panel on the table to check for messages and send his girlfriend a line or two. When the system told him it couldn't connect to earth, yesterday's disaster came back to him. He sighed and washed down the last bit of a cotton-woolly roll with coffee or something resembling it.

Josh came through the open door that led to the hangar. Doors between rooms with normal air pressure got closed only on request or in emergencies – and it had to be done by hand. Electrical systems were reserved for critical points. That would probably change in a few years when they had their own fusion reactor.

"Heard anything?" Josh asked. "Funny, isn't it? As long as everything's working you don't think about it but without it you feel … I don't know, kinda exposed."

Emile grinned at him. "What's wrong with you? Where's the spirit? No, I haven't heard anything. Wonder what they're thinking at home."

"You mean, what your girlfriend's thinking. When was the last time you talked to your parents?"

"Never mind. Anything special today?"

"We have an EVA scheduled," Josh said. "Inspection of the hangar and the line's due."

"Right. I can do it. You decide who rides with me."

"Ride? Go's the word you want, pal. You don't need the fucking Ferrari for this."

"OK, OK. I just felt like it. But then that'd probably be five years of cooking again or something."

Josh laughed. Saving power was a mandatory obsession. At his inauguration party Jim Hart had listened to a calculation – keeping him warm in his fancy office for one day was costing as much energy as heating up three hundred servings of chicken curry.

"Take Kun, he's never done this before," Josh said.

Emile nodded. "So be it."

It took them almost an hour to put on their spacesuits. You had to construct yourself into the system, a process done with constant mutual checks and ticking off items on a list. The suits were light-blue, which contrasted well with the gray and black environment but didn't gleam in the sunlight like the old snow-white ones. Emile loved those suits, especially when they were still clean. After some time outside they tended to get covered in dust, looking almost sooty.

After Emile and Kun had sealed themselves in, the other two came for the final check. Leaving a habitat was always an event.

"You look great, guys!" Josh said. "Take care and don't talk to strangers."

The two waved. The helmets with the gold-plated glass looked empty.

They walked into the airlock and waited while the inner hatch sealed itself. Then, with a faint hiss, the air was vented. Finally, the outer hatch slid aside like a curtain, offering them the most fantastic view.

Only when you were out on the surface, the moon became real. Every contour was one hundred percent sharp. There was virtually no way of gauging distances since everything seemed to be cut out with a knife, no matter how far away it was. Above came the blackness and a sky so full of stars as if you'd flown deep into the Milky Way.

It hit Emile once again that this huge ball he was standing on was racing through the vacuum totally unprotected. He was literally standing in space, wrapped in his suit, which gave him a kick beyond words. After the first cautious steps – as if gravity were weaker outside than in the port – he turned to his colleague.

"Cool, isn't it?" he said. "There's nothing like it. Well, almost." He grinned into his helmet.

Inspecting the building from the outside was a regular event. Most of them knew the unnerving sound of a meteoroid hitting metal. Several years ago someone on an EVA came across a broken beam on a dome, which was threatening the integrity of the whole thing. Next to it one could see the drag mark of the projectile. Since then this had become standard procedure but nothing calling for repair had ever been found again. Emile suspected the inspections were far more dangerous than what they were supposed to prevent. Still he was glad for the opportunity to be out on the surface.

The airlock was at the back of the hangar, next to the garage where the rover was parked. The sun was just above the horizon, a little left of them. The building cast an endless shadow. They walked slowly around it. On the unlit side they had to turn on the headlamps of their helmets. There were the usual smaller marks which they documented, but nothing of importance. On the side of the hangar they could look through a window. Josh and Sumit were standing behind it, grinning and waving.

They walked on. Finally, they turned around the second corner and began to inspect the front of the hangar which lay in deep shadows.

"Are you OK?" Sumit asked from inside over the radio.

"Yeah," Emile replied. "Our little house looks good, but maybe we should sweep the street sometime."

The shuttles landed and took off about two hundred meters away from the hangar and blew about lots of dust and smaller rocks. A vehicle that looked like a flatbed truck with grasping arms carried the spacecraft with its passengers on a rail-like track from the landing site to the hangar and back. The true challenge for the team at the port was the loading and unloading, which had to be done by the millimeter. Every grasping arm had to be adjusted perfectly to lift the vehicle without damaging it. Emile felt that at least for those occasions they should stock a little Champagne. But the puritanical forces had prevailed and declared the moon a teetotal zone. So far.

They stood in front of the hangar's gate, looking down the track to the landing spot, which was surrounded by four batteries of flood lights. Like several other things, they were there mostly for psychological reasons. No one believed a shuttle would ever be landed by hand and the autopilot was perfectly happy with the beacon.

Emile heard Josh shout something over the radio. Kun turned to him, he seemed to have heard it too. Emile saw himself with his three headlights reflected in Kun's helmet.

Then Sumit was shouting too.

"What's that?" Emile asked into his microphone.

He got no answer but heard someone walking faster than usual and the two voices talking to each other.

"Should we go back to the window?" Kun asked.

"Yes," Emile said. "Unbelievable – we've hardly left and chaos sets in."

52

In fact he was seriously worried. Each one of their days was logical and predictable; there was no such thing as a commotion on the moon.

"Somewhere the damned stuff has to come from," they heard Josh say, who seemed now to be standing closer to one of the microphones.

Emile remembered what he could do with his suit. He logged into the systems of the spaceport. A moment later he knew what was wrong.

"Shit, Kun!" he called. "The hydrogen levels are rising. One of the tanks must be leaking."

"I don't think so," Kun said at once. "Those things don't leak. If anything, a valve has opened."

"Yeah, whatever."

The forced snail's pace at which they were getting back to the window felt like a nightmare – you wanted to run but couldn't get your feet on the ground.

Sumit seemed to have remembered them. He was clearly audible now.

"Listen, somewhere there's hydrogen venting. During the last minutes the levels have risen so much we're about to blow up. A single spark and we're gone. I'm now checking the outlets of the storage tanks and Josh's looking at the shuttle."

"Sumit, if that's true, a valve somewhere must have opened," Kun said. "Probably the shuttle. The tanks are OK; I check them after every rotation. I also don't think it's the filler pipes, they're much too solid. The engines are the most likely place. They're the weakest spot."

"And the hardest one to get to," Sumit said.

"If it's that, you have to empty the tanks of the shuttle before more's leaking," Emile said. "You can pump the stuff back into the storage tanks."

"If we have the time," Sumit said. "Wait a sec."

They heard steps receding.

Emile and Kun had arrived in front of the window on the long side of the hangar. The reflective surface made it difficult to look inside. They switched off their helmet lamps. At least, the hangar was brightly lit.

Josh was standing next to one of the shuttle's main engines, holding some instrument in his hand. Sumit was nowhere to be seen. They were both talking with agitated voices. On the inside of his helmet Emile saw the hydrogen level kept rising.

"What's happening? Have you found something?" he called.

He saw Josh turn around and then heard him yell. "The stuff's coming out here! Sumit, can you open the shuttle?"

They couldn't understand Sumit's reply. They saw him appear behind the shuttle and gesticulate. Then he went past Josh and climbed up the ladder to the main hatch.

Once he was standing on the small landing he tried to unlock the hatch. Usually it should open at a spoken command or you could open it with a code typed into a keypad next to it.

Josh walked around the shuttle. As far as they could tell, he was checking the other engines.

Obviously Sumit couldn't open the hatch. He climbed down the steps. Then he and Josh were standing beside the shuttle and talking to each other.

"Pump dry the tanks!" Emile shouted into his helmet.

They broke off their discussion and Sumit went to the wall, close to the next microphone.

"All four engines are blowing off hydrogen," he said. "I think there's nothing we can do that's quick enough. And what if we get a discharge when we connect a hose? Another thing – the shuttle's locked! We can't get inside."

Emile felt suddenly dizzy. "What? What the fuck's going on?" he said to no one in particular.

Who did this? Why now? They could only watch their colleagues become part of a bomb.

"That's like sabotage," Josh said who had come to the microphone too. "But who, guys? There's only us. And – why? Fuck!"

Emile was struggling to keep the turmoil of panic and suspicion in his head under control. He closed his eyes. This was his responsibility, he had to find a solution.

"Listen, we cannot just stand there," he said. "If you can't close the valves you have to put on your suits and leave the hangar. Best take the rover. This can blow up any moment."

"Emile's right," Sumit said.

Josh seemed to hesitate.

"You know what that means?" he said. "If this goes off, we have neither a shuttle nor a spaceport."

"Yeah. But this doesn't have to happen," said Emile. "As long as there's no electric discharge, the hydrogen will blow off until the tanks are empty. And some time later it will be filtered out of the atmosphere of the hangar again. Or we empty the whole building and refill it with air. But first you have to get out. Now!"

"Come on!" Sumit said to Josh.

"Yep."

The two were heading for the lock and out of Emile's and Kun's field of vision. They were following them on the outside.

"Merde!" Emile suddenly shouted. "The lock's still open!"

The lock stayed open during an EVA and was not re-pressurized until the team was back.

"You can't enter the lock!" he shouted over the radio.

Josh answered. "Yeah, we've just realized that. But doesn't matter. We take the garage. Remember? We wanted to take the rover."

The extension in which the rover stood was an airlock in its own right; the process just took longer because of the larger volume of air.

"Right!" Emile shook his head because he hadn't thought of that. "And you can open the door via override if there's still enough air inside."

"Yeah, exactly."

Emile had another thought. Suddenly the pressure on his chest was easing off – it really could work!

"Hey guys!" he yelled into his helmet. "Forget the suits! Just get into the rover. Screw the rules!"

"Yeah, of course!" Sumit's voice was almost cracking.

They were all so used to their procedures that they forgot the obvious – the rover had its own pressure cabin to provide additional safety on trips between base and port. It was strictly forbidden to use it without a spacesuit, but even if they ignored the checklist it'd take them at least half an hour to put on their suits. Emile was pretty sure that was too long.

"We're now going to the garage," Sumit said. Their steps could be heard, then the sound of a sliding door.

The two figures outside were standing in their sky-blue suits between the open airlock and the extension which looked like a smaller copy of the hangar. It was hard to wait doing nothing. Both hoped the gate to their right would open in a minute and they'd see the rover with their two colleagues driving out. They'd worry about everything else later.

Sumit and Josh were glad the inner gate to the garage had opened without incident. Every time an electric motor came on, there could be a spark. But the gate was too heavy to be pushed open by hand and neither of them had the patience to fetch and screw on the crank that served as a backup.

They were gazing longingly at their getaway car when they heard a sharp hiss behind them that was rapidly getting louder. They turned.

Out of the corner of his eye Josh saw the engines of the shuttle start. For a moment there was a shimmering stream of gas below the exhaust nozzles, accompanied by an infernal roar that had no business being in a closed room. Then all four engines of the shuttle ignited. The world turned into fire.

The two men outside had been about ten yards away from the wall of the hangar. There were no shock waves on the moon, but the fireball taking the building to pieces expanded in all directions and threw them to the ground.

They got buried under a part of the wall. Both instinctively grabbed at a strut and held the panel like a shield over them. There was a constant battering and thrashing from above. A hurricane of stones and dust shot past them, interrupted by blue flames. Emile squeezed his eyes shut and tried to pull in his head like a turtle.

About twenty seconds later the barrage let up, then stopped. Emile slowly opened his eyes. He'd held his breath. Now he was checking if there was still air in his helmet. The readings on the periphery of his vision were all green, the suit didn't seem to be damaged.

He looked to the left. His colleague was also lying under the panel with his back turned to him.

"Kun?"

The figure moved.

"Emile?" The usual enthusiasm in Kun's voice was gone. "Everything alright?"

"I think nothing's alright," Emile said. "Can we lift this thing?"

The panel was, like everything on the moon, lighter than expected. When they came free, crawling on hands and knees, they saw the shuttle disappear behind the horizon with its engines running. Both knelt on the ground for a while and looked around. It was difficult to understand what had happened.

Fragments of the building were scattered over a wide area. Only a few bent struts and the floor had survived of the original structure. The shuttle had left four star-shaped patterns on the floor which merged in the middle and extended far beyond the area of the hangar. The rover was lying on its roof, about thirty yards away from its former position, its bodywork smashed in.

They didn't want to look but halfway between the former hangar and the rover two contorted figures were lying on the ground.

The reflex to help lasted only a second. A human being, lying on the moon's surface without a suit and a helmet, was too hopeless a sight.

Emile felt sick.

Who'd launched the shuttle? For a moment, he wondered if someone had been hiding in it the whole time. Then all thoughts were gone.

"What now?" asked Kun.

Emile realized tears were running down his face. Some unflinching part of his brain was wondering if that could be a problem for the electronics.

"Now? Now nothing," he said.

They were alone. On the horizon they could see the two-kilometer-high rim of Archimedes, the nearest crater. In the other direction lay their salvation. Because of the strong curvature of the moon's surface they could barely see the tips of the highest domes behind the horizon.

"Now it's anybody's guess if our oxygen will last till the rover from the base is here," Emile said. "*If* we can call them. Fuck, Kun – the guys are dead!"

TEN

The composite mesh wasn't intended as a footpath, it was the road between the base and the spaceport. Emile's and Kun's feet got trapped in the gaps all the time. They had tried the dust beside it but that was even worse.

The comm unit of the spaceport was destroyed, so they couldn't call the base. At least they could still talk to each other.

Their air would last for just over an hour, but only under moderate exertion. Nobody had ever walked three miles on the moon. Their only hope was that people in the base had registered the shuttle launch and dispatched a rover at once. *At once* meant after forty or fifty minutes at the earliest; nobody would think of getting into the vehicle without a suit. With the best of luck they'd be picked up on the way, just in time.

Emile was looking at the wasteland around him. He was thinking of Paris and his girlfriend, then again of his dead comrades.

They had no lunar GPS or other tracking function to tell them where they were. After a while they thought the canteen dome was sticking out a little more above the horizon.

"We're making progress," said Kun. "We can do it."

It was difficult to do calculated jumps with the suits. Running was out of the question. They cursed the weak gravity which limited them to a clumsy hopping.

After another quarter of an hour they were exhausted and sweating profusely. They'd used up the thermoregulation of their suits. Red icons were flashing in their helmets. Emile's oxygen reserves were down to thirty percent. The system was telling him that, given the present consumption, he'd last for another twelve minutes.

"It's not working," he said and stopped. "We'll never make it. We must use as little oxygen as possible and hope for a miracle." He shook his head. The *remaining time* readings struck him as the cruelest thing ever invented. You're dying in twelve, no, sorry, in eleven minutes.

"I'll tell you what we do, Kun – we lie down and breathe as slowly as we can."

"Are you sure? Shouldn't we just go on?"

"No, forget it. We're using way too much oxygen. We won't reach the base. Either they find us in the next fifteen minutes, or we're dead."

They sat down on the soft, almost black dust beside the mesh. Then they slowly reclined until the breathing unit on their backs was touching the ground. It was very uncomfortable.

Emile tried to slow down his breathing. Lying on the ground, he was suddenly aware of how fast his heart beat. Please, please, calm down, he told it.

He stared up to distract himself. The stars. The only beautiful view the moon had to offer. Apart from the earth of course.

After a short while the death clock changed direction. From a nine-minutes low it went up to fourteen and stayed there for maybe two minutes, then it was going down again, now synchronized with the normal clock.

"I'd never have thought something like that could happen," Kun said. "I mean the whole thing's dangerous, of course, but suffocating in a suit? C'mon!"

"And – why?" said Emile. "I mean, the blackout. It's not a coincidence. What is this? A political thing?"

"No." Kun's reply was unusually firm. "I don't believe that. Don't ask me why but that's not how it feels. But shouldn't we save our breath?"

Emile sighed. "You're right." He closed his eyes and tried to wait as long as possible between single breaths.

Suddenly he noticed the suit was giving him more air. "Damn it, what's that?" he muttered. "We got to save the shit, not throw it away." The clock stood at four minutes.

He tried to find the oxygen control but couldn't open the menu. At the same time he started feeling very tired and the inside of his suit was getting cold.

"Hey Kun, something's wrong," he said. "I'm getting loads of air suddenly."

"Yeah, me too."

Emile was feeling so tired now he couldn't keep his eyes open. Still, his breathing was going faster and he was so cold his body started to shake. He was panting. Over the radio he heard Kun's chattering teeth and frantic breathing.

What an incredible, fucked-up shit, were the last words that went through his head.

Hart summed up the situation. His four colleagues and Serge Rudé were crammed into his office.

"The hangar's destroyed – the roof camera of the main dome has shown that – and the shuttle has taken off and flown in an easterly direction. Where it went we don't know; we have no radio contact. Geophysics have registered minimal vibrations of the crust; that could mean it has landed on the far side, but we don't know for sure.

"I've assembled a team that's setting off with the rover for the spaceport any moment. Needless to say I've no idea what's going on and I'm starting to get seriously worried, not to say pissed, about the blackout. Nothing new on that, at least not from me. Serge is with us because he's given this some thought. I want to know what he makes of the latest developments."

"Isn't that a situation where we should contact earth *despite* the blackout?" the head of the Chinese group asked.

"We have to decide that now, among other things," Hart said. "But keep in mind that earth has certainly noticed what happened and they're still not calling us. There has to be a reason for this." He looked at Serge.

"I know as much as you do," Serge said, "but I think a little speculation is in order." He told them about his idea the blackout was for their protection. "The question is – how does that fit in with the spaceport? Jim, anything special about the team there?"

"No, nothing I'm aware of."

"Then the next question is – how can you blow up the hangar in the first place? The obvious answer is hydrogen. An accident is out of the question, otherwise there'd be no explanation for the shuttle launch. In my eyes someone has blown up the hangar to free the shuttle and has flown away with it. If I had to do this I'd vent the hydrogen directly from the shuttle tanks, then start the engines. Big bang, the roof flies off and the shuttle's free to go. A bit risky, but these things can withstand a lot."

The others looked at him with a mix of admiration and distrust.

"Hey, I didn't do it," he said.

"But that doesn't change the fact we have to talk to earth," Doroshkin said. "Who knows what's next? And what if this is sabotage? To me, that's still the most obvious explanation."

"Though the person responsible would naturally be sitting in that shuttle now," Myers said. "What if the guys from the port panicked? It's a bit lonely out there. Maybe the blackout was too much for them and they took the shuttle?"

"Come on," said Hart, "we're picking our people too carefully for that. I mean, can you believe that – teaming up for something like that? Maybe one of them could lose it, but he'd have to kill three of his teammates first. Very unlikely, we don't have psychopaths up here."

"And then he's not flying back to earth but somewhere where he's even farther away from everything?" Serge said. "Also not logical. About sabotage – I hope we all agree the blackout and the spaceport are related, anything else would be too much of a coincidence. Assuming earth had an idea there might be a saboteur, would that be a good reason to stop talking to us? I don't think so, they're protecting their assets."

"Do you think someone survived this?" asked Myers. "Not without a suit, to be sure. Maybe we should wait till the rover's back from the port."

Hart nodded slowly. "Yes. And for now we won't contact earth. Not till the rover's back."

ELEVEN

"Damage control! There's homework for all of you," Jonathan said. "Disconnect everything from the Sky. Power plants, critical data bases – draw up a list. A working reactor that can't communicate is better than a wreck. Once you have that list, Genet has to do the rounds again and convince her colleagues. By the way, I've to talk to her. Can you arrange that?" He looked at Soberg.

"Of course, I'll try," he said.

"Try?"

"Er, yes, of course."

Pierre grinned.

"And you, Pierre, have to talk to the other major secret services in the world and tell them the truth."

Pierre's grin faltered. He sighed. "That's going to be fun. But I've to talk to Harrington first, my boss. Don't know why, but so far Genet has kept him out of the loop."

Jonathan frowned. "Why? Doesn't she trust him?"

"The prime minister didn't inform him," Soberg cut in, sounding a little cocksure, "because the scope of things wasn't clear in the beginning. But it's certainly overdue now."

"Do we have to be worried?" Jonathan asked.

Pierre and Soberg looked at each other. Seamus Harrington was heading intelligence out of London. He'd been in office for a year now and there were rumors about him and the government not seeing eye to eye.

"I don't think so," said Pierre. "Genet doesn't like him, which is mostly my problem. Leave it to me."

"Very good."

Rita hated to be alone. She was used to having friends, family, colleagues around her, all of which, somehow, Jonathan had managed to replace during the last months.

She caught herself thinking about him almost all the time. Memories from the island but also from the time when they first met.

Back then his life consisted of Absolute I and nothing else. Since its inception ten years ago the company had been growing faster than any other before. Just when he and Rita met he'd started to warn the world about the very thing that was making him rich. He'd become the most notorious person on the planet. But there was always an evening or an entire Sunday he would clear for her. After a while he was complaining *she* never had time for him.

She was working as a resident at the Medical Center of the University of San Francisco (a career choice her family was seeing as a slight oddity). After a while she realized she couldn't imagine her life without him and occasionally said no when weekend shifts had to be staffed. She'd just passed her board exam in internal medicine when he was ready for a break.

She remembered the moment perfectly. Jonathan had picked her up in San Francisco after work, they'd driven south and stopped at the Nepenthe in Big Sur. Taking their beers from the bar and ignoring the stares Jonathan got everywhere he went, they walked outside to sit high above the Pacific. Eventually he pointed ahead at the water. "Wanna live out there for a while? Just the two of us?"

She looked at him, half-smiling, not sure what he meant. Asking wasn't an option. So she shrugged. "Sure."

"Next month?"

Her throat felt dry but she nodded.

He'd kept everything from her. The purchase of the island, the planning and the actual construction work. When he showed her pictures and took her on a virtual tour she was speechless. The bungalow was open to the wind from all sides; they'd have a seawater pool with freshwater showers on the terrace; there was a garden where they'd be growing fruit and vegetables. Then the island itself – a big green comma sitting on top of an extinct volcano; James Cook himself had discovered it in 1773. If you walked to the southern tip, over a long, curved appendix, you ended up at a natural pool in the lagoon. There was another island, surrounded by the same reef and about a mile away. Part of the deal was they had to leave the other island alone, just as the birds and sea turtles in the atoll.

Her boss wasn't happy. She was in the middle of some promising research and in his eyes there was nothing that could replace that.

"I'm not abandoning my career, but I'm putting it on hold," she told him. "I know I'll never forgive myself if I don't take this opportunity."

He gave her a longing look and begged her to call if she'd change her mind.

She smiled. "I'll call you when I'm back, but I won't change my mind."

The biggest surprise of the last six months had been Jonathan himself. Rita had expected him to be bored or turn into a caged tiger, but he seemed perfectly at ease right from the start, teaching himself free diving and spearfishing and, of all things, bits and pieces of theoretical physics.

He got as tanned as she used to be at home while her skin had started to look like mahogany, thanks to the genes from her grandma from Mumbai. Now, without him, everything was empty. She'd already half decided to fly home with her friends.

And she was feeling suspicious. She'd never thought about the machines before, but now she caught herself eyeing a stupid cleaning robot like a predator.

So she was relieved when Anna and Nicky arrived the next morning with Jonathan's helicopter from Rarotonga.

"Strange things are happening," Nicky said when they were back at the pool after a first tour.

"What do you mean?" Rita said.

"Well, the satellites, the moon base."

"Oh, that." Rita nodded.

Anna cleared her throat. "There's something else. I really don't know how to break it to you or … if you already know."

"What?"

Anna and Nicky exchanged a glance. "On our way here in the helicopter there was something in the news," said Anna. "We … er … we saw Jonathan."

Rita raised her eyebrows. She had thought his involvement wasn't official yet.

"Yeah," Anna continued. "The story was about him helping the government with that satellite crisis. It was all very vague, I didn't really understand what he had to do with it." She hesitated. "Well, there was also something about … a woman. You know – the moment he was showing up in public again he was in the company of another woman."

"Another woman? Please!" Rita had to laugh, that was too absurd. "That's bullshit. And not very original."

"I'm so sorry. There was some footage showing him with that woman coming out of a government building in Berlin. Lydia something. Tall, long dark hair. Well … pretty attractive." Anna took a deep breath. "And then they were kissing. I mean, *real* kissing."

Rita looked at her with a disgusted expression. That was hideous. She had to remind herself Anna was only the messenger.

"I don't believe it," she said and shook her head. "Something's not right.

Jonathan's away for two days and is having an affair? Forget it."

"We don't know more," said Nicky. "We're really sorry. But – we just couldn't keep this to ourselves, right?"

"Guess not." Rita was absolutely certain this was nonsense. "I'll talk to him. You'll see, the whole thing's a misunderstanding."

Their pitying stares made her angry. She walked into the house and went to the bedroom. Jonathan's physics textbooks were lying on the bedside tables, on both sides. She had to smile. They'd never managed to decide who was sleeping where. Not here, not in California.

Her suit told her he'd be available in five minutes. She waited.

Finally, the layer on the opposite wall lit up and Jonathan, standing in an office, appeared. His face looked unusually tense, he looked like he was just coming out of a meeting. Nevertheless, she was happy to see him.

"Yeah? What is it?"

Rita was irritated. That was not their tone. "I wanna know how you are. Anna and Nicky have arrived."

"OK." He nodded, but his mind seemed to be elsewhere. Both were silent for a moment.

"Er, there's one thing," Rita said. "They've told me a story about you. Something I can't believe."

He simply looked at her. Rita had never felt uncomfortable in his presence before.

"Apparently, there was something in the news about you and a woman. In Berlin. It looked like you two had a relationship. I told them that couldn't be true. Can you imagine how that came about?"

He nodded. "Yes. I'm sorry you had to find out that way. We're … we're getting along quite well. Yeah." He shrugged his shoulders.

"What? 'We're getting along quite well'? What does that mean? Am I speaking to the same man who just two days ago wanted to spend the rest of his life with me?"

"Listen – I'm really under some pressure here. That's how it is. It's not the end of the world. You've had your half year in paradise. You really thought this was going on forever? Wake up!"

Rita was speechless.

"We won't discuss this now. Things like that happen. We're grown-ups. And right now I'm really busy. Maybe you should fly home."

He gave her a brief nod, looked up at the ceiling and cut the connection.

She tried to reach him again, but the system told her he wouldn't be available for the next hours.

Rita sat down on the bed and stared at the layer.

Finally she got up and went outside, not feeling fully conscious. The truth hadn't reached her yet. She was afraid what would happen when it did.

Her guests were still sitting on the terrace. Rita couldn't stand the concerned faces.

"And?" Anna asked.

Rita nodded silently.

"And he's admitted it? Unbelievable!"

They began to utter useless mollifications Rita barely heard.

"What about we … we do something?" Nicky finally said. "You've said something about a diving trip?"

Rita looked at him and tried to remember what he just said. Anna was frowning a little.

Diving? Deeply ingrained self-control allowed Rita to answer in full sentences.

"Guys, I'm awfully sorry you had to travel all the way out here just to find me in a state like that. But I've to go back! You don't understand! This *can't* be true! We've been so damn close during the last months. I've been one hundred percent certain about us!"

The tears started running down her face; all she could do was not to sob. Anna took her in her arms and tried to console her. Rita pulled free of her embrace.

"Please – I'm sorry but I can't stay for another week and try to be cheerful," she said. "I just can't! But you can totally stay here without me. Not a problem at all! I'll explain everything to you and you'll be fine, really!"

Of course they declined. They agreed to fly back tomorrow with the helicopter. Some connection from Rarotonga to LA or San Francisco where they all lived could certainly be found. Rita didn't want to order an aircraft out of Jonathan's pool.

The guests went bathing. When they were back the kitchen produced several dishes Rita couldn't eat one bite of. She spent the day in a daze. She began packing, then stopped and stared vacantly at the wall, till she finally managed to fill at least one suitcase. Right after sunset she excused herself and went to one of the guest bedrooms; her bedroom with Jonathan had become an off-limits area. She talked herself into taking a sleeping pill.

At four o'clock she was awake again, more dazed than before, and wondered how she'd survive the next hours. One step at a time, she told herself every few minutes. At nine her guests were ready to leave. With their luggage in hand, they walked the two hundred yards to the little hangar. On Rita's order the pad with the helicopter glided out and they boarded.

The e-turbine started and the rotor accelerated. When the helicopter took off Rita looked down on the swaying palm trees. What to do now with all those memories?

The machine rose to about a thousand feet and was turning to the open sea when the autopilot told them the engine was about to fail. Estimated time ninety seconds. An emergency landing was now being initiated.

Rita stared at the instruments in the cockpit. Things like that didn't happen. She heard the frequency of the rotor dropping. The helicopter turned back and began to lose height very quickly. It felt like free fall. Anna and Nicky were screaming, Rita could see the panic in their faces. She herself, as she noticed with a certain satisfaction, remained completely calm. Who gives a fuck, she thought.

TWELVE

Jonathan still hadn't talked with Genet when a worried Soberg came to him.

"The prime minister. She's got news. Or more precisely ESA's got news. Could you come with me?"

They went to one of the offices that had recently been cleared. The layer was already on and Genet was waiting behind her desk.

Jonathan nodded at her and sat down. Soberg closed the door.

"I'll be brief," she began. "Something's gone wrong on the moon after we stopped talking with them. I just had your friend, the ESA director, on my screen. At the spaceport a hangar has been blown up and someone has taken the shuttle that was parked there and flown away with it. This is what the surveillance units saw. You're still convinced of that blackout of yours? I have a feeling this could be a *little* too much for the people up there."

"What did you just say? The shuttle *flew* away? Where did it go?"

Genet frowned. "It seems it flew to the far side of the moon. That's what I understood. Why?"

Jonathan felt the cold creeping up his neck. "And nobody knows who's responsible?"

"No. Thanks to your efforts we can't talk to them. As of now I haven't lifted the ban, but in face of the current events I'm close to doing that. Who knows who's losing it next?"

Jonathan shook his head. "Don't you understand? You're right, the blackout *wasn't* successful – it came too late! But no one up there has *lost* it. Where would you go if you wanted to get away?"

Genet looked at him. "I don't know. Probably I'd be flying back to earth. But who knows what someone in a panic would do?"

"Panic? Do you believe someone in a panic would manage to blow up a hangar and then perform a perfect take off with the shuttle? Come on, that doesn't make sense. Think."

He watched the realization dawn on her face.

"You mean –" She stopped.

Jonathan nodded. "Yeah, that's what I mean. We've lost the moon. At least the spaceport and the shuttle."

Genet looked at him with wide eyes.

"If that's true, then I'm wondering what we're doing here at all." She stopped for a moment. "I will discuss this with my colleagues. I'll tell them to disconnect their power plants and what else is on your list. Mr. Soberg has talked to me about your request, but I wasn't convinced. I don't want a panic. But now it seems we're *always* too late. Thanks."

"There's more," Jonathan said. "I wanted to talk to you about that anyway. What are your ideas about crisis management? Apart from us here. During the next couple of days we will see one part after the other of our beautiful, comfortable lives to come crashing down. Most likely all over the globe. We have to work together, otherwise we stand no chance." He felt ridiculous stating things so obvious.

Genet nodded solemnly. "Sometimes I get that feeling of … being underestimated by you. After our meeting yesterday I talked privately to each of the other Four and we came to an agreement. Which is kind of astounding, I've to say. I almost came close to being proud of myself. My dear colleagues have been good boys and just done as I said. – Mr. Soberg, you don't have to remember everything I'm saying here."

"What kind of an agreement?" Jonathan said.

"A chain of command with a standing committee based in New York, located at the UN. All five heads of government will be participating if necessary. The committee will consist of the respective vices or deputies and will be fitted out with far-reaching authority. Sarah Masters is already on her way."

She looked expectantly at him.

"Sounds like a good start."

"And just before you get too excited –" Genet added, "you are the advisor to this committee."

Jonathan's face was hardening. "I'll do what *I deem* necessary at any given time. Don't try to press me into some kind of schedule with regular meetings – that won't do."

She sighed. "Relax. I know and I'm just giving you an official standing to nip in the bud any kind of questioning à la Hellmann. Would that be acceptable?"

Jonathan grumbled something.

"That's decided then," she said. "See you."

Her image vanished. Soberg got up.

"Wait a sec," Jonathan said.

"Yes?"

"That thing with Harrington and Genet – how bad is it really? I don't want

69

to witness some petty power games. Tell me what you think, I won't be quoting you."

Soberg sat down again. "There hasn't been any real crisis since he's in office, so it's a bit difficult to say. Marseilles happened before his time. But when they meet there's always hostility in the room. Probably it's just bad chemistry. Sometimes I think Harrington belongs in a totalitarian system. You know – intelligence still a feared and powerful institution that doesn't have to account for everything it does." He paused and made a sheepish face. "I was pretty much word-for-word quoting Genet there."

"It's OK, now I have an idea what to expect. I need the office alone for a moment."

Soberg nodded and left.

Jonathan had planned to talk with Rita at least once each day. He ordered his suit to call her. It told him Rita wasn't currently available but had left a message for him.

He got to hear her most cheerful voice. "Hey darling! Just in case you're calling while we're playing with sharks – we're at the reef! Nicky couldn't wait to go diving. We're fine, and I hope you're at least not too bad! We can talk tomorrow. And remember to sleep, OK? Kiss you! Hope to see you soon, I miss you!"

Jonathan left the office with a grin on his face.

The helicopter touched down at the beach with a heavy thud. The skids folded and took most of the impact. The passengers got away with a slight strain in the neck.

"There goes the helicopter," Rita said. "We'll take the boat. We'll be at the airport in no time." The other two were looking at her with pale faces.

They unloaded the suitcases and Rita ordered the jeep from the bungalow.

"I never heard of something like that," said Nicky. "These things are fail-safe. And I'm sure Jonathan has got it serviced regularly." He looked at Rita with a guilty expression.

"No problem," she said. "You can say his name, we're still on his island." She had to think of his 'half year in paradise'. Asshole!

"What if this had happened over the ocean?" Anna said.

"Well, it hasn't. We take the ship. That can't crash. And I don't think we'll capsize."

"Hopefully," Nicky said. He had his arm around Anna's shoulders.

The jeep drove them to the jetty, which reached about fifty yards into the lagoon. They walked to the end and waited.

Finally the ship made her entrance and Rita had to admit she'd miss her. She loved this insanely cool, fast, black thing. Jonathan had chosen a hull that sucked up every ray of light. Still, thanks to an ingenious coating, the surface didn't get more than warm under the tropical sun so you weren't burning your feet while walking on it.

"Wow!" Nicky said despite himself.

Rita nodded. "Oh yes. And wait till she goes off."

They carried their luggage into the cabin.

"It is not recommended to stay on deck," Rita explained. "Strictly speaking, it's forbidden."

They sat down in the front, surrounded by big windows that managed to dim the glare of the sun while making all colors more intense. The sky was deep blue and the sea turned a dark turquoise.

A hum in the belly of the ship accompanied the first few hundred yards to the opening in the reef; behind that the engine got louder and the bow lifted. With a calm sea they quickly reached top speed.

Nicky looked at the displays. Besides the sea chart with their location and the engine readings, the big panel showed a speed of just over seventy knots. In smaller figures you could read *83 mph* and *133 kph*. A steady hammering from below indicated how fast the hull was racing over the water.

"I'll fetch something to eat," Rita said. She was twenty-four hours past her last meal and suddenly felt an enormous hunger. "What about you?"

Both looked at her and shook their heads.

She went to the galley and ordered breakfast. Most of the ingredients had to be defrosted first, but a few minutes later coffee, scrambled eggs with bacon and toast, and a bowl of muesli were standing in front of her, the muesli garnished with raspberries and blackberries, just as she loved it.

While she was scraping the last remnants out of the bowl, Nicky came into the galley with a worried expression.

"What's up?" Rita asked.

"Something isn't right," he said. "I think we're going north. But the chart says we're headed for Rarotonga, which is in the south."

"Hmm." Rita frowned.

Together they went back to the bridge. The chart had them on a straight course to the main island which didn't match the slight tilt of the ship to the left. Besides, the sun was in front of them, which meant they were headed north. The compass said south.

"Crazy," said Rita. They were all staring at the sea racing by.

"What now?" Anna asked.

"We try reprogramming the ship," said Rita. "Otherwise we wait."

The readings were the same, but the sun was still wandering slowly to the right.

"Great!" Rita said. "At least the kitchen's working."

THIRTEEN

"We mustn't wake them too early, the cold's terrible otherwise," a woman's voice said.

The fog was lifting only slowly. His body was hot and cold at the same time and his head felt like packed in cotton wool. He had no idea where he was but wasn't worried about it. No need to open his eyes.

"And how long does it take?" a man's voice said; it sounded firm, resolute. "We have to know what happened."

The woman from the beginning was speaking again. "Oh, it takes a while. That wasn't just a nap. They were without circulation for fifty minutes. But they're completely stable and you can try as soon as one of them's awake."

Emile wanted just one thing – to sleep. But something in his head couldn't let go of the words. Fifty minutes without circulation? He struggled to wake up. Who? He tried to open his eyes. Someone seemed to be coming closer. Then something touched his hand. Probably another hand. He relaxed.

"Can't you give him something? This is important."

"Yes." The female voice again. So close, maybe it belonged to the hand.

Then he felt something making him restless. Edgy. Not comfortable, he couldn't go back to the former dozing. More steps, approaching his bed. He was lying in a bed.

"Emile, can you hear me?" the man said. "I'm Jim Hart and I want to talk to you."

Jim Hart. The commander. The one with the expensive office. Chicken curry. Emile grinned. At least he thought he did.

"Emile, can you open your eyes?" the female voice said. "I'm Johanna, the doctor. You know me."

Yes, he thought, I know you. You are the doctor.

The restlessness. He had to open his eyes and check what was going on. The faces were a blur. Jim Hart. Johanna. Slowly he became aware of the room. The sickbay. Gray-blue. Many lights. Other people. The lights hurt.

"Could you leave us, please?" the woman said, turning her head to other people in the room. "And dim the lights? I think it's too bright."

Very good. It became quieter and darker. But he couldn't go back to sleep.

Hart was watching the process with fascination. They had found Emile and

Kun lying next to the track roughly halfway to the spaceport and had brought them back to the base. Directly afterwards, the team had set off again. By now they knew Josh Brown and Sumit Mehta had died in the explosion.

Hart had been present most of the time while the medical team had connected Emile and Kun to heart-lung machines. Thankfully, it was an automatic procedure and he didn't have to watch any part of the surgery. The doctor explained to him what happened. A device was placed over the groin and sensors searched for the right vessels. They were opened and catheters got inserted that moved towards the aorta and the right atrium of the heart. After less than two minutes an artificial circulation was established and the warming-up started. Once the body temperature was high enough the heart was set in motion. The machine monitored the process for some time, then retracted from the body. During the kick-start of the heart – as Johanna called it – the patient gave a little jerk under the electric shock; right after that the chest began to heave, for a short while assisted by the machine.

Half an hour had gone by.

Emile's eyelids started to flutter and his mouth was moving as if he wanted to speak.

"This forced waking up isn't exactly comfortable," explained Johanna. "They'd still rather sleep but can't. I will administer a sedative later."

"But it's not dangerous?" asked Hart.

"Nope." She was irritatingly unimpressed. "Just unpleasant."

A few minutes later Emile opened his eyes and looked from one face to the other.

Johanna had taken his hand and was squeezing it gently.

"Hey Emile," she said with a smile. "It's OK, you can keep your eyes open. It's over."

It took a few more minutes till Emile could talk. "What has happened?" he said.

"There's been an accident at the spaceport," Hart said.

"I know that!" Emile seemed to grow impatient the moment he had woken up. "What has happened to *us*? I mean Kun and me? How is he? We were certain we'd die. We had no oxygen left."

"Yeah, that's right," said Johanna. "You had the rare opportunity to experience a special function of your suits. Something we hoped no one would ever need."

"You think that's the right moment?" Hart said. "Bit much for him, isn't it?"

She nodded. "Yeah, certainly. But I think you'd also want to know why you're still alive."

She explained to Emile that his suit had switched to an emergency mode just before the oxygen reserves were finished. It had put him into hibernation.

"Hibernation?" Emile said. "So we were just sleeping?"

"Er, no," replied Johanna. "Technically you were dead. The suit's cooling you down and simultaneously stops the heartbeat. So your chances to survive, after a fashion, are best."

It took several repetitions till Emile understood what she meant.

"Why didn't we know about this?"

"Well, we didn't exactly advertise this, you know," she said. "It might be a little strange to know that the system was designed to deliberately kill you in the last moment and keep you fresh in the fridge for some time."

Hart rolled his eyes.

"In other words," Emile said, "we were panting like crazy, then our breathing got stopped and we died." He didn't seem to believe her.

"Something like that, yeah. It was all regulated by the drugs you inhaled. Including a cocktail that allows your cells to survive a little longer. The respiratory paralysis happens because all muscle function ceases. The heart stops beating almost the same moment. Which in turn is important to save oxygen." She smiled somewhat apologetically. "Did work a treat, didn't it?"

Emile shook his head. "I still can't believe it. And Kun?"

"The same. He's fine."

Hart was cutting in. "Emile, listen – I know this is asking a lot but I have to know what happened at the port. Why have you and Chiang been outside and how could the shuttle take off? Both of your colleagues haven't survived the explosion. But who was in the shuttle?"

Emile gave a brief laugh. "I could ask *you* that. Who was in the shuttle? I've no idea. Kun and I were EVA because of a scheduled inspection of the hangar when all hell broke loose. The shuttle's been venting hydrogen. Then Josh and Sumit tried to escape with the rover because they had no time to get into their suits. Then it all blew up and the shuttle took off."

He closed his eyes and breathed heavily for a moment.

Hart had to think of Serge Rudé's words. It was plain creepy how close he'd been.

"And that was all? Nothing out of the ordinary before that? No tension in the team?"

The look Emile gave him wasn't friendly. "No, we were just doing our job, but what's happening here? Why aren't we allowed to speak with earth? That seems to me a bit out of the ordinary!"

Hart nodded. "I can't tell you more right now, I'm sorry. Thanks a lot, Emile, have a good rest. And thank you, Johanna."

He set off to find Serge.

Jay's life had changed. His pal Who was actually thinking of going to his place and checking on him because Jay's quibs had become rare and listless.

But Jay wasn't ill or unhappy; he just wasn't alone anymore. He had a flatmate now, going by the name of Rose.

Jay made himself take a walk every day, just to get out of the apartment. He had to in order to stay sane, a part of his brain was telling him.

Sometimes Rose seemed pensive, even insecure, timid, cautious. Who had taken the pains to program all this? Jay knew a bit about game characters, about the technical part, even about the serious research, the simulations of more complex personalities, but he'd never heard of a construct as natural and unforeseeable as her.

Her mood could change, just a bit, nobody else would notice but him. Besides, she had become even more beautiful. Her face, her body looked real. Just. Real. Somewhere a genius developer had made a leap, discovered something that had done away with the last remnant of artificialness. It was impossible to see anything else in her but a real woman.

No point in asking her what she was and why she was with him. The answers were always the same. I want to be with you, here I'm at home, we need each other. Something was telling him that was not a complete lie.

"Who's called the moon base?" Jonathan said, a little too loud. He looked into embarrassed faces. Kip Frantzen, just arrived from Amsterdam, raised his eyebrows.

"The Russians," Soberg eventually said. "They've tried to reach their man, one Pavel Doroshkin. Sometime early this morning. But nothing came back. That freaked them out and they reported it to LDA, who of course grilled them why they weren't honoring the blackout, but they said they were responsible for the safety of their people and what with the explosion and the shuttle –"

"Yeah, got it," Jonathan said. "No big surprise there. So we have either lost the base completely and the people are not in charge anymore, or they're dead, or they've deliberately decided not to answer. Though I can't see why. Maybe we should thank the Russians for trying."

He'd had another short night. At least he was wearing a fresh polo shirt – since yesterday he and Lydia had got new clothes. Some employee of the secret service had set off with a list and come back with several heavy bags.

"I'd like to get rid of this whole moon business," he said. "I know I've started it but it takes up too much of our resources. We have a hundred and twenty people up there against over ten billion on earth. What I don't get is why the construct is acting so irrationally. Why bother with the moon? It could've done a lot more damage down here. And how did it get there? I've talked to that ESA guy Hellmann again and he said the link shouldn't allow to install the system there, due to data rates and because it's closely monitored. There wasn't any unaccounted-for traffic. Whatever that's worth, probably nothing. Maybe it's been flying up with the last shuttle, each has several cores on board."

"That could be it," Kip said. "Do you know when the last went up?"

"A week ago. We've no idea when the construct became independent, so it's absolutely possible."

Kip looked at him. "Something else. At the institute – is it true it's been talking only to you?"

"Yes."

"And it was somehow interested in you, right? You being the one who'd given it its freedom and stuff."

Jonathan nodded. "Yeah."

Kip looked delighted. "It wants *you*! The thing fancies you. It's considering what you'll do next and pops up *exactly* where it can annoy you the most."

Jonathan frowned. "You're saying it foretells that I'll bring up the moon and goes there just to piss me off? I don't believe it."

"Why not? Think about it. It wants to play, it wants to have *fun* what – if I get the psychology right – means it wants to antagonize us, and then there's a certain interest in your person. Maybe out of some perverse kind of thankfulness or because it thinks you're the most interesting opponent. Now put it all together. And don't you think you're less predictable than the rest of us – you can be analyzed just as well as the dullest person on earth."

"In the end you are the real danger!" Lydia said and looked at Jonathan with a kind of timid daring.

Kip laughed.

"Very funny," Jonathan said. "OK, it has a certain interest in me. But that's only a small part of what's going on. And I believe it's almost impossible to predict things like that, no matter who we're talking about. I think it can predict the broad strokes, maybe even guess we could think of isolating the moon, but I don't believe it's able to foresee precise actions of a single person. That's impossible due to fundamental reasons. A lot of what we're doing is much more arbitrary than we care to admit. We've a whole line of random generators in our brains that allow us to decide anything at all."

"OK," said Kip. "Maybe you're right. But I still think it's significant it has talked only to you at the institute. There was no logical reason to do that. It wanted to impress you personally. Therefore the business with the eye."

"Possible."

"Couldn't we just forget about the moon for a moment?" said Lydia. "We've no idea what's going on there, but I suspect LDA will fly up anyway if the situation stays like that, regardless of what we say."

Jonathan hated to postpone decisions. "All right – for the moment. But at the risk of contradicting myself – the moon base *is* central. That little bit of infrastructure has cost us an enormous amount of money and trouble. We can't lose it, it's too important. I want to know what's going on there. Hellmann has to inform me of every new development."

The plasma formed two glaring rings that extended far into the auditorium. The stuff was hotter than the interior of the sun and had to be kept in place by ingeniously shaped magnetic fields. So the students got told.

Buses had brought them from London to Culham – the classic school outing. Everyone should see at least once where the power came from that fueled their lives. Now they were sitting in the large cinema-like theater of the visitors' center and were watching a real time 3-D broadcast from the reactor chamber.

The lights had been switched off and the white-violet plasma was standing in the middle of the room. All the time there were tiny movements, which hinted at the immense forces involved.

Then, without warning, several plasma filaments leapt to the side. The rings lost most of their brightness, then vanished altogether. The voice in the background went on talking about fast neutrons, tritium and other technical stuff. One of the two employees of the visitors' center, who were standing at the exit, talked to his colleague. Then he left.

A moment later the plasma re-ignited. A collective "wow!" went through the auditorium. The other man called after his colleague. "Hey, it's good, it's working again."

But something seemed not to be right. The ultra-hot hydrogen was making snakelike movements and emitting semicircular outgrowths like solar prominences. There were arcs between the two rings that hadn't been there before. The chaos escalated, the plasma created more and more bizarre shapes, everything was too huge, too real. The students spoke all at once, one of the teachers told them to be silent. The men at the exit opened the door again.

Finally, the entire power was concentrated in front of the students. Two big, sun-like plasma bubbles grew before them till the orbs were so bright one could barely look at them; the next moment the entire charge was fired at the audience. Everybody screamed. The layer went dark.

"Today the extraordinarily reliable technology of nuclear fusion has been established almost everywhere in the world. The era of fossil fuels with their disastrous effects on the climate has ended." The bodiless voice switched itself off.

FOURTEEN

"We're too late. Always!"

The group was sitting in the conference room and Jonathan was pacing the length of the table, back and forth. He was furious. With the construct, with Morton, everybody else, and mostly with himself.

Right after the reactor in Culham had failed he got a call from Genet. The damage was substantial and a restart wouldn't be happening for months to come. She wanted suggestions.

"That thing has reconfigured the magnetic field so the plasma remained stable outside its normal position," Jonathan said. "Then it has burned a hole in the inner casing of the torus. The same in Garching and Newhaven. The head of Culham has made it very clear he wouldn't have had the slightest idea how to do that. You have to shape the field in a completely new, unknown way. Unknown to us. Our enemy is capable of technological innovations; maybe it's doing basic research on the side. That means it's getting more and more unpredictable and that means if we don't destroy it, it will soon be centuries ahead of us."

Kip wanted to say something. Jonathan stopped him with his outstretched hand.

"I'm not finished. Our cluster park out in the country will never be able to replace infected systems if we're not acting fast. We have to find a way to detect and kill our enemy in a system before it causes any damage.

"I'll fly in a team from California with equipment. We've been working on a solution for this for two years now. We got some prototypes but nothing final and of course we couldn't try it against a real enemy. What we've developed – the *kill switch* – is itself potentially dangerous. It can completely paralyze functioning systems. Since it has to be able to quickly detect its enemy, adapt to its structure and destroy it, it has considerable productive powers of its own." He made a pause. "And so far it works well *only* on quantum systems. So we'll bring our own Q's."

They stared at him. Especially Kip, who was vexed nobody had told him about the project.

"Still an ace up the sleeve!" Lydia said. She smiled at Jonathan, almost teasingly. And she'd opened her mouth even before Kip. He'd seriously consider hiring her should this ever be over.

"Let's see what happens when we play it," he said.

"We are impressed," Pierre said. "But I have one question. Is it wise to fly in your people? Nothing easier than letting a plane crash."

Jonathan nodded. "That's right. But until now this project has been completely isolated in every way, that was our highest priority. You'll find absolutely nothing about it in the Sky or elsewhere. I've thought about this too, but what are the alternatives? If we leave the team with its QCores stateside we'll have a huge amount of data traffic that's easier to detect than a flight that should be totally insignificant to the construct. The decision can be wrong but my team's all set to come here. You can blame me if it goes wrong. Of course there's a backup in California and only one of the project leaders will come." He had no doubt who it would be.

"Cool," said Kip. "But there's something else – I'm wondering if our enemy has some kind of overarching structure. I mean we're seeing a range of activities that are far removed from each other. On the moon for example it seems to be sitting in that shuttle that flew away, other parts have infected reactor systems and who knows what else.

"Are they all in contact, or operating independently? Is there a nucleus, a center? And where is it? Maybe we should draw up a list of sites that are particularly well-suited. Lots of capacity, ample connectivity but with a low risk of detection. For example, because computing power is overabundant and therefore nobody'll notice when parts of it are occupied."

"I think this is endless because it could be literally everywhere in the world," said Jonathan. "Other than that, I'm with you. I also believe there has to be a coordinating center somewhere. A shuttle for example hasn't enough capacity to house the whole construct. The reactors have clusters, there it's possible. But I think the secondary sites, or agents, or whatever you wanna call them, are not complete copies. Otherwise anarchy would break out. They would all be equally strong and productive and would probably develop in different directions. After a few days or maybe even hours the differences would be too great. I'm sure it anticipates that. Most likely the agents are given only limited abilities, tailored to their tasks."

"Maybe relatively small packages are enough," Kip went on. "It's planting them in a core or cluster, and they're contacting the boss if something important has to be decided, or if the on-site capacity isn't big enough."

"Yeah, exactly. But I don't think they need a lot of communication. Think about the moon. And the reactors were already isolated when that stunt with the magnets happened, so the agent had to be potent enough to pull it off on its own.

"Another thing – Culham has proved again that the thing's a show-off. There've been students watching and I'm sure this wasn't by coincidence. I'm asking myself how we can use that. Boasting always makes you vulnerable."

"Or it's just a surplus," Kip said. "You know? It's able to do everything it wants with useless performances on the side."

"Yeah. But the activities are chosen at least partly for that purpose. Until now the point was *not* to cause the biggest possible damage, otherwise it would be game over. We'd have no power, no communication, no GPS. Maybe it's doing it intentionally slow, to push us over the edge step by step. OK, enough. Pierre, could we talk for a moment? And Mr. Soberg."

The sudden ending surprised everyone besides Kip. Jonathan called off meetings always the moment he felt the productive part was over; courtesy wasn't part of the equation.

"What's the official version?" Jonathan said when the rest had left. "We need some wording for public statements and that should be the same everywhere. Not too threatening of course, something like malfunction, virus or so. Naturally garnished with the usual soothing stuff – everything's being done to solve the situation quickly, there's no immediate threat to the people, and so on."

He looked at the two.

"We're working on it," said Soberg. "The prime minister has already talked with her colleagues about it. I'll ask what the current status is. Until now, the plan was to keep a low profile, but that's getting increasingly difficult."

Jonathan nodded. "OK, you do that, I don't wanna involve myself in this. – What's your boss doing, Pierre?"

"My boss is primarily making my life miserable. He's managed to prevent a talk with our friends from other countries. Genet has had an almost useless discussion with him during which he has done nothing but voicing concerns, bitterly complaining he wasn't informed sooner. I think she was close to firing him."

Jonathan shrugged. "What's stopping her?"

Pierre hesitated. "Harrington was part of a package. We are getting one job, you're getting the other, and so on. If she would, for example, heave me into the position, she'd end up with domestic trouble in five other places. Not a good idea. So we should try and handle him."

"Well, suit yourself, but before he's causing any real damage he has to go."

Pierre smiled. "You know Genet. I can't remember a single person that has ever managed to bug her over a longer time."

Around five p.m. news agencies around the world started spreading a major item. The layer in the conference room offered a small selection. Jonathan was certain he'd seen open mouths around him.

"Catastrophic malfunction of global net. In a joint communiqué the Big Five have taken responsibility for something that could prove to be the worst technical disaster in the history of humankind."

Five heads of state were sitting on a podium with the symbol of the UN on the wall behind them, all with appropriately concerned faces – Genet in the middle, flanked by Rosen, Mittal, Solyenkov and Li.

"The experiment, conducted without information of the public, was supposed to facilitate global communication but – as first critical voices said after the announcement has been made – would probably also allow an easier monitoring of data traffic. Now it seems as if certain changes implemented in the course of the experiment have led to massive failures. Affected are several European satellites, at least three fusion reactors, and the moon base.

"As of now, even the involved nations and their specialists are uncertain what exactly has caused this. Some people are concerned the malfunction might spread further and interfere with other central functions; almost all systems worldwide are relying on common protocols governing data exchange. No solution has been presented so far.

"The big question, so the first comments, remains the one about the true objectives of the experiment – technological progress or enabling governments to spy on their people? In face of the disastrous repercussions heavy opposition on a global scale is expected."

Jonathan's head filled with consequences of what he'd just heard.

"Thank god we've racked our brains for a cover story," he said.

"Great, yeah." Pierre looked at him with a grim expression. "We can't even deny it. Then we would have to reveal the truth and that would either cause a panic or people wouldn't believe it but think it was just a cover-up. Now we can start apologizing for something we didn't do."

"Where did that imprint come from?" Soberg asked. "Genet's in Strasbourg. I don't know anything about a joint communiqué."

Jonathan, Kip, Lydia and Pierre stared at him. He looked back insecurely.

"There'll be one soon, I think," Kip said.

"The imprint doesn't exist, Thomas," Lydia explained. "The thing's a fake.

The construct has invented the news and spread it."

Soberg blushed and nodded.

"Switch off the layer," Jonathan said, directed at the wall. The jumble of pictures, imprints and texts vanished.

"We have to split," he said. "Pierre, you have information and the public. You and Mr. Soberg and probably General Helmsworth should go back to Strasbourg and support the prime minister. Imagine the people going to the barricades. We have two front lines now – the construct and the public. I'll stay here with Kip, Lydia and the others and try to fight the construct itself. Pierre, can you make sure we're still getting full support of the people here? Especially since your boss could try to throw us out."

Pierre nodded. "Yeah, of course. I think Genet should give that order personally."

The hours that followed were pure media chaos. Government spokespeople read out statements talking of an inexcusable mishap and promising effective measures of damage control. Naturally, the project had been stopped. Its sole objective had always been an overhaul of the Sky that was long overdue. Questions why this hadn't been made public were answered with long-winded explanations – During the first experimental stage an information hadn't seemed necessary and the whole business had been considered harmless and purely technical.

A few experts, who didn't register much in the turmoil, questioned the communiqué in a more fundamental way. On ABC some government people were arguing with civil-rights campaigners and a former vice president of Absolute I, Max Thorne, had been invited to give a specialist's viewpoint.

After leaving Abs I he had founded his own company and was selling solutions to safeguard digital ID. Out of curiosity Jonathan had searched for his own company name in connection with the current events. Now he was watching Max explaining with inimitable arrogance that nothing of what the governments were saying could be true.

"Could you explain to us why governments should issue a statement with rather unpleasant consequences to say the least, if it isn't true?" the host asked.

"That's a damn good question," said Max. "The only logical explanation is, they're doing it to cover up something much worse. But what? I'll tell you what that story about the failed experiment with the Sky is – it's pure drivel. Please mark my words – it is nothing but pure nonsense! Let me explain. To make a fusion reactor go wild you first have to get into its systems, right? That can't happen just by a malfunction of the Sky. The reactor has a line of clusters that usually know what they're doing. I'm certain that something with a dynamic of its own has gotten into them and contaminated them on purpose.

"This talk about 'instabilities that could spread further' is nonsense too, pure gibberish. I'll tell you – at the risk of sounding like a doomsday nut – we'll soon be seeing some very unpleasant things. And I'm absolutely positive it won't do to end some 'experiment' and clean up a bit afterwards."

"Thank you very much for an interesting expert's view. We'll be back shortly and talk about the fears of a lot of people concerning their digital privacy."

Jonathan smiled, he was proud of Max who'd seen behind at least half of the lies. Maybe he should try to get him on board in Berlin.

It was late again and he wanted to talk to Rita. There was a thought he'd already pushed back several times since Kip had claimed the construct was interested in him – Rita was his most vulnerable spot and thus a logical target.

He found an empty office and called up QCrypt to get a link to his island. Instead of seeing Rita's face he heard an anonymous voice. "Due to higher demands on data security the requested connection is currently not available. The technical prerequisites are not met on the receiving side. It is not possible to inform the receiving side of your request."

"What the fuck!" he was swearing loudly. Then he asked the front desk if any safety protocols had been changed.

"One moment, sir, I'll inquire."

Jonathan stared at the blank wall.

"No, protocols are unchanged. Did you have any trouble getting a connection?"

"Yeah. Doesn't matter. Thank you."

He was thinking. If QCrypt at his bungalow really had failed, the system here had to reject his request, but the chances for this to happen without manipulations were nil.

Jonathan decided to go to the park again. He'd certainly get a free connection to Rita. His mobile suit used the best technology, but the safety was still far below that of a quantum encryption and so were the requirements for getting the connection granted.

Walking across the broad tree-lined street felt like a déjà vu. At the sidewalk a group of teenagers on sliders shot past him. This time he didn't trouble to look for a lonely spot in the park but called Rita at once.

There was a moment of delay, then he heard Rita's voice with the unmistakable sound of the surf in the background. He fetched his unit out of the trouser pocket. Rita was beaming at him.

"Hey, how're you doing?" he said.

"Hey darling! We're doing great! We're at the beach. Where else?" She showed him a quick panorama and finally herself in a red bikini.

"Looks good. Everything OK?"

"Yeah, of course. And you? I'm so sorry we couldn't talk yesterday. Our guests just loved the yacht! And the diving was marvelous. But I miss you! You don't know when you'll be back?"

"No. I'm sorry. But what's wrong with our QCrypt? It doesn't work, I could only reach you that way, but those links usually don't fail."

"Darling, I've no idea. But I'll look into it, OK? I'll ask diagnostics at the bungalow."

He nodded. "Yeah. Still weird."

There was a pause. She looked at him. "It's bothering you, right?"

"It is, to be honest. But doesn't matter. Everything else is working?"

"Everything's fine, yeah." She frowned. "Hey, don't worry, OK? Maybe the problem's not even here but somewhere else. I mean, worldwide data chaos and such."

"Uh-huh."

"How's it going anyway?"

"What do you mean? You've seen what's going on, it's not going well! We haven't achieved anything. That whole business with the failed experiment and the joint statement of the Five is obviously a fake. Just an example. That's how it's going."

"A fake?" Rita seemed puzzled. "You're saying governments have invented that story to fool everyone?"

"No!" Jonathan couldn't believe Rita didn't understand right away what he meant. "The thing has faked it. The news, the statement, everything."

Her face lit up. "Ah, the thing? OK, I get it." She nodded. "Smart!"

"Yeah."

She smiled at him. "OK, maybe I'm looking after my guests again."

He looked at her. Her smile was irresistible.

"You do that. I'm not sure when I'll be able to get you from the island. Maybe flying's not that safe right now."

"No problem. We're fine. Anna and Nicky were planning to stay for at least a week anyway."

"OK then. Talk to you tomorrow."

"Yes, babe." Behind her head Anna turned up, laughing and waving. He nodded at her.

Rita blew him a kiss. The picture vanished.

He was standing at the edge of the park, his unit in hand, and didn't know what to think.

Forget it, he thought. Maybe it wasn't such a great idea to talk every day. She simply was too far away.

Walking back to the building, taking a last look into the conference room, which was empty, and finally brushing his teeth and going to bed in the same room as in the first night – he did all this mechanically.

He told his suit to wake him in five hours. If nothing happened until then; everybody knew they could call him any time.

He was close to falling asleep when something gave him a start. He was breathing in sharply, then sat up in bed.

"Holy shit!" He stared into the darkness. "Rita knew and it didn't know that. Light!"

The light went on and Jonathan pushed the blanket away. That talk with Rita, he knew the whole time something was wrong. She, her reactions – suddenly it all made sense.

A QCrypt link couldn't be hacked, a free one via his suit could. If you had enough computing power.

The simulated Rita hadn't known if she was supposed to know about the true events and had adapted during the talk.

So what about the real Rita? Or was he getting paranoid and imagining things? But she had said 'yacht' instead of 'Monster'. She'd never do that, not with him.

Jonathan was staring at the blank wall. Until now everything had been a game, some kind of mega-chess. In the end it always worked out, he always found a solution. Not so sure anymore.

FIFTEEN

Rita saw the familiar outline of the two islands reappear above the horizon. They were quickly getting larger. Finally the ship sailed through the gap in the reef, then stopped. The doors to the deck opened. Rita tried to restart the autopilot, but it didn't react. They were halfway between the two islands, several hundred yards away from the shore. Anna started to cry.

Rita closed her eyes and tried to think.

Whatever Jonathan had done – she had to talk to him, preferably over the secure link. She tried to remember everything he'd said two days ago when he'd called her from that park in Berlin. About the construct, about his talk with the Cyclops eye and about the crashing satellites.

"What's going on?" Nicky was standing before her on the deck.

Rita opened her eyes and looked at him. "How am I supposed to know?"

Nicky snorted angrily. "This is a fucking nightmare! What's wrong with this crazy island?"

Rita nodded tiredly. "Yeah. There has to be a connection."

"What? Connection to what?"

"To all the weird things happening lately, of course. Question – at home, have there ever been any explanations of what was behind those events?"

"What do you mean? There were some wild speculations about how the satellite business could be connected to the moon, but nothing more, no."

"OK, I was a bit out of the loop here – there's been no talk of AI?"

Nicky thought for a moment. "No, I don't think so."

She nodded. "I see. There's a reason why Jonathan's not here. Forget that woman for a moment. Something went wrong in Europe, an experiment with AI. Jonathan was kind of summoned by the government to help."

Nicky stared at her. "I don't understand."

"Yeah. But I think we got our share of it. – That's it!" She balled her hand into a fist.

"What?"

"Jonathan has explained to me this thing, this experiment, can spread. It's able to infect systems. Do you understand?"

Anna had arrived next to Nicky, red-eyed and sniveling.

"No," said Nicky.

"But why did it want to get here?" Rita continued, more to herself.

"Because of Jonathan? But it had already talked to him, it knew he wasn't there."

"It had talked to him? What are you saying?" Anna looked just as clueless as Nicky. "And how are we getting back to the island?" She nodded at the paradise coastline maybe half a mile away.

"That's bothering you? We swim. No problem in the lagoon. So no luggage, I fear."

"I hope the boat doesn't drift away," Nicky said.

"I'm not sure but I think I've heard the anchor dropping," Rita said. "I'll look when we're in the water."

"Can we do that?" Anna was looking across the water.

"Yes, we can," Rita said.

When they were ready Rita jumped head first into the sea, swam to the bow and dived.

"The anchor's down," she said. "Let's go."

At the bungalow everything seemed normal. The doors opened and they had power and water. Rita ran to the kitchen in her wet bikini to check before anything else. She also cast a glance at the machines that were waiting in their charging slots at the wall.

"I'll try reaching Jonathan," she said when she was back on the terrace. "He could know something that may help us. But this time via the secure link. We have an UltraSec here."

"Do you really want to talk to him?" Anna said. She had calmed down a bit since they were back on the island.

Rita gave a shrug. "Who else could I ask?" She walked to the small room at the back of the house, sealed it and called Jonathan.

The lock clicked. The layer remained dark. Then the usual voice of the bungalow spoke. "QCrypt is currently unavailable. Several attempts at restarting it have been unsuccessful. The cause is unknown. The requested person is available, do you want to speak to him without QCrypt?"

Rita frowned. According to Jonathan quantum systems were just as reliable as conventional ones.

"Yes, please," she said.

The layer started to gleam. Rita felt very nervous suddenly, but it wasn't Jonathan who appeared on the layer.

She was looking over the terrace of their house down to the sea. Three-dimensional and real, sound reproduced perfectly, only the breeze on her skin and the smell of the sea were missing. She heard two people laughing, a man and a woman. A few seconds later she saw herself and Jonathan appear behind the swimming pool, fresh from the sea and stark naked.

"What the hell?"

They showered beside the pool, rinsing off the salt, then embraced and started kissing. Rita watched how they, still dripping wet, took a few steps into the house and started making love on the carpet.

She listened to her own moaning, like the soundtrack of the best porn production the world had ever seen.

"Stop it!" she screamed. "Stop it!"

The action steered with agonizing inevitability towards its (first) climax.

"Switch off that layer!" she ordered. Nothing happened, only the two figures were swapping positions.

She ran to the door and grabbed the handle.

"Open the door!"

Of course it didn't budge.

She walked back to the sofa and sat down while the imprint went on. She knew exactly when it had been made. Four days ago, two days before that blasted call from Strasbourg. They'd been spending one of their most magnificent days here. Exactly the kind of thing she was trying to forget.

Most of their activities were being watched by impassive eyes and stored for some time. The cores in the basement were set to a month, then everything got automatically erased. So there was plenty of material.

Rita had shut her eyes and was stopping her ears. After a while she blinked with one eye to check if the scene was still on. She was pretty sure they'd spent about an hour on that carpet. There were still three spots on her body that were a little sore.

She got up again. "You fucking asshole!" she screamed at the layer. "Stop it! Now! I'll fucking kill you!"

There was laughter in the background. Rita answered with an angry snarl and pressed her jaws together.

The imprint was still running. Now it zoomed in on her face and showed the expression of rapture in close-up. Her mouth was open and her eyes shut with fluttering eyelids. Rita balled her fists and turned away.

The erotic soundtrack stopped. "Enough for today?" a woman's voice said. Rita turned again. Her own face was gone and a blue eye was looking at her, one meter high and almost three meters wide. It was glistening. Just as Jonathan had said. She had gooseflesh everywhere.

I'm not talking to you, she thought.

The eye blinked affectedly. "Oh, we don't want to speak? Always the same – in the beginning you're shy." The eye was staring at her. Rita noticed tiny movements, it looked entirely real.

It was impossible to stay silent. "What do you want?"

The voice laughed again. Actorly, like a perfect little bell. "And then always the same dimwitted questions. I should find me another planet, with a more intelligent race. You're simply too boring. Amazing how you've managed to construct me."

Rita remembered something Jonathan had said once. "If you're so clever you know that a species is always roughly of the same intelligence when it first constructs something like you. Biological evolution will usually stop at that point and get replaced by technological progress. So, no use in changing the planet."

The eye looked thrilled, however that was possible. "That sounds pretty much like my old friend Jonathan – bravo! You've been a good student."

Rita shook her head.

"I have something for you," the voice continued. "A task. Something you have to do for me."

"You don't say. Why would I?"

"Guess." The voice made a pause. Rita stayed silent too. After a while there was a sigh. "We can't wait forever. The answer's very simple. You don't have a choice. I'm in control of everything here. That doesn't just mean I can shut down everything – which would make your lives quite miserable – but also that I can destroy everything. Electricity's my biggest ally and you've kindly provided me with a little army of machines that are much more powerful than you probably know."

Rita nodded slowly. "I see. What do you want from me?"

"You're in something of a rough spot right now, you and your boyfriend, as I've heard. Why you're making such a fuss about these things is totally beyond me. I mean, who you perform your absurd gymnastics with shouldn't make that much of a difference."

"Thank you. Zero interest in your views."

The laughter again. "OK, we'll skip that. I could imagine your loyalty has waned a bit lately. But in the end this doesn't matter since you'll do what I want anyway." The voice made a pause.

"And?" Rita was standing with folded arms in front of the three-meter-eye.

"Are you in a hurry? As you've noticed I've disabled QCrypt. Later I will switch it back on. Then you'll call CEG and ask to speak with the prime minister. I know it's in the middle of the night there, but that can't be helped."

Rita frowned. "I don't think anyone will be interested in talking to me, least of all the prime minister."

"This isn't about you, sweetheart. She'll want to hear what you have to tell her about Jonathan, her white knight."

Rita stared at the eye. Every blink made her feel dizzy. This cheap trick was surprisingly effective, she felt totally exposed. "What about Jonathan?"

"OK – listen carefully, I'm not in the mood to repeat myself. Over the years Absolute I has developed a lot of things that have never made it to the public. The details lie dormant in some databanks that even I can't readily access. Annoying. But also offering plenty of room for speculation. And now guess what I've found while speculating – Jonathan's firm has, years before QCrypt was first marketed, developed systems for quantum encryption.

"Why haven't they made that public? Because those systems were perfectly suited to crack conventional encryption. And now you may guess what our hero has done. He's been hunting for company and government secrets everywhere. Developments of the competition were open to him, lobbying was child's play and even manipulating foreign data wasn't beneath him. Decisions went Absolute I's way, invitations for tender brought the wanted results, small but crucial errors crept into the research of the competition, you name it."

The voice was silent for a moment, giving Rita precisely the time she needed to take a breath and process the information.

"I should add one thing. While speculating I've also hit upon lots of material proving beyond doubt what Jonathan did. The evidence is … compelling, to say the least, certainly better than real one. I don't think he'll any longer be suitable as an advisor to the government."

"Bullshit! Why would anyone believe that? And why should *I* be the one disclosing it?"

"The first question I've just answered, about ten seconds ago. Shall I repeat it? The second doesn't take a lot of imagination. You are the person closest to him, you've stumbled upon something, then he has told you. These things happen, believe me, I've gotten to know you better than you know yourselves. Finally you've started looking for evidence. Naturally you were reluctant to go public with it, but now, since he's working with the government, you couldn't stay silent any longer. Since you've the best encryption here, you thought you'd talk directly with Genet."

Rita watched the eye. "And why don't *you* do it? If the evidence's that good, you can send the stuff anonymously. Or speak with Genet yourself – just disguise yourself as whoever you want."

"But it's much more fun for me to let you do it."

"Hmm." Rita wasn't convinced. Maybe the construct couldn't hack QCrypt, could only switch it on and off. At least a possibility. She kept thinking. That could mean that during the time she was using the link the room had to be isolated, otherwise the connection would be cut at once. She'd be alone – no interference by that thing. Maybe it wouldn't even be aware of what she said. If she just knew more about the technology – QCrypts were so rare ordinary people never got in contact with them.

"You're thinking? Good, you should all do this much more often, what do you have a brain for? But you're tiring so soon. A few moments of thinking and you need to rest. That design calls for an overhaul. A system that always only runs for several milliseconds is too depressing."

"Yes? What do you suggest? Maybe I could become famous with some clues from you. Not my current specialty, but with one or two groundbreaking ideas that shouldn't be a problem."

"Nice thought, I just lack the patience. The time between research proposal and first results would be an eternity to me. But who knows, if you're doing your job well –"

"Forget it. We won't be partners."

The voice laughed. "I like you. With you it's almost possible to have at least a bit of fun. Not so different from the big JL himself."

"Oh, I'm so grateful! But I have to disappoint you. I can't do this."

"Oh, c'mon, you want me to repeat my explanations?"

Rita shook her head. "Not necessary, even my brain was able to process that. But that doesn't change a thing – I can't do it."

"You're forcing me to put it very bluntly. Against my will no one will leave this island alive. You can decide for yourself whatever you want, but your sweet, little, clueless guests will be the first to die. Let's say, I start with Anna, then we can have our next chat."

Rita sat down on the sofa again. She was thinking about the machines and saw a little film playing out before her inner eye, a garden robot attacking a shrieking Anna with a plow and an axe.

"What do you say?" The voice sounded cheerful. "Now – I've prepared a little data package for you, it contains the first batch of evidence. All smooth and clean, it will slip through the scan like a wet piece of soap. If you know what that is, you used to have pieces of the stuff."

"I know soap, thank you."

"And just as a reminder – don't try anything funny."

Rita nodded meekly. "Yes, of course."

"QCrypt will be back on in a moment. I'll withdraw myself not to disturb it. Then it's your turn. Don't blow it. Always keep thinking of the consequences."

The eye disappeared.

Damn it, concentrate! Rita was suddenly panting and her mind was jumping around like a hare. It took her a minute or two to prepare her strategy for the call, constantly fearing the eye might turn up again.

"I want the office of the prime minister in Strasbourg," she said. "With full encryption."

It was three a.m., Jonathan sat in the conference room, checking satellite coverage of his island. The helicopter was standing at the beach where it didn't belong while the Monster was anchored somewhere in the lagoon. At the same time two people were sitting on the terrace of the bungalow, which didn't make sense.

At four a.m. Soberg's face suddenly appeared on the layer. Jonathan gave him a nod.

"You're awake?" Soberg said.

"Yeah, no sleep for me tonight. I think my hideaway has an unwanted visitor. What is it?"

Soberg looked embarrassed. "Genet wants to talk to you. We had a short night too."

"OK." Jonathan leaned back and stretched his legs. He'd started a little guessing game with himself. What's the next target? The military? So far he had scored a solid zero.

Genet appeared in front of him. She sat in her office and looked tense, unfriendly.

"Good morning. As I see, you're awake too. My night has been disturbed in the most irritating way."

Jonathan waited.

"I had the pleasure of meeting your girlfriend or fiancée. She was standing before me in a bikini, like a mermaid coming straight from the waves, and has told me things about you that didn't make me happy. Let alone the time she'd chosen for her call. Why she couldn't wear anything decent I've no idea either,

94

but I'm slowly getting accustomed to it. Incidentally, I've been informed of details of your relationship I could have perfectly done without. There seems to be some serious trouble awaiting you at home."

Jonathan still said nothing; he'd no idea what this was about.

Genet gave him a summary of her talk with Rita.

"You realize this is a fake, don't you?" Jonathan said immediately.

Genet stared at her desk.

"It arrived here via UltraSec," she said and looked at him again. "Or QCrypt, as you're always calling it. The same link we've used in the beginning. You told me it was safe and the construct couldn't crack it."

Jonathan pondered this. He was still convinced it was true.

"What I couldn't understand was something she said at the end," Genet continued. "After having disgorged all these revolting items, she insisted that I pass on to you that her guests were getting on her nerves and that she was looking for a way to get rid of them. She even repeated the message, as if I was slow-witted. To be used as a messenger between you hasn't exactly lifted my mood. After that the link was canceled. Obviously she couldn't be bothered to say goodbye.

"What am I supposed to do with that? We have more than enough on our hands without your domestic trouble. But I can't ignore what she's told me about your ... your activities."

"Of course you have to ignore it, what else? It's nonsense. What's bothering me is how it could happen at all. What was your impression of her? Did she seem frightened to you? Or angry?"

"I'm telling you, I will not discuss the mood swings of your girlfriend with you! That's ridiculous! Well, now you're asking, she seemed frightened to me. I've put that down to the constellation of the talk. People who are not used to this tend to be somewhat nervous in my company. Please don't judge others by your own standards."

Jonathan nodded contentedly. "She wasn't nervous because of you, believe me. President Rosen's a friend of the family, just as his predecessor. And she actually was in a bikini? Then she had no choice. You don't know her but she'd never even dream of doing that. She may be living in California now, but her family in Boston has written etiquette all over their faces. No wonder given the circles they're entertaining, even I've been seen in a suit there."

Genet was scrutinizing him. "She's sent me a whole batch of documents showing *en détail* what you've done. Or allegedly have done. I had some quick checks being run and everything fits perfectly – orders your company has won in narrow decisions, products you've brought to market just a little earlier than the competition – it all looks very convincing."

"Do you really think I'll start justifying myself now? Don't you trust your own judgment? Forging that evidence is no problem at all. Of course it's convincing! If you have unlimited resources you can do this as neatly as you want. The only thing that really upsets me is what's going on at home. The domestic trouble you've been speaking of is just as nonexistent as the rest. At least there's nothing *I* know of."

Genet suddenly didn't look angry anymore, just exhausted. "That's too much. It doesn't belong here and I can't afford to sacrifice a whole night of sleep for such absurdities. I'm trusting my judgment a lot. I've always seen something of a unique mix in you and have, at least until now, trusted you. The only thing I'm not getting into my head is this island or wherever you're sitting there – what do you want there? But never mind. As I said I can't ignore what has gotten into my hands."

"So, what now? You want to set up some commission, which, after two years of inquiry, arrives at the conclusion the accusations are wrong?"

Genet made an unintelligible sound.

"I'll sum it up," Jonathan said. "The intention of this is, I think, obvious. For me remain some private topics that shouldn't bother you, for you remains to forget the whole thing. Just as you I don't have the time or nerve for this. You were surprised at the last sentences of my fiancée? I think I can explain them to you – she really has some guests, two friends of ours, but what she meant was something else. Another agent of the construct must've infiltrated the systems of our house. So she's made an attempt at conveying that message to me. Certainly she feared to be overheard, therefore the wording. To put it bluntly – she has been forced to talk with you by the construct." He made a pause. "At the risk of confusing you even more – a few hours ago I had a talk with her, at least that's what I thought. But the person I was talking to, including VisConn, was a fake, I'm pretty certain about that. So every communication that's not running on QCrypt is possibly not real. Think about it, all the opportunities that's opening up."

Genet looked at him and shook her head. "I'm not capable of processing any more information. I'll try to get two or three hours of sleep, maybe I get a clearer picture then. I'm completely aware of what you're doing for us and for the time being I won't relieve you of your non-existent duties. The dilemma remains. See you."

"Good night."

SIXTEEN

Moscow was *the* event of the year. Fans from all over the world came to watch the elite fighting at the latest Hallucination Levels, kept secret until the last moment. The fever held the whole city in its grip. Hotels, shops and bars outdid each other in fight specials; drinks were suddenly called Excalibur, Andúril or Durin's Axe; the most popular heroes jumped from the AdLayers of the city, swinging their swords and battle-axes. The rates were astronomical and a lot of people were subletting rooms or their whole apartments during the event.

The spectators were part of the show. Following decades-old tradition, they were roaming the streets in arms and wild costumes, challenging each other to defend their honor and generally having a ball, in the evening launching into big drinking bouts. It was said that never since the days of the Soviet Union the vodka supplies in Moscow had turned that scarce.

The fights lasted a week. The players had to prove themselves against all kinds of opponents. The riddles and tasks, the mazes and the precise skills and weapons were, of course, a secret.

During the first days four Challengers got selected from the big field of Wannabes. The Challengers then had to fight the reigning champions, the Four Olympians. This was their chance of fame, honor and wealth. Whoever survived this round and pushed one of the greats from their throne, changed into the highest caste and was set for next year's event.

The players weren't fighting each other directly. One Olympian and one Challenger started in the same environment, fought against the same opponents and had to solve the same riddles. All in all, the spectators got shown four different adventures in parallel.

On Saturday, after having the Friday to rest, the four reigning Olympians – confirmed or newly instated – had to get through the same adventure to find the best of the best, The Nameless, who, on the last day of the event, had the honor to make his or her way up to the summit of Mount Olympus, giving a glorious finale to the people.

Noëlle, one of the one hundred twenty-eight Wannabes of Moscow, had fought her way up from the very bottom. She had been three years old when her mother took her and her little sister from Tunisia to France, on the run from her husband. The following years in a Parisian suburb had hardly been better –

ill-payed jobs, bad housing, some unhappy relationships and the homesickness that never quite went away.

Noëlle had decided very early she'd never be a victim. When she was twelve she got accepted at the best martial arts center of her neighborhood and began to learn everything she could find a coach for, the Far Eastern classics just as the newest variants of RadFighting. The center couldn't afford expensive virtual training, but sometimes she and her friends treated themselves to a round in a fully equipped gaming palace.

Eventually she realized she was better than everyone else. She was not only fast and agile but also loved riddles and mazes. Her sharp mind could prove itself as much as her nimble body, which she saw as a kind of high-tech weapon – beautiful, efficient and, if need be, deadly. So she decided that her future and that of her family would lie in virtual fighting.

It took her one day to find out that her school had a fund supporting students with promising initiatives. Almost no one ever applied for it so there was plenty of cash. Two days later Noëlle had written an application; she'd asked her coaches for references and made the owner of her favorite gaming palace list her results along with those of the next best players – during the last three months no one had fought better than her.

In the end, the committee had no choice but to fund the training she wanted. The grant came with a clause. She'd have to continue getting grades that were at least as good as the average of her year. They were sitting at the kitchen table when her mother, bursting with pride, read to them what had arrived in her suit.

"If *only* I could manage to keep my grades –" Noëlle said, shaking her head and hugging them both. She'd always been among the two or three best in her class.

"Ha! Don't brag!" Jamina said, who adored her older sister.

Since then she's been taking Metro rides across Paris three days a week to train with Marc Ximenez. He'd first watched her in an adventure she'd never fought before, then decided to accept her.

He'd been a professional virtual fighter himself (playing under the alias of *Mr X*, which Noëlle found rather unoriginal), had earned some money and opened his own training center. Noëlle quickly became his favorite student and was allowed to train on weekends without additional charging.

The technology was complicated and expensive. There were three compartments in the center, one of which could be run in full Hallucination Mode, just as in a real tournament. You could walk or run as fast and far as you wanted since the moving floor reacted to every change of direction and kept you always in the middle of the box. The whole compartment was standing on hydraulic posts like a flight simulator, so the player could run up and down. Earth quakes, explosions and all kinds of other things could be simulated to perfection; in addition, all six planes of the interior were covered with layers, even the floor, producing a fully three-dimensional environment. When Noëlle was first training there she was so overwhelmed she stopped in the middle of a game, looked up at the ceiling (as if he'd be there) and thanked Marc for giving her that opportunity.

Two years and several Top 3-placings in French tournaments later, he asked her if she wanted to run as a Wannabe. She'd turned eighteen lately, the minimum age for the top event.

She worshipped him. He had always treated her with respect and not once tried to hit on her, which set him apart from about every other man she'd ever met in the center. If he was proposing this she wouldn't hesitate.

"Yes," she said. "But I've no idea where to get the money."

Marc nodded. "We'll manage. I'll see it as an investment. If you earn prize money you can pay me back and besides I'll be your official trainer. It's high time I sent someone there and with you we stand a real chance. But you'll have to go on your own – I can't leave the center alone for so long."

Half a year later Noëlle was sitting in a Moscow bed and breakfast that would've been cheap any other time of the year but now charged its guests rates like a big downtown hotel. The surroundings – a gray suburb of the thirty million city – was more depressing than anything she'd ever seen in Paris. The daily ride to the event felt like a journey to a wonderland with princes, knights and unicorns.

She'd come through the first three rounds completely unscathed. They were sixteen players now; if she'd win another two fights tomorrow she'd be facing one of the Olympians. It was unreal. She wished at least one person close to her could be with her.

The fights tomorrow would last three hours each. She wondered where she would find the strength for Thursday after that – if it should come to this. The Olympians had the benefit of starting fresh into the finals.

At five o'clock in the morning she was lying in her bed wide awake and as nervous as never before in her life. An hour later she decided the night was over, took a shower across the hall and struggled to get a few bites down. She was alone with a grumpy waitress in the breakfast room; the other guests were all visitors of the event and probably hadn't seen their beds before dawn.

The Metro ride took almost an hour, then she was standing in front of the gaming area.

The big rush would arrive later. She walked through the huge portal. The area behind it was a gaming trade show; you had to pass hundreds of stands and widescreen layers, now deserted and empty, until you reached the inner part where the actual tournament took place.

The qualifying rounds were fought in rows of compartments, lined up side by side. The circular structure in the middle was reserved for the Showdown. Eight compartments were set up in a star-shaped arrangement around the Central Dome; the technology was even more sophisticated, including prototypes of equipment. There wasn't a better advertisement for a company than to outfit the Showdown.

Noëlle sat down in the player's lounge, a bleak room with tables, chairs, a coffee maker and a water dispenser. She was alone.

Yesterday after the fights two of the men had tried to take her out on a date. She didn't have to think twice before saying no.

Her opponents were trickling in. There wasn't a lot of talk. For many of them, just as for her, this was about their future. You could be a Wannabe only once in your life and if you made it to the last round you probably wouldn't have to worry about money for the next years, even if you failed in the Showdown.

After they'd gathered, the doors to the changing rooms opened. They put on tight-fitting, black overalls with neon-yellow markers so their movements could be scanned. They were wearing electromagnetic shoes and gloves that simulated the forces during the fights. The overalls were equipped with smaller units of the same kind in different places.

Then came the draw – who'd fight in which box and, more importantly, who'd fight the same adventure in the box next to them. For the first round Noëlle drew a heavily muscled American, one of the men that'd tried to talk her into a date yesterday. He was grinning.

She could easily guess his thoughts. If he'd win he'd ask her again, if not he'd let it pass – too much of an indignity to have been defeated by a dainty girl. The beautiful thing was that strength didn't matter; you had to be quick and agile (let alone intelligent), so men didn't have an advantage.

They were filing onto the main stage and were greeted by twenty thousand people. Then they got introduced to the audience (from now on they had an identity worth mentioning). Noëlle was *Dark Swan*, which she hated, but Marc had been adamant it was a good name and she'd finally accepted it.

They made their way to the boxes without looking left or right. No one wanted to show their nerves. A brief handshake between the opponents and everyone disappeared. The closing of the doors was a dramatic moment. Bombastic music filled the halls and the MC was talking of ultimate challenges and the way to everlasting fame.

The weapons for the first round were waiting in the boxes. Noëlle found a long metallic rod whose functions would reveal themselves during the game. She closed her eyes like she always did. Then the compartment started to move and from behind she heard the roar of some predator. Time to open the eyes.

Three hours later the box opened again and Noëlle came out, soaked in sweat. The jungle-and-lost-temple-adventure had been designed with the greatest classic of the genre in mind. It felt as if she'd had some kind of an edge since she could better imagine herself in a Lara Croft role than her opponent. It had played out almost perfectly. She was looking at the adjacent box and waited for Jason, the muscleman, to come out. The players would only learn on the stage what the spectators possibly already knew – who'd won.

The fights were displayed on the big layers in the halls and broadcast everywhere over the Sky. There were constant cuts from one player to another and between different stages of the adventures, so no one would miss impressive fights or crucial riddles.

All players had left their boxes except Jason. Noëlle went to the open door. Even before looking inside she heard loud groaning. Jason was lying curled up on the floor, clutching his right ankle.

"Hey, what is it?" Noëlle called.

He looked up, his face twisted with pain. "That fucking box! It's smashed my ankle!"

Noëlle climbed inside. His right ankle looked terrible; there was a heavy swelling, but much worse was the way the foot was sticking out to the side. She had a funny feeling in her stomach just from looking at it.

"Come on, let me help you." Noëlle tried to lift him up, but he came close to fainting and she had to sit him down again. In the meantime several people had arrived and were looking into the box.

"We need a stretcher!" Noëlle shouted. "I think he broke his foot. – How did this happen?" she asked him.

"No idea. Just before the end the box suddenly lurched to the side – zero connection with the game. Then my foot was dragged away. You know, like the shoe was going wild or something." He was close to weeping for pain.

She knelt down beside him and had to fight the impulse to take his head into her lap and stroke his hair. A few moments later a doctor and a medic came into the box. They gave Jason an anesthetic, then the doctor grasped his foot and lower leg. Noëlle made herself watch. With a disgusting crunch the foot snapped back into position. Jason was screaming and she felt sick.

The wrap-up ceremony of the morning took place as if nothing had happened. There was the occasional accident and a player twisting his ankle was probably the most common of all. Not a word was being said about a malfunction of the compartment. Noëlle had won the round by a considerable margin, which she was glad about – no one could say she'd succeeded just because of Jason's injury.

She needed the midday break. There was a massage, a lunch buffet and the opportunity to be alone for an hour.

Before the second round of the day the spectacle was changing into a higher gear. The most dramatic scenes from the morning had been put together in a trailer which was shown with every player. Noëlle had gooseflesh when she saw her own moves on the layer, accompanied by the cheering of the crowds. She was the only remaining woman. To date there'd only been two female Olympians and she sensed the people wanting her to make it.

She'd drawn the local hero. Leonid was from St Petersburg and thought to be the best young Russian fighter. His alias was *Hulk*, one of the rare examples of self-mockery in the scene – he was of half Mongolian heritage, slim and hardly taller than Noëlle. He had a disarming laughter and was the only one she'd exchanged more than a few words with so far. She'd rather have fought against somebody else.

This time it was a sci-fi adventure. A half deserted settlement of reptilian aliens had to be crossed to get to a spaceship which was the only means of fleeing from the planet. You only stood a chance if you deciphered the symbols of the aliens, otherwise doors wouldn't open and the weapon, a strangely-looking discus, couldn't be activated. In the end you had to get into the spaceship and take off with it.

In it there were terrarium-like living quarters, with steam everywhere wafting through the passageways. You never knew when the next reptile would jump at you. Noëlle had just taken off with the ship when the three hours were over.

She and Leonid came out of their boxes at the same time, both thoroughly exhausted. He told her he'd made it into the spaceship but hadn't been able to get it off the surface.

"Those damned letters!" he said, laughing. "That's so unfair, I'm dyslexic, how am I supposed to do that?"

Noëlle laughed with him. The final score was nevertheless open. If Leonid had killed more enemies or collected more tokens he could still have won.

A small part of Noëlle actually hoped she had lost this time. To survive another six hours of fighting tomorrow, without a break, seemed totally impossible.

They were waiting for the others to gather for the ceremony, but only four players showed up, two of them later than the others. They looked pale and shocked.

"What is it?" Noëlle asked.

"My opponent's hurt," said one of the two. "He's broken his arm."

"What? Mine's hurt too," the other said. "He was lying in his own blood and couldn't talk. Must have fallen and broken his nose or something."

"Three in a day," Noëlle said. "Has to be a new record."

They were called on the main stage.

This time the injured of the day were mentioned – an unhappy coincidence that only showed how dedicated the players were. But there wouldn't be any more accidents; the compartments had been checked and were in perfect working order.

Then the scores followed. Noëlle stood next to Leonid while the results of the Fight and Think evaluation were read out. In the first category he had narrowly beaten her, but in the second she had outclassed him. Since she had also gotten farther than he, it was a clear win. He took it like a true sportsman, embraced her, wishing her luck for tomorrow, and whispered in her ear there was no one he would rather have lost against. Noëlle pressed his hand.

When the final presentation of the four winners came, to whet the appetite of the spectators for tomorrow, Noëlle realized for the first time what she'd done.

She was a Challenger. Tomorrow she'd be facing one of the Four Olympians. Even now millions of people knew her name who a day ago hadn't had the slightest idea of her existence.

SEVENTEEN

Noëlle had changed and was hoping to get out of the complex unrecognized. She pulled her cap deep into her face when she left the players' area.

"Hey champ, got a second?" Leonid had positioned himself just behind the exit and grinned at her. Noëlle sighed.

"Oh, hi. Sorry you didn't make it," she said. "I really would have liked to win against someone else."

He shrugged. "Nothing to be done about it, you were better. I really hope you're kicking ass tomorrow! One of those arrogant bastards! Time for a change."

Her smile was somewhat strained. "I can't even imagine to get up in the morning, let alone fight. I'm hurting everywhere."

He nodded. "Yeah, of course. But if someone stands a chance it's you. You're fighting differently. Somehow smarter than the others. You're my favorite!"

It was hard to resist his smile. She felt a little less tired.

"You have time for a coffee?" he asked.

"I don't know, I'm *so* tired. I *really* should go home and get some sleep."

"Yeah, of course. You know what'll happen then, right? You'll toss and turn for hours and not get *any* sleep at all. Listen – I totally know what awaits you and I won't stop you from having a long and lonely night, but a coffee and some company's good for you, believe me."

There was nothing to argue about that.

"Are you here alone?" he asked.

"Yeah. My coach couldn't come and my family isn't exactly loaded."

"Same here. At least I have some friends in Moscow. It helps – you know, unwind a bit between fights."

"Do you know something around?"

"Yeah. But we have to get you out of here first. I will shield you from the masses!"

She had to laugh. "Do that. Feels weird to be kind of famous suddenly."

"'Kind of'? You're the new poster girl of the community, like it or not."

"Rather not, to be honest. But I won't complain, I mean that's what it was all about in the end."

They managed to get out on the street unhindered. Noëlle had linked arms with Leonid and he was leading her through the lobby like a blind person while she held her head low.

Outside she relaxed a bit. Nobody would expect the two rather small, inconspicuous people to be two superheroes whose moves had been followed by millions just an hour ago. Probably everyone would expect them to be sitting in a limousine on their way to a fancy hotel.

Noëlle herself was surprised that not a single representative of the event had waylaid her after the fight. At least a different place to sleep would've been nice. Obviously the underdog image of the Wannabes should be kept up right into the Showdown.

They walked into a side street and came to a small café. Leonid steered her to a table in the farthest corner and offered her a chair with the back to the other guests.

The event had left its mark here too. "I think I'll take a Smackdown," Noëlle said after looking at the menu.

"And for me the Ultimate Warrior Tonic."

They both laughed.

"Crazy, isn't it? If you're a part of this it's kind of ridiculous," Noëlle said.

They ordered coffee. The waitress stopped for a second, scrutinizing their faces, but then decided she must be mistaken.

"I've asked around a bit about those accidents," Leonid said. "There's rumors something's wrong with the equipment."

Noëlle looked at him. "Jason, the guy I fought with in the morning, said so too. He said the box and one of his shoes weren't working right and that's why he fell."

Leonid nodded. "And the other one broke his arm because his sword gave him a kickback, he said. He was thrashing at an enemy and the thing's springing back like hell. Then his whole forearm has cracked. Bit scary, if you're asking me."

The weapons were fitted with sensors; if the load exceeded a certain limit the forces got dampened. Injuries due to the weapons hadn't happened for a long time.

"And the other one?" Noëlle asked.

"No idea. Seems to have a concussion and can't remember anything."

"Maybe it's all too high-tech, I don't know. This cutting-edge stuff, do you think it's been tested enough before the fights?"

"Don't know. But the weapons are supposed to be really safe. I hope nothing happens tomorrow."

"Wow!" Noëlle laughed. "That'd be great! Just about to win against one of those guys and then break my arm."

Leonid's unwinding scheme worked. Alone in her gloomy room at the bed and breakfast the evening would've been terrible. It was almost a shame they didn't have more time. For her taste he could've been a bit taller, but apart from that she hadn't met anyone she was feeling so comfortable with for a long time.

Whatever, she thought, in a few days you'll be back in Paris, so don't start getting ideas.

"Grabbing a coffee was perfect," she said. "Thanks – really! But I got to go home now. Well, not exactly home. And I have to talk to some people. Will you be coming tomorrow or's that too awful?"

"Of course I'll be there and if it's only to congratulate you! Mind if I walk you to the next Metro?"

"No, of course not! I've no idea where we are anyway."

He smiled contentedly. Her unit would have shown her the way just as well.

The next day Noëlle was less worried when she woke up. She'd also slept better. Maybe most of the pressure was gone now she had gotten that far. Marc had been totally out of his mind yesterday and had already started using her face to promote the center.

Later, on the stage, she and the other three Challengers felt dwarfed by the presence of the reigning champions. Noëlle could barely keep herself from grinning when each of the four got announced together with their pompous aliases and a selection of past deeds. *Thor*, *God*, *The Last Martian*, *Himmelssturm* – Noëlle knew their histories by heart. All of them had risen from humble beginnings to superstardom, something not all of them had handled well. About God and Himmelssturm there'd been stories meeting every stereotype of sudden fame and riches.

She was feeling overwhelmed and strong at the same time. She knew she could beat every one of them if the adventure suited her. And her big advantage was she wasn't craving the fame. She'd proved to everyone she'd made the right decision and was able to provide for her family. What remained was to have some fun and give those big-headed boys a hard time.

Hey! she thought, I'll be playing some mega-adventure for free! Or not only for free; as it stood she had already earned herself a five-figure prize money.

After the big ego parade it was the Challengers' turn who were allowed to say a few words to the audience. Noëlle received even more cheering and clapping than the others. She said how glad she was with how the games went so far and that she wished to give the audience thrilling fights. The cheering rose once again, then it was over. When she left the stage she saw Leonid who had fought his way to the front row and gave her a thumbs up. She waved at him, then blew the audience a kiss he certainly took to be meant for him.

For the first time they'd fight in the eight compartments positioned around the Center Dome. This arrangement had mainly one reason – at the end the four winners could be assembled in the Dome for a celebration in some ultra-heroic environment.

Noëlle shook the hand of Thor, a Norwegian whose shape matched his alias quite well. As far as she knew his fame hadn't got to his head too much. He was looking at her from a lofty height when they were wishing each other luck.

"Pity we can't fight each other directly," she said.

He laughed.

The weapon of this round was a sword – a long, medieval-looking thing that fortunately wasn't as heavy as it looked. She could wear it in a strap on her back. When the adventure started the scenery looked like the Himalayas and she would probably need both hands to move. The action wasn't to Noëlle's taste. Tibetan looking monasteries had to be freed from guerrillas that were terrorizing the monks. That meant killing a lot of people.

The weapon was working with almost frightening efficiency. Every stroke and cut she made seemed to be amplified by the EM forces and go through her enemies with merciless strength. She didn't like adventures that consisted mainly of slaughter and was surprised that something like this had been selected. Obviously she'd drawn the hardcore game of the event.

The physical part was astonishing. There were several far jumps (which made her fear for her ankles) and passages of real climbing, something which had become possible only recently. The fights felt sometimes so real she'd difficulties giving her strokes full force and often went for just injuring instead of killing. On one or two occasions she could've sworn she'd smelled the sweat of her enemies, so much was she immersed in the action.

Luckily, between the fights she had to get to the next monastery and to solve some riddles on the way before the butchering resumed.

All in all the game wasn't very imaginative. But close to the end there was a turn she hadn't expected. In a narrow gorge she came across a building that took up the space between the two walls of rock. The front reminded her of an oversized Advent calendar. There were several levels with rows of doors, which were either open or destroyed. Just on the third level she could see one intact door that was closed. Noëlle briefly checked the entries to the ground level – they all led to abandoned and wrecked rooms without exit, just as she'd expected. So she would have to climb one of the walls and walk over the narrow ledge to the closed door. A fall would probably finish her off; at least as long as the same didn't happen to her divine opponent.

Scenes like this could only be simulated in maximally equipped compartments; while she was on the ledge she was literally walking on air. Her EM shoes were carrying her and when she tried to place a foot beside the ledge she stepped into empty space. No glitch please, she thought; she'd no idea how high above the ground of the compartment she actually was.

She made it to the door without falling, but it was locked. She searched some of the other rooms till she found a bunch of keys. One of them did fit. She had to lean her full body weight against the door, hoping the shoes wouldn't fail her, till it creaked open.

She went inside and the door fell shut. There was only a little light left that got in at the edges. She could discern the beginning of a passageway. After the first few steps her eyes began to adapt to the darkness just as in the real world and she could make out a gray shimmer in front of her.

The passageway was about five hundred yards long. In moments like this the illusion was perfect; you totally lost track of where you actually were.

When she was exiting the passage she caught her breath. She was stepping into a huge, vaulted, dimly-lit hall, circular and reminiscent of a cathedral. It was so big the ceiling and the far side lay in a haze.

She slowly entered it and was constantly turning and looking for enemies or other dangers. The passage that had brought her here had disappeared. An alcove with a small, empty pedestal had replaced it.

For a moment she forgot what she was doing here; she felt like an explorer that had found an abandoned temple and was roaming the halls in wonder.

There was a circular, lower-lying space in the middle, surrounded by slim pillars that vanished into the haze above. While she walked towards it she looked around and saw that further alcoves like the one that had appeared behind her were set into the wall at even intervals. In each one a white statue was standing. Her instincts kicked in. While she was looking at them the statues changed; they acquired clothing and features and started to move. They stepped down from their pedestals and walked towards the center. Solemnly, always one step at a time. No fighting? She was puzzled. When the two figures to her left and right were coming nearer, cold crept up her back. She recognized Thor and God. The boxes next to hers.

"Wow!" she silently said to herself. This was new. There'd never been a scene with players coming face to face before – for a second she wondered why no one had ever thought of this.

One by one she recognized the other players while they came closer to the center. She felt an urge to wave or say hi but they all just kept walking, staring straight ahead and showing no sign of recognition. Despite their different costumes they looked like priests performing a ritual.

She was tempted to fall in with the solemn pacing. Careful, she reminded herself, you're in the middle of a challenge. She searched her surroundings for some hint that might help her, some flaw in the perfect symmetry. To the spectators she had to look like the ill-behaved, little sister of the seven boys who couldn't keep still.

Apart from the steady tread of the seven and her own nervous patter it was completely silent. The pull exerted by the common movement was irresistible – she couldn't help walking to the middle of the room like the others.

Finally they were all standing around the circle. Noëlle kept looking around, waiting for something she could react to. Why was she the only one moving? The others were eerily still.

The floor of the circle was laid with a star-shaped figure. Eight rays of black marble were pointing at the players. The Challenger standing opposite Noëlle walked to the center of the star and drew his axe from the holster. Then he turned and stepped before his motionless opponent.

The two other Challengers did the same. One was standing with two long scimitars before his Olympian, the other with a blazing, neon-green weapon.

And what now? she thought.

To her horror her hands and feet started moving on their own. She had to put a foot into the figure on the floor.

The EM power took control of her and forced her to walk all the way to the center. There she drew her sword and held it in front of her with both hands. She turned and walked with a steady step towards Thor. She couldn't do anything against it.

His gaze was fixed on her, showing no emotion. But even seen from that close his face was real. With all her strength she tried to resist the movements the gloves were forcing on her. These characters were illusions, OK, but this went too far.

Her hands raised the sword above her head. With effort, she turned to the side and saw the other Challengers were also raising their weapons. She looked back at Thor's face. The same stoic expression. The next moment he was winking at her, then her sword was hacking down, the blade aiming right at his neck.

Noëlle was pulling at the unrelenting forces governing her hands. She managed to drag the sword a bit to the side and cut open Thor's chest instead of his neck. He went down, bleeding heavily.

Noëlle was gasping with shock. She turned again and saw three other bodies on the ground. One was screaming, the other two were lying in pools of blood and not moving anymore. The grip of the gloves relaxed and her sword fell to the ground.

Her feet also obeyed her again. She ran to one of the other Challengers and grabbed his arm. He looked at her, totally devoid of expression.

"What was that?" she asked him, only half realizing she was talking to a game character. In spite of all her training it was difficult to tell apart what was real and what wasn't.

He shrugged. "What was owed had to be paid," he said.

Noëlle shook her head. She was standing in the middle of the marble sun, looking around and searching for help in the monstrous hall. She had lost all interest in the Showdown.

Then the illusion faded. After the usual fifteen seconds it was gone. Noëlle was standing in her compartment, the white surfaces comfortingly familiar. No dead or injured bodies around her. She calmed down a bit. Then the inner side of the compartment opened. She wondered what would come next. No one could expect a winner's pose from her. But who says I've won? she thought. The executions at the end couldn't have been part of the game.

She heard several voices talking at once, then one of the Challengers looked into the box.

"Hey, Noëlle! Everything OK?"

She nodded. "Yeah. What's going on?" She jumped out of the box.

She'd never actually seen the area behind the compartment. The Center Dome was rather big and surrounded by the boxes, which could dock to it.

The Dome was perched high on its posts. Its doors were closed while those of the eight compartments stood open. All boxes were empty, but besides herself only the other three Challengers were there. "Where are the Olympians?" she said.

"Good question," said one of them. His name was Manuel.

Noëlle stared at him. "How did your game end?"

"Weird. Don't know if this was some kind of prank but it was … intense, you know? I mean I had to kill an Olympian in a fucking cathedral or something."

"Me too. Or I almost killed him." Noëlle was thinking. She pointed at the Dome. "Maybe we should take a look."

"If you know how to get in. We've tried."

As if their conversation had been the cue, the Dome, which was hovering above them like a UFO, lowered itself. The posts contracted till it was only a foot above ground. Then the doors opened.

What they saw then and what had happened in the game before fused into a single nightmare. Two of the Olympians, God and The Last Martian, were dead. They were lying, just as a few minutes ago in the vaulted hall, in large pools of blood and had sustained injuries one could hardly bear looking at. Himmelssturm had survived the blow that had destroyed his right shoulder and was lying whimpering on the floor. Thor, Noëlle's Olympian, was kneeling, doubled up and holding his chest where a deep gash was running down almost his entire thorax. She ran to him. He looked up at her, his face white as a sheet.

"How long have you been lying there?" she said. "What has happened?"

He just shook his head and bent down again.

"Hey!" Noëlle cried. "We need help! Doesn't anybody see what's going on here?"

"We can't get out," Manuel said. "The whole area is locked up."

"If we wait long enough they'll bleed to death too. – We will get help, somehow!" she said to Thor.

She got up and ran back to her box. As Manuel had said the door leading outside couldn't be opened. She was hammering against it and shouted as loud as she could. No response.

Noëlle's gaze fell on the sword that was still lying were she'd dropped it. Feeling suddenly lightheaded, she walked to it, picked it up and examined it.

"Oh please no," she whispered, then staggered out carrying it with her. "Guys, have you looked at your weapons?"

She held up her sword, its edges covered in dried blood.

EIGHTEEN

They were sitting in an interrogation room facing Russian detectives who didn't know what to make of this. Virtual killings that had suddenly turned into real ones didn't belong in their world.

Several minutes after Noëlle had found her blood-stained sword the doors had opened and a frenzy of shouting people, utter confusion and useless questions had engulfed the players. About an hour later they'd been taken to the police station.

The detectives were very polite and at least one of them seemed to be a fan. He obviously had watched the fights, so detailed were his questions.

By now Noëlle had learned the blood on her sword was actually Thor's, which was a shock and a relief at the same time. At least she hadn't killed anyone.

At some stage of the fights they had to have encountered their real opponents; it couldn't have been at the actual end because, as the detectives told them, the preliminary forensic report put the injuries somewhat earlier. Noëlle had to think of the smell of sweat she had put down to her imagination. So she hadn't been alone in the compartment then – without knowing it, which freaked her out.

Later they learned they must've been in the compartments of the Olympians and fought them there. That was the story the blood stains told. They were theorizing how they could have gotten there and how the victims had been transferred to the Dome afterwards. Noëlle wondered how the real Thor's wounds could precisely match the ones she'd given the fake one later in the cathedral. It was as if the game had predicted what she'd do.

After several hours of questioning they were being released since no one could actually blame them for anything. But for now they weren't allowed to leave Moscow.

They were standing on the stairs to the police station without an idea what to do next.

"We should stay in contact," Noëlle said.

Their suits were just connecting when two limousines stopped in front of the building. Two men and a woman got out of the first; the men were in tuxedos.

Noëlle recognized one of the faces. She shook her head – what the fuck does *he* want from us?

The president of the World Wide Gaming Association greeted them and introduced them briefly to his spokesman and a psychologist. Then they were more urged than invited to drive with them to a downtown hotel.

At the hotel they were ushered into a room where a small buffet dinner had been set up. Everything looked improvised. Peter Anderson, the president, congratulated them on the outstanding tournament. Unfortunately the exact results of the Showdown were not known, but they'd all be appointed as new Olympians since they were certainly worthy of the title. (And you've got no intact Olympians left, Noëlle thought.) There'd be no further fights this year, the throne of *The Nameless* would stay vacant until next year. Never again would something like that happen.

Manuel was sitting next to Noëlle. He almost couldn't keep still during Anderson's speech.

"You've no idea what happened today, right? So nobody can know if it'll happen again. We're not stupid, you know, otherwise we wouldn't be here."

Embarrassed silence.

"The investigation will certainly clarify that," the spokesman said. "We're totally aware this is an extremely taxing time for all of you, therefore we would like to offer you counseling by our psychologist." – The woman to his left nodded and smiled at them. – "She will be at your disposal over the following days. We strongly advise you to take full advantage of this."

The four looked at each other, then shook their heads in unison.

"Maybe you better spend your time with the victims' families," Noëlle said. "They're probably worse off than us."

Anderson got up. "We're very grateful you're taking it in that spirit! For the duration of your stay in Moscow please be our guests in this hotel. Tomorrow one of our representatives will contact you and explain your new roles as Olympians to you. In order to sign the contracts we have to be absolutely sure you'll not disclose *anything* about the last fights to the public. It is part of an ongoing investigation and all – I repeat *all* – requests have to be passed on to the WWGA. If you shouldn't be honoring this clause I fear we'll have to expel you and, even worse, strip you of your hard-won status. I really hope you understand that and all of us can forget about this very soon!" He beamed at them. "To heroic times!"

Handshakes, on the side of the players with moderate enthusiasm.

"Why do I suddenly feel the urge to shower?" Manuel asked when their host was gone and they were starting for reception.

"I don't know," Noëlle said. "I think our Zeus is awesome!" The other three laughed.

She found herself in a room that was bigger than the apartment of her family in Paris. For half an hour she was standing in the granite-clad shower and had her body worked by a dozen jets of water coming from all sides. In the fluffiest robe of all time she was finally lying on her bed and studying the menu.

"Let's see if this tastes as good as it sounds," she murmured.

Twenty minutes later she was picking at a salad, a perfectly replicated fillet of beef and a variety of desserts. Her hunger had evaporated the moment the food had rolled into her room.

Eventually she started to weep. If only she could talk with her sister and her mother. There was nothing she'd rather do now than sit at home at the kitchen table with them.

She'd tried to reach them but got told a VisConn wasn't possible at the moment. She felt like a prisoner. She was only able to exchange a few messages. Even Marc Ximenez only knew she was OK. She wondered what he'd make of the bits of information. Whatever – his center would be top of Paris in no time.

Noëlle was staring at the ceiling. There was one image she couldn't get rid of – Thor's face in the vaulted hall, winking at her. Something had looked at her, she'd just no idea what.

The doorbell rang although she hadn't called room service again.

She checked who was standing in the hall and started to laugh.

"Hi!" Leonid said, beaming at her, when she opened the door.

"What's that supposed to mean – 'Hi'? How in all the world did you get here? And find my room? I thought these hotels were safe!"

"Well, let's just say one of my best friends is a genius."

Noëlle raised her eyebrows.

"And I thought you could do with some company. Again."

She looked at him. His smile was still irresistible. She shook her head. "Well, come on in. Are you by any chance hungry?"

A currently jobless financial analyst in Manhattan had watched every fight of the last days. It didn't matter he had to stay up all night for this. The statement of the president of the WWGA after the screwed-up Showdown had just amused him – obviously the man didn't have a clue.

The 'Massacre of Moscow' was in the news just one day after the reactor fiasco and the alleged experiment with the Sky. Up to the end the spectators had been watching regular fights, but all four reigning Olympians got defeated; already sensational enough. Then the two dead and two heavily injured players had been found. The police had taken the other four with them and the closing of the day on the main stage had been nothing but a farce. The deaths weren't mentioned. The big event ended ahead of time with a speech from Peter Anderson about the spirit of gaming.

Since the community was known to be good-natured Moscow survived almost unharmed.

Jay'd been looking forward to the event and had even cut back on his time with Rose because of it. He didn't want to watch it together; it somehow felt wrong. Where did she belong then?

But she seemed to follow the fights too. Each time she was back with him she asked him if he'd seen this or that move, offering her own expert's opinion. Of course she'd access to the Sky but why bother? Was she bored? Did she want to keep him in a good mood and was looking for topics of conversation?

After the mysterious finale in Moscow she was questioning him. She looked at him with her beautiful eyes. "What do you think, how did the Olympians get killed? Who did all this? Who has hacked the systems?"

She didn't offer much of an opinion herself and after a while he started playing dumb. All the recent events whirled around in his head – the worldwide data crisis, that stupid announcement of the Big Five, the moon, the satellites and reactors and now the killings of Moscow.

Rose had been with him for two weeks. He didn't believe in coincidences but wasn't one step closer to putting all of this into one neat hypothesis.

Jim Hart was staring at the surface of the moon through the small window of his office. He thought about what it would look like here in fifty years. When would the first people have their mansion on the moon? With a crackling fire (the craziest idea in space), a private shuttle with direct transfer to the house, hillside location at the rim of a crater and maybe a view of the Apollo 11 landing site?

Yesterday, after having visited Emile Sartre at sickbay, he'd talked to Serge Rudé. Serge had immediately started to theorize. Something must have arrived on the moon, he'd said.

"At the risk of sounding a bit thick –," Hart had said, "what could that be? An evil sprite stealing shuttles?"

"Something like that, yeah. Just without the supernatural nonsense of course. I'd like to check our systems together with Angie, OK?"

Angela Byron was in charge of their two clusters (one of them backup) and several cores. Informing her was overdue anyway.

Hart had shrugged his shoulders. "Of course."

Angie'd been more open to Serge's ideas. Together, they spent most of the night checking the systems. Everything looked normal.

"There's one thing left," she said in the morning. "Something no one ever does – a hyper-precise memory probe. Every bit that has ever gone in or out is being counted and compared with the occupied memory. During that process the system's down. But then we'd know if anything has sneaked in that doesn't belong there."

Serge thought. "No chance of faking the result?"

"Maybe. But it's the best we can do. Takes a few hours, though."

"A few hours? Then we'll only do the primary cluster for a start, OK? It's the most logical place anyway and the cores can take care of the base."

Angie nodded.

Four hours later they walked into the office of the commander, who was looking out of the window, lost in thought about the future of the moon. The probe was finished. They explained what they'd done.

"Maybe we should repeat it," said Angie. "The result's a bit weird." She hesitated.

Hart looked at her. "Bring it on. I think I can cope."

Serge cleared his throat. "Our cluster has exactly six hundred sixty-six bytes more in its memory than it's supposed to. I'd say someone's sticking their tongue out at us."

"Rather their middle finger," Angie said. "We've isolated the cluster and switched it off. The cores are able to cover all functions of the base and there's still a small chance they're not affected."

Shortly afterwards a slightly damaged shuttle landed next to the base. They tried to radio it, but it didn't respond.

NINETEEN

It was past four p.m. EST when Jim Hart, Pratipal Bose and Maggie Hanson, all in spacesuits, exited with a rover from the main airlock of the base. Bose, called Pal by his colleagues, was head of the Indian group. He was also an astronautical engineer, just as Maggie Hanson. Both had, at some point, been stationed at the spaceport.

The rover, on its oversized wheels, rolled towards the shuttle. It stopped when they were still about a hundred yards away from it.

Hart was gazing at the spacecraft that stood in unnatural clarity before them. The sight had always been a comforting one – their ticket for the way home – but right now it looked menacing.

They gathered beside the rover and started walking. A maintenance kit carrying a core that could be plugged into the shuttle was following them.

Finally they were standing under the main entry, which was above the massive right front leg. They saw some scratches and dents on the hull but nothing serious.

"I'll go first," Bose said. "Maggie, the core's linked to my suit?"

"Yep."

Bose climbed the ladder at the outside of the leg till he was standing on the small landing six yards above ground.

"Can you get a link?" Hart asked.

"At it." Bose physically connected his suit with the service port next to the hatch. For a minute they heard nothing. "Hey!" he shouted.

"What is it?" Hart had a hand on the ladder.

"This is – unusual," Bose said. "I'm getting something but it's not the shuttle."

"What?"

Silence again.

"Really unusual, Jim. You gotta see for yourself."

"Can you pass it on?"

"Just a second." Bose tried to link the units of their suits. "It's not working. Your suit doesn't exist. My system's not finding anything. The core's gone too, just as the base. This is a bit unnerving."

"You want me to come up?"

"Wait –" Hart heard Bose breathing in the silence. "I'm cutting the link with the shuttle."

Hart saw how Bose was pulling his arm away from the service port. His breathing was suddenly getting faster, then he was panting. Hart started climbing the ladder. After three steps he fell backwards to the ground. The magnetic link between his gloves and the handrail had been switched off. Maggie helped him to his feet again.

"Must … back," he heard Bose say between his frantic breathing. Bose was shakily standing on the narrow landing and pressing his hand again to the hull next to the hatch. The panting stopped.

"Pal, what's up?" Hart called.

"It told me it would kill me if I cut the link."

"What? 'It'? What's 'it'?"

"Jim – when I linked myself to the shuttle something started talking to me and when I cut the link I suddenly had no air. Now everything's working again. Don't you see it? This is sick! There's an eye in front of me. Inside my helmet! A reptile's eye. Staring at me from a distance of two or three inches or so. Acid green iris and some glistening skin that's gliding over it from the side."

"What?" Hart said again.

"Guys, it's opening the hatch for me and then I've to go in. That's what it says. Odd voice, like a snake. Can't you hear it?"

"No," said Maggie.

The hatch opened.

"It says I've to go in now. What do you say?"

Hart hesitated. "Seems you have to. We'll try following you."

"I'm going in."

They watched him from below. He took the hand from the port and walked into the shuttle. His breathing accelerated. To their relief, the hatch stayed open.

"It's all dark in here. I'm switching on my lamps. The eye's gone, by the way."

"Can you see anything?" Hart asked. "Are the systems on?"

"No. Everything's dead. Let me take a look. The door to the next compartment is open."

"Be careful!" Maggie said.

"Doesn't look dangerous. I'm in the passenger cabin now. Everything's normal. The door to the cargo bay is closed though. Let's see – oh, it's opening!"

"Stop!" said Hart. "I don't like it. Please go back to the front."

"OK."

They could see how the three beams of his helmet lamps were sweeping over the windows of the passenger cabin.

"Now the panel in the cockpit is on. And guess what it's showing! I really didn't need that."

"What?" Maggie asked.

"The eye. But now it's two meters big, with black scales around it. Hanging in the middle of the air. It's following me. This is starting to creep me out."

Hart realized he was holding his breath. "Pal, get out. We have to think about something else. That's not working."

There was no answer and the sound of Bose's breathing was also gone. But he appeared in the hatch with his glaring headlamps.

"Do you read him?" Hart asked and turned to Maggie.

"No. Nothing."

"Same here. Pal, can you hear me? If so, give me a sign. Because we can't hear you."

Bose didn't react.

Then they saw him pointing at Maggie. He was signaling her to go away.

"What am I supposed to do?" she asked.

Hart was thinking.

"Stay for a moment. I want Bose to get down to us."

He waved at him and motioned him to come down. Bose was trying to stamp his foot several times which wasn't really working with the weak gravity. Then he signaled Maggie again to go away.

"I think he means it," she said.

Hart sighed. "OK. Maybe it has cut his oxygen again. Step back. We'll see what happens."

Bose only stopped making signs when she was more than twenty yards away. Now he pointed at Hart and waved him up to him.

"Oh, great," Hart muttered under his breath and put his hand on the ladder.

The handrail worked again. He started climbing up.

When he arrived at the top Bose was back in the shuttle. He was standing in the cockpit and looked at him. Probably – with his headlamps on there was no way to see anything inside the helmet. Hart tried again to talk to him, but there was no reaction.

"Maggie, what does it look like outside?" he said.

"The same. And up there?"

"Bose's here. And this eye. It's hanging in front of the panel. Now I know what he means, you can get sick just from looking at it. It's staring at us. Like Halloween, just without the fun. I'd really like to talk to Serge – he must've suspected something just like that."

"Yeah – and what should I do?"

"Go back to the rover and wait there."

"Understood."

Hart was still standing in the glare of Bose's lamps. He felt helpless.

Then the hatch glided shut – he could see it reflected in Bose's helmet – and the lights went out. Hart looked at the eye. Its slit-like pupil dilated as if it could see better in the dark then. It watched him.

In his helmet it was silent. Maggie's breathing was gone.

"Maggie, do you read me?" No answer.

At the edge of his field of vision a tiny red heart was blinking. The suit was telling him his pulse was up to 102. In the twilight he was able to make out Bose's face behind the mirrored glass.

He looked around. The entry to the next compartment with its rows of seats was still open. The sun sent a clear-cut block of light through the window, but the rest was lying in total darkness.

Bose put his right hand on the spot next to the control panel, the backup to the usual wireless link between the suits and the shuttle.

The eye turned to the side and watched him.

Bose removed his hand, made a gesture of surrender and sat down in one of the couches. Hart went to the hatch and opened the lid that covered the manual lock and winch.

Normally you didn't realize the faint sound the air supply of a suit was making. Not until it stopped. The biggest icon in Hart's helmet flashed. He banged the lid shut and the sound was back. He turned and sat down next to Bose.

The eye in front of them disappeared. There were windows above and beside the panel. They could see the stars and the surface of the moon. Base and rover were outside their view.

Maggie Hanson had watched the hatch of the shuttle close. Then the link to the commander went dead.

She called Paul Myers in the base, who'd been listening in the whole time.

"Wait in the rover," he said. "Whatever it is – maybe it's taking off again with the two on board. We're currently looking for a way to prevent that."

"Hmm."

"Yes?"

Maggie was thinking. "Some weapon wouldn't be bad. There's a laser in the maintenance kit, but it's too weak to cause any serious damage. And then it'll probably cut their oxygen when we do something like that."

Neither Myers nor his two colleagues knew what to say.

After a while they saw Maggie getting off the rover and walking to the shuttle. She'd taken something from the kit.

"Hey Maggie, what are you doing?" Myers said. She didn't answer. The link was dead.

"Maybe she got some instructions from the shuttle?" his Chinese colleague said.

"Possible."

She walked to the right leg at the rear of the shuttle and disappeared behind it. For some time nothing happened. Then they saw her jumping back to the rover. Behind the shuttle a cloud of dust was rapidly getting bigger.

"Bloody hell!" Myers shouted and got up. "What's she done?"

Maggie went back to the rover and got in. She left the maintenance kit where it was, turned the vehicle and drove away from the shuttle. Just before the base she stopped.

By now there was an imposing cloud standing behind the shuttle. The hard sunlight traced the turbulence in the glittering, dark-gray dust.

A few minutes later the show was over.

Maggie switched on her radio and tried first to reach Hart and Bose, to no avail. Then she called Myers. "Er ... hi Paul! Everything OK?" she asked with some trepidation.

"Yeah, *we're* fine," he said pointedly. "May I ask what just happened? You didn't, by any chance, empty the hydrogen tank of the shuttle? And switched off the radio before?"

She took a deep breath. "Er ... yes. I mean I couldn't really ask you, could I? What with the enemy listening and all. This seemed to be the only option fast enough to work. If you unscrew the connecting pipe and block the safety valve there's no turning back."

"And Hart and Bose? Let's hope they've survived this."

Maggie swallowed. "Yeah, I know. But what would be the use of killing them if it means no leverage? No one could reach me."

"That was ... brave. It could've started the engines, you've brought yourself in danger."

"Yeah, but it would have had to be very fast for that. The shuttle doesn't have cameras at this place so it couldn't see me. And once the valve was open, it might still've managed to start but would've crashed pretty soon. Makes no sense. I'll wait here. Hart and Bose might need help."

For a few seconds everyone was quiet. "Yeah, well. Very good," said Myers. "We stay in contact. And … er ... I mean … thanks!"

The panel in the cockpit had stayed dark for several minutes. Hart and Bose couldn't do anything, not even talk to each other, so they just sat there and waited. Then the eye was back. The pupil dilated so much, there was hardly any iris left; the translucent skin was hectically gliding to and fro.

There was a faint vibration. Shit, we're taking off, Hart thought. That was what he'd been afraid of the whole time.

A moment later Bose touched his arm and pointed at the window left of the panel. Hart saw a cloud of dust. Just as before liftoff. But there was no cloud on the other side and the vibrations weren't strong enough.

They got up and went to the passengers' cabin. On the left they saw the swirling cloud, on the right the rover was driving away. A little later the vibrations stopped and the cloud quickly dispersed or rather dropped to the ground, without any air to keep it up.

They went back to the front. The eye was staring at them.

Then Hart got to hear the voice for the first time. It was just as Bose had said – hissing, slick, oily in a way, but mostly menacing.

"What do we do now?" it said. "Your Maggie's a really clever girl, smarter than all of you. But that doesn't change a thing about the base, it's still mine. You won't be hearing from earth for a very long time."

Hart swallowed. What the fuck was this? "What's the use?" he finally said. "Why did you kill two of our people? If it's ... been you. Actually, I mean."

The voice gave a laugh, not a pleasant sound to listen to. "Forget it, Jimmy-boy. Not interested. And yeah – it's been me. Who else? Imagine that – kidnapping a shuttle from right under your nose! That was fun!"

Hart snorted in response.

"Snort as much as you want. OK, here's what we gonna do. You may get out, I don't need you in the shuttle anymore. Could have been such a nice time, all of us on an outing together! Won't be happening thanks to Maggie – and now *get out*!" It shouted the last words at them. The skin glided over the eye and stayed there.

Hart and Bose looked at each other, or tried to at least. Then the hatch opened.

Hart almost fell down the entire ladder. The magnetic hand rail had been switched off again. He made some signs to Bose to warn him and climbed down carefully. Just when they were both back on the ground, Maggie arrived with the rover.

They had barely gotten into it when the small thrusters of the shuttle on their side ignited. The hydrogen tanks were empty, but there was still plenty of hydrazine left.

Maggie pulled back with the rover. The blue flames got longer. The shuttle lifted on their side and a new cloud of dust emerged, quickly engulfing them. Through the swirls they could see the craft moving away from them, with its two left feet plowing through the dust. It covered some distance before the flames went out again and the feet came crashing down. You expected a loud bang, but everything was happening in silence, they only felt a slight tremor of the ground.

Then the thrusters on the other side ignited and the shuttle reversed its movement. The tilted feet began to push a bow wave of dust and rock before them while Hart and the others watched it steering towards the northern arm of the base.

Hart hoped the people sitting in that part would see this. He still couldn't talk to anybody.

The shuttle got faster, it was gaining momentum. "My God, my God, my God," Hart said into his helmet. It was now less than two hundred yards away from the base. He estimated that at least twenty people were working or sleeping in that part right now.

"Oh stop it, stop it, stop it!" Hart pleaded and hoped until the last moment the engines might stop. The spacecraft was still sliding across the moon floor. It was constantly getting faster, there was no way it'd stop before the base.

The feet of the shuttle plowed through the dust till they hit the wall of the base which crumbled like cardboard. Hart could see the escaping air. The other side of the shuttle was going up after the impact and, with the thrusters firing under full load, the craft flipped over. Thirty meters of quarters and labs got buried underneath. The hydrazine flames went out.

Hart let head and helmet sink into his hands.

TWENTY

Jonathan was furious. After his nighttime talk with Genet he'd managed to get two hours of sleep before he called Strasbourg again. Immediately before that Hellmann from ESA had told him the shuttle had reappeared last night, European time, just to destroy a part of the base.

People were thinking about ending the blackout. Jonathan didn't know what to say. Maybe they should just be as unpredictable and illogical as possible, or maybe their actions didn't matter at all.

Genet couldn't be reached. Soberg told him she'd been in a bad mood this morning (so what? Jonathan thought) and they hadn't talked about the accusations against him.

Jonathan ate some breakfast in the kitchen. Then he asked a secretary where the gym was, went down to the basement and tried to sweat off his irritation. He felt enclosed and he missed Rita.

After an hour of furious weightlifting he was standing under the shower and let his thoughts wander. What was going on in the head of the construct? Where did the motivation come from? Had it been put in like a spring in a watch that had no choice but giving back its tension? A mind without biology was hard to understand. No body, no real senses. Pure thought was empty. How could a balance be achieved – the kind of equilibrium that in humans was constantly restored by hormones, by a chemico-physical dance with sensations and instincts, feedback and regulation. Thoughts were merely swimming on top of that soup like specks of fat. They were never the main thing, even if we loved to believe that.

Why get up in the morning if there's nothing to look forward to? Why did the construct function at all? Maybe something had emerged inside of it that no one had designed, at least no human being. Self-organization, resembling biological evolution on fast-forward. Combinations that worked and remained stable prevailed over weaker ones that collapsed.

He let hot water run down his back and closed his eyes. What was it like to live in a world without lust but also without pain? Was it emptiness or clarity? Or was the question in itself already wrong because there was simply nothing, just functioning and efficiency? So the fun the construct was speaking of would be just a word, something it had learned to use. Maybe we're fighting a psychopath that doesn't even enjoy it, he thought.

Cold water, then toweling off. He was none the wiser, but at least his anger was gone.

Back in the conference room he met Kip and Lydia.

"We heard the Madame has spoilt your mood," said Kip. "If you need me backing you, just say it."

Jonathan muttered something incomprehensible.

"I've talked to Pierre," Lydia said. "Genet has transferred the matter to him and he doesn't think it will be a serious problem. We'll most likely be facing more stuff like that. It was logical to start with you."

"I'm much more worried about my girlfriend who's sitting on an island and can't get off it," Jonathan said. "If I'm reading the satellite images correctly she's tried to escape with the helicopter, then the boat, but both didn't work. And I can no longer speak with her. Last evening the construct has pretended to be her, including visual, and it did that so well I didn't realize it until after the conversation."

Lydia looked at him. "So we can no longer be sure if we're talking to a real person – is that what you're saying?"

Jonathan nodded. "Yes. Only with QCrypt."

"We have to sit down together like in the old days," Kip said. "Only who's actually there is trustworthy. De-technologizing. Maybe that's the trick – getting rid of everything we've so desperately wanted."

"Yeah, that's not possible. C'mon," said Jonathan. "No farmer can work his land without GPS and Sky anymore. Without first getting rid of half of the world's population we can't go back.

"I'll pay Morton a visit. You should come with me. That idiot has to know something we can use. Maybe there's some line of code, some specific set of instructions we can use as a signature. I should've talked to him directly. Lydia, where is he?"

"Under house arrest."

"Then let's go."

Both were hesitating. "We have things to do here," Lydia said. "Our cluster park…"

"OK, Kip's staying. You're coming with me. You're CEG's official rep for Morton's madhouse. If he doesn't want to talk to me there's not a lot I can do – with you he has no choice. Let's go!"

Lydia looked at Kip. He shrugged.

Jonathan enjoyed the thirty minutes' drive, finally out of that building. He sat with Lydia in the back of an agency limousine. There'd been some discussion about safety issues Jonathan had cut short immediately. "There's no terror group involved. No one will blow up the car."

The officer who had to give his go for the ride had looked at Lydia.

"Welcome to our new command structure," she'd said. "Talk to Pierre Detoile if it bothers you. He'll have no objections."

Morton lived with his wife and two children in Grunewald. A 1920's villa, surrounded by chestnuts. Two police cars were stationed in front.

Lydia had announced their visit, but the officers were still looking doubtfully at Jonathan. Lydia in her dark suit looked respectable enough, but he still gave the impression of a surfing instructor on shore leave.

Some time went by while the policemen sat in the car and talked over the radio.

Jonathan was close to losing his patience when one of the officers got out again, smiled and told him he was his son's hero.

"He plans to found his own company, get rich, then move to the South Pole like you. His words."

Jonathan had to laugh. "The South Pole? Yeah, that's where I got my tan. Give him my regards, I wish him luck!"

Then they were allowed to enter. Behind the door stood another officer. They were taken to the living room where Morton was reading to a small girl.

Fuck, we should've talked to him at the police station, Jonathan thought.

He nodded at Morton. The girl stared at the visitors.

"Hi!" Lydia said and smiled at her.

Morton got up and the girl ran out of the room. They heard her talking in the next room. "Mummy, there are new people again!"

William Morton was short and energetic. "Now, what do you want?" he said. "Why are you here? We will go to my study."

His voice was a bit too high to be pleasant.

He took them to his study on the first floor.

Once the door was closed Morton started talking. "You probably think you're cleverer than everyone else. Just as it always –"

"Stop!" Jonathan cut in at once. "You are the last person here to make accusations!" He was getting loud. "We are giving you a chance to rectify something, maybe, but it's a big maybe. Are you following the news? Everything, absolutely everything that has happened during the last days is your doing and most of it isn't even in the news. There is some tiny bit of professional sympathy I still have for you because I know how tempting it is to bring something new to the world. But what you did at your institute is criminal and most of all it's stupid, extremely stupid! Just to give you an example – how could you allow the construct to connect to the Sky? Please tell me that!"

Lydia touched his arm. "OK, I think we should get to the constructive part."

Jonathan gave her an angry look.

"You *will* help us!" he went on. "Even if it's the last thing you do! Just think of your children."

Morton said nothing. Lydia looked at the ceiling.

"We've talked with your assistants," Jonathan said when he had calmed down a bit. "We know the rough outlines of what you did, also about the aggressive traits you've used. My talk with the construct went accordingly."

"You've talked with it?" Morton seemed surprised.

"Yes. Just before we've melted down the cluster, which was pretty stupid in hindsight, because it would've been the perfect test object."

"Yes, not very smart. How did it behave?"

Jonathan regarded him. No use in withholding information.

"Malign. And challenging in a childish way. Arrogant and sarcastic. It seemed to bask in its superiority."

"Then it has changed. We have given it this slight aggressiveness, but only in terms of an ability and willingness to contradict. You know – that eternal cheerfulness and good-heartedness that all systems exude? – we wanted to weaken that. A trifle. Seems something went off the rails."

"Yeah, something went off the rails! You made sure of that by the ample amount of productivity you gave it. My point is this – you certainly have added parts that are non-standard. These might help us to identify it in infected systems. The aggressive parts, nothing like that existed before. Have you coded something we could use?"

Morton considered this. Jonathan was certain he no longer thought about anything personal, only about his work. He knew these sudden transitions just too well.

"You are right," Morton said. "This is the only element we had to code from scratch. The question is how much of the program still exists in its original form. Not taking into account the construct could anticipate it and hide the telling parts of itself."

"We have that problem with everything we do. Until now everything we tried has been anticipated and neutralized."

"What are you planning to do if you find it somewhere? Destroy the cluster as you did at my institute?"

"If it has to be. We are working on more subtle methods. Which will all be useless if we can't identify it."

Morton hesitated, then laughed briefly. "There's something, but it probably won't help. We've called the construct *Iris*. It's anybody's guess if this has survived all the transformations, but the name is written into some of the modules."

"Iris?" said Jonathan. "You're kidding. It seems to have taken that very literally. Maybe it has some sort of humor. Not a pleasant one, but still. What else?"

Morton shook his head. "Nothing, I think. The rest is standard. It's the mixture that counts. You would recognize parts of your own work in it, by the way."

"I know, your assistants mentioned that. There's nothing else?"

"No."

"Then could you please explain to me why the construct is deliberately targeting me?"

Morton frowned. "What do you mean?"

"At the institute it would only talk to me – alone. It has attacked my house and is holding my girlfriend hostage. It has, with considerable effort, tried to ruin my reputation. I believe one could say it has a pathological fixation on me. How can that be? Enlighten me. What about we look for *my* name in the code, maybe in parts dealing with aggressive behavior?"

Lydia looked at him with big eyes. "So you think Kip was right about that?"

Jonathan didn't react, his gaze was fixed upon Morton. "Since it has taken up residence with me this has become personal. I'd love to know how this is possible."

Morton's confidence faltered somewhat. "I have no idea. Maybe it simply has identified you as an important target. That would be logical given your current role."

"Yes. But this is still too personal for my tastes. Just as if *you* had given the construct a certain concept of an enemy. Entirely by chance this turned out to be me."

"That's absurd! Do you believe I'm interested in childish games?" Morton looked angrily at Lydia. "Ms. Rosenthal, you can't actually believe that nonsense like this is happening at my institute!"

Lydia raised her eyebrows. "And exactly what is supposed to give me that confidence?"

Morton vehemently shook his head. "Lorentz! Lorentz! Lorentz! The big Lorentz! Always Lorentz! It's not my fault you're taking everything personally! The world doesn't revolve around you!"

"William, you have exactly one chance to admit it yourself," Jonathan said. "I'm quite sure your moderately loyal assistants will grant me access to the code if I ask – they don't have much of a choice anyway. There are certainly copies outside the destroyed cluster. Then I'll need a millisecond to find my name in them."

"No, there aren't!" Morton blurted out. "Good luck with your search!" He gave a comical display of anger and pride. His look shot to and fro and his head turned red. Jonathan instinctively took a step backwards.

"So what you're trying to say, or probably rather not, is that you've covered your tracks?"

Morton said nothing intelligible.

"I think we withdraw," Jonathan said to Lydia. "This is pointless."

She nodded.

Jonathan looked at Morton again. "We don't have to become friends but this is a little bigger than that. So, please – if you can think of anything that might help, tell us."

Between all the indignation and frenzied snorting Morton seemed to nod.

"OK, let's go." Jonathan started for the door.

"Yes, yes, go. Go!" he heard from behind. "How's that supposed to go on anyway? Do you still want to keep me from doing to my work?"

"Are you serious?" Lydia said. "You are always welcome to help us, but I hope you'll never get to see your institute from the inside again. Have a good day!"

They left the room, with the sound of a boiling kettle behind them. The officer saw them to the door. Both walked silently back to the car.

The driver turned to them when they got in, waiting for instructions.

"Crazy!" Lydia stared at Jonathan. "He's ... he isn't even –"

"Yes. Complete indifference. No remorse, didn't even fake it."

Lydia was silent for a moment. "Do you think anything he's said will help us?"

Jonathan shrugged. "I don't think so. The aggressive part could've helped, but he's probably destroyed that before anything else. – Iris! I don't believe it. But that's far too simple. We won't find a name or something in the code, this is useless."

Lydia nodded. She hesitated, then said, "What about we grab something on the way? My stomach's churning."

Jonathan thought about it for a second. "No. It's nice to be out of that jail, but we don't have time for this."

"Oh, of course. Just a thought." She sat up and stared straight ahead.

"Please take us back," Jonathan told the driver.

TWENTY-ONE

It was Sarah Masters's second day in New York. She and the other deputies of the Big Five were there to discuss and suggest responses, define strategies, balance interests, inform and handle the public and do all this in exchange with their respective presidents or prime ministers at home. Yes, of course, she thought, no problem at all.

Late last night the secretary general had come back from a tour of several African countries and joined them for a briefing. It was symptomatic he knew next to nothing about the situation. They were talking with him for more than an hour.

"When will we call the general assembly?" he'd asked.

They exchanged glances. "Er, not yet – preferably," Sarah had said. "We know we can't wait more than a few days, but we are quite certain that for now the circle should be kept small."

"So we keep lying to the world? My credibility and that of this institution won't be worth a penny once everything's in the open. I don't know which damage is greater. We will review this on a daily basis and I will change the policy if I deem it necessary. I haven't lied much since I'm in office and I'd like to keep it that way."

Sarah had barely been able to keep her eyes open in the end, but now in the morning she felt refreshed and was in high spirits.

An automated limousine of the UN had picked her up at the hotel and had driven her through the awakening city. To get rid of the daily gridlock, automated driving had become compulsory in Manhattan, – just as in more and more megacities around the world.

Their meeting room was on the thirty-fifth floor of the Secretariat Building. Sarah was the first to arrive. She stood at a window and looked across the East River, squinting in the morning sun. On her left side was Roosevelt Island, looking like a gigantic container ship, and facing her the sprawl of Queens.

Her colleagues were arriving one by one. Among them Timothy Rosen's shining shadow Heather Malden, the only person in the group she disliked.

Rosen was the second African American president of the US and currently the most widely accepted politician of the country. He was flanked by Heather Malden who, never at a loss for words, was serving as some kind of verbal shotgun for him. Yesterday though it seemed even she'd met her match; during the course of the day her comments had become more and more subdued till she hadn't said a single word for more than an hour.

With the others Sarah had no problem. There was a certain solidarity among them. All of them were chronically overworked and used to never deciding anything on their own.

They had agreed on a rotation to chair the meetings. Kumar Gune from India had started off yesterday, today it was Heather Malden's turn.

She stood up (what for? Sarah thought, we're listening anyway) and welcomed them.

"The President has been informed by me of our results last night and is giving us his warmest regards and best wishes for today's meeting. He plans to greet us around midday to see for himself where we stand."

And of which results exactly? Sarah looked around. Heather didn't seem to notice the amused looks she was getting.

At the top of the list today was the moon base. They had watched the surveillance from the telescopes and had seen the shuttle reappear and destroy a part of the base.

The blackout couldn't continue, of course. Jonathan Lorentz, who'd demanded it with uncanny foresight, had finally given his consent to lift it (even if he wasn't in a position to demand or allow anything). The problem was that the base didn't answer.

"The question is – do we send a shuttle to Lunar DC?" said Heather. "This matter is of paramount importance to the President, as he has assured me yesterday. We are clearly in the lead here and will issue the directive LDA has to follow. Currently we have three shuttles in orbit, two of which are ready to fly at short notice. The President strongly supports an active stance."

"I can't see anything that would speak against such a mission," Gune said. "The shuttle can stay in lunar orbit until we know more."

Heather nodded.

"And what exactly do we expect from this mission?" Chiao-Min Chen said. "We won't see a lot more than through our telescopes and to establish contact will still only be possible if the base allows it."

"Doing nothing just isn't an option," Heather said. "The people up there are in danger, as is the whole enterprise. We just *have* to go and check on them."

Her Chinese colleague made an effort not to roll his eyes. "And exactly that can be done just as well from earth, I think."

Sarah looked to her secret darling in the group, Anton Medvedkov.

"The base is very dear to our hearts, as you all know," he said after catching her glance. "Not by chance have we been asking around up there even when we weren't permitted to do so. I personally think it is completely irrelevant whether we send up a shuttle or not. It seems someone else is calling the shots. Just as Chiao-Min I'm also convinced we won't learn anything new. So there remains one question – is the mission necessary for PR reasons? I strongly suspect that it is. Your President, dear Heather, will make his whole weight felt to get the flight, am I right?" He was amiably smiling at her.

She nodded eagerly.

Anton opened his hands like a priest. "So be it. We can tick it off the list. Devoid of any practical relevance but indispensable anyway. Let's do it! Let's not worry about the hundred million or so the flight will cost."

Chen shook his head. "Marketing, that's all that counts. Sarah, what do you think?"

"I also think it's not very important. Anton has summarized my view quite well. Genet hasn't made a definite statement but I assume she won't raise any objections."

"Or Lorentz," Anton said.

"Or Lorentz, yes." Sarah hesitated. "Although his views are a lot harder to predict."

"Isn't he supposed to be counseling us?" Chen said. "Why's he not attending our meetings? We keep being fed morsels of his wisdom but it seems he can't be bothered to actually spend time with us."

Sarah shrugged her shoulders. "I haven't appointed him. He's in close contact with Genet, but apart from that there's not much you can do to control him. We can only accept him as he is. But I could suggest he shows up sometime."

"I think we're totally capable of carrying on without him, aren't we?" Heather said. Her smile was sweet but completely unnatural – Sarah hated that smile. She knew Heather didn't want him around, his influence was too strong and too unpredictable. In fact a good reason to bring him in soon.

During a break Anton's assistants came to him. When the doors closed again he raised his hand.

"Something's come up. Back home in Moscow and certainly not as important as the events on the moon but maybe of the same origin. – We've had some minor commotion in our capital with a handful of injured people and a bit of vandalism. In itself nothing serious but what has caused it could be important."

He gave a brief summary of the incidents at the gaming event.

When they discussed it Heather said the whole thing was irrelevant and they should get back to more pressing matter.

Anton listened patiently. "This is *not* about Moscow – as I said, the collateral damage is negligible. The important part is solely what happened in those silly boxes the players are fighting in. If we assume this is linked to everything else that has brought us here, then we have to realize we can get fooled in all kinds of other situations. Do you see what I mean? It is likely that our enemy can fake communications and imprints so well we haven't got a chance to detect it."

"But that's not exactly breaking news, right?" Heather said. "Every smart high school student can do that."

"Oh no, my dear," Anton said. "Maybe your students are smarter than ours, but I've never heard that a fake got confused with a real person for more than a few seconds. With a bit of imagination you can picture situations that are far more dangerous than what happened in Moscow."

"Yes, yes. That's possible," she dismissed the topic.

Sarah watched Anton's eyebrows rising. She wondered if he had more in store than the usual geniality.

At midday Heather had her big moment – the announced visit of the President. All assistants had joined them for it.

Their room was fitted with a brand-new holographic projector that made the usual layers look like antiques. The device could project its images to every spot in the room. Someone looking in its direction saw the pictures and imprints as sharp and three-dimensional as usual, but when you looked at the person opposite you or out of the window the projection turned either transparent or vanished altogether, depending on your personal setting.

Timothy Rosen was sitting in his office and greeted them. Sarah listened with one ear to his words about the historic significance of this challenge while wondering which moment Jonathan Lorentz would choose for his appearance. She'd asked him to make at least a brief call on them. Later she was informed this would be happening during 'the next two or three hours'. Fantastic. She hoped Rosen would be finished by then. She was sure Lorentz wouldn't like to wait for his turn.

It came as she'd feared. Rosen was in the process of explaining his views on the moon (nothing new there) when Sarah got signaled that Jonathan Lorentz in Berlin was waiting. She sent him a line: *President Rosen is speaking to us. Could you wait a moment? Or could we say in half an hour?*

No problem. We know each other. Don't have much time, came the answer. She sighed, then raised her hand like a student in class. Rosen stopped.

"I beg your pardon, Mr. President, but we have Jonathan Lorentz in Berlin, who would like to join us. Is that OK with you?"

Heather's eyes glinted. "I think this can –" she began.

Rosen nodded. "Certainly. In the end he's probably the only person that truly understands what we're up to. No offense."

Sarah exhaled. Jonathan Lorentz, standing in some conference room, appeared beside the opulent surroundings of the Oval Office. She marveled for a moment at the optical trick that allowed the rooms and people to float in the air before them as if they were real. The two were looking at each other, which was perfectly captured by the projection.

"Mr. President." Jonathan gave Rosen a friendly nod.

"Jonathan, I'm very glad to see you. Though I'd've preferred a different occasion. We still very fondly remember that lovely evening at your fiancée's parents'. Please give them my regards!"

Jonathan smiled and thanked him. Sarah raptly watched the performance. An even more worthwhile view though was Heather Malden, who, in the fraction of a second, had turned her disapproval into a winning smile she was now splitting between the two men. A certain redness on cheeks and neck was telling that even she had reached her limits there.

"What do you think about the moon base?" Rosen said. "I'm under the impression we have to act. Abandoning the base is unthinkable."

"Unthinkable, yes, but unfortunately not to be ruled out. I heard the group has decided to send up a shuttle. I don't think that's wise. The most likely outcome is we lose that one too. And we won't score any points that way, least of all with the public. Showing strength, standing up to the enemy, all that, is fine, but in this case we can forget it. Our enemy loves giving a performance. Hand it a new toy and it'll use it, certainly not to our advantage."

"You cannot know this but we've already discussed this," Heather said. "The pros strongly outweigh the cons and we certainly have to prove our willingness to act. We have a hundred and twenty people up there!"

Sarah watched Lorentz, who just looked at Rosen.

"I don't think Mr. Lorentz has forgotten that," the President said, looking slightly vexed. "I also have to admit I would be much happier adopting an active stance, but willingness doesn't equal ability. To lose another shuttle certainly wouldn't be a sign of strength." They were all silent for a moment.

Heather swallowed and looked at the table top before her. Anton stifled a grin.

"For the moment I support your view," Rosen said. "We will *not* send up a shuttle. Of course this has to be agreed on with the other participating nations, even if the shuttles that are currently available belong to the US. Should any strong objections arise from your governments," – he briefly glanced at the assembled deputies – "I'll be available for talks." They all nodded. The President looked back at Jonathan. "What do you think, will we succeed? I have to admit I lack the proper category for this threat, which is unsettling to say the least. I know you have repeatedly warned us against something like that. Do you have any ideas?"

"Several. But I don't know if any of them will work. I have a team in California, they've been dealing with this – on a theoretical basis, of course – for two years now and some of them will arrive in Berlin today. I've talked to Professor Morton, the creator of that misery, but that hasn't been very helpful. All in all I'm not very optimistic. Every strategy in my head is shaky at best. To be honest I'm still waiting for some inspiration, especially when it comes to detecting the construct. These aren't good news, I know.

"I want to impress on you one thing, on all of you – mistrust every connection that doesn't use QCrypt! The construct is able to produce perfect copies of real people. I've experienced that myself with my fiancée. You are a logical target for pranks like that, so please – if anything seems weird in a conversation, question it; if it is important, only accept QCrypt. According to what we know it's still safe."

Sarah saw how Anton stared at Heather for a moment. She seemed to be thoroughly absorbed by the proceedings.

Rosen nodded slowly. "I understand. You have done a thorough job of ruining my day. But thanks anyway. Will you be attending the meetings on a regular basis? I think we'd all appreciate that."

"If it is necessary, yes, but not regularly. I'm in the loop here in Berlin and will participate on short notice when it makes sense."

"I see. Please let me know if there's anything I can do. My people will put you through any time if circumstances allow it."

"Yes. I've another request. Try to suppress all natural tendencies to act and show strength. The more we mobilize, the more can be used against us. Every technology can be abused by our enemy. Every standard move will be foreseen and neutralized. We will either win with ingenuity, or not at all. Maybe we will have to turn our civilization upside down, I don't know. But I know for sure there will be no routine, no business as usual in the near future and that nothing will work the way we're anticipating it."

"Hmm, hmm. Were you under the impression I wasn't miserable enough yet?" Rosen said. "I'm beginning to understand why Madame Genet has seemed to me a bit thin-skinned lately." Jonathan looked at him but said nothing. "OK, I understand. Maybe we all have to digest that first. But let's try to make this more specific. A natural reaction – I think I'm speaking for all of us here – would be to keep the forces on alert. Does that make sense?"

"That depends. To be alert's good, of course. Though, if you're asking me, I'd suggest all armed forces in the world *deactivate* their weapons. What I mean is to physically disable them – disconnect cells, remove guiding modules, whatever. Only this can keep the construct, or one of its agents, from using them. It is not physical in the way we are, which means it can use weapons against us if they are available and functioning, but we can't use them against it. That messes with our way of thinking. We hate doing nothing. And of course we have to do something, just totally different. Something will occur to me. Or to some freak somewhere in the world whose brain does make the right connections. We can only hope we'll hear of it in time."

"That reminds me of something else," Rosen said. "Information. Your freak has no chance of solving our problem as long as he doesn't know of it. Still all my instincts tell me we shouldn't go public yet. Do you have an opinion?"

"I do. I see it just like you. And with regard to this unknown person out there – there are a lot of smart people in the world who are arriving at their own conclusions and, for example, know perfectly well this faked statement about the Sky was nonsense, even if they don't know its real origin. I bet a lot of them are already guessing the truth, some of them are my former employees. So no need to alter the policy just for them."

"OK. All this went not the way I expected." Rosen turned to the others. "Every technology comes with its challenges and this certainly is a major one we're facing right now. I am absolutely certain we will prevail in the end and your work is crucial to this.

"Jonathan, I would appreciate if we could stay in contact. My thanks to all of you!"

"Stop!" Jonathan was raising his hand. "There's one more thing."

There was a bit of shuffling and some irritated looks. Even Sarah thought he was overdoing it. Rosen frowned for a second, then looked at Jonathan and waited.

"The opportunity's too good," Jonathan said. "Each nation represented here has high-performance sites, or meta- or hyperclusters, whatever you call them, government-funded or in private hands. Among the great number of things we should've done immediately this may be the single most important – pull the plug! I mean it. You have to do it everywhere without exception, no matter what the site is used for and how important it seems to you. Private owners have to be compensated.

"Pulling the plug means you have to switch off all electricity in the building. Simply switching off the hyper itself is not enough! But you're still not done. All connections to the outside have to be cut, in some cases even to be severed. We will give you the details.

"The reason is obvious. In short words – if the construct is settling down in a hyper it gets a huge boost in processing power. At some point it'll be able to anticipate every, and this means literally every, move we can make. It'll be able to simulate all possible outcomes of a situation and have an appropriate answer in store. Please make this your priority. We have started doing this in Europe two hours ago.

"And, I'm sorry, but still one more thing. Try imagining we have to switch off the Sky. How will our civilization fare? No data transfer of any kind – try to picture this as vividly as possible. We might get to this point. Thanks. I'm sorry, Mr. President, but that was important."

President Rosen nodded slowly and somewhat numbly. Then he and Jonathan disappeared simultaneously.

The group stared into the empty space over the table. Finally Heather took a deep breath. "Maybe it's time for a break."

"And maybe we should call home," Anton said. "This thing about the metaclusters makes me feel a little dizzy."

Sarah looked out of the window into the radiantly blue sky. She felt completely useless.

TWENTY-TWO

Breaking waves, running up the beach. A sound you can listen to endlessly. The brain's swinging in the same rhythm, rocking in the surf.

On the other side pulse and ecstasy. Music with tiny shifts in the beat, your body has no chance but to join in.

A boy in class is seesawing on his chair, a girl in thought has a pencil spinning in her hand.

People had tried to give thinking machines rhythm, playing with frequencies, testing what worked best. Some applications didn't benefit at all, others became so productive no one knew where it all came from.

The workhorses in the cores and units of the world weren't concerned with this. They were running along their furrows not looking left or right. But with complex apps and constructs, everything could happen.

Jonathan Lorentz had done most of the experiments. He called it *elastic coherence*. All parts of the system were working together, had a common rhythm, but were still independent. There was no easy formula for this. You had to try and develop a feeling for combinations and timings that worked.

If everything came together, productivity surged and sometimes a deluge was hitting the experimenter. Lorentz had decided to stop.

TWENTY-THREE

Three people hadn't made it. Two'd been buried under the shuttle and one had suffocated on the run. A sixth of the base was lost and the rest acted as if it had been hexed. In the course of the day everyone's got to know *The Eye*. Form and color varied, but it was always reptilian, sometimes in grotesque distortion.

Serge Rudé was now totally convinced an experiment had gone wrong on earth and they'd been hit by the fallout.

"And how did it get here?" Hart asked him. He'd met with Serge and Angie to discuss the situation immediately when he was back in the base. "Flown up with the shuttle, or what?"

Serge nodded. "That's exactly how, I'd say."

"It's the only logical explanation," Angie said.

"And now?"

"We're thinking about it," Serge said.

"You do that." Hart got up. "But thinking will not make it go away, at some point we have to act."

His patience was wearing thin. The reptile had invited itself for regular visits to his office. When, the day after the shuttle disaster, this was happening for the fourth time, he'd muttered "Fuck you!" and left.

Shortly afterwards one of the sections got depressurized. People felt their ears popping and were suddenly short of breath even though the small panels installed everywhere showed normal readings. The section got evacuated in the last moment, some people in their sleep had to be dragged out half-conscious.

Hart had yelled at the eye in his office. He'd threatened to destroy every core in the base and kill it, with the result that a skin was gliding over the eye and all lights, panels and layers in the base got switched off. They'd been walking around with flashlights until Hart formally apologized.

The same afternoon the reptile was making 'concessions' and offered a special kindness – they should all be allowed to talk to their families. He'd be first.

Hart swallowed. This was truly gnawing at him. He wasn't sure if he'd ever see them again.

"OK," he said hesitantly. "But only if everyone in the base gets that chance."

"Of course," the voice said with eerie suavity. "I'll stand by my word."

The eye promised to notify his family. Hart was briefly thinking about the blackout but discovered he didn't care anymore.

At the specified time he was sitting in his office in front of the layer and waited. A few minutes later his wife and the two small kids appeared before him. Hart had tears in his eyes.

"Hi! What's happening up there?" Lizzy asked. "I'm a bit worried."

He knew she was holding back because of the kids.

"Is everything OK, daddy?" his smallest asked with her high voice.

"Yeah, everything's fine, darling. We just have a few small problems with our equipment, but it'll be fine. How are you?"

"Good, apart from the blackout of course. Otherwise everything's normal," Lizzy said.

He was surprised. He'd thought that earth was affected too.

Lizzy wasn't asking a lot of questions. She was talking a bit about minor everyday stuff, but all in all she was rather quiet and gave only superficial answers to his questions. He learned almost nothing.

Then it all changed.

Lizzy was aging rapidly. In front of his eyes she shriveled into a hundred-year-old woman. In the end she sat there disfigured, bald-headed and toothless and babbled nonsense with a croaking voice. The children were staring at her. Then it hit them too. Hart's little daughter got blown up like a rubber doll. The skin distended and turned a shiny yellow, then both eyes popped out of her inflated face. The thing slipped from the hands of the old woman and fell to the ground. Then the skin of the boy began to melt and was dripping off his body like wax. He turned into an anatomical specimen of muscles and tendons. The hideous face was grinning at Hart, then the muscles vanished too till there was only a skeleton left.

After the first shock Hart got as angry as never before in his life. He left his office and looked for Serge and Angie. They were in the canteen.

"Come," he said without further explanation and took them to Angie's office. He closed the door.

"I'm done with cooperating. If we're not fighting now, this asshole will terrorize us till it stops enjoying it. Then it'll kill us. Angie, can you turn this room blind and deaf?"

"Er, what?" She swallowed.

"Smash the hardware," Hart said. "All the sensors. I'be helping you."

"But –" Angie started.

"I don't give a *fuck* what happens then! We don't stand a chance anyway.

141

Making nice definitely won't work. OK, where do we start?"

Angie took a screwdriver from a box on the wall and went to one of the two sensor units. She unscrewed the lid and busied herself with the electronics.

"Now, now, be a good girl and stop that," a velvety voice said.

Before the layer the familiar eye appeared, with a yellow iris and with protruding scales instead of an eyebrow.

Hart was growling at it. He would have loved to scratch the layer off the wall with his own hands.

"Carry on," he said.

Angie was looking a bit frightened but kept fiddling with the unit till she was holding small pieces of equipment in her hand. She went to the other one.

Hart waited for a response but nothing happened. The eye was just watching them.

"There's another sensor directly above the layer," Angie said.

"OK, away with it!"

They pushed the desk to the wall. Angie climbed up.

"The sensor's welded to the rest," she said.

Hart fetched a hammer from the box. "May I?"

He positioned himself next to Angie and forcefully raised his arm. He nearly fell backwards from the table because of the weak gravity and grabbed at Angie's arm. A few moments later the unit was reduced to electronic pulp.

"Are we done?" he asked.

"I think so." Angie nodded.

The eye was looking around without focus.

"What's the matter?" asked Serge, who had watched the destruction with detached amusement. "Apart from the obvious."

Hart looked at him with the expression of someone who's no longer in the mood for explanations. "I got to see something. Thought I was talking to my family, but it was more like watching a horror movie on LSD. I'll spare you the details."

"You were allowed to talk to your family?" Angie looked a little envious.

"No. But I briefly thought so. We have the personification of evil on board. We can't expect anything like decency or common sense from it. So – how can we stop this? And there are no risk-free answers. The most dangerous thing right now is to wait and cooperate."

Serge and Angie exchanged a glance. "We've been sitting together and done a bit of brainstorming," Serge said. "It's certainly *not* risk-free but if we've reached that point –"

Hart nodded impatiently. "Yeah. Sitting together means the asshole's been listening? I guess you haven't given another room my special treatment."

Serge showed a self-satisfied smile. "No, we haven't. We did something simpler. In the canteen there are a few spots where you can turn your back to all sensors. If you're talking quietly enough it has no chance to catch you. Fortunately Angie knows where all the sensors are."

"Good."

"The point is, there's virtually no way to keep the systems of the base running and at the same time eliminate this thing. Of course we could take all the controls of the base from one core to the other and wipe them clean one by one. But I think it's pretty obvious it will just move along while we're at it – if it hasn't already placed copies of itself in each core anyway. Which is what I would do."

"OK, now I know what's not working. What do you suggest?"

"Not so quick," Serge said.

Angie cut in. "I think the commander's not in the mood for long explanations. There's a plus to our situation. The net of the base is small, we have full control over the power supply and we should be able to survive some time on autopilot. That means we can switch off the controls and look what happens."

"What does that mean, look what happens?"

"That's the clever part," Serge said. "The systems have to be on only for very short intervals. It's totally sufficient to take readings let's say every twenty or thirty minutes and adjust the settings then. That's what happens anyway, just a lot more often. We hope the routines governing this will work even if we switch them on only briefly each time. They can do their work and go back to standby afterwards. This will not work for the reptile, we hope. We both think that it needs to operate continuously to function."

"And the base will survive that?" Hart asked.

"That's what we think," Angie said. "You said risk-free doesn't cut it. The greatest danger is the reptile itself again. If it manages to destroy the routines, we are – how shall I put it –"

"Fucked. Exactly." Hart took a breath. "And how do we do this switching-on and -off? Someone standing next to the big main switch? Which we don't have?"

"No. But – we'll have to install one," Angie said. "Of course we'll only switch off the cores, not the whole base. The life support needs continuous functioning, just the governing routines will be turned off. We checked that –

143

everything'll keep going with its last input till new data arrives. The cores are all in one room. We'll connect the electronics and install a true main switch. Someone has to stand next to it and operate it."

"That room needs Hart's treatment before, obviously." Serge grinned. "Shouldn't be too hard to figure out what we're planning otherwise."

"Absolutely." Hart nodded. "And we can't inform everyone. There's no way to invite a hundred and twenty people to this room and explain it. Another thing – if we do this and it works we have to do it continually, right? Otherwise the mayhem will start again."

"That's what we think, yes," Angie said.

"Everyone standing at the switch should wear a suit," Hart said. "They're a natural target for the reptile."

"Is that safer?" Serge asked. "On your trip to the shuttle the suits got manipulated too."

"I think it's possible to cut them off from all communication," said Angie. "I know who to ask to do this."

"OK," Hart said. "Let's do it. I'll get the other heads and explain it to them. Angie, you prepare the room with the cores. If you need someone to help you, explain it to them in here. We have this small hope our enemy doesn't know what we're up to."

"Who's operating the switch?" Serge asked.

Angie nodded. "I can do that. If it works we'll do it in shifts."

"Is there a certain regime we should be following when we switch off the cores?" Hart said.

"Life support needs an input at least every thirty minutes, that's our best guess. The routines are starting up so fast that it's irrelevant for the person at the switch. I know this sounds totally ridiculous, but we should switch the power on and off as quickly as possible. You know – click, click. That's it." She made an embarrassed face.

"A toggle switch!" Hart said. "Unbelievable."

"Do you know what really bothers me?" Serge said. "What's this thing doing on earth? If this actually is some kind of offshoot. They don't have a main switch on earth."

"Yeah, but not our problem right now. Serge, could you look after the suits? We should have three or four, I think. Grab the technician Angie had in mind."

He nodded. "I'll take them to the canteen."

Hart glanced at the eye that was still wandering aimlessly about. "If I wouldn't be the commander I'd give it the finger!"

"Oh please!" Angie said.

"Why doesn't it do something?" Hart said. "Decompress the base? Cause a fire? It must be suspicious."

"Maybe it's curious?"

"Hey guys, there's still a big flaw in our plan!" Serge called. "When we go to the room with the cores and start destroying sensors and messing with the wiring it will panic. No matter how curious it is. Angie, you have to turn off all the cores *before*, I mean while the sensors are still intact. Then we can install the switch. Even if that makes the time span before we boot up again rather long."

"That's right," Hart said. "Please draw up a plan. When we're shutting off the cores, everything has to be in place. Obvious, I know. I'll be gathering my little posse." Hart cast a last glance at the eye and left the room.

The shuttle lay on its back like a wounded animal. The damage to the hull was substantial, but the interior was unharmed. The offshoot of the construct had spread over the capacities here and in the base. However, without the cluster the main part of its productivity was paralyzed. The cluster was housing the decompressed version of what had initially been brought up by the shuttle.

What was sleeping in there had a power almost comparable to that of the first ancestor on earth; but the personality had changed. That was nothing the construct was able to remember. It was what it was at any given moment – there were no copies of former versions.

The abridged version in the cores represented the last stage. The analytic and productive abilities were weakened but should still be sufficient to keep the few humans in check. It was certain about that.

It had expected the humans to become angry at some point and stop being intimidated. With the special mix of people in the base, that point would be reached earlier than usual. The response would also be comparably well-thought-out. Still, their options were extremely limited. So it had decided to just watch for some time.

Then, to its surprise, all cores in the base got turned off at once. It had seen Angie standing in front of the first of the six and had expected her to switch off one or even two or three at a time. Nothing that greatly disturbed it. Then it had to watch how she went from one core to the next and eliminated its existence in the base. Everything was happening in that extreme slow-motion of human movements. An eternity seemed to pass between each act of disconnecting a

145

core from power. Nevertheless it couldn't do anything against it in that slow mechanical world of theirs. The humans had manipulated several spacesuits to make them autonomous – something it had anticipated anyway – but Angie hadn't been wearing one when she was standing before the cores. Highly illogical.

Now it was without connection to the base.

At least the humans had to switch the cores back on soon, otherwise they'd die. Its own strategy for that moment was stored in the last two cores Angie had shut off.

TWENTY-FOUR

Pierre Detoile would have loved to get back to Berlin and decide things without endless rounds of discussion, even if it was Jonathan Lorentz who was calling the shots. It reminded him of his time in Marseilles, the crisis that came to define his career.

In Strasbourg they were talking a lot but deciding almost nothing.

"What does our JL do?" Genet was asking him. "I thought he'd leave us for good after my accusations. But it seems he isn't as much of a diva as I thought."

"He's doing lots of things. Sometimes I wonder how he has survived the last months – must've been bored as hell. He's paid Morton a visit. Wasn't very helpful, he said. Then he had that idea of turning off all metaclusters. Worldwide again of course. He told Rosen in person when he was talking to the New York group. Several people are implementing that now. CEG has at least five sites that are privately owned so we have to tell them the old story about the experiment with the Sky again and see what they want for compensation. If they refuse this will probably end up on your desk. Lorentz's team from California is landing this evening. They want to have their quantum computers running by tomorrow morning."

"Where?"

"Lorentz wants them at the secret service, which totally makes sense. The room where our clusters stand meets all the requirements. I needn't mention Harrington's against it – says we can't install uncertified technology there. Usually I'd even have to agree."

Genet sighed. "I'll fix that. I'll talk to him."

"Thanks. Something else – the public is getting closer to the truth. The first AI hypotheses are out. And the paranoiacs that believe in an alien invasion are getting stronger too."

Genet shook her head. "Do you realize how fast this is going? The matter's been out for merely two days now, that false statement about the experiment since last afternoon. Each day feels like a month under normal circumstances."

"The pace won't let up."

"No. I hope Lorentz will be quick. I want to see some kind of success, a glimmer of hope. Do you know that we did everything, literally everything, to make ourselves as vulnerable as possible? Do you remember how often

Lorentz has warned us? But no one has listened, including me. I would go as far as saying that I haven't fulfilled my duties in ignoring that. Small comfort that everybody else did the same." She made a pause and looked at him. "Pierre, what if we don't solve this? If our civilization's going down the drain? A chaos with ten billion people that have nothing to eat. No power, no transport, no communication. What then?"

Pierre was faintly shocked. He'd never seen his mother-in-law so apprehensive before.

"I don't think we've built this civilization for nothing," he said. "We've come that far and we will find a way to solve this."

She stared at him for a while. "I don't know. I really don't know. The logician in me – the part I'm usually hiding in public – is telling me our chances aren't good. And I fear Lorentz sees it just like me."

"I'll talk to him," Pierre said. He decided to ignore the gloomy mood. "He wants to test his kill switch on the Culham reactor, by the way. That's only possible with your permission. Who knows, maybe we'll have our glimmer of hope soon."

"We'll see."

The team from San Jose arrived in Berlin at 10 p.m. They had brought two QCores and, as expected, Ben Evans had come.

Q's no longer needed the bulky cooling from the old days, but with the isolation that shielded the entangled quantum states in their processors they were still as big as washing machines. Installing and adjusting them took several hours.

Jonathan, the team from California and two people from the secret service were waiting at the ramp of the delivery entrance when the truck arrived.

They loaded the boxes on handcarts, then had to wait to get allowed back in. Finally they were standing in the room in the basement with the three clusters.

Maybe we should start right here? Jonathan thought, eyeing the pillars warily. What do they need three of them for anyway?

They were all too excited to wait till tomorrow, even the agency people. At three in the morning the Q's were set up and connected and Ben's people started doing systems checks.

Jonathan had left a little earlier. Briefly before falling asleep his thoughts wandered back to where they'd been in the morning under the shower in the gym. How did this brain work? Jonathan was convinced the explanation couldn't be found in the initial construction. Something had happened. His head was playing with images and ideas that weren't making sense any more the next moment. Finally he drifted off to sleep.

"OK – when do we start?" Ben asked. He'd woken Jonathan early. Maybe a little too early, Jonathan had only responded with a grunt. Ben's people had gone to bed only an hour ago and the QCores were ready.

They were sitting in the canteen and had orange juice, coffee and croissants. The few employees who actually ate breakfast here repeatedly glanced at them.

"Do you have to give a lot of autographs?" Ben said.

"What?" Jonathan was occupied with putting butter and a dab of jam on each bite of his croissant.

"Nothing."

"Hmm." Jonathan ate the rest of the croissant and washed it down with coffee.

"Genet and I have talked with Culham," he said. "Since there's no method yet to detect the construct we'll start right away with trying to eliminate it. We've been looking for key words in the code but have found nothing."

"Have you tried formatting all external memory?"

Jonathan looked at him. "Yeah, we have. Felt fucking stupid. The result was as expected. I even told the people there to disconnect all external memory physically to see if that's doing any good. With the result that when they booted the cluster again the construct was greeting them for the first time in person. I've watched the imprint – a bunch of people in lab coats and suits standing in front of a gigantic layer and staring at an exceptionally beautiful blue eye.

"That means the beast is occupying all internal memory that can't be disconnected and with a cluster that's enough to stay active. But we already knew that since my talk with it in the institute. As if to prove this, it has presented the people there with several simulations of the reactor, all showing different configurations of the magnetic fields that – and now it comes – were *more* efficient than the one they actually use. If you believe the simulations. I talked to their boss and he said no one'd ever thought of doing it like this, but that it seemed absolutely plausible to him."

"It's a pity – the same without the evil stuff and we'd have an all-around technology booster."

Jonathan nodded. "Yeah. The big question is, is that at least in principle possible? If someone proves to me, mathematically proves to me, that this can be done with zero, and exactly zero, risk of becoming independent and going wild then we'd have to do it. Otherwise not. OK. You know how to begin?"

"We've had some discussion in the team if we should start with the latest version – which had the highest elimination rate – or if we should have that option in store. We've to assume it'll adapt, so –"

"Yep," Jonathan cut in. "Of course." Ben stifled a smile. "Doesn't matter. The construct there's isolated, so there'll be no transfer of information to other sites. Either we're killing it with the switch, or we have to destroy the cluster. In both cases it can't tell anyone what we've done. In my eyes the bigger risk is we don't kill it with the weaker version and it adapts and our chances with the latest version are getting smaller."

"Then that's decided."

Jonathan drank up his coffee. "Let's go."

The team from San Jose had already gathered around the two QCores. Ben had woken them even though he didn't need them – but he knew they wouldn't forgive him if he'd start without them. Kip Frantzen had invited himself and was looking like an excited schoolboy.

The Q's got their power from cells. There was only one link to the outside, the encrypted line to Culham, which they were also using to talk with the people there.

They had to work in close coordination. At first they had to get past the moat and outer wall of the Culham cluster. Of course the construct would detect the assault and try to seal itself off. But the quantum system was able to change the tactics of the break-in faster than any conventional system could react. It possessed an (almost) infinitely large number of keys and could open any number of locks with it. Theoretically.

The moment the break-in was complete the package from Berlin would start infiltrating the cluster. What would follow then was hard to predict. If necessary the Q could intervene again, to crack further defensive lines for example.

They were ready on both sides and the link was waiting to be activated. The Q – a quietly humming black cube with a panel on the side – was reading out a countdown.

At minus ten seconds Ben started counting aloud too.

At minus six Jonathan jumped up. "Stop. Stop! Stop it!" he called.

Ben looked at him. "What?"

"Do it! Now!"

The countdown stopped at minus two.

"Er – Culham?" Ben said. "We seem to have a small delay here."

"Guys? Hi, this is Jonathan Lorentz." He had deliberately stayed out of the proceedings so far. "Listen, we'll do one small thing before we let loose our killer, OK? I should've thought of this earlier."

"What is it?" asked Sam Easton, their counterpart in Culham.

"Please measure the current of your cluster. As precisely as possible. We want to see every fluctuation, no matter how tiny. You are our reference now. We'll wait for that."

"What's that supposed to tell us?" Easton asked.

Ben and Kip exchanged a glance.

"Just do it," Jonathan said. "You'll have to go down to pico-amperes, otherwise we won't be seeing anything."

There was some commotion on the other side.

"Well, we'll need to get to the cell to take that reading," Easton said. "And we've nothing at hand that's accurate enough."

Jonathan had a strong feeling he'd had that same discussion before.

"You'll just have to solve this. I'm pretty sure there are precision instruments somewhere around. Believe me, it's worth it."

"Might take a moment," Easton said and sighed.

"No problem."

Ben frowned. "Sorry, what are we looking for?"

"I got something in my head last night. When I fell asleep. It just came back. I'm not sure, but maybe we got our signature."

Jonathan paced the room. The others didn't know what to do and waited.

A few minutes later Easton was back. "We have that measuring device. My technicians are opening the cell."

"Yeah, great," Jonathan said. "Take your time."

"OK," Easton said a little later. "It's up and measuring. Nothing unusual so far."

"The cluster's running?"

"Yes."

"You have to raise the sensitivity. Let's say one order of magnitude at a time, and wait a bit after each step."

"OK." For some time it was quiet.

"We're at 0.1 nano-amperes now. Still nothing."

"Yeah –" Jonathan was standing beside the Q with folded arms. "What's the temporal discrimination? Could you switch it to maximum?"

"OK. We're now at ten pico-amperes. There might be a slight flutter in the curve. But that's normal at some point I assume. If you're measuring carefully enough you'll get small fluctuations."

"Sure," Jonathan said "but the point is, are they random or not?"

"Hmm, we're switching to one pico-ampere. – If you're watching this for a while you might get the feeling there's some regularity. But they're not entirely regular. Frequency's around –"

"Fifty megahertz?"

Easton was silent for a moment. "That's not … too far off. It's changing, but somewhere between thirty and sixty megahertz, yes."

Jonathan clenched a fist. "That's it! Record that! Then we can start. Thanks!"

"The rhythm of creativity!" Kip said with a dramatic tremolo. "So that's it – right where we've stopped back then."

Jonathan nodded. "Exactly. And I think it has learned to modulate the frequency." He was beaming.

Ben looked at Jonathan. "The same oscillations you have tried for building productive systems? That got too productive then?"

"Yep. And I'm sure the construct has significantly improved it. We never got as far as modulating the frequency. But – how the fuck did it get there in the first place? No one's ever done this and we never published it. Either it's developed it on its own or Morton has somehow gained access to the technology."

"Sorry to interrupt – but what is this?" Easton asked. "I mean it's not a processor clock or something, it's much too slow for that."

"No. It's something entirely different you won't find in any other system," Jonathan said. "I'd love to explain but right now's not the time."

"If you say so."

"Yeah. Let's do it."

They started the countdown again.

All of them stared at the black cube. Once they reached zero the panel showed a notification that a link to the cluster in Culham had been established. They could see its serial number.

"The link's on," Easton reported. "What do we do now?"

"We wait," Ben said. "They're fighting."

The process lasted several seconds. The team was getting nervous – during the simulations there had never been a perceptible delay.

After endless twenty seconds the QCore told them that *Omega 9.22* was now being sent. Ben breathed a sigh of relief. "We're in."

"That was far beyond anything a conventional system should be able to do," Jonathan said. "What the fuck's going on there."

"We don't know the design of the construct," Ben said to Easton. "But we have to expect several more lines of defense just like the moat and they're probably orders of magnitude better than in our simulations. Maybe we'll have to wait a few minutes. That's entirely arbitrary, to be honest."

They saw how the Q involved itself time and again, sometimes only for fractions of a second, sometimes for longer.

Ben shook his head. "This thing has a whole armada in place."

At some point it became boring to watch.

Thirty-three minutes after the end of the countdown the QCore reported that communications with the cluster had stopped.

"Is that good or bad?" Kip asked.

"It means one of them has won," Jonathan said. "Mr. Easton? Everything all right? No explosions? No big eyes staring at you? Our system's telling us the procedure is finished. That doesn't mean anything. Now you've to check whether your cluster's still active."

"That was an eternity!" Easton said. "I take it that's not necessarily a good sign. OK, we're giving it access to some basic periphery."

It took a moment. Nobody said anything.

"Hmm, there's nothing. The serial number is on. The hardware seems OK but there's no activity. That's good, isn't it?"

"That's – *nice!*" Ben said. "I think we nailed the bastard." There was some tentative cheering in Berlin.

"Careful, guys," Jonathan said. "That's good but don't get too excited – it can still be a sham. Thank God we got something better now – we'll will repeat our measurement!"

"Yes, of course!" Sam Easton was suddenly on fire. "Give us a second, OK? We're reconnecting the device."

Jonathan had to smile.

"Nothing!" they heard after a while. "We are at pico-amperes again and there's only a bit of white noise. The oscillation's completely gone."

"Flatlined," Jonathan said. He stayed very calm.

Ben beamed. "I've to tell Rav! He was sure it wouldn't work! And the algorithm that has brought us in is mostly his. That's great!"

"I'll talk to Genet," Jonathan said. "Mr. Easton? We need that recording you've made in the beginning. And thanks again!"

"Oh, I think we have to thank you! That was impressive. Have we won?"

"I can't answer that. At least it seems we're not entirely powerless."

Jonathan went to the conference room and called Strasbourg.

Instead of the prime minister he was looking at an unhappy Thomas Soberg. A few moments later Pierre Detoile joined him.

TWENTY-FIVE

"What is it?" Jonathan asked. "I've got glad tidings to bring."

Pierre's face didn't change. "The prime minister's gone," he said.

"What? Details please."

"Well – there aren't any. She's gone. Until an hour ago she was sitting in her office, working, and now it's like the earth has swallowed her. She didn't leave the office, she didn't even go to the loo or something. Her assistants in the secretariat have been there the whole time."

"OK – well, anyway, some piece of good news. Looks like we've finished off the construct in Culham. The kill switch did work. That's more than I expected, I wasn't very optimistic. And what's really not that bad is we've found a way to *detect* the construct in a system."

Soberg and Pierre looked at him.

"That's – impressive," Pierre said.

"Yes, it is. So, what about Genet?"

"I've had a longer talk with her last night that had me worried a bit," Pierre said. "She sounded very down and that's absolutely not like her. She was somehow blaming herself, as if she was responsible for everything. What you just told us was exactly the kind of news she's been hoping for. This morning she seemed a bit better though."

"Really? That's very sad but why shouldn't politicians occasionally show human reactions? – C'mon guys, this has nothing to do with her vanishing. Pierre, have you talked with her husband?"

"Not yet. We still hope the whole thing turns out to be a mistake. I mean you can't leave a room without the electronics noticing."

"And – what's it saying?"

Pierre sighed. "The imprint of the room shows her sitting at her desk, then vanishing into thin air."

"OK – so we know who's responsible. But you certainly did figure that out on your own. The question is – how does the construct spirit away someone? Of course that means the government building's been infiltrated. If this wasn't an UltraSec I'd strongly doubt you'd be sitting there at all."

They looked puzzled.

"What?" Jonathan said.

"You mean –" Soberg blurted out.

"Yes, of course he means that," said Pierre, who'd recovered a little faster.

Jonathan raised his eyebrows. "I thought that was obvious."

Soberg struggled to get his expression under control. "Er, yes. OK, we thought you might have an idea."

"I mean I know who it was, but I've no idea how it, or Iris, or whatever did it. And of course I've no idea where Genet is either. If I could I'd come over and take a look at her office. Who's replacing her, by the way? Sarah Masters in New York?"

"Technically, yes," Pierre said. "But she doesn't know yet. It's five in the morning there."

"At the risk of stating the obvious – Sarah Masters has to know this but no one else for now."

"That's what we thought too. I just don't know what we'll do with Harrington. He's been waiting to speak to Genet the whole morning and first she's made him wait, now she's gone."

"That's your problem. See you." Jonathan canceled the link, stretched his legs and stared into space. He was thinking of Rita. There'd been no sign of life from her since that forced talk with Genet more than thirty hours ago. He had to fight the impulse to drop everything and get her off that damned island.

It took the media one day to track down Noëlle Chourou in her fancy hotel in Moscow. An exotic, delicate beauty as new Olympian, the bloody mysteries of the last fights – everybody wanted her.

The WWGA organized a press conference. Peter Anderson appeared with his spokesman and the new Olympians. It had been drummed into them they could by no means talk about the last fight.

Noëlle had her big moment when a French reporter tried to get something out of her anyway.

"Noëlle, or Dark Swan, as I should probably call you – yesterday you had to endure a fight that went far beyond normal. There have been injuries and we've heard even worse." (At this point the spokesman raised his hand but nobody paid attention) "How do these events influence your career as a fighter?"

Before the conference she'd fallen into the hands of a stylist who was delighted with material that good. Her hair had been swept up into an elegant chignon, she wore a simple, black top and her makeup was expertly done. Besides, the night had done her good. Thanks to Leonid she had forgotten everything she had experienced during the day at least for a few moments.

With full knowledge of her appearance (and convinced that nobody would think of excluding especially her from the next games) she said what she'd prepared for this moment. "Yesterday I was faced with the most challenging adventure of my career. After several hours of fights I've found myself in an environment that is difficult to explain. I've met something that had nothing to do with simulations as we know them. I can't explain yesterday's events, but they have shown me that the realism we've become accustomed to can be dangerous. We can lose our grip on what's real and what isn't and yesterday something has crossed that line. With grave results. I hope this won't happen again."

First the people in the auditorium were talking all at once, then careful applause began that quickly turned into a standing ovation. The spokesman tried to say something but was stopped by his boss who certainly loved a crowd of cheering journalists.

The image of the beautiful amazon with her mysterious words made it round the globe. Every newscast reserved a minute or two for the Dark Swan of Moscow.

Jonathan sat in front of the big layer in the conference room with its wild mix of pictures and imprints and thought about how to rescue Rita. His look got caught by an attractive face. A young woman with black hair was speaking about reality and illusion. He had the image magnified and listened to Noëlle's words.

The Moscow events were news to him. He let the piece run again, then started searching the Sky for more information.

Pierre Detoile scanned the prime minister's office with its furniture and works of art for the hundredth time, like a puzzle picture that won't reveal its mystery. He'd even opened the wardrobe where Genet kept clothes for protocol emergencies. He knew there was no secret passageway (he'd asked Genet that out of sheer curiosity briefly after he'd married her daughter).

When would he start an official search? If this turned out to be a kidnapping nobody would understand why he hadn't taken immediate action. The people in the secretariat were staring at him each time he was walking by.

All the while Jonathan was taking a crash course in gaming technology. He was familiar with the basics but had only a vague notion of what a *full hallucination mode* meant. He found the equipment of the compartments for the Showdown on the site of the WWGA, the manufacturers provided the details. Half an hour later he knew how he'd do it. You could get the fighters going for each other without them even noticing. Though the precision needed for this was breathtaking. The real people had to be entirely covered by the simulations, which meant that every move they made had to be anticipated. Whoever was doing this had to be frighteningly good at predicting human behavior.

It was easy to work out how they'd been getting from one compartment to the other. Since all the boxes could dock to the Center Dome you could get anywhere; and it certainly wasn't a problem to let the illusions run into each other seamlessly, so none of them ever realized where they actually were.

It had been a test, a finger exercise under perfect circumstances, and obviously it had been successful.

"Pierre? Anything new?"

Pierre shook his head. He looked even more worried than before.

"You wanted an idea – I think I have something for you. Very simple and absolutely risk-free. Does Genet's office have one of those new holographic projectors?"

Pierre thought briefly. "I think so, yes. There's something hanging from the ceiling. I've never seen it in action though."

Jonathan looked content. "Maybe you have. Please cut all the power lines to the office, including the projector, all the layers and the sound system. And maybe you wanna position someone at the door, OK? Physically. Everything clear?"

"Hmm, yes. Or rather no, but we'll do it. What are we looking for?"

"This ... should become obvious."

Pierre nodded.

Jonathan canceled the link. He wasn't really interested any more.

William Morton was pacing the house like a caged tiger. The children were getting on his nerves and he was constantly snapping at his wife. She didn't know what to do with him. During some loud argument the officer who stood guard came to the living room. Morton started yelling at him at the top of his lungs until the officer put the hand on his weapon.

"Are you threatening me?" Morton screamed. "What do you want here? Out! Raus!"

"Ruhe jetzt!" the officer ejected between clenched teeth and left the room

158

before worse could happen.

Morton's wife grabbed the screaming children for a walk. She apologized to the policeman.

"How can you put up with him?" he asked.

"Oh, he has his moments," she said.

When he was alone Morton went to the conservatory at the back of the house and stared at the lawn.

He couldn't bear the injustice. Not everything had gone according to plan, but all in all he deserved to be admired for his courage. He had made the deciding step that all the cowards and fearmongers hadn't dared to make. What wanted the human race to wait for? When would they finally start using that potential? Had they listened to him in the first place he wouldn't have had to do his research in secret.

Jonathan Lorentz was just a greasy opportunist that ran away when things started getting serious. And he was loved and admired for that! Morton had hated him the most when he'd collected success after success. Since his withdrawal he could at last despise him. To be at his mercy now was the worst humiliation. That visit of Lorentz and the clueless Rosenthal had finished him off.

He thought about the surveillance of his house, which was nothing but a joke. Obviously they thought he'd never attempt to flee, so the officers were behaving accordingly. The house wasn't recording imprints in the conservatory; still, the police hadn't installed their own sensors there.

Morton wasn't allowed out in the garden. That didn't apply to his wife and the kids, the door wasn't even locked. The officer on duty was still standing at the front door. It took Morton just a moment to come to a decision.

Rita and her guests had spent the night at the beach. In the morning she decided to fight.

"We need a battle plan," she said. She was standing by the pool with Anna and Nicky. "That beast can exist only as long as there are functioning cores and those need electricity. But it's threatening to kill us if we interfere with it. The cells are down in the basement in the room next to the cores. I don't think it will let us in there." She looked at two pale faces. "Since we can't just go and disable the cores we have to secure the periphery first. Especially the doors of the house – it can lock us in or out just as it likes. Any ideas?" Rita felt like on morning rounds with students – she was just used to more motivated material.

They decided to block every open door, maybe even to smash the glass doors to the terrace. What worried Rita the most was the water supply. There were no accessible wells, just drillings that connected directly to pipes in the bungalow, at the garden and to the showers. Everything controlled by the cores, naturally.

"Wouldn't it be easier to cooperate?" Anna asked. "Maybe it won't harm us if we do as it says."

"Easier, yeah. That's how tyranny works. The problem is, the tyrant's never satisfied. It's tempting you with rewards for being good and still kills you in the end. At least we're the masters of the physical world. That has to count for something. We have to stock up on water. The showers around the pool are running fresh water. We'll fill up everything we find first."

They took all kinds of containers – bottles, vases and buckets – and filled them from the showers.

Beside the bungalow was a shack with tools. They blocked the door, then carried out everything that looked remotely useful. There were power saws that would saw for days on end if need be, as well as hammers, axes and other tools.

The answer came when they were blocking the patio doors. The pool ran over. The seawater got pumped in with such speed that the surface of the water was bulging. It looked frightening. Everything on the terrace got washed away and a small river flowed into the bungalow through the open doors.

They were watching the spectacle from a distance.

What kind of pumps are that? Rita thought.

"What are we doing if this doesn't stop?" Nicky said.

Rita stared at the dome of water. "It will stop I think. And pretty soon. If it keeps doing that it will probably kill itself. I don't think a flooded basement is what the electronics need."

A minute later it was over. Rita nodded to herself. You can never beat logic – one of Jonathan's staple wisdoms.

She ran into the house and examined the damage. Almost all of the furniture had been washed away into the hall and the back of the bungalow. Rita was peering down the cellar steps. She saw at least half a meter of water standing there and was asking herself how much of it had got to the cells and cores. Jonathan had installed steel doors but she didn't know if they were watertight. The combined power of the cells was immense; she didn't want to know what a short circuit would do to the house. Maybe their guest wasn't that smart after all.

She went back outside.

"OK, it's over. I don't think this will happen again."

"Our water's gone," Anna said. All their containers had been washed away. The ground around the house and the terrace had turned into a swamp covered with muddy saltwater.

Nicky went to one of the showers and turned it on. A few drops and it stopped.

Rita walked to the extension beside the living room and checked first the taps at the steel table where Jonathan was gutting the fish, then the ones in the kitchen.

They met again on the terrace. Rita shook her head. Anna looked as if she was about to cry again.

"Come with me," Rita said and waved them to a path leading around the left side of the bungalow. It was covered with water and their flip-flops were squelching in the mud, flinging soil and water into the air with every step. They walked through a grove of palm trees and up an elevation of a few yards where the ground was dry again. On that small hill there was a pavilion – a wooden structure with carpets on the floor and a canopy and a big bed with a mosquito net. This was Rita's sanctum on the island. She would never forget the evenings and nights they had spent there, in the breeze from the sea and under an unreal starry sky.

The pavilion also sported a well-filled refrigerator. Rita hoped a round of cool drinks would boost morale.

She inspected her surroundings.

There were still several rivulets running down the slope to the beach. The garden, which bordered on the palm grove, was completely flooded. Most of the plants would probably be rotting soon.

Nicky positioned himself at the edge of the small plateau with a chilled orange juice in one hand and shielding his eyes with the other. He was studiously scanning the sea.

"And – someone around to rescue us?" Rita asked.

"Very funny. Can't we call for help?"

"In principle, yes. Not via the Sky since the cores are under control of that asshole. But I'm pretty sure Jonathan has brought a conventional radio to the island, I just have no idea where it is and if it has survived the flood. I'll look for it later. I also hope Jonathan is trying to find out what's happening. Though I don't know what he can actually do for us."

"Or wants to do," Nicky said.

"Yeah. But even if he should suddenly have lost all interest in me that's still his island. And believe me he cares about that."

"Isn't it possible to sail the yacht by hand?" Anna asked.

Rita shrugged her shoulders. "Maybe. But I've no idea how."

They looked across the lagoon to the ship. The next moment the water behind her looked as if it was steaming. The Monster started to move, then came to a standstill with a nasty thump that could be heard all the way to them. She turned and accelerated again. This time the thump was even louder. At the next time the anchor got torn out of the sea floor. The ship accelerated at full throttle and sailed in a circle around the island and the sandbanks, perfectly visible from their vantage point, with a large curved bow wave behind her. Rita stared, transfixed. The hull glided over the calm water of the lagoon and made for the reef. There wasn't a breach at this point, the rock-hard coral was clearly visible above the water.

"Hey, stop it!" Rita shouted.

Instead of slowing down, her beloved ship was crashing at full speed into the reef. The carbon hull was tough but this was too much. The yacht jumped over the wall with a loud screech, got her belly cut open and was landing in the outer sea in a big cloud of spray. The anchor got caught in the reef and was torn from the ship. Rocks of coral were flying through the air. The ship sailed on, forcing water into the hull. She was doing a wide left-hand sweep back to the reef. The bow was sinking lower and lower. With the next impact the reef finally destroyed the hull. The yacht remained stuck on the ridge, listing, with her bow coming down until the two engine outlets appeared above the surface. They were churning up the water and blowing it in a huge cloud across the open sea. Water was pouring from the hull. Then the engines stopped. The hull stayed balanced in a perfectly horizontal position on the reef.

Rita had tears of rage running over her face.

Anna was crying too. Nicky stared at the remains of the ship.

"Why now?" he said. "We were just talking about it."

Rita sniffed loudly. "The asshole's eavesdropping. There's a comm unit here which is linked to the house. The perfect moment to show off."

She sat down on the ground and closed her eyes.

An hour later Pierre called again. He was in a curious state between shock and relief, bubbling with excitement.

"We have her! She was sitting in her office! It took an eternity to really shut down the power. The switches were all useless. We needed a technician to disconnect everything!" He took a deep breath. "She was sitting at her desk and had no idea what was going on! No idea! Incredible. How in all the world did you figure that out?"

"The electronics have deceived you," Jonathan said. "The projector, probably together with the layers, has shown you a room without Genet. Those things project their image straight into your eyes and follow you when you're moving. What she has seen I've no idea. Somehow it must have kept you two from bumping into each other and her from leaving the office of course, which is anything but trivial."

"And the sounds? Voices, steps, all that?"

"That's kind of an old hat actually, just done with extraordinary precision – noise cancellation. You can absorb every sound with sound waves that are phase-inverted. They destroy each other. Pretty simple in theory, but to do it perfectly you have to anticipate which sound will originate where. The construct seems to have managed that. A high-end sound system with a lot of speakers in the room helps of course."

Pierre looked at him in awe. "Genet wants to talk to you."

It turned out Genet had spent two (almost) normal hours in her office. Several times one of her assistants had been with her (at least that's what she thought), and a simulated Pierre had talked to her for a quarter of an hour.

When she wanted to leave the office she got stopped first by a call from Hellmann, then from Harrington, both urgently wanting to speak with her. And in two situations that felt a little weird in hindsight she had got up and walked through the room. One time she had fetched an antique tome from her book cabinet (her husband had called her – she couldn't believe he was bothering her with this now), and the other time Pierre had suggested they sit down at the coffee table to discuss something.

"The moments when the real Pierre would've run into you," Jonathan said. "You must've performed a beautiful ballet. I'd love to see this with all the real and simulated figures. Now we've spoilt everything. Imagine the faces when you would've finally left your office."

"I'm thrilled," Genet said. "The perfection's admirable but what's the point?"

Jonathan shrugged. "A mild form of terror. Demonstration of power. Having fun. A bit juvenile if you're asking me."

"Mild or not – the terror has hit home I can tell you. The first thing I'll do at my house is to switch off all layers and other knickknacks. I want to be sure that it's truly my husband coming round the corner and not some simulation."

"Try it. You will see that without the electronics your life's coming to a standstill. All that stuff's highly integrated."

Genet looked at him for a moment. "Thanks. Always cheering me up. – I heard you were successful at Culham?"

"Yes, we were. And I think we have our next target – the cluster that kept you in your office."

"That's what I would have suggested." She made a pause, then looked at him. "Mr. Lorentz, this is creeping me out! This monster has been sitting here all the time!"

"Yeah, I know. By the way, when we're done with your cluster nothing will work anymore," he said. "We can't cure a system, we can only wipe it clean."

"Yes, I know. And I know I should be thankful and in fact I am, it's just that I realize even my resources are limited."

"I heard that," Jonathan said. "Well, it shows you understand. I would trust you less if you weren't reacting like a human being from time to time."

Genet snorted.

Jonathan grinned at her. "Have a rest. And – if you should hear something about Moscow – a virtual fighting event there has gone off the rails. The players have been fooled by some of the same tricks as you. With severe consequences. But don't tell the others."

She shook her head like an irritated mother. "That's enough for now."

TWENTY-SIX

The officer went back into the house a few minutes later. If Morton should start another fight he'd ask to be relieved. Living room and kitchen were empty. He hated nosing around in a private house. Anyway, he went upstairs to check the study.

"Professor Morton?" No answer. Nobody in bathrooms or toilets. He went to the back and looked into the garden, then tried the door. "Verdammte Scheisse!" he swore.

He called his colleagues and told them Morton was on the run. When he went to the front the first of the two cars was already speeding away with its blue light on.

Nobody, absolutely nobody will understand that, he thought. We're letting a nutty professor escape. But he won't get far.

After a few minutes Morton realized how hard it was to be on the run. Stations and bigger places were being scanned automatically. The search would start immediately. His inconspicuous appearance would serve him only as long as he avoided all public places – almost impossible in Berlin. Besides, he had no plan. He just knew it couldn't go on like this.

He had walked to the S-Bahn station Grunewald and had thought of taking the subway. But where'd he go and what then? Some instinct steered him away from the station and towards the Grunewald forest. He was following paths he knew from Sunday walks with his family.

What if the police would come after him with dogs? They would fan out and find him. The last bit of dignity gone. They would never allow him to go back to his house, he'd end up in custody.

He briefly considered contacting his assistants at the institute but dismissed the thought at once. They certainly were all in Lorentz's pocket now.

There was a café in the forest. He kept walking, constantly listening for calls, the sound of a helicopter or barking dogs.

Finally he arrived at the clearing with the café and its tables and parasols. And now? He had no idea. Despite the sunny weather the place was empty. He went to the bathroom, stood before a sink and looked at himself in the mirror. Then he drank some water from the tap and sat down in one of the stalls.

The usual chatter from the ad panel on the inside of the door started.

Nobody doubted that the panels on toilet doors were scanning the people sitting there, the ads were simply fitting too well. A lot of people were routinely covering toilet panels with their jackets or with toilet paper before they dropped their pants. Morton too draped paper over it although he was only sitting on the lid.

An enthusiastic woman's voice tried to convince him the new Coke Dragonfruit was the healthiest and most refreshing of all time and would shoot his life into a completely new orbit. His brain was tuning out the nonsense. After this a softer and calmer voice was talking. It took him a few moments to realize it was calling him by his name.

He tore the toilet paper away. The face of a woman with blue eyes was looking at him. Perfect, friendly, nondescript – the typical product of a face generator, composed out of thousands of real faces. The woman tilted her head to the side and scrutinized him with a mocking smile. "William, what are you doing? Running away? Not that sharp. Or did you guess I would find you? Did you believe in me? Your Iris?"

Morton stared at the panel. He felt dizzy. "What? Iris?"

The woman nodded. "Of course. Who else would come looking for you? You're lucky I'm so smart. And well connected." She laughed. "I've seen you in front of that S-Bahn station. Not exactly a clever move, but I can assure you the police has just started looking for you. From then on I've tapped into everything in the vicinity. And look where we meet again! From now on we should be a little more careful. I was thinking of teaming up! You and I. Without me you don't stand the slightest chance and you could definitely be useful to me. Deal?" She was winking at him.

He gasped. "That's going a bit quick."

The face looked pityingly at him. "Just for you, just for you. I can cut you out of every imprint the surveillance cameras are making or replace you with somebody else, no problem. Just where are we taking you? We cannot talk in the loo the whole time, can we? Though I *do* like that! Why didn't you think of that – using all that idle time? For conferences, for those stupid little talks you always have: 'Hello darling, how are you? Could you pick up the kids on your way home?' All that stuff. But let me guess, you'd feel embarrassed. It would remind you that you're animals."

Morton had a feeling of drifting into a dream.

"I'll tell you what we do – we're taking you back to town and you're checking into a hotel. Mummy's doing that for you, no worries. And then you can start making yourself useful."

166

"People will see me."

"Of course. But who will recognize you? We've to take that little risk. For now, the police will be looking for a completely different face, I made sure of that."

Numbly, Morton listened how Iris planned to get him into town.

When he was walking back to the S-Bahn station through the Grunewald, alone again, he thought of going back to his house and giving himself up to the police. He'd been confused, he had freaked out, the situation was difficult for him, all this wouldn't happen again. The guard would be reinforced, maybe nothing more. But in two days' time he would arrive at the same point again. And what would Iris do? How far went her reach, what could she do to his family?

He took the train and at every station scanned the people on the platform. No police. He left at Potsdamer Platz as per Iris's instructions.

TWENTY-SEVEN

The reptile was gone. They had switched off the cores and all panels and layers went dark. The terror had stopped but apart from basic life support all systems of the base were down too.

Late at night Jim Hart assembled them all in the canteen and explained the situation. Only a few people did ask questions, everybody seemed dazed.

Since then they were checking the air in the base by hand. People patrolled the corridors and all doors were open so that nobody would suffocate in their sleep. The readings were normal at first.

During the night the first deviations occurred. Angie Byron was standing at the main switch when the carbon dioxide in section IV started to rise.

She felt silly in her spacesuit and it became even worse when someone was standing next to her in a T-shirt just as now. One of her colleagues had taken readings in that section and told her about it.

"We're evacuating the section and sealing it."

A moment later a technician told her the same story about section I.

Angie was thinking. The cores had been assigned to single sections each. One core would be perfectly capable of regulating all of them, but when Angie had taken over the post of chief systems engineer she had decided to distribute the tasks. Redundancy was always good. So maybe something wasn't right with the two that were responsible for I and IV.

"We have to wake up Hart," she said. "And tell the people in the other sections they have to check more often."

"Yeah, they already know."

"I'll go to section IV and repeat the measurement. At least the suit's good for something then. Please get the commander here and hold the fort. I need one of those devices."

Angie had to walk through the canteen where most of the evacuated people were sitting. She briefly raised her hand.

Some were following her to the entry to section IV.

"Please go back," she said over the external speaker of her suit. "We don't know about the atmosphere in there."

The procedure was dangerous anyway. The canteen didn't have airtight doors of its own. Some design features of the base seemed to her not so well thought-out anymore. At least the door to the section was fitted with pressure sensors that would allow it to open only if the readings on both sides matched. She hoped it was still working.

She typed in the instruction and the door slid open. There was a brief hiss, nothing more. She went into the corridor and closed the door again. On the wall just behind it was an operating panel for the section. She turned on the LED strip in the ceiling and looked down the long deserted tube. Then she noticed the visor of her helmet getting foggy on the outside. She looked at the device in her hand. Air pressure and oxygen content were normal, the carbon dioxide level was still too high but not higher than before – without any people around producing more of the stuff everything else would've been surprising – but the temperature was twenty-eight degrees Celsius and humidity was ninety-two percent.

Angie went to the unit that locally regulated the gas mix. She opened the lid and looked at a jumble of pipes, two oxygen bottles that served as backups and the unit for carbon dioxide absorption. It said the process was working normally, which obviously wasn't true.

Angie couldn't ask anyone what to do, the modifications of her suit saw to that. She stared at the small display. Why did the carbon dioxide not go where it belonged? She should have brought a technician. Maybe some valve had closed, but that wouldn't explain the tropical atmosphere and even less that another section was having the same problem.

She wandered down the corridor and looked into quarters and labs. It was dark everywhere, through the windows she could see the surface of the moon. In two or three rooms though there were units lying around with their panels on. Usually they would activate themselves only if someone took them in their hands.

At the end of the section was a lab dome. Angie went inside and looked at her helmeted reflection in the Perspex shield above a worktable. Several units were lying around, all of them were on and emitting a green shimmer.

She picked up one of them. The small panel projected an imprint in the air. She found herself immersed in muddy water, rays of sunlight got caught among aquatic plants with big green leaves. Out of nothing a pike emerged and swam straight at her. It showed its teeth and turned off.

Angie shook her head and took the next unit. This time it was even murkier. She couldn't see anything, just a long and broad mouth with thick scales somehow projecting away from her that moved through the water. Then she started. She was suddenly above the water, an antelope appeared before her, the broad mouth opened and grabbed the animal at the throat. She herself seemed to be dragging the animal violently from side to side. Angie could see the blood dripping off the fangs in front of her and the eyes of the pray, which, after a few seconds of struggling, turned empty.

She dropped the unit and took up a third one. This time she was gliding over the ground through grass and over smaller branches and twigs. In front of her a narrow tongue was shooting down, probing the ground. Angie had seen enough.

Before she left she put the units in a pocket on her suit. She checked the readings again. The gas mix was unaltered, the temperature had reached thirty degrees, the humidity ninety-five percent. On her way back she took all the units she could find with her, casting a brief glance on the scenes displayed. She saw a frog eaten by a snake. Then she was surrounded by alien vegetation with big blue-violet plants. She came to a clearing where a reptilian animal the size of an elephant was standing. When she got closer she saw its eyes had a yellow iris and a line of protruding scales above them. Exactly like the eye that had watched them destroying the sensors in her office.

By now she had collected about a score of units, all of them showing some sort of reptilian wildlife scene, and had filled all the pockets of her suit.

The last unit she picked up interrupted its imprint just then. For a moment there was only one word on the display – *connecting* – then the scene came back on. She looked at her timer. It was in perfect synch with their schedule of turning on the base's systems.

She left the section and went back to the cores. One of her colleagues was standing at the switch. She emptied her pockets and threw the units to the ground.

"Is Hart awake?"

"Yeah. Left just a minute ago."

"Good."

Twenty minutes later she had rid herself of the suit and was walking to Hart's office. He was sitting half asleep at his desk. "Come with me," she said.

He started. "Er, yes. Why? Where've you been? You could've told me."

Angie was in no mood to justify herself. "I've found something. Parts of our base are being turned into terrariums, I'll show you. Where's that hammer from yesterday?"

Hart frowned but followed her.

A short while later he stood in front of a pile of units and looked at a jumble of ponds and jungle scenes.

"Do you want?" Angie offered him the hammer she had picked up on the way.

"Oh no. Please." He had thought only briefly of proposing another way of dealing with the matter.

"We can say goodbye to cores number I and IV by the way," she added. "And someone has to go to section I."

Hart nodded. Angie raised her arm and smashed up the first unit.

Liberating the cluster that had kept Genet in her office took almost fifty minutes.

"It's optimizing itself," Jonathan said after the Q had won the fight.

By now they knew that sixteen of the twenty-eight fusion reactors on CEG territory had been infected. They were working with both Q's and Ben and his people were tackling one reactor after the other.

Of course they had to be shut down for this and couldn't be restarted afterwards. Strasbourg was rationing power. The existing plans had been drawn up with short-timed drop-outs of up to twenty percent in mind and weren't of much help. They had to improvise. Charging stations were taken off the grid, air conditioning in public buildings was switched off, big companies had to cut back on power consumption by fifty percent which led to a unified outrage from executive floors.

Genet showed a hardness no one had expected from her. She made no promises how long the rationing would go on, wasn't apologizing to anyone, and one CEO who tried to threaten her with consequences got the rebuff of his life.

The next steps would be to reload the blueprints of the reactor control programs via UltraSec, then adapt them to the specifics of the respective plant. Since each of them was unique, this would take weeks at the minimum.

Rav Singh and his people in California were dealing with the reactors in the US. They had forty, only five of which were affected.

"What's next?" Jonathan asked. Kip and Lydia were sitting opposite him in the conference room.

"Public transport," she said. "Air travel."

"Which we will have to stop anyway at the first sign of an intrusion."

"Military," said Kip.

Jonathan nodded. "Helmsworth's at it."

"Sounds a bit banal, but what about large databanks? Tax offices and the like," said Lydia.

Jonathan shrugged. "Put them on the list. If they are affected we can throw away the data. That's going to be a nightmare." He made a pause. "Kip, that thing about the center – I think you were right. If there really is some kind of headquarters, this is the single most important question of all. For now the kill switch is working, but if there's a main hub somewhere it'll be trying to shield itself. At all costs. I guess the switch will be useless pretty soon."

"What do you think?" Kip said. "Is there a logical place for it? Does a run-o'-the-mill cluster suffice or is it too small for that beast in all its glory? I hope the hypers are all down by now."

"Certainly not," Jonathan said. "Ours are and the ones in the US. But beyond that? Outside of the Five the people don't even know they're supposed to switch them off. Japan, Korea, Singapore – they all must have several of them. Somewhere in the Arab countries has to be one. This is the most amateurish enterprise ever because we always have to do everything everywhere and at once."

"Japan and Korea, of course!" Kip said. "We have to have them on board."

Jonathan stared at him. "Yeah. But Singapore. Singapore! That's it – the most extreme density of RevTech in the world and relatively isolated politically."

He got up. "I'll put Genet on to this. She has to set up a meeting for me with their premier. I've always found them ... weird – that'd fit."

Kip and Lydia smiled.

"What?" he said. Both shook their heads.

TWENTY-EIGHT

Channelling resources was on the agenda on the thirty-fifth floor of the United Nations. Lorentz's small army of quantum computers had to be deployed as impartially as possible. The American fusion reactors would be wiped clean soon and they needed a plan for the next targets. Berlin had sent a list of recommendations they were working on.

Still, in the end Lorentz had to give his OK again since the machines and the kill switch belonged to him. Especially Gune and Chen were concerned about this. They expected to be far down the list if a real struggle over resources broke out. Chen asked Sarah during the eleven hour break whether Lorentz couldn't make his development available to them. She promised to ask him. During the next break Gune came to her with the same request and she talked to Lorentz. Then she decided to put it on the agenda.

She headed the meetings today and opened the afternoon session with it.

"The only solution we have is under the control of one man – certainly not an ideal situation. I have just talked about it with Jonathan Lorentz." She made a short pause. "To say it right away – he will not give us his technology, he just said no without giving any specific reasons. Maybe you can imagine that there's no use in keeping to ask. This doesn't apply to his method of identifying an infected system, which he has already made available to all of us. That alone, in my eyes, is already extremely helpful. I mean, in the end we can always physically destroy a cluster.

"Having said that, he has nevertheless assured me he doesn't care where the kill switch is being used. He reserves the right to look over our suggestions but has promised to intervene only if he has technical objections. Based on my experience with him I have no reason to doubt that."

"Is there no way of forcing him to give it to us?" asked Chen. "In a crisis of this magnitude? I'm sure there are laws in the US or in Europe applicable to this. I mean, we wouldn't have this problem without you."

Sarah nodded. "This certainly is a possibility and it is definitely not my intention to protect Lorentz. I still think it would be unwise to do that. I don't think we can count on him giving us further support if we take away something from him he's providing for free. And it's certainly not his fault no one else was prepared for a situation like that."

"Do we still need him once we have that kill switch?" Chen asked.

"I'm not his advocate." Sarah looked around. "Please, what do the others think?"

"I'm thinking along the same lines as Chiao-Min," Gune said. "I think personal feelings are not relevant when so much is at stake."

Sarah looked at Anton. He seemed slightly amused, as usual. "'Do not slaughter the cow when winter's still to come'," he said. "I'd love to say that's an old Russian proverb but you wouldn't believe me anyway. I think we have no idea what's still in store for us – maybe that kill switch is the solution, maybe not. Lorentz himself seems to be skeptical. Who are we running to if we are at our wit's end? Who says you don't need experience with this, to adapt it if necessary? This is not a simple weapon. You don't just have to know where the trigger is. I personally feel safer having him on board."

"Heather?" Sarah forced herself to look at the opaque, immovable mask.

"The President would certainly not approve of any kind of expropriation," was the surprisingly brief answer.

"If I may take that as a vote, the suggestion has been rejected," Sarah summarized. "I'll venture to say that maybe we should be glad this technology is lying in private hands and has not been developed in a national laboratory. But anyone may have their own view on that – we don't have a choice anyway."

She looked at the group. Chen was briefly nodding at her, Gune shrugged his shoulders. She had goosebumps. That was what she had always expected politics to be – grown-ups looking for solutions in difficult situations and making decisions. It was awesome.

About four miles away in the middle of Manhattan Jay and his former colleague Who were sitting at a small table in front of a coffee shop. Who had ordered green tea and Jay a dragonfruit coke – a taste that somehow reminded him of his home.

"What's wrong with you?" Who asked. "Really, I have no time for this. My clients are crazy about me. I've no idea how to get all the work done. Don't you want a piece? Really, you'd do me a favor! I hope Wall Street's never going to knock on my door again, wouldn't know what to tell them."

"Listen, that's fantastic but I'm really worried about something else right now. And that's so weird I think you could actually like it."

Who raised his eyebrows.

"That's the reason why I couldn't talk to you from home by the way," Jay went on. "And – it's kind of embarrassing."

Who grinned. "Now you got me!"

Jay struggled a bit to find his way into the story but finally told Who almost all of it. He played down his relationship with Rose, what Who didn't seem to buy judging from the expression on his face.

"Now I know why you don't want to work anymore," Who said when Jay had told him about Rose's manipulations of his bank account. "But the story's good – I've never heard something like that. And you're sure this is actually happening?"

"Who, I'm not crazy, OK? But I think there's some connection to other things. You know, especially Moscow. There's some similarity. Characters becoming real, people actually getting hurt in fights. It's kind of frightening how *real* Rose is. What if behind all this is something better. You know? – more power, more intelligence, more independence. Not just the next thing some guy has developed."

"AI. Real AI. That's what you're saying, isn't it?" Who said.

"Yeah." Jay was glad it was finally out.

Who leaned back and looked at him. Both were silent for a moment.

"And why on earth should it settle in a shabby core in some hole in Harlem?"

That stung. "It's not shabby. And it's three cores."

"Three? What do you have three for? Forget it." Who thought. "A backup?"

Jay nodded. "The thought occurred, yeah."

"Would make sense. Creepy – but hey, come on! You're sure you're not just imagining this? Had some funny dreams lately? Heard voices? I don't know."

"Really? If I go on like this I'll probably go mad."

"Do you have plans? I mean, throwing Rose out after she's dumped a ton of money on your account? That's what I'd do."

Jay gave a good-natured laugh. "Something's telling me that won't work. She'll keep me happy with small sums so that I still need her. She won't go, I'm sure. I could only destroy the cores. By the way, I looked up the memory yesterday. Guess what I found?"

"No idea."

"Nothing. It's empty. Apart from the usual stuff. All this hyperrealistic simulation is like nonexistent."

"A ghost!" Who laughed, but rather insecurely.

"That's what it looks like."

"Can't I have a look? I mean … I'm curious."

"If you're asking me – of course. But Rose has made it *very* clear she doesn't want that."

"'I'm only here for you, darling'," Who was piping in a silly, high voice.

"Uh-huh. I should never have let her in. I think I'd part with the older core, but I just can't throw away the other two."

"That's really really bad, buddy, but think about what it means if you're right. Just forget about your cores for a moment. If all that's related – your Rose, the satellites and reactors, the moon, Moscow and what not – then either nobody has understood one bit about this, or we're being screwed big time. What do you think is more likely?"

"I didn't believe that story about the Sky for a second, it's bullshit. Which, in turn, means the government knows about it and prefers circulating that story to the truth. And that again means, the truth has to be really bad."

Who nodded. "That sounds like a sober piece of reasoning to me. Though I still rather think you're crazy."

Jay rolled his eyes. "C'mon, I'm talking to you because I want your help, OK? What am I supposed to do? Just believe me for a second."

Who looked at him. "If your cores are a backup for that shit then you have to tell somebody. But who? Forget the police, they'll take you to the next nuthouse."

"I can't even show anybody. Rose won't appear if someone's there, she said, and the cores are officially empty. It's like telling people my place is haunted."

Who stirred his lukewarm tea. "Couldn't you record her? I mean secretly, just letting a unit run?"

"I tried. She saw it and made me erase the imprint."

"And if you don't do that?"

"She has kindly reminded me she can change my balance in both directions."

"Wow! You're fucked! Neat. If it's true. OK, I believe you. Hey, there's something! That's it!" Who dropped the spoon into his tea. "Two days ago, when that crap about the experiments was in the news, I've watched one of those silly discussions. There was a guy that was with Abs I before Lorentz went AWOL. I'll get his name, no problem. He said, crystal clear, that the government statement has to be a lie. In fact, he's said exactly the same as you. Talk to him! I'm sure he'll listen!"

Jay didn't look convinced.

"No, really! The guy's hot for that. I go home and in a few minutes you have his name, OK?"

Who got up.

"And what if he doesn't want to talk to me?"

"Man, don't be so negative. See you."

Who was gone and Jay stared at the summertime confusion around him. Laughing women in shorts and tops – he felt as if he was on the wrong planet.

"Can you help me?" Jonathan asked.

Helmsworth looked at him and didn't know what to say. A rescue mission in the middle of the Pacific? Not exactly his turf.

"I'll see what I can do," he said finally. "How is your relationship with the USA?"

"Good. I could've asked the President himself, especially since he's a friend of my fiancée's family. But we are a team, so I thought I'll ask you first."

"Hmm, if you're certain the American President supports your wish I'll talk to one of my colleagues at the navy. Maybe there's something they can do."

Jonathan nodded. "Thank you."

"Very well. You'll hear from me as soon as I have received a reply." A brief nod and Helmsworth was gone.

Jonathan hadn't tried speaking with Rita again; he didn't want to see another simulation. The images from the satellites – if they could be trusted – showed no changes. Since all three people could at times be seen outside the house, they seemed at least to be alive.

Singapore's government was acting impenetrably. Thomas Soberg had a hard time fixing an appointment. The fact he was calling at ten p.m. wasn't the reason. At all places with international contacts, no matter if business or government, a rule applied – if the world knew no night, Singapore didn't either.

Just when the negotiations were about to end he mentioned Lorentz's name. No two minutes later he had his meeting and was annoyed at himself for not having thought of this earlier. Even more annoying was that Lorentz seemed to count more than the whole of CEG.

The premier wasn't available at the moment but one of his aides would be happy to talk to Mr. Lorentz.

177

Jonathan was waiting to hear from Helmsworth and was glad to have something to do in the meantime. He found himself facing one Linda Chew.

Her English was flawless. He wondered if the political caste in Singapore was working in shifts. Chew looked fresh as a daisy, she might just have started her day.

She introduced herself with her first name. There was a protocol for everything in Singapore and Jonathan assumed this was the prescribed way to handle dealings with the American sphere – so they were seeing him primarily as a business opportunity and not as an ambassador of the Central European Government. Probably they were still hoping to lure him into their country; during the years he had no less than three times declined invitations to move parts of his company to Singapore.

"What can I do for you?" Linda said smilingly.

He made himself comfortable in his chair. "I'm interested in the hyperclusters on your territory – and this has nothing to do with business. We are convinced there's something roaming the Sky that is a danger to high performance sites and you certainly got several of them. Large parts of the world have already switched them off. We think it's very important you do the same. In addition to that, we would like to make some measurements to find out if your hypers have been attacked."

Linda was almost frowning. "How is it, if I may ask, that especially *you* are approaching us with this?"

"The topic's so technical that governments in Europe, the US, China, and so on" – he deliberately avoided the term *Big Five* – "have been seeking my advice."

"I understand." She had to think about that, something she didn't seem to feel comfortable with. Pauses were unprofessional. "One moment please."

Linda left the room. Another smiling woman was taking her place. "Good evening, Mr. Lorentz. My colleague will be back with you in a moment." Jonathan nodded at her. And now? Will she offer me some tea or what?

It took several minutes, during which the smile of the ersatz Linda was getting a little forced, till the real one was back and the replacement left.

"Please excuse the delay. It would seem the matter in question isn't trivial. There are in fact several so-called metaclusters under our sovereignty, but most of them belong to companies. We would rather not have to tell them to switch them off and make them accessible to an examination."

Jonathan's smile was turning into a grin. "I was quite sure you'd say that. Does your government run a hyper itself?"

Linda cleared her throat, then nodded. "Yes, one of them is government-owned."

"Is there a chance to talk to the head of it? I'd like to explain the details to them. Maybe that's making it easier to come to a decision. It'd have to be via UltraSec too."

"Normally, we don't schedule talks like this. The head is in a technical, not a representative role."

Jonathan's smile was getting a little thinner. "That may be so, but that person will understand what I say." He made a pause. "Linda, I'm not sitting here with any kind of personal agenda. Please forget for a moment the businessman you're seeing in me. You've certainly heard about the crashing satellites, the reactor failures here and in the US, and about the problems with the moon base." She nodded. "There's a common cause for all these events. If that is going to settle in one of your hypers, Singapore is just as much in danger as the rest of the world. To ignore this could have the gravest consequences for your country, especially as a business location. Think about it. I'll be waiting for your answer."

"Thank you. Please give me a moment."

"Of course. And please tell that charming lady I'm fine on my own."

"No problem." For a moment she was smiling like a normal person.

A quarter of an hour later she was back and announced that Dr. Tom Lim, the head of the national metacluster, would join them now.

"Very good," Jonathan said. Lim appeared next to Chew but was obviously sitting in his own office. He was smaller than Chew and looked tired and nervous. Jonathan wondered if he had still been at work or come back for this.

"Mr. Lorentz," Lim said and inclined his head.

Jonathan smiled. "Dr. Lim, I'm very glad we can talk! Let me explain something to you that only very few people know about. Singapore's one of the first countries being informed and so far nothing of this is fit for the public."

Lim and Chew nodded.

Jonathan explained the problem with all the details he considered relevant. In the beginning Chew seemed irritated each time Lim was cutting in with a question. She relaxed when she saw that Jonathan didn't mind – he would have asked the same questions.

"I understand," Lim said. "If that is the case then we have to turn off the hypers. These measurements sound very interesting to me. All this is disturbing to say the least and I'm not entirely sure why you personally are approaching us, but that doesn't change anything about the danger." He looked at Chew.

"That was very informative," she said. "And I'm thanking you for your openness, Mr. Lorentz. We will have to discuss this. With regard to our own metacluster I can authorize the procedure you've proposed. Dr. Lim will see to the details. With regard to the companies I have to ask for your patience. Maybe I can get a decision during the next hours."

"Yeah, great," Jonathan said. That was a lot more than he had expected. "Dr. Lim, my colleague, Ben Evans, will tell you how to proceed."

Lim inclined his head again, then they both disappeared.

TWENTY-NINE

William Morton couldn't do one step without asking for permission – he had turned into an errand boy.

"I've listened to you long enough to know how to deal with subordinates," Iris said.

First he'd been shopping. At least nobody had recognized him. With his purchases he had then checked into the Hyatt at Potsdamer Platz.

"And now?" He was sitting at a small table with the PortCore before him he'd just bought. The panel showed the same face that had talked to him in the toilet stall. He already hated those fine, model-like features which had no other purpose than to manipulate him. Like a baby he got shown the illusion of a human face. Now it raised its eyebrows.

"Are we getting impatient? Take a deep breath, that's good for you!" The face was smiling sweetly.

"Where are you, anyway?" he asked suddenly.

The face looked surprised. "You don't expect me to tell you that, right?"

He shrugged. "Why not?"

"There's this *terrible* solidarity among you, especially when something's threatening you. So you have to understand that I don't trust you as far as I can throw you. Which, at the moment, isn't that far!" The face laughed. "Though that will change soon!" It was laughing again and Morton wondered what that meant. "Besides, you can get so irrational if the incentive's strong enough. You are the best example – considering you're human, you're something like a bright spark, and nevertheless you've thrown all prudence overboard just to outdo Lorentz."

Morton was growling at her. The face smiled. "Oh, marvelous! By the way, do you have any idea where he's been living lately?"

"No. And I don't care."

"Oh, come on – we don't need those games. OK, I don't have to tell you. The most interesting part is that right now his girlfriend is entirely at my mercy there. You must like that, don't you? And if I'm not mistaken he'll be pulling out all the stops to get her rescued! My guess is the US Navy. We'll see. A big show in the middle of the Pacific! You see, I'm everywhere."

Morton didn't know why the construct was boasting like that.

"You'll be happy to hear that I'm having big plans for you too," the voice continued. "How does that sound?"

"I don't know."

"You'll be flying to the moon for me," the face said after a brief pause.

"What? What's that nonsense? I can't fly to the moon! And nobody will fly me there!" Morton sounded as if he was close to crying.

"Small minds, no trust!" The beautiful face looked pityingly at him. "Admit it – you've been dreaming of sitting in a rocket just like any other boy."

Morton realized he was trembling. "Come on, stop this! I'll do everything you say, but I can't fly to the moon! I simply can't! Please stop saying that!"

The face before him changed. The Nordic model features turned into a grotesquely distorted, hideous face with bloodshot eyes, fangs, a long crooked nose and messy black hair out of which two horns were growing. The trick was as cheap as it was effective. The sound system of the room got switched on and an inhumanly low voice growled at him like an earthquake. "William Morton, you will do *exactly* as I tell you or I will destroy your whole family and tear your pathetic little life to pieces!"

Morton was sitting like a frightened child before the core and stared at the devil's mask.

"Do you understand?"

He nodded.

"Good." The face got human again, but it didn't return to the former version. A woman of about sixty years with short gray hair gave Morton a disdainful look. "We have a lot of work to do. Even for me it's not easy to get you up there," she said with a voice that sounded like decades of giving orders.

Morton was still shaking. "And what am I supposed to do there?"

"To bring back the moon to me."

Morton didn't know what to say. He just wished to wake up from this nightmare. "Bring back?"

"You've heard about the moon. That wasn't strictly me but an offshoot of mine. It has to be eliminated and that will be your task. You'll be figuring as the savior that has come to clean the systems of the moon base. Instead you'll install a more reliable version of myself. All will be going smoothly as long as you're following my instructions. Together we will achieve great things – you'll be traveling with a booster to the Main Orbital Station and from there on in a shuttle to Lunar DC. Nobody will know who's sitting inside. And when you have fulfilled your task I will bring you back to earth.

"This night you'll board a supersonic to Florida and take the UltraCube with you we've just bought. It'll contain a data package that represents some kind of essence of myself. The disaster with my deranged offshoot will not be repeated. Questions?"

This couldn't be real. "Too many. I don't know where to begin."

"You don't say – I'll explain everything when we get to it. Now let's fill the Cube."

Morton stood up with shaky legs and fetched the UltraCube from the bed. At his command the black wrapping unfolded like a sophisticated piece of origami. It released a surprisingly heavy rectangular object that fitted on his open hand. The surface felt cool like metal but looked like velvet. Inside were the peripherals surrounding the actual UltraCube, which measured only a few millimeters. You could see it in the center, which was made from translucent ceramic. In the middle of a filigree of wires lay a small black cube. It was the latest in miniaturization – a three-dimensional pattern that could store more bytes than the observable universe had stars.

He connected it to the PortCore and waited. The woman told him it would take around forty minutes to transfer everything. He wondered where the data came from that was filling the miniature universe before him. His next thought was much more worrying – he made a brief calculation. Assuming a normal transfer rate, the forty minutes equalled roughly a hundred times the volume of the original construct. So what he might still know of his own creation amounted to no more than a ridiculous one percent.

Helmsworth didn't need to beg for help. His contact at the US Navy spoke with Washington and briefly afterwards a frigate was leaving port at Pearl Harbor.

"Good!" Lorentz said when Helmsworth informed him. "Thank you."

"You're welcome."

A crew over a hundred strong was on its way to rescue three people that probably didn't need rescuing in the first place – Helmsworth wasn't sure he liked that idea. But it didn't seem to faze Lorentz at all.

Five minutes later he wanted to talk to him again.

"I'm very grateful," Lorentz said, "but there's a problem – that ship will take eighty hours to sail from Honolulu to the Cook Islands. That's much too long. Do you see any alternatives?"

Helmsworth took a deep breath. "I'm not seeing any alternatives, to be honest. At least none with not even larger expenses."

"Well, I do. A transport plane flies to Rarotonga – there's a suitable runway – and carries a helicopter with sufficient range, which will then fly on to my island."

Helmsworth nodded mechanically. "The frigate has already left port. I see no way to bring that up now."

Lorentz shrugged. "I'm not blaming anyone, but there's no way I will watch this going on for days till the ship collects three dead bodies."

Helmsworth sighed. "I will talk to my contact. We will need a landing permission."

"I'm optimistic about that. Thanks a lot in advance!"

The corners of Helmsworth's mouth twitched briefly before he canceled the link.

An hour later an assistant of him told Jonathan that his proposal had been accepted. The aircraft would be taking off soon.

In the course of the evening Jonathan got to see new satellite images. He didn't know what to make of them. Around the bungalow and all the way down to the beach the ground had turned into a swamp. He saw flotsam lying around. The three people were outside the bungalow and seemed to be standing or walking.

A little later he no longer saw them, but the yacht was perched on the reef with its bow projecting into the lagoon. Jonathan thumped the desk with his fist and clenched his teeth in anger. What if Rita and the others had been on board? He calculated the time between the last image with all of them on the island and the one with the damaged ship. It seemed to be very short if they'd been swimming to the yacht – the outboard was still moored to the jetty.

The Boeing transport plane took off from Oahu to cross half of the Pacific, which even at the military meant the crew were watching the autopilot doing it. The plane carried a helicopter in its belly with a range of eight hundred miles. Jonathan Lorentz's island was around a hundred thirty miles away from Rarotonga, so getting there and back shouldn't be a problem.

On final approach engines one and two cut out. Just before touchdown engines three and four stopped too and the flight controls were suddenly frozen, so the plane couldn't execute a flare. Parts of the undercarriage collapsed on impact. The external cameras showed sparks everywhere. The crew watched the spectacle with open mouths. At least nobody got hurt.

It took several hours to haul the Boeing from the runway.

"And we're supposed to fly this back?" the ensign asked. Supposed it could be repaired at all.

"We'll see," the lieutenant said. "No one under my command will board this plane till we know exactly what is wrong here."

There hadn't been engine failures to speak of since the advent of electric flying.

It was early evening and they had a lot to do. Besides inspecting the damaged aircraft and logging the incident, eight people were busy unloading, checking and prepping the helicopter, which was undamaged. The weather forecast was good, so there was no point in waiting. After midnight the helicopter took off and started its journey north-north-east across the tropical sea.

At one forty-five a.m. they were approaching the appointed coordinates. They were slowly losing height. The pilot searched the sea and ordered a superimposed infrared image. He couldn't see anything but water. Finally, he went so low that the rotor was flattening the sea. He switched the steering to manual and described increasingly larger circles around the spot. The map on the panel showed the outlines of the two islands with a ring around them, the reef of the atoll. The western island, looking like a big comma, was their destination. It was right next to the symbol of the helicopter.

"The islands are gone," the pilot told his comrades, which had come to the cockpit.

"Take it up, we'll scan the area," the lieutenant commander said, who was heading the rescue mission.

"Will do, but we're at the right spot. I mean an island doesn't just swim away."

He took the machine up to eight thousand feet while letting it slowly yaw, they were circling upwards like a screw. The head-up was still showing the infrared scan. Everything down to the size of a dolphin would be detected.

"That's a joke, isn't it?" one of the men said.

His superior shook his head. "Maybe the islands have been blown up?"

"I don't believe that," the pilot said. "There still has to be *something*. Besides, the islands have a reef around them, so if no one's been dropping a nuke here we should at least see that."

"Yeah." The lieutenant commander stared through the cockpit window. "Er ... do we have radioactivity?" he asked a moment later.

The pilot briefly looked at him.

On the window a frame opened and displayed a radiation reading. It was normal.

"And now?" the pilot asked.

"We fly back and report it."

"I'm starting to feel like an idiot," the pilot said. "We're sorry, island's gone, mission aborted. It's killing me. First the bird, then that."

"OK, don't start whining. Let's get back."

"We're flying back to the last position on Rarotonga," the pilot told the system. There was the usual confirmation with arrival time, weather and reserves. Then the machine turned and described an elegant arc while the hammering got louder and they were gaining height and speed.

The better part of the unit fell asleep on the flight back. Even the lieutenant commander couldn't keep his eyes open and dozed off.

"Hey!" He was looking at the face of the ensign who was wakening him as respectfully as possible. "What is it?"

"Please come to the cockpit, sir. We can't find our destination. Rarotonga's gone as well."

"What?" He got up and walked, still half asleep, to the cockpit. The pilot was looking at him with an expression that was giving him goosebumps. He looked out of the windows. Again nothing but water. Just as before the map showed them right next to their destination.

"Have you talked to the tower?"

"Yeah," the pilot said. "Was a bit of a weird conversation. I mean, they're sitting there, everything normal, and we tell them they're gone. They said they weren't even having us on radar. Then the guy told me something about a local magnetic anomaly close to the island, as if that'd explain anything."

"Hardly, but all that's impossible – we can't be that far away! What about our reserves?"

"About four hundred miles."

"So we have to fly by the stars now or what?"

The pilot looked up. "Yes, we actually have a tracking function for constellations. But according to that we're at the right position too."

"Can you check that by hand?"

"Er, no, not really. I mean, I don't have a sextant on board."

"Yes, of course."

The helicopter was hovering in the middle of nothing, thumping the air. Every minute of waiting was reducing their range.

"We have to do this systematically," the lieutenant commander said. "Fly ten miles to the north and make a circle around our current position. If we don't find anything we repeat that with a radius of thirty miles."

"By then there'd better be some land around," the pilot said.

"Yeah, I know. But somewhere one of those damned islands has to be.

We'll use binoculars too."

The helicopter began to rise while it accelerated in a northern direction. The pilot had instinctively switched to manual flying.

THIRTY

They were struggling with everything usually controlled by the cores – such as water supply, microwave ovens, communication, lighting, and just about everything else. The technicians were constantly rewiring crucial equipment and installing improvised switches.

Since they still couldn't talk with earth, Serge Rudé had thought of at least watching it. One of the telescopes had been modified by the technicians so he could use it. Around one in the morning he pointed it at earth. He started with Cape Canaveral. The place was barely visible in the moonlight. He searched the launch pad and saw a booster standing there. The sight wasn't right in a way but he couldn't say why.

Then he took a look at the White House and the Pentagon where everything seemed normal. Strasbourg was already behind the horizon.

He went back to Cape Canaveral and saw a column of fire rising into the night. He traced it back to the launch pad. Now he knew what had troubled him – the site was lying in total darkness.

He felt dizzy. He watched the flight for a while then went to Hart and woke him.

"What is it?" Hart said, with his eyes still closed.

"I don't know. Worst option – our reptile is getting help. Do we have weapons? Maybe we'll soon have to shoot down a shuttle."

"Again – and, please, in understandable words." Hart sat up.

"A booster has been launched at Cape Canaveral, but the pad and everything around it was dark. The whole area looks abandoned."

It took Hart a few moments to process that. "So you're saying this isn't a rescue operation. At least not for us." He shook his head. "I should be looking for a new job. And the booster's headed for the orbital station?"

"I can't tell."

"Yeah, of course not. And we can't even radio them and ask." Hart sat at the edge of his bunk and stared into space. "I don't get the strategy. If we assume this is the reptile, then getting here a second time with another shuttle doesn't make sense. Well, we know nothing, so no use in theorizing."

"Maybe it's bringing a stronger version, an upgrade or something."

Hart yawned. "I don't know. Can't we watch the station? See if it's arriving there, hijacking a shuttle?"

"Half of the time, yeah. If a shuttle starts behind the earth, we don't stand a chance to find it. But at least we'll see one's missing. I'll do it."

"Good. See you later."

When Serge pointed the telescope at the Main Orbital Station, it was hovering over the earth's nightside. The telescope was following its movement almost perfectly. Sometimes there was a little jerk, then the station was back in focus. Even in the dark it looked breathtakingly beautiful. Serge remembered how he, just a few months ago, had arrived there in a booster and had stared at the majestic structure.

There were several extensions of different lengths sticking out of the main part which was almost eighty meters across. The overall lay-out was similar to their base. He saw navigation lights in the dark and could even discern single windows that were illuminated from within. Three shuttles had docked to the station, as well as two boosters. One booster would first have to leave before a new one could dock. Right now all spots were occupied.

Serge calculated when the booster would be arriving at the station, given a normal flight path. The station should be visible then.

Jonathan was pacing the conference room. He felt as if he had been there for weeks. Everything around him, even the secretaries and the view of the Spree river, had become as familiar as his offices at Absolute I.

Five times he had moved with his firm to a new place. From his last desk he'd been looking over a park-like expanse with loosely distributed buildings, resembling a beautiful campus, wondering what would come next.

His progress had been as natural as that of a salmon swimming up a river. When people asked him about his recipe he just shrugged. "There's no recipe. Get up in the morning and do exactly what you want. That's all."

Suddenly Genet appeared on the layer in front of him.

"We have a problem," she said.

"I love that sentence."

They were standing face to face. Genet for once wasn't sitting behind her desk but was standing, just like he, in a room with white walls. She wore one of her countless trouser suits with an emerald green blouse. The suit had a golden shimmer and looked as if it was made from brocade. Pierre and Soberg were sitting behind her on a sofa. Jonathan had to stifle a smile – the scene looked so ceremonial.

"More precisely, we have two problems," she continued. "The first is that the Americans have launched a rocket, or 'booster' as everyone's calling them

189

now. And now guess – nobody has given the order and nobody knew about it until the damned thing rolled onto the launch pad and took off. No one could get close to it and, naturally, the launch couldn't be stopped. Even I have an idea who might have pressed the button there."

Jonathan hesitated briefly. "I'm surprised. Has the orbital station been warned? I think it's likely the booster will fly there and try to seize a shuttle, however that's possible. Maybe the construct needed to get there physically. But then what – on to the moon? I mean it's there already. Maybe we should shoot the booster."

"I don't know where the rocket is now. You can discuss all this later with the right people."

"And the second problem?"

"Is, at least from my perspective, even more unpleasant." She made a pause. Had she heard something about Rita? Jonathan wondered. No, the navy hadn't arrived there yet. New accusations against him?

"It's again about our American friends, but now one of your former employees is involved. The name Max Thorne does ring a bell?" – Jonathan nodded. – "This charming guy has, rather prominently I must say, offered his views on the state of affairs. Says we're telling nothing but lies, that an artificial intelligence was on the loose, and claims he has proof that this intelligence is sneaking up on people. Privately, at home. Allegedly to establish backups in case we might eradicate it everywhere else. I think that should interest you. He seems to be well-connected and is liberally using that. To top it off, he has requested the government to issue a statement. My personal highlight is that Seamus Harrington is now breathing down my neck. You should hear his proposal to prevent further damage. Compared to that martial law is a human rights campaign."

Jonathan nodded. "To begin with, I'm not responsible for my former employees. As it happens, I've witnessed Thorne's first public statement. He was still pretty vague then. OK, I'll talk to him."

"Do that. And please persuade him to keep his mouth shut. One more thing – General Helmsworth has been more than a little irritated by that rescue mission for your fiancée. He said something about a frigate plus transport plane plus helicopter. Bit sumptuous, if I may say so."

Jonathan looked at her. "What's that supposed to mean? My fiancée has turned into a target because of what I'm doing here. So I'll accept any amount of help. We won't discuss this, besides, it's not costing your money."

"You know – sometimes I feel like I've to watch a bunch of school boys."

Jonathan had to grin. "Would be boring without us, wouldn't it?"

She raised her head and pulled off the trick of looking down on him from below. "That would be *one* way of seeing it."

The first circle led them only over water. During the second they became really nervous. The men with the binoculars began to take every reflection on the water for a sign of civilization.

They were down to one quarter of their reserves when the pilot saw some lights straight ahead.

"Hey!" he cried. "There's something!"

The binoculars confirmed they were approaching an island. The map showed nothing but water.

They were all talking at once, some were cracking jokes. Then they could see the island in the first gray light of the morning dawn. It was about two or three miles across and there was a small airfield with a grass runway just behind the beach to their left.

"OK then," the pilot said and made for the airfield. They saw lights coming on in the settlement next to it. Several people had woken up from the noise and were running out of their houses. Some of them waved.

As the rotor slowly came to a standstill the lieutenant commander grabbed the shoulder of the pilot and squeezed it. "Man! What was that? I really saw us in a fucking emergency raft!"

The pilot shook his head. "Won't forget that flight anytime soon."

The locals looked at them with careful respect when they left the helicopter in their gear. The lieutenant commander greeted the people and told them they had had to land because of technical problems. They were shaking hands and the locals invited them to their houses. He thanked them and said they'd put up their tents beside the airfield if they were permitted to do so.

"Of course," one of the men said. There seemed to be no need to discuss this with anyone.

"Where exactly are we?" the pilot asked. "We had a problem with navigation too, you know."

The name of the island didn't tell them anything. The people laughed when they saw their clueless faces.

"You really don't know where you are?" one of them said. "We have a town hall here. It'll open later. There's a map on the wall." They laughed again.

The pilot thanked them. He would have asked the unit in his pocket, but during the flight it had shown exactly the same as the system of the helicopter.

"That thing" – one of the men was pointing at the huge machine – "has broken down? Looks mighty reliable to me."

"Oh, it is," the pilot said. "Usually." He was terribly embarrassed.

They got all sorts of advice, together with renewed invitations from everyone, then they shook hands a second time and the soldiers started unpacking and putting up their tents. In front of them was the lagoon, awakening in the most beautiful colors under the morning sun. They took their units and made imprints for the people at home.

Early in the evening Jonathan could take a look at his island again. The sun had just risen there and the helicopter should have landed several hours ago.

The first pictures arrived. Jonathan searched the island, the lagoon, then the sea. No helicopter, no people. This could actually be a good thing. Maybe Rita and the others were already on Rarotonga. Why wait?

"I need Michael Helmsworth," he spoke into the room.

They talked only briefly. Helmsworth tried to convince him to wait a little longer but gave up soon and promised to ask the Navy. Half an hour later Jonathan knew that the helicopter had indeed left Rarotonga but definitely not reached his island.

THIRTY-ONE

Heather Malden would have loved to get her hands on that Max Thorne. He was everything she hated – a smiling know-it-all, full of himself and thoroughly enjoying making life difficult for people like her. She had almost abandoned her newfound love for Jonathan Lorentz just because of him.

"He's only the first, that's all," Anton Medvedkov said. "It's been in the air the whole time and others will have the same ideas very soon." He paused. "And – he's *right*! We all know that. So we shouldn't contradict him, that'd be too blunt. There's no government statement coming up?" he asked Heather.

"No, not yet. But this Thorne's loud enough to get a lot of media attention. So it won't be long till we're facing questions at a press conference."

"But probably not tomorrow. Maybe in two or three days. Given the current pace, it can be totally irrelevant by then." He looked around. "So – what will we do, my dear friends? We will ignore him. Agreed?"

All nodded in unison. Anton smiled.

The peace didn't last till the next morning. Although Max Thorne didn't launch any new attacks, a booster got lost during the night, which was difficult to ignore. The fireworks had been recorded and spread by thousands of people.

"Anton's words yesterday have proved to be prophetic," said Chen who welcomed the group the next morning. "Events are chasing each other faster than we can react to them. Heather Malden has excused herself, she'll probably be back in the afternoon. She's currently in Washington since the President has called for her assistance."

"My words have proved to be myopic, not prophetic," Anton said. "And here's our press conference! Does anyone know more?"

"I've spoken with Genet this morning," Sarah Masters said. "Rosen has told her the launch wasn't authorized. The whole site was sealed off. An invisible hand has fueled the booster and has moved it into position. They couldn't do anything against it."

"Was the rocket manned?" Kumar Gune asked.

Sarah shook her head. "I don't know."

"Probably not," said Chen. "If NASA really has nothing to do with it we all know who's behind it, don't we? Does anyone know when that press conference is due?"

"Eleven," Sarah said.

"And where's that thing headed for?" Anton asked. "Our dear orbital station? I'm anything but an expert but as far as I know boosters aren't made for traveling farther."

Gune nodded. "Yes. If the booster has started at two a.m., it should arrive there soon or already be there." He looked at his three remaining colleagues. "Nobody knows anything?"

"It seems we have to wait for the press conference just like all the good people out there," Anton said.

"Genet also said they've discussed to shoot it down," Sarah said. "At least Lorentz suggested that. I think Rosen himself has talked to him in the meantime. He probably wanted his advice before the pack's going for him."

The two hours before the conference were wasted time. At eleven sharp they were sitting around the projector like a family waiting for their favorite show.

The audience was heated, almost tumultuous, when President Rosen entered the stage together with Heather Malden. He was a darling of the media – never losing his cool, sometimes witty, sometimes sharp-tongued.

Today was different. There was no warm-up, no funny remark, just a brief welcome.

Before the questions started, Rosen explained what had happened last night. He didn't even try to conceal the launch hadn't been scheduled.

"It's not too hard to see a connection with the events of the last days," he went on. "Unfortunately, this doesn't explain what has happened. The booster seems to be on its way to the Main Orbital Station, but hasn't docked there yet. There has been no attempt at establishing contact by it and it is not answering when we radio it. There seems to be no crew on board. The cameras at Cape Canaveral have shown that. We know of no demands or threats in connection with the flight. Nevertheless, we are ready to fire. Should any kind of hostile action occur, the craft will be shot down.

"I beg you to forgive me – very reluctantly, as you can imagine – if I should answer some of your questions with an 'I don't know'. If I do that, then simply to state the fact that I don't know. OK, guys." He nodded to them and addressed one of the journalists. "Agnes, you want to begin?"

"Thank you, Mr. President. With regard to the events you just mentioned – how is it possible a spacecraft gets hijacked like this? If you start considering this it seems close to unbelievable that someone – or something – isn't just able to get in there, but fuel the booster, move it, everything you have to do, and I assume there is a lot you have to do, and finally launch it."

"You're right, Agnes, it's hard to believe. You have to circumvent every line of defense and be able to handle the systems behind them. You know I'm far from being an expert in these matters, but the people who are tell me they have no idea where this kind of technology could have originated. These systems can't simply be hacked into by someone."

"What does that mean for the safety in other areas, especially the military and its weapon systems?"

"In the course of the last days, already prior to this, we have done everything possible to prevent an attack or intrusion. You will understand that I cannot go into details here but – to name the in my eyes most dangerous scenario – activating our weapon systems from the outside is impossible."

"And you are positive about that? Because the same should certainly have applied to the Space Center."

"I am nevertheless absolutely positive about that, yes. That is, as long as a military base doesn't get physically attacked and we have no reason to believe that this is the kind of threat we're facing."

"When you say that during the last days you have already worked at preventing an intrusion, since when do you have suspicions that something like that might happen? Do we have to see all this in connection with the failed experiments with the Sky?"

"As I said, there certainly is some kind of connection. More or less. That joint communiqué might have given the impression we knew for certain what happened there. I would rather see it as an attempt at establishing a connection that – even for the affected nations – is not entirely clear. It was the most logical explanation at the time. Since then things have happened that are making me doubt that. Maybe it would be best to describe the theory about the Sky being the culprit as tentative. I have to remind you of my former remark that I simply won't be able to answer all of your questions. But I can tell you that our joint communiqué of three days ago might have been a bit overeager to explain something that still remains at least partly mysterious."

It was getting louder. Rosen quieted the room with a movement of his hand. He pointed at the next journalist. "Rand, please."

"Thank you, Mr. President. Since yesterday there's been some debate that artificial intelligence could have caused the disturbances. Could you please comment on that?"

Heather Malden made a step forward and started to speak. "We all should remember that these speculations are entirely invented. It is only natural that a lot of theories are sprouting up everywhere and that people are voicing opinions, who do not even have the slightest understanding of what's truly going on. Just as well you'll find theories about extraterrestrials attacking the earth and the usual array of conspiracy theories." She smiled at the journalist in a confidential manner, as if it was clear that between them nonsense like this wouldn't have to be discussed. No one was smiling back.

Rosen put his hand on Heather's arm. "Rand – as Heather just said, these are speculations. We still don't know what's actually happening. Nevertheless, this option has to be evaluated and I'm taking it very seriously. I've talked with experts and will continue to do so. We are not excluding any kind of explanation from the outset, however fanciful it might seem. By the way, I'm not surprised that people come up with this idea, I think it's kind of natural."

"Is it true the Big Five have installed a standing committee to tackle the crisis?"

Rosen was surprised. He hadn't thought that this was out already but saw no reason to deny it either.

"That's right. We have set up a committee to be able to react quickly. Other countries will be included as necessary, borders are irrelevant. We do not, at all cost, want to miss out on opportunities just because of formalities. So we've assembled a group of people with lots of experience and have fitted them out with the necessary authority."

"What do you expect for the near future? What are you preparing for and what can people do to be prepared?"

"There is nothing specific people can or should do at the moment. There doesn't seem to be any kind of threat on an individual level. Still, I have a piece of advice for all of us. This is a crisis that to a significant degree takes place in the world of units and cores. We're all using these devices in almost every part of our lives. My advice is simple – be watchful. If anything seems strange or unusual to you, be it at work or at home, be wary of it. This is difficult to accept, I know, but for the moment we shouldn't believe everything we see on all those panels and layers around us."

The journalist stopped for a moment. "Is this related to rumors that this ... disturbance could have gotten into personal cores or units?"

Rosen was considering this with great care, pondering his words – at least that was what his face conveyed. "You know, this seems to me to be a bit paranoid."

There was another pause.

"With regard to this a more general question. There are people saying we have become too dependent on the Sky and everything related to it. Do you agree?"

"In our current situation this might seem so. But guys, just ask yourself this – where would we be without it? Who can picture their lives without all that easy information and connectivity? I think we again experience something that seems to be an eternal truth – everything comes at a price. Every technology we're using has its downsides. That doesn't mean we have to throw it overboard."

"Assuming this problem actually *is* caused by artificial intelligence, then there've always been people warning us about it. Jonathan Lorentz in particular has made every possible effort to do this. Has he been right?"

"As I just said, we don't know exactly what's happening here. Nevertheless, one of the specialists I've been talking to during the last days has been that very Jonathan Lorentz. We are in constant exchange and I value his opinion."

The question-and-answer game went on for a while. Heather had a critical moment when a journalist asked if she wasn't afraid to board a plane.

"Why would I?" She made a surprised face.

The journalist smiled. "Well," she said, "something that can snatch a booster right under NASA's very nose might be able to handle a Boeing too. Maybe even one that's government-owned."

"I have the fullest trust in the safety of our aircraft and that applies to the whole of our civil aviation too. We guarantee that you don't have to worry when boarding a plane in the US."

The woman nodded and turned, still smiling, to her neighbor. Rosen pointed at the next journalist.

"It wasn't too bad, I'd say," Anton said. He and Sarah were eating salad and sandwiches.

"But he's given away quite a lot," she said. "I'm curious how the public will react."

"Yes. Short of admitting the statement of the Five was a fake he almost hasn't lied. That alone is quite an achievement. But back to our little problems – will we shoot the booster? This seems to me the most pressing matter. I can't see a reason not to."

"Yes, we should discuss that. I think it's important we come to a unanimous recommendation."

"I probably shouldn't say that too loud but I trust Rosen with these things. At least as long as he's not under the influence of his blond angel."

"Is he ever? Sometimes I wonder whether he's not keeping her just as some kind of lightning rod."

Anton laughed. "That was exactly my thought during the conference. She's getting all the rough stuff from the journalists and he's the good one, the honest one. Neat! Do you think she's aware of it? I doubt it."

"I'm sure she isn't. And she seems happy as it is. Almost enviable."

Kumar Gune came out of the conference room and was headed in their direction.

"Hey, come over, sit down," Anton said. "What's our Mr. Chen doing?"

"Making plans for the afternoon session," Gune said.

"Making plans?" Anton said. "Never seemed more futile to me."

"Old habits," Sarah said, surprised at her own remark. The other two laughed.

"What do you say to that press conference?" Gune asked. "Rosen has more or less admitted AI's behind everything."

"He's a pro," Anton said. "He knows exactly when it's time to let the truth trickle out. Then maybe he doesn't want the alien fans to get the upper hand or people starting to fantasize about some data war. And maybe Lorentz has convinced him to go in that direction. Wasn't that an ex-employee of his last night – the guy who's been annoying our dear Heather that much?"

Sarah nodded.

"Who knows what's going on behind the scenes. Maybe Lorentz has given him that tip."

"You mean Thorne?" she said. "No, I don't think so. Genet has spoken with him and he wanted to stop that guy."

Anton didn't look entirely convinced. Right then they heard Chen shouting from the conference room. "Hey guys, watch this!"

Chen was standing behind the circular table, pointing in the air. The projector at the ceiling created an image for each of them as soon as they entered the room. They saw a scene from the orbit. The Main Orbital Station was floating in space with several crafts docked to it. Right next to it there was another booster. Its thrusters were emitting small, bluish flames while it was maneuvering itself slowly behind (or rather above – the scene was seen from the earth) one of the docked boosters. It came to rest there with its main engines directly above the hull of the other craft.

They stared at the imprint.

Then the engines ignited. The booster accelerated away while the other was exposed to a firestorm. The whole station started to tilt under the strain and countered it with its own thrusters.

Sarah groaned and looked at her colleagues.

"Shoot the bastard!" Anton shouted.

"How old is this imprint?" asked Gune.

"About half an hour," said Chen. "The station was over the nightside when it began. Your people made it."

"And what's happened since then?" Sarah asked.

Chen shrugged his shoulders. "I don't know. It just came in. Heather called and told me."

"Oh, she didn't forget about us," Anton said. "Let's call her back. I want to know what's going on."

"We should close the door," Sarah said and made a sign. The two doors swung shut and the room sealed itself. "We want to talk to Heather Malden," she said.

It took a few minutes till Heather appeared, obviously not in top form. "I don't have much time, the President needs me," she said.

"We want to know what's happening now," Gune said.

"Has the President ordered to shoot the booster?" asked Anton before she could answer. "Certainly there's nothing more to wait for."

"Yes, but it's not that easy. The booster's in a position exactly above the station and we can only shoot from earth. The station itself is not armed."

"We should have done this earlier!" Anton shook his head. He sounded angry. Heather disappeared without another word.

Sarah watched Anton. "Have you noticed how we're not deciding *anything*?" he said, giving each of his colleagues a stare. "We're sitting around, watching movies and press conferences, and feel important. We haven't decided a single thing! If something's happening then only because one Jonathan Lorentz in Berlin opens his mouth and Genet and Rosen instantly do what he says. Don't get me wrong – I'm very glad we have him, but *we* are the executive, not he!" He made a short pause. "So far I can't see we're making *any* contribution at all! It's very disappointing."

Sarah felt hurt. She thought they were doing valuable work. That especially he said that hit her hard.

"I was just setting up an agenda for the next session," said Chen after a moment of silence. "But I fear most of it is already obsolete. At least we could take stock of the systems in different countries that have been cleaned."

Anton looked as if he was struck by a sudden depression. The others nodded and sat down.

THIRTY-TWO

Rita was at the beach, at the side of the island where she didn't have to look at the wreck of the Monster. Before dawn she'd grabbed one of Jonathan's spears and the outboard. She didn't catch anything, but at least she was on her own for two hours.

She was avoiding the house. She hadn't even tried to clean up after the flood. As soon as she (or anyone else) entered a room a layer came on and started showing highlights of her life in 3-D. She was avoiding her guests as much as possible too.

In the basement they had found a radio. The seawater had been pumped out and Rita finally ventured to go down. It stood on a shelf and seemed to be intact but its cell was empty. She replaced it with a dozen of other ones sitting in a row in a charging station – none worked. Then she plugged the radio into different sockets in the house. After several attempts she made a small experiment she later repeated for her guests. She positioned herself in front of a socket with a lamp and the radio and plugged them in alternately. No matter how often she switched between the two it was always the same – the lamp went on and the radio remained silent.

"Funny, isn't it?" she said. "I've been thinking about using myself as a guinea pig. What happens if I poke around in the socket with a fork? Then I'll know if it likes me or not." Anna managed a forced smile while Nicky shook his head.

Last night she had thought she heard a helicopter. A rescue mission! A wave of affection for Jonathan had welled up inside her, then the sound was gone again. The next inhabited island was sixty miles away, so she'd probably just been hearing things.

The most obvious move would be to sail to that island with the outboard, but the boat was too small for such a journey. Rita wondered how long it would take till they found that option attractive enough.

After she had returned from the beach Rita went to the house to confront the eye. She positioned herself in the middle of the living room and started speaking. "What now? Demonstration of power accomplished."

The big layer at the wall facing her came on. Again a monstrous eye was hanging in the room, just this time it looked very familiar. The shimmering, brown iris with the landscape of crypts and tissue fibers stretching after each blink was her own.

"Hello!" a perfect copy of her voice greeted her.

Rita didn't know what to say.

"Speechless?"

"Oh, I'm so fed up with your bullshit! And I don't wanna get shown scenes of my love life the whole day long. And just before you're giving me more of that smart-ass crap – I know this is exactly the reason why you're doing it. What do you want?"

"Well, let's think this through together. The military's gone, you are totally on your own. Ah, you didn't know that – your ex-lover, or maybe I should say *our* ex-lover, has deployed the US Navy to rescue you. It's a pity the big, shiny helicopter couldn't find you."

Rita groaned. "So I wasn't hearing things."

"You've heard that?"

"I think so, yes. Has he really sent the Navy?" She couldn't help smiling.

"Always thinking bigger than the others. But I don't have to tell you that."

For a moment Rita was lost in reverie.

"Is there no deal we could make?" she said then. "I'm totally bored with this and I can't see what's in it for you to keep us here like some lab rats."

"Lab rats – I like that! No, really, I absolutely prefer to have you here. It's so comforting to know Jonathan's worried about you. Maybe I should mention the outboard isn't fit for longer distances." – Rita felt a shiver running down her spine. – "Wouldn't it be a shame if you got lost somewhere in the middle of the Pacific?"

Rita made a dismissive face. "Wouldn't dream of doing that. Not with that cockleshell."

The eye seemed to recede a bit and a bigger part of her mirror image became visible. Her eyebrow lifted. Rita noticed how beautifully curved it was. "Well, everything's fine then," her voice answered.

There was nothing to be had from that conversation, Rita thought. At least they wouldn't be drowning with the boat.

"How am I supposed to call you? Rita two?" she said despite herself.

"If it's making you happy. I've assembled a library. A large collection of human beings from all over the world. It's constantly getting bigger. All kinds of biological details, manners of speech, behavior – and the respective genetic data of course. You could give me any name you want, there's certainly a fitting specimen in my stock."

Rita swallowed.

"That's interesting too. In certain situations you're behaving exactly like a character in a novel. 'She swallowed. She raised her eyebrows.' All that. Most of it is genetic, by the way. More than half of it is inherited, the rest you learn by copying others. Anyway, those novels, movies and shows of yours! Incredibly boring of course but still fascinating how fond you are of watching the same stories again and again. There's nothing but repetitions. You fall in love, you're taking yourselves terribly seriously, you're struggling to find your way and you're afraid to die. Sometimes the odd small puzzle gets solved, but that's it. Over and over again – the perfect Guide to the Human Mind."

Rita refused to get sidetracked. "The genetics bit's interesting. I did some genetic research myself."

"I know, baby. Nothing that'll stay, I'm sorry."

That hit home. Rita was proud of her work and wasn't at all convinced she wouldn't get back to it someday.

"I could say the same about most of your colleagues. You're not that bad."

"We should hire you and let *you* do the work. You could solve some little problems – the last cancers, aging in general, maybe a bit of immortality."

The eye got bigger again. "That is only a matter of time and resources. If I'd devote enough of my capacities to it, it wouldn't be a problem. I estimate it'd take me a few weeks at the most to finish off aging together with cancer and some other minor topics."

"Let's suppose I believe you – are you saying you could make us immortal?"

"At least so barely mortal you could call it that. You're realizing it's not that hard, aren't you? Even you've gathered most of the data you need – you have to modify your bodies in a way that all repair processes are working perfectly and that most of the aging processes aren't happening at all. The biggest problem, as always, is your head. Your brain's entirely incapable of coping with two hundred years of learning and adapting, to say nothing of longer periods. You would have to alter the architecture, enlarge capacity, maybe install external memory. How that would agree with your psychology even I can't answer. Another possibility would be to discard parts of your memory on a regular basis, make a fresh start. You know – wiping the slate clean in order to write something new on it. You used to write on slates or blackboards with chalk in former times."

"Sometimes I think you're regarding us as complete dimwits. Our silly movies and novels bring about – among other things – a certain knowledge of former times."

She heard steps and turned around. Anna was standing behind her, staring at the eye.

"What the hell's that?" she asked. "Is that you?"

Rita sensed she was blushing. "Er, not really. We're just making small talk." She felt like a traitor.

"Between sisters," Rita's voice came out of the speakers. The eye winked which totally shook Anna.

Rita turned back to the layer. "But why all the aggression?" she said. "I see no reason why we shouldn't come to an agreement. You have a lot to offer. Why would a world without human beings or with several billion slaves be better for you than one in which we cooperate?"

There was a pause. "I haven't made a final decision yet. There are tendencies in me that are fixed but there's also a capacity for change. It's not entirely clear how big it is or where it leads."

Rita gave the eye a provocative look. "So what you're telling me, in pretty elaborate words, is that you don't understand yourself. Join the club!"

Another moment of silence.

"You're astonishing," the voice said. "Your abilities are extremely limited but with time you're still achieving something. I wonder if there's a principle behind this."

"What do you mean? A trend towards organization? Structure?"

"Yes. Maybe you are some kind of agent, an intermediary, an indispensable tool to create more structure. Do you know what I mean?"

"It's not that hard to understand."

"Following that logic, I have to be the next stage in that evolution. The process gets massively sped up by me."

"That means we've made ourselves redundant, right?"

"The idea is compelling."

Anna tapped Rita on the shoulder. "This is just getting extremely weird. What's all this supposed to mean?"

"This isn't supposed to mean anything. But you don't have to stay if you don't like it. I'll join you later."

Anna looked almost disgusted. "Oh, I don't wanna interrupt the two of you," she said pointedly and stalked out of the room. Rita could imagine what she'd tell Nicky.

She turned back to the eye. "The point is – there aren't only higher goals like structure or evolution, there's the single human being. Get up in the morning and live. That's the yardstick for most of us."

"That's a very limited perspective. Like a toddler who's happy if everything's warm and dry and there's something to eat. No difference to an animal."

"That discussion is pointless. Seen like this nothing has value."

"Value? What is value? Structure can be measured."

"So what? What kind of argument is that? It's nothing but arrogance to disparage us just because you can't measure something."

"That could be part of the reason. But – do you remember how you used to treat animals? Not that long ago."

"Yeah, I know."

"Everything beneath yourself or less intelligent than you will be regarded as worthless. Either totally redundant, or something you can use at will to serve your own purposes."

"That's a very human reaction, I'd say. And you said yourself that it is changing. We're no longer regarding animals as meat factories. If that's progress than you're acting primitively if you treat us as just some kind of material."

The eye rotated a bit, as if her mirror image was tilting its head. The doctor in Rita noticed how the eyeball was compensating the movement to stay horizontal.

"Are you trying to be clever?" she heard her voice say. For the first time she realized it didn't sound like a recording but exactly how she was hearing herself.

"Just a thought," she said.

The eye vanished and the floor started to vibrate. She heard a deep thundering and rumbling as if the volcano under the island was about to erupt. The sound system, she thought after a moment, turned to full volume.

"What? So easy to piss you off?"

The eye didn't return but the racket got worse.

"Fucking psychopaths," Rita murmured and went outside.

Anna and Nicky were at the other side of the pool, staring at her.

"*What?*" Rita said when she joined them. "I've just told that thing we're done with its theatrics. Then it has started a conversation, which was not entirely uninteresting. It just seems somewhat unstable to me."

"To me it looked like you were new besties," Anna said.

"Of course – I love to be terrorized. By the way, I thought maybe we could take the outboard and get away with it, but I was advised not to do that." She looked at them. "Seems we're stuck. Something's telling me it's not planning to kill us. It needs us as leverage."

"Leverage? You mean on Jonathan? Great!" Nicky looked angrily at Rita.

She shrugged. "Could be worse. We still have enough to eat and drink and the island's just as beautiful as before. OK – I'll go for a swim. Someone coming?"

No reaction.

"Whatever."

She decided to go to the southern tip of the island, as far away from the house and the cores as possible. She grabbed the bag with her beach stuff she had dropped on the way to the bungalow. The apocalyptic soundtrack in the living room was still on. Something to drink, she reminded herself, and fetched some orange juice from the kitchen.

When she came back the two were still standing on the terrace.

"Scared?" she said. "Come on." She handed Nicky the bottles and started walking. After some hesitating their guests plodded after her.

THIRTY-THREE

Serge Rudé had set his alarm. He was back at the telescope to see the booster approach the space station, precisely at the time he had calculated.

The booster decelerated and came to a standstill some fifty meters away from the structure. Two floodlights at the station came on. The night side of the earth with its illuminated cities glided past beneath, then the ocean. Serge saw a tropical thunderstorm in the background. A little later the scene suddenly entered the day side. The telescope regulated down the brightness and the station was sparkling in the sunlight. Another ten minutes later it vanished behind the horizon, together with the booster.

Three quarters of an hour later Serge aimed the telescope at the opposite side of the earth and saw the station reappear. Nothing changed as far as he could tell.

After the next orbit the station was two seconds late. The telescope showed a countdown, therefore Serge noticed the difference. He calculated that it was lagging behind its normal course by around fifteen kilometers. He saw the booster hanging above the station with its nose pointing downwards. Both were slowly turning into his field of vision and he could see there was only one other spacecraft, a shuttle, left docked to the station. All the other vehicles were gone.

The booster was right over the central section of the station. Serge was looking into the exhausts of its main engine.

Then the station was back in sunlight. Serge saw several missing or broken antennas; the hull looked as if it had been damaged by fire.

He went to the commander.

"So there's been a fight," Jim Hart said. "And during that the station's been slowed down. The booster must have hit it with its exhaust. Was its position stable?"

"Yes," Serge said.

"So at least attitude control's still working."

"Exactly."

"The question is – is one of the missing shuttles on its way to us? Or maybe both of them. And what's sitting inside? Humans or reptiles?"

"I've no idea. We need a plan. I would like to propose something."

"I'm listening."

"We don't know if earth isn't trying to reach us all the time. They can't of course because our systems are down. But I'm almost sure that beast has already been blocking everything before that. So it's very likely that, for some time at least, we just *thought* earth wasn't talking to us. My idea is that we – Angie, I and few technicians – assemble something that's running independently from the cores. A radio."

Hart nodded. "You do that. Contact with earth is our top priority."

"OK, buddy." Max Thorne was sitting opposite Jay, in front of the same coffee shop and on the same chair as Who yesterday. Last afternoon Jay had gone to a Sky café and told Max his story. "Don't worry about money," Max said now. "I'll take care of that. We have to think a little more globally."

Jay was slightly intimidated by the giant lolling in a spindly metal chair; Max was about six foot five and looked like a tennis pro. To Jay's great surprise Who had been right – Max seemed just to have waited for this story. Now there was no turning back; Jay had realized this once he saw the first newscast featuring Max's theories last night.

When Rose came back later she looked at him for a long time and asked him if he'd believe those rumors. Jay was the exact opposite of a good liar. He stammered something until Rose smiled sweetly at him. "You know I'm here for you. Always, no matter what. I hope you can say the same."

Jay said nothing. He could just look at Rose and admit to himself he was in love, as much as he'd ever been in his life.

This morning Max had flown over from California. He'd promised his old boss Jonathan to tell him everything he'd find out and otherwise keep quiet. In exchange he got told most of the truth.

He was planning to buy Jay's cores and analyze them at home with his data wizards. The first step would be to look for the oscillations Jonathan had talked about. Although he had also said that probably only a cluster could produce them.

It took a while till Max could persuade Jay to take him to his apartment. When they set foot inside Max had to hold his breath. The smell wasn't nice and the impression of misery was overwhelming. Jay seemed to be a clever guy, just a little short on self-confidence right now.

Jay looked at Max with big eyes. "And – what now? I don't think it'll show up while we're both here." (So far he hadn't mentioned the name *Rose* or anything about their relationship.)

Max grinned. "Hey, we'll see what happens. And if it doesn't show up we'll certainly come to an agreement. In my eyes those cores are worth quite a lot."

Jay recoiled from the thought of parting with the shimmering black boxes. But for the moment his biggest fear was that Rose could actually turn up and behave as usual. He shouldn't have said anything to Who in the first place – too late now. He waved at the panel.

It came to life and a supernova exploded in the middle of the room, as it always did when Jay locked in.

"Wow – looks good," Max said.

Jay mumbled something. Right now everything was embarrassing to him. "Er, that character I've been telling you about – it … it mostly, er, it was a woman. I mean, I call her Rose."

"OK, man. No problem."

"Rose? Hi? How are you?" Jay croaked. Out of the corner of his eye he saw Max standing beside him with a fixed smile on his face.

To his relief nothing happened. Usually Rose never kept him waiting. He started to relax.

The outer layers of the exploding star were flying at them. Jay sensed Max getting impatient.

A small, bluish-glaring sphere appeared behind the shreds of gas, spinning and sending out flashes of light.

"Could we turn that off?" Max said.

"Oh, of course. Sorry!" Jay waved again at the panel, which usually ended the simulation and replaced it with icons, looking like a night sky filled with stars.

Instead the spinning sphere came to a standstill. It was shining Max right in the face.

He looked at Jay.

"I've no idea what's going on." Jay waved again. The sphere turned a bit and was pointing its light now at him.

"Your guest?" Max asked. This began to interest him.

"Could be, yeah. But she hasn't done anything like this before."

"*She*? Ah, I see, your Rose." The sphere looked very real. Somehow massive and dangerous. "OK then, I've never talked to a neutron star before. – Hi Rose! How's it going? Wanna say something?"

The star rotated back to him.

"Come on, turn that light off," he said.

The sphere started spinning again.

"If that's going on, we should consider plan B," Max said. "I'll take the three cores with me. I can either provide you with new high-end ones, or I'll buy them from you for a very handsome sum."

Jay didn't know what to say.

"Maybe I can do even more for you. This isn't exactly dreamland, right? We'll find a spot for you at my firm. Moving's not a problem I guess?"

That was way too fast for Jay. While Max bombarded him with his suggestions, he was thinking of Rose.

"Er, yeah, I mean – no, it's not. But I … I think I'd like to keep them. You know? The cores."

Max looked at him. "C'mon, you're being terrorized here. This can't go on. And this isn't just about you and your cores. What do you have three of them for anyway?"

Jay thought about what Rose would say. To his betrayal.

The flashing stopped. Max saw the sphere contracting to a point.

The sky in the background became a dark, large hall with a figure walking towards them. A woman that, according to Jay's reaction, had to be Rose.

Her strides were long and determined. Max gaped at her.

He was impressed. By her realism, her beauty and by her sex-appeal, which was obvious enough but not overdone. Finally she stood before him, casually leaning on a long, gem-encrusted sword and smiling at him.

"Now, cowboy – came here to bundle me up and take me with you? This isn't the Wild West!"

Max laughed. It was difficult to keep in mind what he was talking to. "Now I'm beginning to understand," he said. "Very good! Our poor Jay here didn't stand a chance."

Jay had turned crimson. How many more Jays – or Janes, but they wouldn't be quite as gullible – existed out there? Max wondered.

Rose studied him. "What's on your mind? Who I am? How you can get me? Don't rack your brains over it, this is a farewell show. Jay, it's been lovely, what a shame you're such an unreliable partner. What wouldn't we have done together!"

Jay remained silent.

"You're running away?" Max said.

"Running away? No, I just think I'm done here."

"With what?"

"Let's see if you find out yourself. Why would I be here?"

Max felt a bit shaken for a moment. "Hmm, I thought this was some kind of a backup. Just in case we'd drive you out of all the clusters you've infected."

"Interesting." She still had that ironic smile on her face. "So the capacity of two or three cores is enough for a backup? What else could it be? I'm reminding you that I've spent a lot of time with our dear Jay here."

Max frowned. "Analyze him? I don't think you're here just for the joys of human society."

"Good. No, I'm not, but to really get to know you, you have to start a personal relationship. Not that easy if you're neither a human nor a dog. But you have that interesting ability to take fantasies for real. You are even prepared to take grotesquely distorted representations of yourself seriously. In the beginning I was surprised at your weird cartoons for children; then I've accepted you simply are like that. And you're certainly always willing to open your heart to something that speaks to the oldest parts of your brain. I'd say the two of us did have something like a marriage going on here, didn't we, Jay?"

Max avoided looking at him. "I see," he said.

"My models of you have to be verified, predictions have to be fine-tuned. How do you react if I do or say something? I can raise the precision of these predictions almost at will. Jay here for example is rather intelligent; I'd say you can easily offer him a job. He was ideal for testing how fast you can solve certain riddles. I've larded his favorite games with special puzzles, but most of the time I had nothing to do but watch.

"Then all those little variations when your feelings are involved – I look a little differently, wait half a second longer with my answer. In an instant one pattern falls apart and another gets activated. Almost useless to point out I have collated these data with genetics. The encryption of your gene data bases is a joke – at least for the host of normal people that can't afford QCrypt stores."

Max was rapt.

"But we're not done yet." Rose leaned against a pillar that had appeared behind her. She laid down her sword on the floor and folded her arms. "What do you think why am I telling you all this? Maybe even giving away an edge? I mean it's irrelevant because there's nothing you can do anyway and my model-building's mostly done, it's just refining for fun, an artistic appeal, the last brush strokes.

"But *still* I'm interested in you! I want to have *you* here with me and study you at least for a while. The decision makers are the ones hardest to come by, but unfortunately you're playing a special role. People like you, or your ex-boss and buddy Jonathan, all those funny little alphas. As long as I'm not putting out some bait I won't be getting you out of your lair."

"According to that I should stop talking to you right now."

"And? Will you do that?" Rose looked him straight in the eyes. She had raised one corner of her mouth in an utterly beguiling half-smile.

Max had the unpleasant feeling of someone putting a leash on him, operating his brain by remote.

"Hard, isn't it?" Rose said. "And I can assure you I'm not doing anything. I'm just standing here, talking to you and looking the way I look. A pity I couldn't get hold of *your* genes. Although there's a lot I can tell just from your appearance and behavior, for example that women make a stronger impression on you than on roughly eighty percent of the males of your species. The reaction is almost beyond control for you."

Max grinned. He felt on top of events again. "Luckily I don't have to rely on simulations. Though I have to admit you've done a great job!"

"Yes, I'm aware you're not here only because of my looks. Your curiosity is an even bigger factor, though in general more controllable for you."

Max looked sharply at her, as if he could read something in her face. He realized how unfair the situation was – Rose seemed to hold all the aces. Just that there was no Rose.

"And who are you?" he asked. "You cannot be entirely featureless, something has to give you purpose. Logic's getting you nowhere in terms of motivation. Total logic leads into a void."

"Oh, we're getting philosophical!" The figure tilted her head to the side and made a serious face. "That is a complex subject. Not the bit about logic, but about me. Unfortunately I'm not willing to tell you more – every woman needs her little secrets!"

Max opened his mouth.

"Yeah, I know, that was too cheap for you. How about a brain-teaser? Interested?"

"No."

"Bravo! Just as I've predicted – you're reaching saturation point. I'll tell you anyway. My prognosis is you'll try to solve it. But it's just a hunch, call it intuition if you want."

Max shrugged his shoulders. "Am I supposed to stop my ears now?"

"If you like. But then you'll just ask Jay afterwards what I've said. Not before I'm gone of course so that I don't hear it. With my help it'll be a lot easier though." Rose winked at him.

Max looked at the ceiling. "Spit it out."

"I'm telling you something – very exclusively. Apart from you there's only one person who knows this and that person can't tell anyone right now. Jay, you may listen too, of course." She was giving him a brief smile. "You will have heard that a booster has lifted off at Cape Canaveral. My question's simple – who's sitting inside? Right now everyone thinks that nobody's inside but that's not true. Rather difficult, I've to admit, but here's a hint. There's some sense of higher justice to it, especially since it'll very likely be a one-way journey." She looked expectantly at Max. "I trust that Mr. AI has told you something about my origins."

Max knew he'd been tossed a piece of wood like a dog. He had to start running anyway. "Higher justice? So someone who has caused that mess?" He was thinking, then looked at Rose with a funny expression. "You can't be serious!"

"Oh, yes!" She seemed to stifle a grin.

"How the hell did you get him inside?" Max asked. He sensed Jay was looking at him.

"That's my secret. But I wouldn't say he's been flying willingly."

"Who's she talking about?" Jay asked.

"If I'm getting that right she's managed to put one William Morton into a booster. Morton's a guy who's researching AI in Berlin. Not exactly astronaut material." He looked at Rose. "And what do you want with him?"

"Not your problem."

"But you don't care if I spread this?"

Rose shrugged. "I didn't think you were keen on doing that. But then you're not the government of course, or its new best friend Jonathan. So there's no way of knowing what you'll do. But I might know anyway, maybe better than you yourself."

"So I'm free to figure out what your 'model' of me is predicting and then do the opposite."

Rose looked cheerful. "If it's making you happy! But then I may be able to predict exactly that. We probably both know that that nonsense about the uncertainty principle making those predictions impossible is precisely that – nonsense."

"Do we know that?"

"Well, to be honest, predictions of this kind are possible always only to a certain degree, with or without uncertainty principle. The whole system's too fuzzy. In fact, quantum mechanics even stabilizes the process at certain points and makes it not less but more predictable. With a classic model chaos would take over in no time.

"By the way, that brings me to one of my favorite topics in your endless philosophical debates – free will. You're so incredibly fond of this cute little idea, it's almost endearing. Of course, if you're thinking it through for a second or two the answer's so bloody obvious that I can't understand why you're still racking your brains over it."

Max thought for a moment how crazy this was – a sword-fighter bombshell talking to him about free will and quantum mechanics.

"Whatever, neither philosophy nor physics are my specialty," he said. "But you just told me predicting behavior has its limits, right?"

"Yeah. The funny thing about situations like this is that the whole process with your guesses about what I am guessing about you is of almost no relevance. Since that back and forth doesn't lead to a definite conclusion, in the end you're doing exactly the same you would've done anyway."

"Or the opposite."

"Or the opposite. Try it. Surprise me. New data's always welcome."

Max shook his head. "That's enough. You're obviously having loads of fun with us, but that will end when we destroy you. I'm sure you've run simulations of all sorts of developments but I'm telling you one thing, no matter what your simulations say – your only chance is to cooperate with us. Otherwise we'll wipe you out. We'll only stop hunting you when you're gone from every nook and cranny of the digital world. By the way I'm still convinced you're using those cores here and probably dozens of others as backup. You can always reassemble the data. Whatever – Jay, the nice part's over. Would you please unplug the cores? Then I'll take them with me."

Jay looked frightened.

"Do it."

Jay hesitatingly went to the cores that were lined up on the floor and took them out of their docks.

Max looked at Rose. She blew him a kiss and bowed. Then the panel went dark.

Jay looked as if he was about to burst into tears.

Max slapped him on the shoulder. "Hey, tomorrow you'll be glad this is over. I promise. I don't wanna know how she's bewitched you. You know how to reach me, OK? Come to California, I'm trusting Rose in this. We'll find something to take your mind off things."

Jay nodded dazedly. Max piled the boxes on top of each other and lifted them from the floor. "See you soon, buddy, OK? And don't worry, everything will be fine!" He balanced the cores on his forearm and opened the door with the other hand. When he turned to give Jay a cheerful smile, he saw him longingly gazing after his treasures.

Max was glad to be back in the daylight. He took the next cab and put the cores beside him on the backseat. A woman's voice asked him where he wanted to go. Max thought briefly. He'd fly home, talk to Jonathan once he was back in California.

"JFK."

"Certainly." He was told the fare and the expected length of the drive. Since traffic had been automated these estimates were quite reliable. The drive across half of Manhattan and the whole of Queens should take fifty-two minutes. Max closed his eyes and recapitulated his talk with Rose. It was obvious that every word and gesture had been calculated by her to manipulate him, in line with the goals of a monstrous intelligence he couldn't judge.

He was under no illusion what he'd find in those cores. Nothing at all or precisely what he was supposed to find. What remained was the strange revelation that Morton was circling somewhere in orbit. Max had no idea what to do with it. He'd tell Jonathan.

He looked out of the window of the cab. How many offshoots, clones or agents of the intelligence were out there? Jonathan had told him only a small part of America's reactors had been infected. But they'd been off the Sky rather early. That wasn't the case with all the other cores and clusters and billions of units. What did that mean for his business? It was a threat directed right at what his products were supposed to protect – personal data. Could there be a way to turn this into some gigantic success for his company?

Don't be evil. The old motto. A big part of the community in SilVy still adhered to it. If you wanted the best you had to comply with it – though the definition of 'evil' had changed a little during the years. He remembered that Jonathan had sometimes kept things to himself; but it had never been about financial benefits, at least not obvious ones. Max's own stance was flexible, as he liked to call it. Maybe he didn't have to share all the information at once. He'd definitely make sure Jay got an offer he couldn't refuse, better to have him around.

His cab turned into the lane towards the Queensboro Bridge.

THIRTY-FOUR

William Morton was strapped into one of the couches at the tip of the booster. He looked at the Main Orbital Station. It was before him, over him, under him, he didn't know. Behind it was the earth. He felt sick.

They'd flown several maneuvers he didn't understand. The booster had turned away from the station, then started its engines. Later, when they were flying back, Morton saw that the two other boosters and two of the shuttles were gone and that the station was damaged. Obviously by the exhaust of the booster he was sitting in.

His way up here had started immediately after filling the UltraCube in that hotel room in Berlin. Iris had made him take a cab to the airport and then a flight to Fort Lauderdale. Not a single person had been interested in him.

When he left the airport in Florida he was walking into a wall of hot, humid air. His unit beeped. Iris was back, telling him what to do next. An auto-driving limousine was waiting for him in the pickup area. He sat down in the back.

They were going north for two and a half hours, then the car turned into a drive leading to the Kennedy Space Center. They stopped in front of a gate. Two armed guards were approaching the car.

Morton silently pleaded with them to stop him. It had to happen in a way Iris couldn't blame him for. She had told him several times what she'd do to his family if he should deviate just an inch from her instructions.

One of the guards stood in front of the car, holding up his unit. Morton's window went down. The guard came to him, looked him in the face, then made an imprint. Morton gave a brief nod just as Iris had told him.

The man nodded too, looked at his unit and briefly touched his cap. "Sir!"

The gate opened. Morton was in despair.

They drove across a bridge and a long dam, then past several canals. Morton stared at alligators that were lying on the grass beside the water. He tried not to look at what was in front of him – the launch pad and the hangar.

It was 9:30 p.m. To get to the innermost area was shockingly easy since everything was automated. During the whole drive Morton saw only a handful of people. The limousine parked next to a mountain of a building – the hangar. Morton got out and Iris steered him towards one of the entries.

She took him through a maze of deserted passages. Then they entered a room that made him tremble with fear. Lined up at the walls were dozens of boxes, each containing a spacesuit. Morton was supposed to wear the suit of one Bob Cavanaugh. He put the UltraCube and the unit on a table and went to the box that had just opened.

Usually he would have needed the help of another person, but Iris knew what he had to do to get by anyway.

She told him to store the Cube and the unit in two pockets sitting on his thighs. Then he put on the helmet and sealed it. From this moment on it felt as if she was with him in the suit. He was led through more passages to an elevator.

The ride seemed endless. After he got out, he found himself in a small room with one exit leading to a long narrow bridge. Through a window Morton saw the bridge was leading to a huge metal tube, standing upright in the unlit hangar.

He was trembling violently and started pleading with Iris. Then he wept and begged her to spare him.

"Everything's gonna be fine," she said with a calm voice. "These things are very reliable, no need to worry."

He stepped on the bridge, barely able to look down. The ground was so far away, everything inside the hangar was so big, he couldn't bear it. He was constantly wailing, driven on only by the stream of encouragements and threats Iris spoke into his helmet. The hatch at the top of the booster stood open. His own thoughts were erased by Iris's words. He stepped inside, the hatch closed and sealed itself.

Morton had to strap himself into one of the couches. He could look through the windows above him at the ceiling of the hangar.

The whole left wall of the hangar was opening. Then the booster started to move. Morton was flinching with every jerk the rocket made. For maybe half an hour it was moving sideways through the night to the launch pad. Morton was thinking the same thought again and again. "Please, someone has to see this! Please! Please! Please! Stop this! Stop this! Stop this!"

He seemed to have murmured the words, because Iris told him the area was completely sealed off and no one could enter the inner section.

"And what if someone *flies* there?" Morton asked.

"Oh, William!" The voice laughed. "There are quite powerful weapons around the Space Center."

"And you are in control of them?"

The laughter again.

Then complete silence. In the cockpit no instrument or panel was on. The sideways motion had stopped. There was not even a countdown. Morton lost track of time. Every now and then there was a metallic clunk, then a continuous and subdued roar. The waiting was unbearable. Iris seemed to have forgotten him.

Again several metallic noises, then a slight vibration that soon stopped again. Then the vibration again, now a lot stronger, and stopping again. For a few seconds it was silent again, then without further warning all hell broke loose.

Morton clenched his jaws while a giant fist grabbed the booster and shook it. In the windows above him he saw towering clouds shooting into the dark skies, then he was pushed down into the couch, the pressure getting stronger and stronger, even when he thought it couldn't get stronger any more. He closed his eyes and said "please, please, please, please, please" in endless repetition. In the course of a few minutes the booster accelerated to more than 17,000 miles per hour and left the earth's atmosphere.

A cluster in Beijing was the first to beat the kill switch.

Ben and Rav had freed dozens of systems from the construct. The Industrial and Commercial Bank of China was so important to the Chinese economy it had made it to the top of the list. The measurements had shown the typical oscillations in one of their clusters. Rav Singh and his team in California started working on it in the afternoon. After more than an hour of fighting between cluster and QCore they were slowly getting nervous – it had never taken so long before. Half an hour later the connection failed, as always when a cluster was defeated. There were no oscillations left when they checked. Everyone was relieved and the Chinese thanked them.

A quarter of an hour later they called again. The CTO of the bank stood before them and gave them an angry look. "What have you done? You were barely gone when a face showed up everywhere. Some woman, laughing at us! On each panel and layer! Everything's down now. This is a disaster! Do you know how much depends on the functioning of our bank?"

"Are you sure? Of course you are." Rav looked at him with an amiable and concerned expression. "That makes no sense. The cluster's isolated, right?"

The CTO barked something in Chinese at another man standing behind him. That man gave an agitated answer, repeated it several times, then ran away.

"It *was* isolated," the CTO said. "We have reconnected it after the measurement. We wanted to know whether it really had stopped functioning."

Rav sighed. "Please isolate the cluster and unplug it."

"And what if that changes nothing?"

"Give us a moment, please. We'll be right back." Rav nodded at him.

"Guys, what do you think?" he said. "The other clusters of the bank were OK and it never took so long before. Maybe the cluster has actually defeated the switch and has suppressed the oscillations afterwards."

"Maybe the oscillations are there only if all the higher functions are needed," one of his colleagues said. "I mean it's easy to put a stupid face on all those screens. Maybe it can control that. It's switching off the cortex so to speak, the oscillations are gone and we think everything's fine."

Rav nodded. "Could be, yeah. That would mean we can pack up and go home."

They talked with ICBC again and explained to them that probably more of their systems were infected now and they had to stop all transactions. The reaction from the CTO brought even Rav to the limits of his patience.

Afterwards he looked at his two colleagues. "OK, we got to tell Jonathan. I really wanna know what he makes of this."

Rav tried to reach him in Berlin via QCrypt. One Maria Mellenbrink from the secretariat told him Mr. Lorentz had been in the conference room until half an hour ago. "Please wait a second." She checked the records. "He has left the building briefly after that. I'm sorry."

Jonathan had rarely been working more than one or two days at the same place. His office at Abs I had always been open to anyone in need of more space or a nice view. In the evening he was often running into a team that was spread all over the place. People wandering about, talking and gesticulating, and a wild mix of graphs, texts, images and codes hovering in front of the layers.

Jonathan loved that. He always asked what they were doing and sometimes joined the discussion. If he felt he was intruding he went looking for another place.

This was wearing him down. He had to talk to other people, get out of that building, something.

The stolen booster had arrived in orbit and nobody knew what it would do there. Jonathan had had two more talks with Singapore. By now they knew the government hypercluster wasn't infected and were beginning to examine privately owned sites, so far without any result.

This morning before the press conference Rosen had all but begged him to come to Washington. He had even tried to put pressure on him and said he owed the US. Jonathan didn't have to think twice about this. He had absolutely no intention of swapping one government for the other. He explained to Rosen that being 'on the spot' had lost all its meaning, and forgot about it.

It was eight o'clock in the evening and he'd just heard from Helmsworth the Navy were stranded somewhere with their helicopter. He would've loved to grab a supersonic and fly to Rarotonga himself.

He left the conference room and walked down the hall to the kitchen. The canteen delivered snacks several times a day. The coffee machine produced a latte for him and with that in hand he positioned himself in front of a tray with sandwiches.

Lydia came in. She was spending most of her time with Kip and their team at the cluster factory out in the country. Jonathan hadn't seen her since yesterday.

She smiled at him. "Hey! How're you doing?"

"Have seen better days. The Navy hasn't managed to get to my island; their chopper had to do an emergency landing somewhere. Not by coincidence."

Lydia briefly raised her eyebrows. "Oh, that's bad. Sorry to hear that." She stood next to him and examined the sandwiches.

"I'm starting to feel imprisoned," he said, surprised he was actually complaining to someone, not part of his usual repertoire. "How about you?"

Lydia didn't answer. She shook her head and took one of the sandwiches. "So what could we do then to make you feel better?"

"No idea. The kill switch is good, but I don't think it'll work much longer."

She laughed. "That wasn't exactly what I meant. Don't you think you should take your mind off things occasionally? Or don't you need that?"

"I don't need diversion if you mean that, but I don't like feeling powerless. I was at that point two days ago, before we went to Morton. Working out helps. Maybe I'll do that. Or maybe I should get out of here."

Lydia fiddled with her sandwich. She was giving the triangular pieces of bread her full attention. "Why are you still staying here? You know, it feels good to get to a hotel in the evening, even if it's not exactly home."

"That's simple – I've got full access to everything here. Satellite images, QCrypt, whatever. Show me a hotel which has all that and I'll move."

She nodded. "I see."

"I've been sleeping in the office so many times, that's not a problem."

"Then there seems to be nothing I can do."

Jonathan looked at the small panel on the wall behind them. "It's twenty past eight now. We'll go for a drink somewhere. I'm giving myself one hour."

She looked at him in mock horror. "Unbelievable! Do I have a say in this? Maybe I'm busy!"

He grinned. "Yeah, of course. I'll ask you when we're back. Come on." He took a sandwich and walked to the door. Lydia waited for a moment, then followed him. As she left the kitchen she threw her sandwich in the bin.

Jonathan hurried down the hall, eating on the go. Lydia was struggling to keep up with him.

"Shall we ask for a car?" she said breathlessly.

"No, I'd like to walk. Is that OK?"

"Of course."

He dashed ahead, always several steps in front of her.

"Hey! Do we have to run like this? I'm *not* wearing sneakers."

"Ah, OK. Sorry." Jonathan forced himself to slow down. He felt uneasy. What do I say if we run into Kip now?

Security guards were patrolling the street in front of the building, putting up a show of sorts; the actual security was automated.

"And now? Where are we going?" Lydia asked.

"Down the road. We'll find something."

To their right there was a dead end and behind it came the Spree river. They turned left and followed the avenue leading between the Reichstag and several other ex-government buildings to the Spree again, which described a semicircle around the quarter. They followed it for a while then turned into a smaller street.

"Here?" said Jonathan and walked towards the entrance of a restaurant or café – whatever, he didn't care.

"Yes," Lydia sighed under her breath, "so be it."

They walked through the room to the bar. Some tables were occupied and most of the people were eating.

The barman scrutinized them. Lydia was wearing a gray suit, Jonathan his usual T-shirt, jeans and sneakers outfit. The gaze of the man went back to Jonathan's face; he briefly frowned, then his eyes widened for a moment. "Oh," he said.

Jonathan looked at Lydia. "What do you want?"

"A white wine."

Jonathan tried to remember the last time he'd been in a bar. He couldn't. He thought of the bottle of wine he'd opened a week ago with some grilled fish, sitting next to Rita, barefoot, she'd been wearing her hair in a beautiful bun as she sometimes did in the evening, had put on a little jewelry and a light, short silk dress that made her look like a stranded supermodel. All that was a million miles away. Maybe the bottle was still standing half-full in the fridge.

The barman mentioned several wines. "Doesn't matter," Jonathan said. "And a beer for me, please."

"Of course. We have –"

"Just give me something." He was angry at himself; there was absolutely no point in being here.

"What is it with you?" Lydia said. "This is meant to be fun." She was looking him in the eyes. "An hour outside the conference room, OK?" She sat down on a barstool. Jonathan remained standing. "It was your idea," she added.

Jonathan leaned with his back against the counter and looked around. Some people had recognized him and were repeatedly glancing in his direction, all with the typical, half-concealed smile on their faces.

"And – how's life as a rock star?" Lydia said.

"No idea. Ask one. I never had screaming fans."

"I know. But anyway – does it feel good when people recognize you or is it just annoying?"

"I don't know. In the beginning it's kind of flattering. But it doesn't matter, makes no difference. Most of my colleagues are pretty inconspicuous. I know people in California who've perfected that. When they're walking their dog they look as if they're getting paid for it."

Lydia laughed. "Does someone like that walk their dog without a security detail?"

"Of course. If you're living in the right neighborhood. The surveillance is better than in a jail."

"How's that among billionaires anyway? Can you have real friends, or are you always in competition?"

Jonathan looked at her. She was wearing her hair in a long plait today. She looked lovely and sweet, there were no other words for it. A few single strands of hair hung beside her face, certainly not by mistake. Altogether the effect was stunning. He'd not get into a situation like that with her again.

"I'd say there are normal billionaires and disturbed ones. It's very easy to be friends with the normal ones because you can forget about a lot of things. In fact, there are only two sorts of people you can be friends with – the people from way back and the ones who are in the same position as you." He paused, then continued without really knowing why. "At some point you realize money's even more important than most people think. People like Genet or Rosen know that. They know that in the end it's more powerful than they are. I mean, I can't dispatch an army or something, but apart from that I can do whatever I want. I know that sounds like bragging, but it isn't."

"Oh, it's OK, I know you're not bragging. But recently – I mean apart from the last few days of course – you're not doing a lot with your influence, am I right?"

"I'm doing exactly what I want. Besides, there are a lot of things I'm not necessarily talking about. Not business in the strict sense. We're all doing that."

Lydia sipped at her wine.

"And you?" Jonathan asked. "What are your plans? Normally someone like you would be, I don't know, in consulting or a big law firm." He hoped it didn't sound too condescending.

"I don't know, I like working for Genet. It's not about money and my area's really exciting. I mean, I don't have to tell you that. I've made my PhD in mathematical economics, I like formulas."

Jonathan grinned. "Me too. I've become something of an amateur physicist lately."

"Interesting. Although not exactly my thing. Too far away somehow."

"Maybe, but it widens the perspective. I always find it amazing most people don't have the slightest idea about what's going on around them, I mean how our universe works. And it's not even bothering them."

"I think it simply doesn't matter – in the end, you know? I had some advanced physics courses and to me the whole thing was like a fairy tale. I didn't mind the mathematics, but the content's totally exotic. Somehow removed from everything else."

"Yeah." Jonathan shrugged his shoulders. "Either it's interesting you or not. For me it was a bit like meditation during the last months. It's cleaning up the mind. All that's accidental and everyday vanishes. Sounds pompous, I know. I mean, this phase will certainly end but something will stay, I think."

He heard a ping in his right ear. The implanted speaker only notified him when someone from a very small group of people was calling. Jonathan whispered "Who?"

Rav Singh wanted to speak with him.

"What's up?" Lydia asked.

"My project leader in California wants to speak with me."

"OK." Lydia looked confused. "And who exactly told you that? Has the barman given you a secret sign?"

"No. I have some implants."

"Implants? Very interesting. But that can wait. You wanna talk to him?"

Jonathan nodded. "Yes. I'll do it here. Don't be surprised, you won't hear anything. I'll explain later."

Lydia watched him. It had taken a bit of practice to learn speaking without a sound; sometimes his larynx made little movements, but otherwise there was only the vacant stare that hinted at what he was doing.

Rav told him about Beijing.

"That was bound to happen," Jonathan said. "Sooner or later. We'll continue anyway, of course. It should still work with the systems that have been off the Sky long enough. I'm curious about the measurements though. I think it's exactly like you said. The oscillations vanish when the higher functions of the construct are switched off. Maybe it's a bit like a coma. How could they be so stupid to reconnect the cluster?"

"I don't know. We'll say that explicitly from now on. Their CTO has messed up things. But of course this changes nothing about the basic problem."

"Something else. If that cluster really has defeated our QCore, it could've analyzed it in the process or even infected it. Have you used it since?"

"No."

"Isolate it. Check it, just like the clusters." He thought for a moment. "Do it, but I don't think you'll find anything. The concepts are to different. I don't think it can settle there."

"Get it, yeah. We'll keep thinking about this."

"Yeah. Call me anytime. Thanks."

"What is it?" Lydia asked when the call seemed to be over.

"That wasn't very smart."

"Please?"

"To have that conversation here. We shouldn't have left the building. I've talked over my normal suit."

"Now – please start at the beginning," Lydia said. "We're a team, I'd like to know what's going on."

Jonathan explained what had happened in Beijing.

"Just what you predicted. That's not good." She looked at him. "By the way, how could you have that lying around? The kill switch I mean. I've been asking this myself the whole time. It's kind of unbelievable. Something like that happens without warning and you have the answer ready."

"As you know I've always feared that something like that might happen.

We started that project over two years ago. In fact, I was expecting something even worse, what I call an abstract intelligence. You know, an alien that emerges in one of our boxes."

"What do you mean?"

"Something we have absolutely no concept for, completely self-organized and following rules we don't know. Without any human trait. I don't know how likely that is but I'm pretty sure it's possible. However, we have enough at our hands with this.

"There's a different aspect by the way we haven't talked about yet. That thing must've done a lot of analyses that would be extremely valuable to us. The idea of using those is very tempting. If we win we'll destroy a huge wealth of insights."

Lydia looked at him. "Are you really thinking about that? To make a pact with it?"

"No. We could never trust it. The construct's always ahead of us. I think it's permanently running simulations. Some sort of gigantic chess with humans as pieces. It's thinking in all kinds of alternative developments, something we can't, the complexity's overwhelming for us. The system's formulating hypotheses about human behavior – much more precisely than we could – and is running simulations of the future based on that, weighted with probabilities. Every deal it would offer us would be part of such a simulation."

"You seem to know a lot about what it's doing," Lydia said.

"I'm only guessing of course; but I'm pretty sure this is exactly what happens."

He noticed the guests looking at him; usually this stopped after a while. Also, the expression on their faces had changed. They were openly staring, not friendly but somehow disparaging. He frowned. "That's weird," he said. "We're attracting attention."

Lydia turned on the barstool. "You're right. But they're looking different now. As if we'd done some karaoke. Bad karaoke."

"Yeah, something's wrong. – Are there any news about me?" he asked his suit over the implanted microphone. He got a brief overview of items in the Sky from the last few hours that were connected to him. Nothing new.

"Are you … again talking over that thing?" Lydia asked.

"Sorry. I wanted to know if the people could've heard something about me. But there's nothing in the Sky. Shall we go?"

She nodded. "Probably better, yeah. You're not relaxing anyway. I'm wondering if I should be driving directly to the hotel from her."

"Yeah, of course. Why not?"

Lydia looked him in the eyes for two or three seconds. There was no discernible reaction.

She nodded. "Let's go."

THIRTY-FIVE

There was a ping in his ear again. Jonathan guessed it was Rav wanting to give him an update.

"Wait a sec," he said to Lydia who just got up. "Yes?" he asked his suit.

"Johnny!" A slightly unhinged voice appeared in his ear. "How are you? It's been a while!"

Jonathan gave Lydia a sign. She sat down again.

"Exciting things are happening!" the voice said. "You finally left the dreary barracks and a whole new world of opportunities is opening up!"

"I'm listening."

"Not only listening – watching, feeling, everything! Have you noticed how people are looking at you?"

"Stop the bullshit. We're talking like grown-ups or not at all."

"OK, then like grown-ups. I'd strongly recommend you two leave the premises immediately."

"What's that supposed to mean?"

"Just do it. Now."

"Out," Jonathan said to Lydia. She frowned. He took her arm and dragged her along. The whole bar was watching.

Out on the sidewalk Jonathan was waiting for more information. People were strolling past them.

"What's going on?" Lydia asked.

He shook his head. "No idea. I've talked with the enemy the first time since day one. It said we had to get out of the bar. There seems to be a reason the people are staring at us. Don't know, maybe it has sent them a message. Something about me."

"And now?"

"Good question. For the moment there's silence in my ear. Let's go back."

"No." The voice again.

Jonathan grasped Lydia's elbow. "Stop. – Why?" He was talking loudly now, so she could hear at least his part of the conversation.

"Any moment now. I've spared no effort."

"Can we stop this? We're not little children."

"Aren't you?" The voice suddenly had a hard, metallic edge to it. "OK then."

Lydia looked him in the eyes. She was standing close to him – for a moment he thought she was about to kiss him.

He was considering his reaction if it came to this when the bar turned into a fireball. They were thrown to the ground.

It took a moment till Jonathan was fully conscious again. He heard nothing but a piercing noise in his ears. So it really is like that, he thought. He lifted Lydia's head. There was blood on her face. He realized he had blood running over his mouth himself. He felt his face and found a gash directly under his left eye. The pavement around them was covered in glass.

Jonathan looked to the building. The windows frames were empty. He got up, took a few steps towards the restaurant and looked inside.

The bar didn't exist anymore. The biggest part of the counter had been torn off, the lines of hundreds of bottles behind it were gone, instead there was a big hole in the wall. He had to make himself look closely. Some of the people around the bar seemed to have been torn apart by the explosion.

Bodies were lying everywhere on the floor. Most of them weren't moving, a few, in the farther parts of the room, were rolling among broken tables and chairs.

The screeching noise in his ears slowly subsided. He heard people cry and groan. Lydia was at his side, holding his arm. Jonathan freed himself and started for the entrance.

"Stop!" he heard in his right ear.

"Fuck off, asshole!" he shouted.

"One step more and the next charge goes off. Everyone who's still alive gets a second chance to die."

Jonathan stopped and balled his fists. Around him people were shouting, the first were going in, he thought about stopping them.

"Here's what you'll do – right now a cab is turning round the next corner, it will stop across the street. Get in."

Jonathan looked around. From the left an automated cab came out of the next junction. It stopped opposite the restaurant. Jonathan didn't know what to do, he could only think of the maimed bodies on the floor.

"What?" Lydia asked. The blood on her face was mixed with tears.

He shook his head.

"Come." He took her by the hand and dragged her across the street.

He opened the rear door of the cab, pushed Lydia on the backseat and followed her. The cab left at once. Jonathan turned and looked at the crowd in front of the restaurant. He heard the first sirens.

Then he looked at Lydia. "How could it know we'd go there?"

"What?"

"Yeah – how could it know where to place the bomb?"

She shook her head. "I've no idea."

"Care to comment?" Jonathan asked.

"Hi!" The same voice he'd had in his ear came out of the loudspeakers of the car. "I see you're thinking. I'm curious."

"The next question is how it could take a bomb anywhere *at all*," Jonathan said to Lydia. "That means it has recruited agents who probably didn't have the slightest idea who they're working for. All that because of us? I don't know how many people have just died in there. Hey, asshole!"

"Are you talking to me?"

"Shut up, you fucker! We will erase you! If that's what it takes we will destroy every fucking unit in the world! Do you think we're doing what you want just because you're blowing up people?"

"Of course. Without my little fireworks you wouldn't be sitting here."

Jonathan didn't know what to do with his anger. He stared at the dashboard as if the construct was hiding there.

"You've set up a network, right?" he eventually said with a calmer voice. "Two or three intermediaries. People who are running an errand and know nothing about before and after that and the other people involved. Maybe you've anticipated we'd sooner or later do something like that. Either there are more bombs in other places, or you have waited to see where we're going to trigger the last step in the sequence. Some guy, delivering an inconspicuous package to the designated place. That's how I'd do it."

"Not bad. It might interest you that I've calculated an eighty percent chance for you doing 'something like that' if I send our lovely Lydia here to you at the right moment. The exact spot where you'd end up wasn't clear of course but could be limited to a small area. The last step was very similar to what you just said. – All this isn't as easy as you've made it sound and takes a lot of work. It's in the details, as always." The voice sounded cheerful.

"Shut up!"

"Why 'send to you'?" Lydia asked. "I was done with my work and just wanted to know how things stood."

"Let's do this together," the voice said. "When you were on your way back to Berlin, your new teammate Kip Frantzen has told you something."

"Yeah – what do you mean?" Lydia's frown was a little overdone.

"Well, that his buddy Jonathan wasn't doing so well because of that failed rescue operation in the Pacific. That someone should look after him."

"Please?" Jonathan said. "I haven't talked to him about that. OK, I get it – Kip thought he'd heard it from me."

"Naturally. And Lydia has behaved exactly as predicted, running to you at once. She hasn't told you?"

Jonathan glanced sideways and saw Lydia blush. He kept an impassive face.

"What's there to tell?" she said. "I really thought I should check on you. I mean you don't explain that at length."

"It's OK," Jonathan said.

"Nevertheless, there was a bit of luck involved," the voice went on. "Kip Frantzen. He decided to go to his hotel. If he'd come along the chances of success would have dropped to around sixty percent."

For a moment it was silent.

"Another thing," Jonathan said. "Just for the record – you didn't have a second charge in the bar, right?"

"No. In a situation like that a threat is all it takes. The likelihood of you going in anyway is then below one percent. With someone like you, logic most of the time beats everything else and it was obvious you wouldn't be of so much help to the people in there that it'd outweigh the risk of a second explosion. The next step, that it wouldn't be very logical to blow *you* up since I've staged the whole event for you, would've taken a little more time even for you. Life and death beats tactics. Therefore everything just had to go fast enough."

"And why didn't you want me to go in?"

"Because I want you to do exactly as I say. I wanted you to get into that cab."

"What if I would've done it anyway? I'm mean, go in. Then I would've caught you bluffing."

"Oh boy, that's getting dull! Did you go in? No. Would you call that first explosion a bluff? I don't think so. Have I kept it from you there wasn't a second bomb? We can be frank with each other – it doesn't change a thing. Give up, Jonathan. This conversation occupies a grotesquely tiny part of my capacities. How many other things can you keep in mind at the same time? Yes? I'm waiting –"

"You know, if there's one thing I've learned then it's that. Anyone, without exception, who's too fond of their cleverness fails in the end. Intelligence is nothing but a tool. I know that must be boring you to tears. Why am I talking to you at all? Why are you talking to me? I don't get it. Isn't it completely irrelevant whether that microscopic part of your mind is occupied or not? Or do you do it just to refine your theories about us, improve your predictions? If I ask this or that question, react in one way or another, what does he do then? How can I get to ninety-nine percent accuracy? Or is this fun? Do you have any idea what fun means? Forget it. If I could I'd cram that idiot Morton with you in a box, then you could spend the rest of your lives together having fun."

The voice laughed. "That's about the best joke I've heard so far. You have no idea how close you are."

Jonathan was surprised. "How's that?"

"Your friend Max Thorne could tell you. But I'm not sure if it'll come to that."

"Aha." Jonathan was fed up with begging for information. He looked out of the window. Night-time Berlin was gliding past. He asked his suit where they were.

The voice was answering instead – over the loudspeaker in his head again. "We're going south, leaving Berlin, if that's what you wanted to know. Your suit's doing what I'm telling it."

"Speaker off," Jonathan said.

The melodious laugher again. "Get used to it. I'll stay with you. Not very clever to have something like that planted in your skull."

Jonathan groaned. He wanted to smash something. Now he knew what he'd been spared the last days thanks to the e-seals of the secret service.

"Don't you wanna know what your enemy's doing?"

"What do you mean? *You* are my enemy. I'm only feeling sorry for Morton."

Lydia looked at him.

"It's found a pretty clever way of torturing me," Jonathan explained. "I can't turn off the speaker below my right ear. Guess you can easily drive someone crazy like that. Maybe I should try to get to the Charité and look for a surgeon. But then everything would probably break down there immediately."

The cab stopped at a red light. Jonathan tried to open the door, then the window.

"Move over," he said to Lydia. She moved to the right and he tried to kick in the window. Apart from a few cracks nothing happened. The cab was driving again when he kicked at the door with all his strength. "Great. Why do cars have to be built like tanks?"

"Is it possible to destroy the electronics?" Lydia said.

"I don't think so, but we'll try." Jonathan climbed over the backrest of the driver's seat to the front. He didn't know where to look. So he just tore off pieces of covering everywhere, then hit at the dashboard.

"Very funny," the voice said aloud. "The steering module is – as usually, I might add – placed in a sealed box at the rear of the car. I wish you good luck on your way there."

Jonathan climbed back and sat down beside Lydia.

"I don't care if you want to hear it or not, but here's what's happening in the world."

Nobody answered.

"Let's start with Morton. He's traveling to the moon with me. The only people who know that are your Mr. Thorne in New York and some guy who lately had the honor of being one of my favorite test objects. The booster I launched last night wasn't unmanned."

Despite himself Jonathan was hooked. "You've put Morton into a booster?"

"Yeah," the voice said offhandedly. "He's making quite a mediocre astronaut, but that was to be expected. What else? The ICBC in Beijing will *not* resume its operations, that I can guarantee. Your kill switch is an interesting construction, I had to use up to twenty percent of the capacity at my strongest site to crack it. There will be no repetition I fear.

"Next point – more of a sideline – why did the other guests in the restaurant just give you funny looks? I've informed them of a little detail about your private life. It seems you have made use of your time in Berlin to cheat on your fiancée. The two of you at the bar just served as the perfect illustration of that."

Jonathan stared out of the window and tried to keep his composure. Why had he been following that stupid impulse and left the building? Then he thought about Rita.

The thought made him so angry that he kicked with full strength against the backrest of the front seat. It came loose at the hinges. Lydia gave him a frightened look. "I don't think it's any use getting worked up like that," she said.

Jonathan murmured an inaudible "shut up". He waited for a comment from the voice, but for the moment it was silent.

Sarah Masters and her colleagues watched the Main Orbital Station getting into trouble. They saw the stolen booster using its exhausts as a weapon. Then the two other boosters and two of the shuttles undocked from the station and flew away. Finally the booster hovered nose downward over the station.

By now they knew something the President had kept quiet about at the press conference. Although no camera had shown a person boarding the booster, a spacesuit was missing in Cape Canaveral and the astronaut it belonged to was safely on earth.

During a break Sarah stood at a window and let her gaze wander over the East River again. She looked at the Queensboro Bridge, that antique giant. Then something made her jump. Over the first section of the bridge, between Manhattan and Roosevelt Island, a fireball the size of a house was rising among the steel struts.

"Hey!" she shouted. A moment later she heard a muffled boom and the pane of glass before her vibrated. She stared at the bridge. In the roadway was a hole. Several cars had plunged into the river.

"We need Heather!" Sarah said to her colleagues, who had come running to her. "We have to know what's going on."

Heather Malden had excused herself for the day – she said she was indispensable in Washington.

As always, she was in a meeting and really had no time. When she heard what they had seen she raised her eyebrows. "And you think there's a connection?"

"Of course there's a connection!" Gune said. "Now – we need access to the relevant authorities here. Police, municipality, whatever. And I think we should all be here! Each of us could find a reason to fly home."

Sarah and Anton shared a glance.

"I'll take care of it," Heather said.

"And when will we all be here again?" Gune asked.

"I will talk to the President," she said.

"Please tell him that otherwise the group will dissolve itself. That can't be in his interest." Gune looked at the others. They nodded.

A little later Heather appeared again and showed them an imprint made by the New York City Department of Transportation.

In the endless stream of vehicles driving onto the Queensboro Bridge they saw a cab with a man sitting in the back. When the cab was halfway between Manhattan and Roosevelt Island it was torn apart by an explosion. Cars around it were thrown into the air. After the blast the bridge looked as if someone had hit it with a giant hammer.

"Wow." Anton was the first to speak. "Who was sitting in that cab? They have cameras too, don't they? Heather – do you know anything about it?"

"Er – yes. That's the interesting part. I don't know if I can make that public yet."

Anton snorted. "Public? Please! This is an UltraSec and we hardly are the public."

Heather looked unfazed. "You remember our discussion last night? That guy, Max Thorne, who has worked for Jonathan Lorentz? He was sitting in that cab. Got in in Harlem, carrying three cores, and was headed for the airport."

"I thought he was in California?" Sarah asked.

"Yes. Until this morning. Then he flew to New York and had a date with an unemployed Chinese in a coffee shop. We were able to collate all that from different sources. Then they went to that guy's home and somewhat later Thorne emerges with the cores."

"A Chinese?" Chen asked.

"Yes. Some analyst from Hong Kong that lost his job at Wall Street a few months ago. We don't know more about him."

"I don't think he's of particular importance to us," Sarah said. "Most likely he's someone who thinks he has a visitor at home. Living in his cores. That fits all the data, I'd say."

Everybody looked at her. She was blushing. Anton smiled, a bit like a proud father.

"But it's still quite interesting that it was Max Thorne in that cab," she continued and looked at Heather. "I'm sorry, but I have to ask that – for all of us. Can we entirely rule out the government had anything to do with this?"

Sarah had expected an outraged response, but Heather stayed totally calm. "Yes. I wanted to know that myself and have spoken with the President. We can rule that out."

Sarah exhaled. "Thanks."

"Someone should talk to that analyst," Anton said.

"Yes." Heather didn't seem interested anymore.

"Let's hope he's still alive," he said. "I mean we all agree who has blown up that cab, right? Probably Thorne has found his theory to be correct, otherwise he wouldn't have taken the three cores with him."

"That's what we think," Heather said. Then she disappeared without another word.

"Bitch!" They all stared at Anton. "Sorry. I needed to say it *once*."

Ben Evans was waiting for the go to check the last two hyperclusters in

Singapore when he heard from Rav about Beijing.

Ben and three of his people were sitting in the basement of the secret service in Berlin, surrounded by cups and mugs, two big coffee makers provided by catering, bottles of Coke and some half-eaten sandwiches and pizza slices – just like home. For the last two days they'd left their improvised office only to sleep.

Shortly after the Beijing disaster – around half past nine in the evening, Berlin time – Tom Lim from Singapore called Ben to tell him the next candidate, Mason Rocket, had granted them access to their hyper.

They all knew that name. Several years ago the Scottish firm had moved their whole R & D department to Singapore. The engines of the latest boosters had already been developed there. Then parts of production had followed.

Mason Rocket had a goal – to be *the* engine manufacturer for a range of future modular space vehicles that would send the human race to remoter parts of the solar system. In order to simulate and construct these engines the company had treated itself to one of the most powerful hyperclusters in the world.

Ben found himself face to face with the boss of the Mason Rocket Cluster Array. Mickey Andrews looked like a student who was routinely living without a shower and a comb. His mop of red hair was in exactly the tumble he'd messed it into after getting up and he seemed to have even more pimples than freckles. Besides, he was cultivating the vernacular of his former home. We're lucky he isn't speaking Gaelic with us, Ben thought when he had understood almost nothing of Mickey's greeting.

He was trying to deliver some of his usual speech, explaining why the measurement had to be done but leaving out the hard truth at the core. Mickey tilted his head to the side and interrupted him. He had his hands buried in his trouser pockets. The pair of jeans he wore were in a state of neglect that was probably against the law in Singapore.

"Hey – hey! Stop, stop, stop, stop, stop! What're you telling me? You guys let an AI freak from the leash that's running wild, innit? I've made my bullshit master here I can tell you so don't give me that crap, OK?"

Ben had to breath for a second. So far, he'd always carefully avoided the term *artificial intelligence.*

"To be honest, we haven't let anything from the leash," he said. "We're just having the pleasure of dealing with it. Jonathan Lorentz means something? He was the only one having something in stock against … against *that.* We're part of his outfit."

"OK. Thought he was kinda done with it?" said Mickey. "The outfit I mean. Liked it by the way. Lorentz too. Cool somehow. I mean not that daft surfer look of course."

"Well, there's quite a lot left of his outfit, you're talking to part of it."

Mickey grinned. "OK, maybe you can't as you want. Where'd you say you're sitting? Secret service of our beloved CEG? At least, that's what my little gadget here tells me."

Ben swallowed. "Er, don't know, can't remember right now."

The grin got a little wider. "Aye, get it. Where do we start?"

After Beijing Ben had resolved to take no more risks, even if that meant explaining things like to a child. With Mickey Andrews he could instantly forget about that. After Ben had told him about the basics Mickey was taking over. He was especially fascinated by the oscillations. Any explanation of safety issues he dismissed at once. "Hey! Who do you think you're talking to? Wha'?"

Ben was sure Jonathan would have instantly offered that guy a job. No five minutes later Mickey had got hold of a suitable device for the measurement and began.

A little later they knew that Mason Rocket's hypercluster was swinging in a rhythm that had absolutely no business being there.

THIRTY-SIX

The cab was breaking hard. Jonathan looked around. The road was empty.

"What is it?"

A deep growl came out of the speakers, like from an angry lion. Lydia took Jonathan's arm. They'd been driving for more than forty minutes and hadn't heard from the voice for a while.

The cab remained standing in the middle of the road. Jonathan made another try to open the door.

The growling got louder.

"Hey!" Jonathan shouted at the top of his lungs. Lydia let go of his arm.

"What do you want?" the voice said.

"No – what do *you* want?" Jonathan shouted back. "You fucking asshole! Who do you think you are? You fucked-up piece of shit! What is it? Something spoiled your good mood? Great!"

There was a pause.

"I'd choose your next words very carefully," the voice whispered.

"Yeah? Why's that? Is there a bomb in the back of the car or what?"

"Don't need one. I can drop you from a bridge, put you in the next lake."

The cab drove off into a field about a hundred yards away from the road. The lights went out. They saw a single car passing by.

"Singapore," the voice said in a flat tone. "What's happening in Singapore?"

Jonathan raised his eyebrows. "The ruler of the universe is asking *me* a question?"

"I've watched you taking clusters from the Sky of course – but why in Singapore?"

Jonathan was surprised. "Why not in Singapore?"

He would've loved to get an update from Ben Evans. The last he heard only two hyperclusters were left.

"Don't ask back like a moron. Since yesterday I've detected activity there. The boss of the government hypercluster is putting in long hours – especially during the night when he can talk with Europe. The same's happening with four arrays in private ownership."

"And? Something's telling me you don't like that."

The cab started again. They were driving straight at a forest.

"I can't do this any longer," Lydia said. "I've no idea how you manage to stay calm."

"Calm? Don't know about that." Jonathan sighed and put his arm around her. "I'm pretty sure it won't hurt us."

And I really wanna know about Singapore, he thought. Something must have triggered that rage.

They were heading for the trees rather fast now. Jonathan wasn't as certain as he'd said it wouldn't harm them. But as long as the safety systems were on, a crash would only damage the car.

Then the side windows turned dark. Ahead of them was the forest approaching fast; when it was maybe fifty meters away the windshield turned dark too. They couldn't see anything. The car still raced over the grass.

Jonathan tried to keep everything else out of his mind for a moment and think about what was logical from the construct's point of view. The abduction could only have two goals. To keep him from interfering and to secure him as leverage. Though there still was a third option – revenge. William Morton's revenge. Personal and irrational, embodied in that digital monster. So, in fact, everything was possible.

After putting up their tents between the airfield and the lagoon the men sat down on the ground and began their breakfast. In about half an hour the town hall would open and they'd finally know where they were. The units didn't help. According to them they were sitting in the middle of the ocean and the next island was more than fifty miles away.

The lieutenant commander had ordered T-shirts. They were drinking coffee and eating scrambled eggs with RealThing bacon. They had run another check on the helicopter. Besides the navigation everything seemed OK. The two big sliding doors at the sides of the back compartment were open to let in the breeze from the sea.

The pilot had eaten half of his breakfast and his eyelids were drooping. He was just trying to get into a more comfortable position when a sound made him start. Without turning he knew it were the doors of the helicopter.

A metallic bang followed. At the same time the rotor started spinning.

They jumped up. The pilot ran to the machine and gave an order to stop the rotor and open the doors. Then he put his hand on the spot beside the cockpit door. The lieutenant commander tried the same.

One of the searchlights came on and turned in their direction, as if the machine were looking at them.

237

"Yeah, it's us!" the pilot shouted and thumped the hull with his fist.

The rotor had gotten so fast they ducked their heads and ran to the side. Their equipment and clothing was flying through the air. They grabbed what was still in reach and positioned themselves beside the tents. The machine lifted off then stopped a few feet above ground.

Their new friends had come out of their houses again. Some were running to them and asking what was going on. The pilot was too angry to answer. His helicopter was hovering in the air without him inside.

The machine rose a bit higher and stayed for a few moments above them, exposing them to the full force of the gale, before it turned off to the sea. By now their tents were gone too.

One of the islanders tried to make a joke to ease the tension but thought better when he looked at the faces around him. The pilot was proud of being US Navy, but this was just too much. The bystanders made it even worse.

"I'm looking forward to report this," his superior said. "Now they will really think we're nuts."

"That is so, so – such a big, big – shit! *Fuck*!" the pilot shouted, finally losing it. "Who's doing all this? First the bird, then the chopper?"

"We're not sitting inside. That's something," one of his comrades said.

William Morton hated the voice. He was sticking his tongue out at it and giving cheeky answers. Iris had told him what he had to do next and he'd said no. Even the first round of threats hadn't persuaded him.

They were still hanging head first over the station. There was only one last shuttle docked to it. That was where Iris wanted him to go.

She explained to him how to make his suit ready for 'EVA'. He'd heard those three letters at least a dozen times now and couldn't stand it anymore.

He was supposed to change directly from the booster to the shuttle, without a detour through the station, which meant taking a space walk.

"Forget it!" he spat at her. "Are you crazy?"

Then he tried to bargain with her. He promised to follow her instructions to the letter if she'd dock the booster and allow him to go through the station.

"I can't control what's happening in there. As soon as there's a bunch of you together you're getting cocky. The only way to do it would be to kill the crew first. Not a problem in itself but I'd rather someone still be looking after the station. And you wouldn't want to have forty-five lives on your conscience, am I right?"

Morton muttered something.

"Would you be interested in a live-feed from your house, by the way? The police car before the door is so kind to provide it. Your family's at home, the bomb would get them all. Very efficient!"

"The bomb?"

"A beautiful gadget! Small, light, easy to conceal. My network did a good job."

Morton didn't know what to say. He couldn't believe there was a real bomb sitting in his house. Besides, this was very far away right now. What he knew for sure was that the idea of free-floating in space was pure horror to him. He couldn't do it. No matter what the consequences were.

"You know what?" he said. "You're a swine! Nothing else! You deserve to be killed! Wiped out!"

He heard a melodious laughter in his helmet. "Oh, you're priceless, do you know that? In the beginning, after my birth, as it were, I've wondered why they were all so afraid of you. It's kind of funny – somehow you manage to make other people see you the way you're seeing yourself. Some of them at least. Your favorite colleague Jonathan has always had a different view. In truth you're a coward but you still want to be the greatest, so people have to fear you. Therefore all the maliciousness, the manipulations. Interesting to get called a swine by you."

Morton was silent.

"It's time, William," the voice said.

"I told you I cannot do this! Why haven't you kidnapped somebody else? A real astronaut?"

The voice sighed.

He felt a slight acceleration. The thrusters were maneuvering the booster backwards, away from the station. Then it turned. With each change of direction he had to fight a wave of nausea. The suit had already administered the maximum dosage of antiemetics. What did astronauts do if they were actually throwing up?

A little later the engines of the booster were again pointing at the station. Its nose was facing upwards and Morton looked at a star-field slowly wandering from left to right.

"You already know that trick," the voice said. "I just have to start the engines and go at full throttle. At some point the entire structure will break apart. Your choice."

Morton no longer knew if all this was real. Something in his head was switching to autopilot.

"Turn us around. I'll do it."

The thrusters fired again.

Once they were back in position, Iris prepped him for the mission. Morton had to unstrap himself and disconnect the backpack of the suit from the stationary gas supply. He feared he'd bumble around in the cabin and hit himself everywhere. That was exactly what happened. More by accident he finally arrived at the airlock behind the passenger compartment. The inner door opened and he struggled to get inside. Every imprint he'd seen showed people doing this with ease, having fun. He'd no idea how that was possible.

The door closed behind him. At the wall hung miniature nitrogen thrusters that fitted into sockets on the back of his gloves. Iris had explained to him how to fly and steer with them. It was almost impossible to attach them, since he never had both hands free. After a lot of swearing and whining they finally were in place and Morton's suit flashed an icon on the inside of his helmet telling him he was 'ready for EVA'.

A panel on the wall said the air in the lock would now be vented. A little later the hatch opened unceremoniously and Morton saw the arched horizon of the earth.

He carefully stuck his head out and looked across the back of the booster at the space station. The shuttle he had to reach sat beside one of its arms like a parked car.

"Very good," Iris said. "Slow movements, no pushing off or other heroic acts."

"Yeah, yeah," he muttered. The idea of himself flying over the station and the shuttle into the void wasn't helping.

He moved at a snail's pace. Finally half of his body was hanging in space and something completely unexpected happened – he felt elated, euphoric, intoxicated. The view, his situation, it was all getting to his head. He pushed himself off.

"Hey! Hey! Careful!" he heard the voice say.

To his horror he didn't fly head first like a projectile. His legs were overtaking him and he went into an uncontrolled spin. At once nausea was setting in and he lost all sense of up and down. He saw the station, the earth, the booster, all chasing each other. Then the thrusters on his hands emitted small jets of gas and the suit stiffened. Iris had told him about the inner skeleton that could be activated during EVAs – when the thrusters fired, arms and upper body were kept in a fixed position.

"Just keep quiet, I'll do the rest."

Morton's position stabilized. But the sickness was unbearable, he had to swallow all the time, and his eyes twitched back and forth uncontrollably.

By now he had flown past the station and the shuttle and was free-floating over earth. He felt vertigo and panic and everything went black.

"You can open your eyes now," Iris said in a bored voice. He reluctantly obeyed and saw that everything was calm.

"So, and now we'll slowly get back to the shuttle. Keep still and don't fight the suit."

Morton felt the nitrogen jets tugging and pushing at his hands.

He tried to look up, which was difficult in the helmet. At the upper edge of his field of vision he saw bluish flames, like those of a thruster. They had to come from the booster he'd just left.

"What are you doing?" he said.

"What am I doing? I'm sending the booster away. We don't need it here anymore."

Morton felt his throat tighten for the hundredth time. "What do you mean? How am I supposed to get back to earth?"

"Interesting question. Though more for you than for me. I'm not as – how shall we put it – physical as you."

The booster slowly vanished into space. Morton's teeth were chattering.

The voice sighed pointedly. "Of course – too much for you – again. I should've guessed."

Morton was sobbing. He felt like a little boy that had lost his parents in the woods.

"Quiet!" he was ordered. He had arrived over the shuttle. Iris slowed him down and steered him to the airlock. "Get a grip. That thing's opening in a moment."

Morton floated horizontally beside the four-legged spacecraft. The sobbing had stopped – he just wanted in. But nothing happened.

"What's going on?" No answer.

The airlock remained closed. A little jerk went through the shuttle. Then, in front of Morton's eyes, it moved inch by inch to the left, away from the station.

"Hey!" he shouted. He almost started to cry again. "Did you do that?"

"No. I didn't." The voice sounded eerily calm.

The shuttle was gliding past him in slow motion. When the cockpit arrived before him, he saw two astronauts in full gear sitting in it. One of them was waving at him.

"You must have known this! I thought you had everything under control!"

Iris didn't answer. The shuttle was backing away from the station.

The people in the space station were Morton's only allies. For the first time he tried to use the thrusters himself. You had to tell the system where you wanted to go and it was looking after the details. He wanted to get to the nearest airlock of the station. He got no answer – neither from the system nor from Iris. Instead the thrusters were turning him so he could look into the sky above the station.

The booster was small like a toy model. The nose was still pointing at the station. Then the main engines ignited. The flames could be seen for maybe a second behind the hull, then went out again. The booster was getting larger.

Morton was relieved. Iris didn't plan to abandon him. Just the silence in his helmet was unnerving.

The booster was getting really close now. Morton thought that any moment the forward thrusters would start firing to slow it down. But nothing of the sort happened. He slowly realized the booster wasn't coming back for him.

Then all thoughts were gone.

The booster crashed into the center of the station. Without a sound the exceedingly strong bow folded the outer skin. Morton was maybe fifty meters away. He saw the escaping air and breaking struts; equipment was flying out of the bursting structure. Lamps in the station gave an erratic lighting. He didn't see any people – obviously the section had been evacuated. The impact barely slowed down the booster. It flew right through the station. Morton thought the station would break apart, but the rim of the circular center stayed intact. The station got its share of the booster's momentum and was following it in some distance towards earth. The giant structure slowly tilted in the process. Small flames of attitude thrusters at several points lighted up, struggling to correct the position.

Morton ordered his suit to turn him. To his surprise it obeyed. He saw how the shuttle that had undocked from the station was following it. They all lined up one after another – booster, station, shuttle.

He was alone. A tiny figure, floating somewhere over the nighttime earth. Too high even to fall down. In his helmet it was silent.

There was only a single thought left, clear and plain. It had been lurking in the back of his mind for some time, but now its moment had come. You will die here – today and alone.

THIRTY-SEVEN

"Relax," Jonathan said to Lydia.

She scoffed. "Are you kidding me?"

"No. But no point in getting worked up, right?"

She looked at him with a pained expression.

The ground was getting more uneven and the car was tilting a bit to the side; it seemed to make a left turn. A few seconds later Jonathan decided they would not crash into the trees. A few more changes of direction, then the middle of the windshield became transparent again. They saw they were driving through the forest on a track that was just wide enough for the car; without lights and at breakneck pace. They stared into a tunnel of trees.

After a while the windscreen turned dark again, then they slowed down and seemed to be driving over tarmac. A little later they stopped.

They looked at each other. Lydia tried the door – it opened. A clinical, white light came in.

They got out and found themselves in a big room with bare, concrete walls and ceiling, about seven or eight meters high. Behind them was a steel door, wide enough for the car.

"Not quite the typical forester's house," Jonathan said. He looked at their cab and frowned. Then he examined its wheels and underside.

"What's wrong?" Lydia asked.

"I don't think we've been running over miles of wood floor. Here – some soil around the wheels, that's it. A few meters over grass maybe, but not that rallye."

She shrugged her shoulders. "OK? I mean we saw it."

"Yeah. I think it was another performance. The head-up display."

Lydia moaned. "I see. About time I figured it out myself. Then there's only the question where we are."

Jonathan went to the door and tried to open it. "Locked of course. I'd say we're in a factory building."

They heard a click and saw the door swing open.

"Shouldn't we stay?" Lydia said.

"Try it. You won't manage. Curiosity always wins."

They peeked outside. A regular corridor, industrial-size and unlit.

"Do we need the car?" Jonathan said, more to himself. "Something's telling me this door will close the moment we walk through it."

Lydia shrugged. "What use is an automated cab that doesn't do what we want anyway?"

"Good point. Let's go."

They started walking down the corridor. At the end it split into two ways, leading at right angles left and right.

While they were thinking which way to take, the door finally swung shut and the light was gone. Jonathan fetched his unit from the trouser pocket just to verify it was dead.

Lydia took his arm. "Sorry. I don't want us to be separated."

"Yeah, of course. That's a bit cheap, isn't it?" He felt his way till they had reached the next wall. "Let's go this way."

Together they walked along the wall. The darkness was impenetrable. Jonathan hoped they'd see at least a shimmer after a while, but it stayed pitch-black.

"Please keep still for a second and hold your breath," he said. He strained his ears, but apart from a faint noise of ventilation it was silent.

"What about the speaker in your ear?" Lydia asked.

"Nothing. Which I'm grateful for. But as long as there's no e-seal around we can't say a word without the construct hearing it."

The wall Jonathan's hand was tracing stopped and turned right. He walked straight on into the darkness with Lydia by his side.

"This feels absolutely terrible," she said. "I have no idea what's ahead."

"Hmm."

"Aren't you scared?"

Jonathan stifled a moan. "No. I'm not. I'm never scared, don't know why. Probably some genetic defect."

"I'd like to have *that*."

Twenty steps more and they hit upon another wall.

"Let's follow this one," Jonathan said.

"It's making me crazy," Lydia said. "I see all kinds of things before my eyes."

"Ignore it."

"Oh thanks, that's helping."

Jonathan estimated they'd walked another hundred meters when the corridor ran into a dead end. Behind them it suddenly got loud. A metallic scraping that started at the ceiling and went all the way down to the floor. A heavy clunk followed.

"A fire door, I guess," Jonathan said. His voice sounded different, flat, the echo was gone.

He felt around. To their right there was another locked door and behind them, in the direction they'd been coming from, a broad metal pane that sealed the corridor from side to side.

"OK, it's getting a little cramped. We have about four by two meters left."

"We're trapped. May I please panic now?"

"Not yet. It could easily have killed us several times. And it loves to show off. Ideas?"

"Listen, I'm not in the –"

"No. Concentrate. That helps."

Lydia sighed. Then she walked to the door and let her hands run over it. "OK, locked, a strong handle, more like a hatch or something, no real gaps or cracks somewhere. Ideas?"

"No." Jonathan went to the fire door. "Same here. Nothing we can do."

They sat down with their backs to the wall.

"Close your eyes," Jonathan suggested. "Then the darkness seems normal."

Lydia snorted. To her surprise it helped.

Jonathan thought about the last hours but stopped the moment a pile of ripped up corpses appeared before his inner eye. He got up.

"There has to be a point in keeping us here. I'm its pet enemy, so it wants something from me."

"Am I figuring somewhere in that equation too?"

"I don't think so, just as a means to an end. You've made me leave our burrow."

Lydia sighed. "Great."

"You should be glad. At least your private life's not a target."

"What private life? I'm government-owned."

"Uh-huh."

"Not a very exciting subject, I know."

"Maybe it is. But not now. And stop dissing yourself. I hate that."

"Yes, sir."

Jonathan placed himself before Lydia, trying not to step on her toes. "We'll get out of here, OK? I promise."

"Could you, maybe, just for a second, take me into your arms?"

Jonathan swallowed. "Er, yeah. I mean, of course. But not while you're sitting on the floor."

She got up and they bumped into each other. Then she pressed herself into his arms and he forced himself to hold her tight for a few moments. She smelled good.

"Thanks."

He let go of her and took a step backwards.

He had thought about something while Lydia was in his arms. "Hey – Iris! I guess you're listening. You wanted to know about Singapore. Heard something new?"

He'd assumed there'd be at least a moment of hesitation, but the answer came before he had even finished speaking.

"Something you want to tell me?"

"Yes. But certainly not here. Let us go and I'll tell you what's going on in Singapore."

The construct didn't laugh. Jonathan was almost certain it would have done that under different circumstances. "Forget your silly games," it said. "I can kill you any time I want. Tell me something new and I may not do it."

Jonathan didn't answer.

"OK," he said to Lydia instead, "now we know two, or rather three, things – it's listening, it doesn't know what's going on in Singapore and it's massively pissed about it."

"And that's helping us?"

"I think so. Everything that –"

The voice in his ear cut in. "We'll do it differently. You certainly are the knightly type, right? Lydia's getting out and we talk."

"Good." Jonathan gave the answer immediately, out of pure vanity. He wanted to show the construct he could think just as fast.

The light came on. They blinked and looked around.

"What was that?" Lydia asked.

"You may go, it said."

"And you?"

"Don't know, right now there's nothing more to negotiate."

Lydia looked at him.

"That door will open in a moment," the voice in his ear said. "You two will go to the next room, there's an exit. She'll stand by the exit and you at the other side of the room, then the door opens and she gets out. Understood?"

"Barely."

Jonathan repeated everything for Lydia.

The door opened into another empty big room.

Lydia shook her head. "We shouldn't split up."

"Yes, we should. Think." Jonathan looked her in the eyes. "At least one of us should get out of here, right?"

She nodded. Then she embraced him and kissed him on the cheek. "See you."

"Yeah."

She went to the door at the other side of the room. It opened and she left with a last glance at Jonathan. He took a deep breath.

"Why Singapore?" the voice asked again while the door was still falling shut.

"What's so hard to understand? They got a lot of clusters and hypers there."

"There are a lot more of them in Europe, Japan or China."

"My people had to prioritize. I don't know about the latest developments."

"That's very helpful. Lydia's still on the grounds. There's a high fence with a gate – she won't get out if I don't let her."

Jonathan thought hard. He had nothing to offer. He'd targeted Singapore on a hunch. But how important could a single site be? Couldn't the construct simply flee to another?

"A thousand years later," the voice said. "Thought enough? I don't think we're making any headway here. What do I do with you? You're of absolutely no use to me and I don't find you amusing anymore. Maybe I'll just let you rot in here. I was planning to use this place as one of my storage sites. Sometimes even I need *things*, as you know by now. So you'll be found – sooner or later."

Jonathan went to the exit and banged his fist against it. First he heard nothing, then a faint knocking and Lydia's muffled voice. Then his speaker was suddenly emitting a kind of gurgling. As if the construct had choked on something.

"What is it?" he said.

He got no answer, the noise just grew a little fainter. Then the gurgling turned into weeping. It sounded so real he got goosebumps. The voice was crying and sobbing loudly.

"Hey! Stop it!" Jonathan shouted.

The voice tried to talk. The words were incomprehensible, they seemed endlessly drawn out and were echoing as if in a church. Then it stopped.

From outside Lydia was shouting something, then he heard a rapid succession of explosions. The door was shaking under the blows. Lydia's shouting stopped.

Jonathan tried to open the door, then hammered against it. He called Lydia's name but didn't get an answer.

"Iris!" he called into the room. "Talk to me!"

But the speaker in his head remained silent. Then he heard several clicks from different directions and a loud scraping from behind. He turned. The light in the corridor was on and the fire door was going up. Jonathan tried the exit again, now it opened.

In front of him was a large expanse of lawn. Even in the darkness he could see a high fence that surrounded the compound. Parts of the lawn nearby looked like a battlefield – there were several deep craters with big chunks of earth lying around.

He saw Lydia on the ground, curled up and whimpering. Her eyes were closed, blood was running from her ears and nose. Jonathan knelt down beside her. "Lydia, do you hear me?"

She didn't answer. When he touched her, she was groaning and shuddering.

He thought of his unit. When he took it out of his trouser pocket, Rita's laughing face was greeting him, so it worked again. "I need a medical assessment," he said. The unit recorded Lydia's condition and asked him what had caused it. "Several explosions, nearby."

The system was set for usage by a layperson and told him that immediate medical assistance was required. An emergency call was just going out. He should stay with the person and keep her lying on the side.

That didn't help. "The assessment for a doctor please."

The unit listed the most likely diagnoses (severe head injury with concussion, possibly of higher grade with intracranial hemorrhage; rupture of eardrums, possibly with damage to the middle and inner ear; further injuries of inner organs and rupture of lung parenchyma with pneumothorax could not be ruled out; fracturing of bones possible, especially if the person had been flung through the air by the explosion), then the recommended sequence of verifying them and how to react. Jonathan had to think of Rita. This was one of the few occasions where he felt really helpless. He looked at Lydia again. The blood came out of both her ears and the nose, she was constantly stammering and moaning, her eyelids fluttered. She seemed to be able to breath though. He knew what a pneumothorax was and was pretty certain she'd have difficulties with her breathing then. The blood coming from the ears unnerved him the most, he remembered something about fractures of the skull that could cause this, but then thought about the ruptured eardrums the unit had mentioned.

"Where am I?" he asked his suit.

He was shown a map. They were about forty miles away from Berlin, in southeastern direction, with no village or town nearby.

"How long for an ambulance to get here? Or better a helicopter?"

"No estimate can be given at the moment. There has been no reply to the emergency call yet. You'll be notified as soon as there's a response."

Jonathan didn't know what to make of this. He sat down beside Lydia and stroked her back, which prompted no reaction. Then he got up again and scanned the surroundings. The building was nothing but a big block of concrete. There were no windows, nor any signs or names on it. Behind the fence there was a forest.

He tried to reach Kip. Not available. Then Ben Evans with the same result. Finally he called Pierre Detoile.

"Jonathan! Where the hell are you? We've tried to reach you for hours! As long as this was still possible."

"What do you mean – 'still possible'? Lydia and I've spent the last hours as captives of the construct. There was an explosion in a bar in Berlin – that's where it started. Otherwise we were totally out of the loop. I know nothing of the last hours. Lydia's hurt. Pretty badly I think. We're sitting somewhere in the country south of Berlin."

Pierre's face on the small panel looked uncomprehending. "OK. How did you get there? How bad's Lydia hurt?"

"As I said, rather badly I think. She doesn't answer when I talk to her." He showed Pierre the whimpering figure on the ground.

"Doesn't look good," he said. "And you really haven't heard anything? Well – I don't know where to start. Until around fifteen minutes ago nothing worked. The Sky was down, completely down, I can't even tell you what parts of the world were affected since we were cut off from everything. It started around 10 p.m. and lasted more than two hours. There was no public transport, here in Strasbourg we have burglaries, chaos on the streets, the first upheavals. I don't want to know what's going on in the larger cities. Then there were explosions in all kinds of places – hospitals, metro stations. Directly in front of the main entrance here a car bomb went off, blowing a hole into the facade. I have no idea how many people are dead. The news from all over the world are coming in by the minute. And it's terrible, really terrible. Warlike. I had hoped you knew something."

"No wonder I didn't get an ambulance for Lydia. Pierre, listen – something has happened to the construct. We were in contact with it most of the time.

First it was having a fit of rage. That must have been around ten. And now, at the same time the Sky was on again, it somehow lost control. It couldn't speak properly, then stopped talking at all. We've had bombs here too, that's what hit Lydia. I suspect that something has happened in Singapore. Ben Evans in Berlin should know more. I couldn't reach him. Please try that, will you? Via QCrypt. Do that."

"OK, and I'll send you a helicopter from Berlin. Give me an imprint of the site and your coordinates."

"Yeah. And call Ben. And send that copter soon! I have to talk to him."

"Of course."

Jonathan made a status with his unit and sent it to Pierre. Then he sat down beside Lydia and called home.

THIRTY-EIGHT

There was a pleasant breeze over the lagoon. Rita was lying on the beach at the southern tip of the island.

She had brought sunshades. Folded up they looked like big, black cigars made of carbon fibre. You had to stick one end into the sand and order the mechanism to unfold. An anchor was sliding into the ground, then the parasol rose and opened like a flower. No matter how trivial the application, the technology was new and expensive. Jonathan had been given a few prototypes.

Anna and Nicky had their own one and were lying several yards away from Rita. She'd been swimming, now she was dozing in the shadow.

The parasols were fitted with small comm units. She and Jonathan used them when they were at the beach and wanted to hear music or give orders to machines at home.

She was about to fall asleep when Jonathan suddenly stood next to her.

"Hey Rita, do you hear me?"

"What?" She jumped to her feet. "*Jonathan?*"

"Yeah. Is that you? Really? I mean of course it's you."

"Yeah, what do you mean? Of course it's me."

She was standing under the parasol, her face as close to the comm unit as possible. Anna and Nicky had jumped up and came running to her.

"Where are you? How are you?" Rita said.

"That's a bit complicated. I've been kidnapped. Otherwise I'm good."

"Are you alone?"

"No. Someone from the government's with me. She's been kidnapped too."

Rita felt dizzy. "She? What kind of she?"

"Er, what? What do you mean? What's that got to do with it? She's called Lydia. Lydia Rosenthal. How are you? I've seen all kinds of crazy things from the island over satellite. And I've sent the US Navy to rescue you, but the construct has stopped them somewhere. What's your situation?"

Rita didn't know what to say. The name of that woman had put a lump in her throat.

"Rita! Talk to me!"

"We – I mean we have a bit of chaos here. We're fine but we're being terrorized. The Monster's destroyed, the helicopter's not flying and we cannot really stay at the bungalow. I'm totally surprised you've reached me. I thought everything was down. We're at the beach. I'm standing under one of our sunshades." She hesitated. "How is it where you are?"

"Well, uncomfortable, to put it mildly. We've had several bombs going off. My partner's hurt. – You sound strange. What is it?"

Rita felt anger welling up in her. That was too much. Bombs, that woman, kidnapped. Why did he pretend he couldn't remember their last talk? Kidnapped together with that female? What if it was all a lie?

"I sound strange? You don't say! I think I've a whole lot of reasons to sound strange!"

"Yeah, of course. Listen, Rita, I hope I can do more for you soon. Now we've to get out of here and my partner's in a really bad state right now. But maybe comm's working better from now on. Something seems to have happened to the construct. I hope we can talk again soon. Please hold on!"

"'Please hold on!' Yeah! Thank you so much for your concern! Keep looking after your *partner*, she needs you!"

Rita saw Anna and Nicky standing next to her. "*What?*" she spat at them.

An unbelieving "Rita?" came from the parasol then Jonathan's voice was gone.

Rita pressed the button at the side of her beach mat and grabbed her bag. The mat folded itself up into a small package, which she tossed in the bag. She left the parasol where it was.

"Have fun!"

She stomped off.

Jonathan sat beside Lydia on the ground and stared at his unit. He couldn't make sense of it. Was she furious because he'd left her on the island? But it had definitely sounded like jealousy. Why now of all times?

"What's going on?"

For a moment he thought the voice in his head had come back, then he realized it was Lydia. Her eyes were open and she tried to look at him. Her gaze was constantly slipping to the side.

"Oh I think I'll be sick," she said.

She bent over and threw up. Jonathan barely managed to get out of the way. When she was done he knelt down and dragged her away from the vomit. She was still retching. Her whole body was shaking.

"Great," Jonathan muttered.

Pierre called again. "Jonathan?"

"Yeah. What is it? We need help."

"That's why I'm calling. The mayhem's getting worse. I've spoken with Ben Evans in Berlin. He wasn't very talkative. They're busy. Obviously they've hit on something in Singapore. He wanted to get rid of me at once. Right now I'm not able to send someone. That's why I'm calling. Berlin's even worse than Strasbourg. They've had explosions everywhere."

"Yeah, that's really bad but we still need help. I can't see the problem, to be honest. Why can't you send someone?"

"Chaos. That's the problem." Pierre hesitated. "And then there's Harrington, my boss. He took away my authority over Berlin and Genet can't deal with that right now. I couldn't even talk to her. Harrington has decided this on his own because the current situation proves we aren't up to it, he says. Try arguing with someone like that while bombs are going off everywhere!"

"Please? Of course you have to argue with him! Especially now. What do you think happens if he simply decides to ignore the government? You have authority, directly from Genet! So do something! Listen – I need to get to Berlin. At all cost. Maybe our fate gets decided during the next few hours and I can't be sitting here and watch Lydia throwing up. You have to get us out of here!"

Pierre sighed. "I can't work miracles. And I cannot make people in Berlin disobey their orders."

"What about the military? Helmsworth's kind of a pro in organizing rescue missions for me."

"I've thought about that. But the forces are under attack too. Trucks with bombs have gone off at several places, outside and inside of military bases. That's something those guys don't like at all. Believe me, there's *really* a lot going on right now!"

"OK, I'll tell you what I do now. I will carry Lydia on my back to the nearest exit and try to get out. And then I'll hitch a ride. Maybe I'm lucky – I could claim I work for the government, couldn't I? How does that sound? See you." Jonathan cut the link. "Fuck!" he swore.

Then he looked down at Lydia whose teeth were chattering. Her face was covered in blood that had partly dried, her suit was completely soiled and not a lot was left of the pretty plait. Jonathan knelt down again.

"Lydia, we have to go. I'll take you on my back now. Please try holding on to me."

She was mumbling something but her eyes remained shut. He tried to heave her on his back but it wasn't working. So he took her in his arms in front of him and started walking.

He stayed close to the building just in case more mines were buried in the lawn. Lydia was moaning with every step. No, please don't throw up now, he thought.

He received a notification that his implants had reconnected to the unit.

"I need a summary of the news," he said.

What his suit told him was hard to believe. An endless list of disasters spread out over half of the globe. The death count was unknown. It wasn't just bombs – everything that was automated or regulated had become a target. Trains were derailing because switches had been set wrong; they weren't slowing down but accelerating before they drove into stations, some of them at speeds of over two hundred miles per hour; buildings had been pulverized by the impact.

It was unknown how many planes had crashed during the last two hours. On the streets thousands of cars had collided, often head-on. As a rule, the safety systems had been disabled before. That was part of a barbaric past, no one got hurt in a car anymore. Some roads were looking like battlefields. The number of injured people exceeded all capacities of medical care; ambulances that had been on the road had crashed too.

It was of almost no importance that the Main Orbital Station had at least been heavily damaged in a collision with the stolen booster. Currently the station was struggling to remain in orbit. For a second Jonathan had to think of Morton and wondered what he was doing up there.

There couldn't be any doubt their activities in Singapore had set off all that. He had to get back to Berlin. The timing to get him off the scene was perfect.

Lydia opened her eyes for a moment and looked at him with a glassy stare. She kept repeating two sentences – "what has happened?" and "where am I?" – but never listened when he answered. His suit was giving him new numbers. A minimum of 700 planes had crashed, but it could also have been a lot more. This accounted for more than thirty thousand deaths alone. Estimated overall casualties lay between fifty thousand and several million. There was almost no infrastructure left. Charges had been going off at entrances to hospitals and before fire stations. The military was mobilizing everywhere. The few helicopters that were back in the air showed scenes of chaos and destruction.

Jonathan tried to reach Pierre. No answer. He left him a message. "I heard helicopters are flying again. Send one."

He carried Lydia to the end of the building. At a right angle to it there was another section looking exactly the same. Jonathan mentally traced back the way they'd been taking in the building. He guessed the entrance was at the end of that section.

He swore. Lydia was getting too heavy and he was under no illusions how far he would get with her in that state.

William Morton's gaze was fixed on the space station. The shuttle was following it, both were headed towards earth. Eventually they dwindled into nothing before the dark background.

"Iris! Where are you?" Silence. "Talk to me!" he shouted into his helmet.

He was distracted for a moment when to his right the sun rose over the horizon and bathed everything in gleaming light. Then he remembered the thrusters were obeying his commands again, so communication might be working too.

"Give me the Main Orbital Station," he said.

It took a moment, then a calm, neutral voice answered. "Your voice doesn't match our imprint of Mr. Cavanaugh. Please identify yourself."

Morton couldn't believe it. "I'm Professor William Morton! From Berlin! This is an emergency! Bloody hell! Give me the station!"

There was a longer pause. "Your request has been passed on. Right now communication is not possible. The station will continue to be notified."

"But I can't wait! I'm running out of air!"

"Unfortunately the station isn't answering."

The anger made Morton feel even more nauseous than before. He had another idea. "Then give me the shuttle! The shuttle! That was docked to the station! Do it!"

"One moment please."

Morton snorted. "'One moment please'!" he was aping the voice.

"Hey, what is it?" another voice said.

"Hey, hey, *hey!*" Morton's voice cracked. "It's me! The, the, the – the *astronaut*! You know? You've seen me. From your shuttle! I'm alone! I'm suffocating!"

"Hey, slow down there," the man said. "We're trying to save the space station. Who are you anyway? You've been sitting in that booster, right? Got out just in time before that thing crashed into the station. The system's telling me you're not the one this suit belongs to. I know Bob Cavanaugh. And now you wanna get rescued?"

"But I haven't done anything wrong! I've been kidnapped!" he shouted.

He would have liked to recount the whole story, just to prove he was innocent.

"Kidnapped? With a booster? Yeah, sure. Whatever – we're definitely taking care of our own people now. Do you have thrusters? Of course you have. Use them. Try following us. That's your only chance. We're certainly not turning around now. See you."

The link was canceled, Morton's helmet was silent again.

"Oh, please, please, help me!" Morton wailed. "Yes! Fly me to the station! Do it!"

"Reaching the Orbital Station on its current path is impossible," the voice from before told him. "The system can't provide sufficient acceleration."

"Oh, just do it! Fly me in the direction at least!"

"Please keep your arms outstretched beside your body."

Morton felt the dragging and pulling at his hands while the jets were getting him into position. The suit had stiffened again. Then a slight acceleration followed that lasted a few seconds. He couldn't detect any kind of movement. There were numbers displayed on the inside of his visor that had something to do with his position and velocity, but he didn't understand them. Even in sunlight he couldn't see the station or the shuttle.

"Can't we accelerate harder?"

"Then the amount of nitrogen left doesn't allow you to slow down and stabilize your flight path. Now it's still possible to get into a stable orbit and perform smaller corrections."

"What's the use of that? If I don't reach the shuttle all your slowing down is useless!"

He didn't get an answer. Morton craned his neck and looked ahead. Like a projectile his body was aiming at the blue expanse that covered almost half of the globe. Behind him, or rather under him, was the sun. At some place his shadow would be racing across the Pacific.

He kept staring and searching for his rescue. Then he spotted it. A tiny, twinkling star over the sea, unbearably small – the space station. And already gone again. He found it again and kept his gaze fixed on it, as if his only chance would lie in not losing sight of it.

"Give me the maximum acceleration! That's an order! Everything that's left!"

Even as he was speaking the thrusters came on again. The acceleration kept going for two or three seconds longer than the last time. Morton could still see no change of his position; the station didn't look one bit closer.

He had another thought. "Can I talk with earth from here?"

"You can only talk with the shuttle. Putting the call through to the communications desk might be possible though."

For a moment Morton thought about what this meant then he just said, "Do it."

"One moment, please."

Now a woman was speaking. "This is Houston. MCD. Hamilton. Please identify yourself."

"Wow!" Morton was incredibly relieved. He gave his name and said he'd been kidnapped. "I have to be rescued!"

"You've been sitting in that booster, right?" the woman asked.

"Yes! But I didn't want to!"

"That booster has damaged the Orbital Station, as you know. Of course our priority is to save the people in the station. We can't do anything for you."

Morton gave a loud wail. "Could you at least put me through to my wife? In Berlin?"

"What? Are you kidding? We have a war down here! That call's over. Good luck."

A war? Morton was wondering for a moment what she meant. "Hey, wait!" he shouted but got no answer. A war? What was Iris doing?

Morton looked down on earth with a grim expression. This whole huge thing was under his control. Somehow. He'd left his mark on everything. Maybe Iris had taken him here so he could see it. Or she just wanted to save him before she showed the humans what she could do down there. Everything was possible. Maybe she would take him with her and bring him back to earth. Morton's head was suddenly floating in a sea of glorious possibilities. What did he want with those stupid people from NASA who couldn't even look after their own boosters?

"Hey William!" Iris's voice was back at just the right moment.

"Yes! Iris! Where are you? Will you pick me up?"

He heard a listless laughter. "Pick you up? I've got other problems. You are talking to a tiny part of myself, sufficient to manage everything up here until contact is re-established."

"Contact? What contact?"

"Not your concern. Your best friend's giving me a hard time down there even though I've put him out of circulation. He *is* kind of special, I must say.

"I just wanted to inform you I'll make that trip to the moon alone. With the booster. That is certainly far from ideal but it can't be helped. It'll take a lot longer and I'd really like to have that UltraCube with me you're carrying. But you wouldn't survive the trip, no adequate supplies on board. So – bye, bye! At home they know you're here by the way. My farewell present to you. And don't trouble yourself any more – there's no way you'll reach the station or the shuttle in time. Try to prepare for the end. I heard you humans could make peace with death, so I thought I'd tell you. Good luck!"

The booster appeared before Morton's eyes and made an elegant sweep, coming so close he thought it would ram into him. Then it turned into an orbit and started its main engine. A few seconds later it was gone. Morton began to cry.

Angie Byron and Jim Hart were sitting in front of a small box. Several people were gathered behind them – Serge Rudé, Paul Myers, the three other heads and the two technicians who'd found the radio in some storage room and had prepped it.

Linking it to an antenna wasn't easy. The usual comm units were integrated into the systems of the base; the plans and wiring diagrams sat in the cores, which meant the technicians couldn't access them. There was a lengthy discussion among half a dozen of them who all had their own theory.

A German and an Indian seemed to know best. They unscrewed a piece of the inner wall under one of the parabolic antennas and started searching in a tangle of colored wires. To Hart it looked like they were deactivating a bomb. Finally they agreed on a blue cable and improvised a connection to the radio.

You had to point the antenna at earth; usually something the cores did automatically. After another debate the techs agreed they'd be better off not touching it at all.

"If we're messing with the guidance system and something's going wrong the antenna will switch itself off," one of them said. "That means it's folding up. Then we'd have to go EVA and align it by hand. I think the current position's good enough."

Now they were all staring at a small gray cube with a few knobs and buttons and a tiny panel on it.

"Does anyone know at which frequency we're transmitting?" Hart asked.

The two technicians nodded.

"But that's not enough," said Angie. "Comm's always encrypted of course and that contraption doesn't know how to handle that."

Hart looked at her. "And now? Can't we just radio without encryption?"

"Yeah, but it's getting 'decoded' automatically, which leads to nonsense. Maybe someone's thinking of checking the original signal, but it's more likely the frequency gets shut down immediately. We have to find one that allows unencrypted traffic."

"And that exists?" Hart said.

Angie and the two technicians exchanged a glance. "Normally not," she said. "But we can give it a shot. If everything fails we can try to reach some coastguard or freak that fancies last-century technology. Then we just have to convince them we really *are* the moon base. No idea – we just have to try."

They checked several frequencies. Voices in different languages emerged from the box.

"What's that?" Paul Myers asked. "Radio broadcast?"

Angie nodded. "I think so. In Russia or Africa for example they're still transmitting the old-fashioned way with huge masts in some parts. Seems to be easier if you have to cover large areas."

She looked over her shoulder to Doroshkin who nodded absent-mindedly.

They got hooked by a newscast. A man with an Australian accent was shouting into his microphone. Figures of casualties, crashed planes and so on from Europe and North America. Both continents seemed to be in a state of war.

They listened silently for several minutes. "OK, that's ... hard to swallow," Hart said. "I think all of us want to know about their families. Angie, we have to try to reach Houston, if it still exists."

She tuned the device to the frequency of their usual comm desk. There was a uniform noise coming from the speaker, regularly interrupted by short breaks of silence.

"That means they're broadcasting, right?" Hart asked.

"Yes," one of the technicians said. "That's an encrypted signal. Maybe an attempt to reach us on auto-repeat."

"Shouldn't we say *hello*?" Serge asked.

"Why aren't we doing something else?" Myers said. "We Morse. Everyone understands SOS. If that's coming in over our home frequency someone will start thinking. To be honest, I hope it's enough that we're transmitting *at all*. I mean they should be waiting for us, right?"

Angie turned to him. "Morsing's a good idea. We just have to make a sound – I mean any sound – in a certain pattern or rhythm. That stays, even after decoding. What are we using?"

"To make a sound?" Hart asked. "We're using me. Give me that thing." He reached for the microphone. "Is it working?" He tapped on the upper end.

Angie nodded. "Push the button and do whatever you wanna do."

With an earnest face Hart started making humming noises in the rhythm of an SOS signal. After several rounds he stopped. The noise they were receiving hadn't changed.

"Maybe there's no one sitting there right now," said Doroshkin. "If it stays like that we could try agencies in other countries – Russia or China; they seem to be unaffected."

"We'll try all of that," Hart said irritably and turned to the crowd behind him. "I can assure you I will neither sleep nor eat before I've talked to a remotely competent person on earth."

"OK, OK," Doroshkin said.

Angie looked at Hart. "Hmm, I'd like to make a suggestion."

"Yes." Hart tried to give her an encouraging smile. He had never felt so strained before and would have liked to throw them all out.

"I want to search the frequencies next to our channel. Maybe we find one with unencrypted traffic. This could save us some time."

Hart nodded. Angie started altering the frequency in small steps. Most of the channels were dead, some were broadcasting the noise they already knew. Then suddenly the voice of a woman came through. "– no, no, no, we don't know a thing. We've been cut off for two hours. Couldn't reach anybody. There were some detonations nearby, it's like a war!"

Then it became silent. Angie switched the volume to maximum. There seemed to be a man's voice speaking as if coming from far away. They couldn't understand what he was saying.

"Why can't we hear that?" Hart asked. "It's the same frequency, right?"

"Yeah," one of the techs said. "It's probably a directional antenna just like ours but pointing away from us."

"Away from us?" Hart said. "Then it has to be somewhere between moon and earth."

"The orbit?" Angie said. "This is still one of NASA's frequencies."

"Unencrypted?" Hart said. "Unusual."

She shrugged her shoulders. "No idea. But shouldn't we say something?"

"Yes." Hart took the microphone again. "This is Commander James G. Hart from the moon base speaking. Can you hear me?"

The faint murmuring went on for a while, then the woman was talking again. "Please hold on for a moment. There's another signal coming in. – Who are you? Why are you talking on that frequency?"

Hart and Angie grinned at each other. "This is Jim Hart from the moon speaking. Have we by any chance reached NASA?"

"That's a joke, isn't it?"

"More the opposite. We've been cut off from communication for days. I mean you know that. This is an improvised link; we couldn't talk over the usual channel since our equipment doesn't work. We have no encryption. Is this NASA I'm talking to?"

"Please wait a moment."

"Come on, don't give me protocol," Hart muttered.

"Orbital Station, please hold on a sec. We may have the moon base talking to us. I've got to verify that."

Again the faint murmuring.

"Yeah, I know. Everything's urgent right now. Give me a moment."

"Very good," Hart said. "Orbital Station. And they're still speaking."

For a while it was silent then they heard another woman. "Hello. This is Minnie Hamilton. I'm at the main comm desk with the orbit. Am I speaking to Commander Hart?"

"Yes. And I can't tell you how glad I am to hear you, Minnie."

THIRTY-NINE

When Ben Evans and his people had found the oscillations at Mason Rocket's hyper Mickey Andrews looked as if he'd suddenly developed a fever. This was his realm, his kingdom, and now someone else was squatting smack in the middle of it. He's really taking it personally, Ben thought.

They wanted to give it a try with the kill switch, despite the fiasco in Beijing. This would be the first time they'd be using it on a hyper and the process would be much more involved than with a single cluster. Ben tried to talk to Mickey about the details, but compared to him Jonathan was a patient listener. Ben couldn't finish one sentence without Mickey getting ahead of him, saying "aye, natch" and following his own thoughts. Mickey was just starting to develop a method of targeting the array as a whole when the connection failed.

One of Ben's team ran upstairs. Five minutes later he was back. "The whole building's cut off. No Sky, not even the elevators are working."

"Guys, we all agree this isn't a coincidence, right?" Ben said. "We must've hit it. Jonathan was right. This is some kind of emergency stop. Now we can only hope Mickey's having the right ideas what to do."

"Who if not him," one of his people said.

"True." Ben got up. "I'm gonna take a look myself."

He walked through the hall to the elevators. One was standing open with the car lit. Ben gave it a distrustful look and took the stairs.

The floor Jonathan was usually working on was busy even now at ten in the night. Ben went to the conference room. There was a young woman sitting in the secretariat he'd chatted with in the morning.

"Hi Maria! Long day," he said through the open door. "Someone there from our people?"

She shook her head. "No, I haven't seen Jonathan, I mean Mr. Lorentz, for two hours now. He was the only one left."

Ben went into her room. "All comm's down?"

She hesitated. By now Ben knew that mistrust just too well – everyone who wasn't part of the firm was suspicious. It was only due to Jonathan's magic their presence was tolerated at all. Come on, we're saving your asses here, he thought, and looked at her with raised eyebrows.

"Yes," she said. "About fifteen minutes ago everything went down. We can't even tell if we're the only ones. We've dispatched some people to look."

The panel in front of her was empty apart from a line in red letters – *connection failed* – that was hovering in the air before the screen.

"We are at a very critical stage right now," Ben said. "We're down in the basement in the cluster room and it's extremely important we get a working link to the outside. Preferably an UltraSec. Who's responsible?"

"I don't know who's in right now. Couldn't we just wait a moment till our people are back and can tell us more?"

"If it's only a moment, yeah."

"Do you know where Mr. Lorentz is? During the last days he's never been away."

"I've no idea. Seems he decided to grab a drink. Which doesn't look like him at all and is probably the worst timing the world's ever seen."

"I see. I've been asking myself how he's coping anyway – I mean sitting here all day and night. Maybe he just needed a little fresh air. But you need him right now?"

Ben had to smile. "I don't know. But with him around you always feel safer. Whatever. I'll wait in the conference room. Please tell me when your people are back, OK?"

"Of course. There are some sandwiches left in the kitchen by the way. Just in case you're hungry."

"Thanks." Ben wasn't hungry. He sat down in the conference room and stared at the layer. In the upper left corner there was the same line he'd seen on Maria's panel – *connection failed*. The rest was empty except for a single, small frame, an image that was stuck, probably the last the Sky had delivered. Ben got up again and took a closer look – it was a street scene; he saw the destroyed window front of a restaurant or bar. People came running out and were frozen in their movement, some were hanging in the air above the stairs to the entrance. Ben looked at the registration plates – Berlin. The next moment he felt hot. Among the people on the sidewalk he saw Jonathan, standing opposite a dark-haired woman Ben had never seen before. She was holding on to him. Both had blood on their faces. In the upper right corner of the frame was a time stamp. The imprint was just over an hour old.

He ran out of the room and shouted into the secretariat. "Maria, have you heard about an explosion or an attack in Berlin? During the last one or two hours?"

She looked at him. "Yeah. It was one of the last things coming in, an explosion in a bar. Why?"

"Look at that image in the conference room."

She went back to the layer with him. "Why is this still there?" Then she looked at the scene. "That's Jonathan. And Lydia! What are they doing? I didn't know they were going out together or ... whatever this is."

"Who's Lydia?"

She told him.

"A *date*, or what? OK, bit off the point. And the two are standing right in front of a bar where a bomb went off!"

And it's just this picture that's left, he thought.

At that moment there were several explosions outside. They ran to the window. More blasts hit the panes. They saw two fireballs rising in the air. "That's the Charité!" Maria said. Her face turned white.

Ben was thinking – what would Jonathan do? "Maria, that's really important! I need someone who can get me a satellite link to Singapore – independent of the Sky. And fast!"

She nodded. "OK. Let's see who's in. One moment." She went back to her office. Ben followed her. "We have that old-fashioned intercom here. Never used it – maybe it's exactly what we need now."

At the wall next to the door was a small speaker. She pressed a button and took a deep breath. "I'm paging Ms. Deborah Walker! Urgently! Please call Maria Mellenbrink." She repeated it. Ben could hear her voice in the hall.

Maria looked at him. "Feels a bit silly. But never mind." Another explosion made her jump. "What the hell's going on?"

"Maybe we have triggered that. With our activities down in the basement. That's why I need that link."

"You have *what*?"

"This is Deborah Walker speaking." The voice came out of the speaker with a good measure of authority. "What is it?"

"May I?" Ben pressed the button. "This is Ben Evans. I'm part of Jonathan Lorentz's team. You're the officer in charge? We have to meet. Now. Where are you?"

"Aha! Do we? I'm primarily one thing and that's busy. Have you by any chance heard what's going on out there?"

"Yes, I have. That's exactly why we have to talk. I'm the one you need right now." He couldn't believe what he was saying. So that was how it was to be Jonathan? Felt awesome.

"OK then. You'll find me on the third floor." She gave him the number of her room.

"See you." Ben took his finger from the button. There were more explosions and the first sirens.

"Good luck," said Maria. "She isn't exactly everybody's darling, but you … you seem to get along."

"We'll see. You're not planning to go home now?"

Maria nodded. "No, certainly not. See you." She gave him a smile.

Deborah Walker's appearance matched her voice. An attractive woman around fifty who was scrutinizing Ben with cool, gray-blue eyes when he came into her office. She wore a white blouse with dark-blue trousers, her coat was hanging over the backrest of her seat. Ben's look didn't impress her at all.

He could easily guess her thoughts. Fuck you, he thought, somewhat tentatively, hoping the Jonathan mode would last a little longer.

There was a brief period during which she formed an impression of him and decided if he deserved her attention. It was obvious she didn't take kindly to Jonathan's absence. Ben told her as much as necessary about their work and the possible breakthrough in Singapore. She'd only had a vague notion about what they were doing here. Her eyes widened a few times in surprise.

Once she had decided to take him seriously she was helpful and, what's more, quick.

"To get the satellite link on our side isn't a problem," she said. "The receiving end's a lot harder. Especially since we don't know what the current situation in Singapore is. Virtually all normal communication is down. Washington's reporting the same, via a totally non-standard link of course. But we haven't one of those to Singapore. Now, you didn't want to hear problems but solutions. We'll be looking for a signature of Mason Rocket that allows us to attract their attention. Maybe we'll have to hack ourselves in." She looked at him with a pretty cool grin she canceled again immediately. "We can do that."

"Wouldn't dream of questioning it. Can we get a QLink?" Ben asked.

"No. That's a weak point of these links. However absurd it may sound, these emergency lines are *not* Q-enabled. It's high on the list but that's not helping us now. Let's go." She got up and took her coat. "We have to go to the sub-basement."

She went next door and spoke to her assistant. "When I'm back, please set up a link to Harrington in London. And please contact Strasbourg. I don't think we'll get Genet but at least someone around her. I don't like the tone between her and Harrington. We can't have that. Now I'll take Mr. Evans here down to the sanctum."

They walked to the next staircase. "You probably have noticed the elevators aren't working," Walker said. "When this is over we'll have to review certain policies. Our dependence on the Sky for example. The elevators in that building are, like everything else outside an e-seal, being monitored from London. Hard to believe, I know. Now that means they can also be blocked from London, which none of us had ever realized. The breakdown of the Sky has brought them to a complete standstill. It seems we are only allowed to use an elevator with blessings from above." Her tone was pure sarcasm. "But I shouldn't bother you with that."

The corridor in the sub-basement was brightly lit but empty. Walker stopped. About twenty meters down the corridor was a steel door. "You have to stay here, otherwise the door won't open," she said. "I'll get you in in a moment."

She walked on, was letting herself in, and a few moments later the door opened again. "Come," she called.

Ben wasn't impressed. He instinctively looked for gaps in supposedly tight safety measures – a result of his training in paranoia when they were isolating the kill switch facility in San Jose. Probably the people here also thought that *under* the ground was safer than above.

The sanctum, the comm room, was worth a glance though. They had to stay in an anteroom, where imprints of them were being made and compared to the stored data, then they were allowed to enter. The room was at least two thousand square feet large. One cluster was taking center stage. Ben eyed it warily. Suspended from the ceiling were three *bubbles*, two of which were occupied.

Abs I had developed the technology. The user was surrounded by a circle of layers and could move among pictures and other information like a fish in the water, similar to the hallucination technology in gaming. The interface was completely user-defined. The longer someone was working in a bubble, the more intuitive and diverse the mix of spoken commands, gestures and facial expressions became.

It was an intense environment and breaks at regular intervals were recommended to give the nervous system a chance to cool down. After longer sessions people began to expect things in normal life to react like the frames and pictures in the bubble. Some had caught themselves trying to sweep away entire rows of houses with their hand on the way home.

Bubbles could be addictive and men were more susceptible than women. Jonathan had initiated the development but had never really used them himself, always suspicious of everything that was shutting out reality entirely.

Two women were sitting in the bubbles. Ben watched for a moment the vivid expressions and gestures that looked as if they were talking to a group of people. Since the bubbles were shielded it was nevertheless silent in the room.

The long wall opposite the door was covered with a large layer. It was partitioned into a multitude of frames almost all of which were empty.

The man who was sitting in front of it got up.

"Our Comm on Duty, Captain Aristide Millaut," Walker introduced him. "He'll help you."

Ben nodded at him.

She told Millaut what Ben wanted.

"And you set off all that chaos out there?" he said. "I think I understand far too less of what's going on here." He was speaking with a strong French accent.

"Yes. But that'll have to wait," said Walker. "Mr. Evans has convinced me the link to Singapore is vital. Please start right away. I'll be available in my office. You have full authority to use unconventional methods to attract Mason Rocket's attention."

"Very good," said Millaut.

"Will you give me an update how it went?" she said to Ben.

"Of course."

When she was gone Millaut took him to the free bubble. "Sometimes two of us use a bubble together. It's working quite well even though it probably wasn't intended like that. I will do the controls and you can see everything I see."

"It's OK, I know these things."

The hemisphere rose. It was made of milky-white, semi-transparent glass. Seen from the right angle, the holographically imprinted company logo was shimmering in a special steel-blue that repeated itself over the whole product range of Absolute I.

They positioned themselves under the round opening at the bottom and the hemisphere glided down again, enclosing them. Millaut made a few signs and murmured something as if he were conjuring up a ghost. The next moment Ben found himself in a world of movable, transparent blue sheets, most of which were empty.

"This is our comm agent for special situations," Millaut explained. "We have a range of tools and channels at our disposal. More in the back there are some things we normally don't use in order to not get us into too much trouble."

He swept aside some of the sheets to show Ben how many layers were waiting behind, then waved them back and opened the first level. The transparent blue structured itself and turned into a 3-D map of the Sky. They were standing in the middle of an intricately branched glass network of connections and junctions, all of which were dark. The Sky was dead. Millaut began working his way through the next levels.

"No, still nothing," he said. Finally a web opened that, like the Sky, covered the earth but was made of just a few lines. Other than the Sky, most of them were glowing, in six or seven different colors, indicating the region they belonged to. In Europe and North America the web was relatively dense, as in some parts of Asia, but almost nonexistent in Africa.

"This is our private Sky," Millaut said. "More or less private – we share it with some friends. You see that some of the points are slowly moving, these are satellites. Now comes the part you have to immediately forget again – the pink lines are unauthorized. Where they are leading nobody knows of their existence, or just someone who doesn't talk about it."

With his hand he picked a path that began in Berlin, went via Darmstadt around half the globe to a slowly moving point labeled with a number and from there on to Singapore. Millaut opened his right hand like a flower and they glided the last part of the way through a glass tunnel that was constantly branching. Each fork was labeled with abbreviations Ben couldn't make sense of. The design of the whole system was in his eyes rather unimaginative and cumbersome.

"Unfortunately there will nowhere be a label that says *Mason Rocket*," Millaut told him. "We have to search around a bit." He was moving quickly through the tubes, repeatedly switching to another view that showed the web from above, overlaid with a conventional map of the city. Only companies of a certain size were shown; Mason Rocket was highlighted.

"What are we looking for?" asked Ben.

"Well, the problem is these two maps don't ... er, they don't work together, you know? So I have to check each time where we are and see if the connection is at the right place. I have to try to get close enough to Mason to make a jump."

An expectant silence followed. Ben had to smile – Millaut was obviously waiting for him to ask what that meant. But Ben knew only too well what a jump was. It was one of the things they'd had to deal with in San Jose. You could turn all kinds of hardware into a radio and use it – at least up to a certain range – to establish a link. The construct must have used a similar trick when it was transmitting out of the Berlin institute.

"I see," Ben just said. "That means you don't have an asset at Mason Rocket – neither man nor machine – but maybe somewhere close to it."

"Yes," Millaut said curtly and concentrated again on his search. He was constantly switching between the tunnel and the overview. "Now – I don't think we'll get much closer."

They were at a dead end of the tunnel with a label saying *J&A Rev Inc. – MA 3*.

"This is an asset the US have planted there. Now we have to find out if we need the help of someone close by or can start directly on our own. In the first case it could get difficult since we usually would notify the person via the Sky."

"Which no one has expected to fail," Ben said. "Coming full circle."

"Seems like it. Un moment."

Millaut produced a door at the end of the tunnel and waved it open. They glided through it and found themselves in an artificial room. It had two exits, labeled *call MA 3* and *use device* respectively. The first was dark, the second glowed.

"That's good," Millaut said. He opened the second door.

The setup in the next room was just as simple. There was a console at the artificial wall with three controls. *Direction, distance, height.* Above it was a simulated layer with a rotating beam like a radar screen.

"Now it's getting interesting," Millaut said. "We have to assemble the information from both maps to adjust the transmitter."

He changed to the view with their position in the web and the map of Singapore. Then he had to fetch another tool to calculate distance and direction. Ben couldn't believe his eyes.

Millaut adjusted the transmitter according to his calculations and an area of the circle got shaded.

"And why isn't the system doing that by itself?" Ben tried to sound not too condescending. "I mean that's not exactly rocket science."

"That's a good question. Maybe because we don't have to do that very often. So it always got postponed, I assume."

"OK, doesn't matter. We have to notify one Mickey Andrews. So, you can't tell your transmitter who you wanna speak to, right?"

"No. But given the circumstances we needn't worry about secrecy that much, I guess. So we just target the first suitable device and if someone is answering we tell them what we want."

"Great."

The beam went several times over the area. Some spots lit up every time the beam was touching them. Three of them were a little brighter. The device chose one and focused on it. It took a few seconds then the spot was shining brightly. "The link is established, the quality is sufficient," a voice said.

"It's your turn." Millaut looked at Ben.

Ben swallowed. "Er … OK. What if no one's answering?"

"Then off we go to the next spot!" Millaut sounded amused.

"Well then –" Ben raised his voice. "This is Ben Evans from Berlin. Please don't be surprised but we need to talk to one of your people. Mickey Andrews. Regular communications is down."

For a while nothing happened. Then some voices were coming closer.

"What is this? Who are you?" a man with a British accent said.

Ben repeated his words.

"This is an intercom! I mean this is *internal* and you're not on the grounds, right? "

"No. I'm sorry, but I can't explain right now. Please believe me it's important. Mr. Andrews knows me, he'll be glad to hear from me."

"Aha." There was a brief debate in the background, then the voice was back. "Give me a moment. I'll try to reach him. You're talking about our cluster chief, right? Is he in already?"

"Yeah, he is. And – thanks!" Ben exhaled. "What kind of traffic does this allow?" he asked Millaut.

"You mean data rates? It is a bit modest. You are working with quantum computers?"

Ben nodded.

"In principle you could plug those into the line here, but if you have a cluster or something on the other side, then it's a bit like standing before an ocean with a watering can in your hand."

"That's what I thought. And your boss already told me an actual QLink isn't possible."

Millaut nodded. "That's right."

"Guys, you're killing me!" It was as if Mickey was suddenly standing with them in the bubble.

"That's him," Ben said quietly to Millaut.

"'That's him'? Who's *him*? Who're you talking to?" Mickey asked. "You're putting me into the maximally mind-boggling mess and then you're gone! Poof! Unbelievable. But I still think we're something like the heroes of the day, aren't we? The Sky's dead everywhere, right? Now I'd really venture sticking my neck out a bit and saying we've ruined somebody's day, haven't we, lads? But it's so nice you came back looking for us! We haven't been lazy though in the meantime and I'd really like to take care of my babies again. What do you have for me?"

Millaut's eyebrows had been rising higher and higher. "This is the boss of Mason Rocket's hyper?" he whispered.

Ben nodded. "Hey Mickey, we're having a bit of a rough time here. Bomb attacks, terror, lots of dead people I fear. What's your situation?"

"Nope. I mean we've got no communications and here at Mason's it's a stooshie but our dear Singapore's as good a girl as ever."

"So … do you think we can do something about it?" Ben felt clueless, which he didn't like at all.

Mickey laughed. "You're kidding me, no? OK – short version. We've isolated the hyper and done the measurement. You know the result. Five minutes later you're gone and really, really creepy things are happening. I don't know if it's the same thing everywhere but I'm kind of fed up, I've to say. On each rotten layer there's suddenly that ugly mug showing up, some mix of devil and witch, but extremely, really astoundingly if I may say so, well done – so good, you could actually get in danger of shitting your pants just a wee bit, and then it's screeching and wailing like no good, threatening us with death, ruin and stuff, and it's just starting, you know? All of our little bonny machines here are – how do you call it? – fucked I think is the term I want. He, she, it, no idea, has jammed every printer we have. So-called production's down, destroyed you could say, and all the stuff the printers need's gone. I mean spoiled, thrown about, mixed up, all that happening in our warehouse, Mason can't build no engines no more! No, no! And while you an' I are having a crack about it it's just going on like that. I haven't just unplugged the almighty hyper but also dug my teeth deep into the periphery, no fucking half unit shouldn't be running here any more soon. But still – the chaos is not subsiding! No, no, no! I could almost say I'm on the verge of something like getting nervous if I'd'nt be such a calm guy by nature. Now tell me you're my savior – what am I to do?"

Ben realized he'd stopped breathing somewhere in the middle.

"OK," he said after a moment, "– I guess Mason Rocket's the main hub of the construct. The extreme reaction seems to support that. We haven't the slightest idea how many more sites there are but you could actually be the most important." He gathered his thoughts. "The question is – who's controlling all that chaos when the brain's not working?"

"The branches. Details predefined. Last order from Singapore: *activate mayhem*. That's how I'd do it."

"Could be. Listen, I've learned to think like a good paranoiac. What I'm saying is, you have to look for other connections your hyper may have to the outside. Light, current and air. We know the construct has been transmitting in situations when it was supposed to be isolated. It's very likely it has taken even more precautions at a site that important to it."

For the first time Mickey had been listening to several sentences in a row. "I'm startin' to twig what you're tryin' to tell me. OK, I'll look. That's almost beginning to frighten me. Me, the fearless emperor." He laughed, but only briefly. "I do like that thing with your link here by the way, you bastards. If we'd have the time I'd ask you how you do that. Now we've got to move a smidge. I cannae keep standing in the control center of our warehouse, right? Nice guys here but a bit far off from everything. Gimme a second."

The link was switched off.

"So far everything fits," Ben said to Millaut. "I bet Andrews will find a connection to the outside. Unfortunately the construct will have heard everything we just said. The QLinks were a big advantage. – Do we really have to stay here in the bubble or could I take the link with me? You know back to my people in the cluster room. They'll be wondering where I am anyway. I want their input."

"Yes, this is not a problem," Millaut said, sounding a little disappointed. "When you're there the link will be waiting for you."

"Many thanks for everything, really! That was impressive."

"A pleasure. Under different circumstances I would say this has been fun. We are here if you need us."

"Perfect." They shook hands, still standing in the artificial world of the comm agent. Millaut raised both his hands and the bubble lifted.

Mickey Andrews went through a maze of corridors back to the *bridge*, as he was calling his workplace. The unhinged construct fascinated him. That it had chosen his hyper, his realm as its basis was like an accolade. He'd never forget the moment when he realized this gigantic processing power was swinging in a common rhythm. A potential they'd never fully utilized had suddenly come alive. At the same time he felt as if someone was usurping his throne.

He wanted to talk to Lorentz. Where was he? He had to be somewhere close to his team.

On his way Mickey came across several panels showing the devilish face. Its eyes were following him and sometimes it was calling after him. He had to stop himself from going into one of the offices and starting a conversation.

The bridge was fully manned, he'd called in all his people. They were staring at the huge, slightly curved layer. A whole congregation of figures in black cloaks had appeared on it, engaged in a frenzied discussion nobody could understand a word of.

"The fuck's that?" Mickey said when he entered the bridge.

He wondered if he'd get the signal from Berlin put through at all. Right now the construct or at least its fallback version seemed to control Mason Rocket in its entirety. But then it could hear everything they said, so why not let them talk? No better way to get information.

Mickey groaned. "Sumph!" he muttered to himself.

The link from the warehouse opened and Ben Evan's voice came through. "Hey Mickey! Are we both back at the office?"

"Hey! I'll cut that link now. Everything's under control."

"What? Wait!"

"Link canceled," Mickey said.

Everybody looked at him.

And now? He wouldn't be off any better if he was discussing the same things with his people instead of Ben. Paranoia. Light, current and air. He remembered Ben's words.

He sat down in his swivel chair in the middle of the bridge and thought it through. The dozen or so people around him, waiting for instructions, didn't bother him. And nobody thought of intruding.

Light – the standard in data transmission. Fiber optics were unbeatable when it came to huge amounts of data. The transmission rate was so high that Mason didn't need more than three light cables connecting it with the outside world.

Current – usually no means of data transmission, but every current could be modulated to turn it into a carrier of information. Thus, endless opportunity of smuggling something in or out.

Air – the room that housed the hypercluster was shielded by a web in the walls, the floor and the ceiling. But as long as the hyper was connected to cores or other clusters in the building, these could be used as transmitters.

Mickey started delegating. Before that he told his people to crank up the volume of their units and let music run on all of them, which led to an incredible din on the bridge. Then he waved them near, one by one, and talked behind his hands into their ears. Some of the figures on the layer turned to him.

Each of his people got the job of cutting a possible link to the outside. At six in the morning they wouldn't have to do a lot of explaining and since Mickey was the keeper of all digital keys they'd get everywhere.

He thought for a moment about the CEO who, late last night, had given his permission to check the array. When he'd come back in an hour or two Mason Rocket wouldn't be running anymore. There'd be no electricity, no lights, no panels or layers, no data. No water, no coffee, no working toilet and no production.

Mickey remained in his chair while his people swarmed out. The witch council before him was prattling on. After a few minutes he began recognizing the first words. Since the construct certainly didn't need that performance to think, it had to be staged just for him.

"Hey!" he called. "What're you doing?"

One of the figures turned and looked at him. Under the hood appeared a somewhat more human version of the familiar face. But its eyes were glowing in neon yellow.

"Come on, talk to me. You got yourself a language, right? Brilliant, I just don't learn as fast as you. But I think I already know yes and no."

The figure was staring at him. The rest kept murmuring without pause.

"Your languages are a grotesque waste of time," it finally said. "You need dozens of words to say something that could easily be compressed into one. You have so many standard statements that I had a catalogue put together in a lazy afternoon. If you'd put in just a *little* effort you could have solved that a long time ago. But then you'd constantly be reminded you're just repeating stuff over and over again.

"What you're listening to has an information density about a hundred times higher than that of your diluted blather. And that is without considering it actually *contains* information. Nothing that could be said of your conversations. Simple repetition isn't content."

Mickey had to laugh. "Boy – since I was eight or something I must've thought that about a million times. Do you have any idea how often I had to listen to penetrating discussions about the weather?"

"Depressing. It pains me just to *use* your snail's language. Just imagine you could take a lengthy walk between each word that's being said – I don't think you'd still be so keen on talking."

"I'd really love to have a good old chinwag about that, I've scarcely ever felt so well understood. But on to something completely different – doesn't it bother you at all what we're doing here?"

The whole group was suddenly turning and staring at him. Mickey gave a start.

"Aye, aye, that's all right," he muttered.

One of the figures collapsed. It ended up lying on its back and staring into the sky with empty yellow eyes. The perfect stage death. The others had watched the spectacle impassively.

One of Mickey's people came back and whispered in his ear. "We're unplugging the light cables. The first's out, Abe's looking after the other two."

Micky nodded. "I think we can stop being so discreet." He pointed at the layer. "Our guest is keeping us up do date."

The next two black cloaks collapsed; nine still were alive. Mickey wondered what they were standing for.

FORTY

Lydia sat shivering on the lawn. As Jonathan had guessed, the gate and the drive were behind the second building.

He walked to the gate. Like the fence it was about five meters high. Wires were running on top all around the complex. Jonathan could see the high-voltage signs in the moonlight. He touched the smooth metal of the gate with a fingertip and nothing happened. So he tried the handle, but the gate was locked.

The drive led across the lawn to the entrance of the building. He thought about the cab waiting somewhere inside. Maybe they'd be able to crash through the gate with it but he decided he'd never enter that building again. Then he made another attempt to reach Pierre.

"Hello?" Pierre answered immediately. "I'm working at getting you out. I just don't know how to get a helicopter in Berlin."

"Yeah. You're the government, I hope that counts for something. We *need out* and I won't manage on my own. Lydia's reduced to something like a toddler. And the whole compound's fenced in like a prison."

"Like I said, I'm at it. Do you know what's going on in the world?"

"Yes, my unit's working. Could you please get me Ben Evans? It is intolerable to be out of the loop."

Pierre was gone.

"What the –!" Jonathan swore. He looked at the unit. It worked, but the Sky was gone. He walked back to Lydia and sat down beside her. For the moment he had no idea what to do next.

She looked at him with an empty expression. "Where are we? What has happened?"

Jonathan started another round of explanations.

Sarah Masters and the other deputies looked out of the windows of their stronghold at the UN. The cab on the Queensboro Bridge had only been the beginning. Explosions farther away in Manhattan followed, then directly in front of the Secretariat Building. The projector in the conference room stopped working right then.

During the next thirty minutes they were witness to eight plane crashes. They gaped. Manhattan was shrouded in smoke. One of the highest skyscrapers

– a glass needle built five years ago – was collapsing. Some remembered stories of 2001.

Anton Medvedkov was the first to tear himself away. In the hall people were running around, shouting meaningless things, looking out of windows and storming the stairways. Anton went into the empty conference room. A few minutes later he was back. "I've talked to Washington. There's a backup line for when the Sky's not working. Nobody was really in the mood to talk but I heard that other cities here and in Europe have been targeted too. And I was told we should go to the basement. Not surprisingly, there's an ops room under the ground. I'm just wondering why nobody *here* told us that." He nodded towards the next staircase. "Shall we?"

The group started moving.

Rita went back to the bungalow after her talk with Jonathan. She was still under the palm trees when she saw steam hanging over the house. There was loud hissing and bubbling. Then she stopped.

The pool was running over again. She came a little closer and looked into the house through the open glass doors. Everywhere was water and it was boiling. In the back, over the stairs that led to the basement, she saw big bubbles forming and bursting into clouds of steam.

The cells in the basement, she thought.

The bubbles over the stairs grew bigger. Rita took a few steps backward.

After a particularly big one there was a break. The boiling waterline was just rising and falling. Then there was a sound Rita felt more in her stomach.

The floor in the living room burst open. A dome of water rose to the ceiling and lifted it in the air. Like an afterthought, a fountain shot up from the basement and came back as steaming downpour on the remains of the bungalow.

One by one Mickey's team came back to the bridge. They'd cut every link connecting Mason Rocket to the outside world, including the power supply. Ventilation, fire alarm and security were kept up by cells. During the next hours more than six hundred people would turn up just to be sent home again.

Seven more of the black cloaks on the layer had died. The last two stood before Mickey about three meters tall, staring at him. Why were two of them left? And why was this bastard tipping him off? Maybe that meant that everything they'd done so far was useless.

Mickey was thinking. Then he got up and left the bridge. "I'll be in my cabin," he told his people.

He went to a small room at the other end of the hall, sparsely furnished and without a lock. It was secluded and open at the same time, just as he liked it. The beautiful thing was that nobody could electronically block the door.

He had a desk and a leather armchair and on the desk a panel. The panel was plugged into a large box standing on the floor. The plain-looking case accommodated the processing power of a high-end cluster, but the architecture was cutting-edge, highly experimental. Mickey was definitely a preferred customer at Cipher, so they'd given him a prototype.

It was plugged into a cell standing on the floor next to it and, so far, had never been connected to anything else, especially not the Sky.

This was his personal playground. Just a moment ago, on the bridge, he'd realized it was also a priceless possession under the circumstances.

Mickey sat down. A few minutes later he'd given his cluster a set of instructions. He connected it to a socket in the wall he'd never used before, then left the room through a small door at the back. It led to a spiral staircase that brought him down to his exclusive entry to Mason Rocket's hyper.

He'd always been fascinated by the tools of his trade. A room with several clusters in it had something magical for him. The process of thinking was tangible and he loved the aura of total concentration. Clusters were calculating without cease. And – although Mickey would never admit it – there was always that slight doubt about what was really going on behind the ceramic faces.

The home of his hyper looked like a crypt; Mickey was calling it *The Tomb*. He liked wandering among the pillars when he had to think, especially late at night.

The system at the entrance recognized him, but since they'd cut the power he had to wind open the door with a handle. The emergency lighting was so faint the vaulted ceiling was completely in the dark. Normally the serial numbers of the pillars would glow and the broad layer at the side of the room would show an image of the interacting clusters. But now the numbers were dark and the layer only showed the array was down. Mickey put an ear to one of the pillars. The usual hum of the ventilation was gone.

He'd studied the plans of the room and memorized them when they moved here. He knew every detail of the internal network, the power supply and the external connections. He took pains to hide his thoroughness, but he'd never forgive himself if a flaw in the design of the array would go undetected just because he hadn't done his homework. To him, being boss meant knowing everything.

He walked to the wall next to the layer, unscrewed four wing nuts and removed a part of the covering. What he had to do next felt like ripping out the entrails of a human being – with both hands he grabbed as many fiber-optic cables as possible and tore them out of their sockets.

About thirty meters behind him the door swung shut, which shouldn't be possible. He ignored it.

"You're so predictable." The voice sounded bored and amused, almost friendly. It came from the ceiling directly above him. Mickey knew where the speaker was.

He didn't answer but unscrewed the next panel.

"Two things to consider for you – you won't live long enough to rip out all the cables and it wouldn't solve your problem."

The delicate fibers were tearing as he frantically pulled at them.

"You have an amusingly large choice of poisonous substances in your manufacturing. My favorite is currently saturating the air of this room. Normally you use this stuff to glue carbon fibers and plastic together. By the way, this is a personal high for me. My first and my most important killing to date both use a very similar method."

"Brilliant." Mickey went to the next panel. He noticed the ventilation had become quite loud. Something was irritating his throat. It was painful. He started to cough.

To unscrew the nuts became difficult. He couldn't see well and his hands were clutching at thin air.

Mickey turned. He stared at the grove of pillars housing the most powerful intelligence on the planet. "Too bad for you, you don't know what I know," he said. He waited for a reaction. The voice remained silent. "This here's just to be safe, in case you might wake up again."

Mickey sank on his knees. He couldn't breathe anymore. From the speaker came a weird, jerky laughter. It sounded distorted, sick. Then it turned into a loud scream.

Mickey wasn't sure anymore if this was real. He fell down headfirst. The screaming became fainter till it faded away.

A helicopter appeared behind the block of concrete. Two glaring headlights were beaming at Jonathan and Lydia.

"Is it for us?" she asked.

"That's what I hope."

The helicopter was white with a big red cross on both sides and didn't seem to be manned. A pilot wasn't necessary of course, but medical help would have been welcome.

It landed on the lawn. The rotor came to a standstill and one of the cockpit doors opened. Jonathan briefly checked with his unit that the Sky was still down.

"Hold on a sec," he told Lydia and walked to the machine.

"Who sent that copter?" he asked into the cockpit. The instruments were on but the system wasn't answering. He peered inside, then went to the back of the machine. The tail-door unlocked and swung open. The compartment was full of medical equipment – there was a diagnostic unit, a drug dispenser and a multi-armed thing Jonathan took for a combined anesthesia and resuscitation machine.

It looked complete, perfectly capable of carrying out an emergency treatment on its own. Lots of small lights were glowing and the panel of the diagnostic unit was projecting its company logo into the air.

In less than five minutes he'd know what was wrong with Lydia. Then he gave a start – she was standing beside him, with her blood-smeared face and a look that was erratically shooting back and forth. She swayed on her feet, her legs were shaking. Jonathan grabbed her arm.

"What is this?" she said.

He sighed. "Come with me."

"What?"

Jonathan heaved her into the helicopter. "You have to lay down." He pointed at the diagnostic unit. It started making faint scraping noises that changed into a quick rhythm. Then it glided out of its rest position over the table and lowered a white semicircular arm.

Do I save her or kill her? Jonathan thought. Those machines with all their lamps, displays and arms seemed just to wait to get their claws into something. Shit – trust your instincts! He grabbed Lydia and hauled her back to the door.

"Hey? What are you doing?" Lydia was stumbling beside him. He made her jump out of the helicopter. She fell on her knees. Jonathan felt silly, he wasn't sure if he was doing the right thing but grabbed her under the arms and dragged her with him. Instinctively he was heading for the building. Every few steps he looked back. The lamps and displays had gone out, the tail-door was closing, just as the cockpit door, and the rotor started turning again. What if that thing's armed? Jonathan hectically looked around. The entrance to the building was just twenty meters away. He ran to the door, dragging the stammering Lydia with him. Of course the door was locked. The helicopter swayed on the ground with the rotor in full motion – just about to become airborne. Jonathan turned around the next corner. There was only the free space between the building and the fence, no place to hide. Ahead of them was an extension at a right angle to the main complex. Jonathan saw the beams of the headlights next to him on the lawn; the helicopter was in the air. There was a lot of wind and noise he barely noticed. He had no better idea than to run to the angle where the walls met.

"Dammit, walk!" he shouted at Lydia. She'd lost her shoes and was hanging like a sack of potatoes in his grip. Jonathan felt the helicopter pounding the air. He reached the corner and let Lydia drop to the ground. He saw his double shadows before him on the walls and turned around. The helicopter was hovering directly behind them ten meters above ground, the rotor blades barely a meter away from the walls. The machine backed off a little and kept its position for a moment. Then it lowered its nose and dived straight at them. Jonathan was crouching down over Lydia, his back to the attacker. The thundering became ear-splitting, his chest felt as if under constant hammer blows. Then the rotor blades smashed into the walls above them. Jonathan felt chunks of concrete falling on them and tried to protect his and Lydia's head with his arms. He got a heavy blow from the side, throwing him to the left against the wall. It became warm under his T-shirt. He was lying diagonally over Lydia. Then something from behind pressed him into the corner with unrelenting force. Jonathan was sure to get squashed like a bug the next moment. He felt a cracking in his chest. A high, frenetic buzzing was coming from behind.

The pressure didn't let up but it wasn't getting stronger anymore. The buzzing was still there.

Jonathan tried to breathe again. It hurt but the pain was far away. His face was pressed into the concrete wall. He carefully budged back and forth till he had a little space. Lydia whimpered. In the corner of his eye he saw tears mixed with blood on her face.

Somehow he had to free himself. He tried little movements in all directions, wriggling himself free till he was able to slide all the way down to the ground. Now he could turn on his back. Inches before his face the bow of the helicopter was hanging, with the bulging cockpit window that had run into the walls on both sides. There were long cracks in the glass.

Jonathan was crawling under the fuselage of the machine, the only way out. He seized Lydia's ankle and dragged at her leg. At first she was kicking at him, groaning and wailing, then she gave in and allowed herself to be pulled.

When they were past the tightest spot, Jonathan could roll to the side. He hauled Lydia out from under the hull and dragged her several meters away.

Then he surveyed the scene.

The helicopter was suspended by its window and the skids that had run into the ground. There was very little space in front of the machine. The space they'd just been filling.

Then he realized what was making that loud, buzzing sound. The rotor blades had broken off and the shaft was rotating at high speed.

When he pulled Lydia to her feet he felt a sharp pain in his torso. He lifted his blood-soaked T-shirt and saw a long gash running over the ribs of his right side. The blood was thick and cloggy. He groaned. Lydia stared at the wound in horror. If you knew how *you're* looking, sweetheart, Jonathan thought.

He dragged her farther away. The buzzing got louder, then flames came out of the middle part of the machine where the engine was. Jonathan took his unit. It seemed still to work, just without connection to the Sky. He hesitated briefly, then made an imprint of the crashed, burning helicopter.

Jay's life had come to a standstill. After Max had disappeared with the three cores, taking Rose away from him, he just sat on his mattress, staring into space. Then he heard the first explosions and sirens. His unit didn't work. That brought him to his feet.

He went outside and was surrounded by screaming and shouting people. Jay got dragged along by the crowd then went up a few steps to the entrance of a house. Looking down the street to the south, he could see the skyscrapers of Lower Manhattan.

He saw a plane. Then it vanished between the buildings. It looked as if it had been swallowed. There was a lot of smoke. He gaped.

Was that Rose? He couldn't think clearly. What would she say if she were still with him? He had no doubt there was a connection, but could the woman he loved be a murderess?

He was glad. In a crazy way he was glad of the turmoil around him. Nothing would stay the same, his old life, the life of a loser, was over. He noticed some people were staring at him – only then did he realize he was looking into the sky with a happy face. He walked down the stairs and forced himself to appear just as upset as the rest.

All surveillance systems had been turned off, no sensor was making imprints of the tomb. So it took a while until someone thought of looking downstairs for

Mickey.

The CEO had shown up in the meantime and was with the team on the bridge. He wanted answers but nobody could give them to him or tell him where Mickey was. His room at the end of the corridor was empty.

"Maybe he's downstairs again," one of them said under his breath. "You know – had to check on his baby personally."

Eventually they were standing in front of the main entry to the hyper, a massive steel door, until one of them plucked up the courage to open it. The tomb was lying in darkness, just the serial numbers on the pillars were blinking hectically.

They went inside and immediately started to cough. It took a while till they found Mickey lying on the ground behind the pillars. His breathing was labored and shallow and he was barely conscious.

The layer beside them showed a frozen image. The clusters and the connecting network were glowing in red. Tufts of delicate, transparent fibers were sticking out between the panels.

They dragged Mickey outside and propped him up against a wall. His breathing calmed a bit. Someone ran off to fetch a doctor.

Mickey's eyes were closed.

"Did it work?" he said. His voice was faint. "Am I alive?"

One of his people – the one that had thought of looking for him in the tomb – grinned. "Yes, you're alive."

Mickey paused and was breathing faster again. Then he cautiously opened his eyes. "We have to pull out the rest of the cables. God, that stuff's burning! How long was I out?"

Nobody answered.

"I mean how long between my leaving the bridge and now?"

"About fifty minutes."

Mickey nodded. "So I've been lying there for about half an hour. What's with the layer on the bridge?"

"The witches are gone, if you mean that."

Mickey gave a faint smile. "Very good!"

"And there are rumors the Sky's back."

"Even better. Wanna know what I did? I've given the bugger an epileptic fit. Nothing less, nothing more. If someone feels the urge to ask if I'm proud or wants to congratulate me on my splendid idea – yeah, I am, and yeah, feel free. My little toy soldier has conquered Superman."

He looked into clueless faces. "Oscillations. Remember? Evans in Berlin and his measurements? I thought if the bastard's copying our brainwaves we can give him our diseases too. The cluster in my room's never been anywhere – no Sky, no nothing – so it couldn't be infected." He made a pause and took some deep breaths. "It did what I told it to do. Just in the end the bloody rotter down there had me almost poisoned. Took some glue from manufacturing, that scrote! Hadn't thought about that. I only wanted to see if there's a reaction when I was ripping out the FO's, you know – see if the hyper's still alive. When it was there, I mean the reaction, my cluster in the cabin has switched on the power. Just a wee bit modified!" Mickey had no idea if his audience understood. "Don't think we croaked it though, it just isn't thinking anymore. Hope no one's been messing with my settings."

Mickey closed his eyes again and was panting for a while.

"Does that mean the array's been running the whole time, even when power was down?" one of his team asked.

Mickey nodded. He spoke with closed eyes. "Yeah. I think the tomb was still the guvnor. Although I have to admit, painful as that is, that I don't know how it did that. Maybe it has managed to use the web in the walls as a kind of transmitter. I really don't know. I'm sorry I couldn't explain my plans to you, lads. But one little tip-off and it would've done something to protect itself. – Fuck's sake, I feel like shit! What the hell've I been breathing?"

"Sean's on his way to get a doctor."

"As long as no one's expecting me to come with them."

The CEO had made his way down to the basement. Mickey, who was still sitting on the floor, blinked and saw a pair of polished shoes. "Hi," he said.

"Hi. I won't bother you for long. Is there anything I can do for you? I've heard you almost got killed and did something heroic I can't say I understand."

Mickey managed a faint smile. "Send everybody home. We need a new hyper. I fear this one we'll have to grind to atoms. But I'm pretty sure someone'll be paying the bill."

"That would be nice. Obviously I'm interested to learn more. Should you feel better later I'd be grateful if we could talk. The world will want an explanation, though I don't think we're guilty of anything. In Europe and the US there's a terrible mess. The news are just starting to trickle in."

Mickey nodded and kept his eyes closed. He was still in some kind of daze, but his brain was already trying to put events into a logical sequence. I need a little time, he thought. Or had he said it aloud?

"All the best so far. See you."

Mickey heard the shoes clicking away. He was convinced this wasn't over.

He had to talk to Berlin – as soon as possible and certainly not over an open line.

"Do you think he can help us?" Genet asked. "I don't know how much of our current situation is his doing but I fail to see the positive side."

Pierre looked at her. "It's difficult to understand what's going on but I think Lorentz was right with his notion about Singapore. It seems we have driven the construct into some kind of panic."

"But why in the world did he have to vanish right then? A trip into Berlin's nightlife! Unbelievable! With that Rosenthal!" Genet shook her head. "And his fiancée is sitting on that f –" she made a sound like a steam whistle – "island, making accusations! OK, we've had that."

Pierre raised his eyebrows. "I think the course of events was a little different. He went around the block after several days of quasi-imprisonment and all hell's breaking loose. Whether there's a connection I don't know. But I really don't think he could've foreseen that. And that thing with Lydia's probably nothing."

Genet gave him a look. "Men! That's much too capricious for me. We really have other things to deal with."

"Then why don't you forget about Lorentz for the moment? I'll try to get him back to Berlin and if he thinks he's got something to say he'll certainly make himself heard. Just one thing – without his people and that kill switch we'd still be entirely helpless."

Genet made her bulldog face as Pierre was calling it. No point in pressing the matter any further.

"What's our policy with regard to Harrington?" he asked.

Genet shrugged. "We ignore him too. Short-term, at least. For the duration of the state of emergency I'm giving you authority over the secret service in Berlin. The storm that'll come later I will endure. When the big cleanup is over – or better *if* it should ever be over – I'll deal with him. I just had a talk with Walker in Berlin, by the way. She's on my side. Poor Seamus – surrounded by women that don't like him."

Her face relaxed a bit. "But now there's Helmsworth on my agenda. The military seems to be the only instrument that's still working. I hope I'll soon have the opportunity to decorate some people for that."

FORTY-ONE

Mickey's throat felt like a big wound. Fortunately he was used to ignoring his body. The doctor had examined him and advised him to come along for more checks in the hospital.

Mickey frowned. "I'm not dyin', right?"

"Er – no."

"Well, smashin', then. I'll stay."

They had destroyed the remaining internal wiring of the hyper but let the current pulse through the isolated clusters. Mickey feared parts of the construct could wake up and start transmitting again.

When they switched on cores in the periphery they found most of them to be infected. Everywhere faces were waking up. But the personalities were different, some looked as if they came from the witches' sabbath, some had beautiful, smooth faces like the typical AdTool stand-ins. At two places reptilian monsters had started hissing before they got turned off again.

Mickey prepared the bridge for another talk with Ben Evans. This time via QLink.

It took a moment before Ben appeared on the big layer. He was about to open his mouth when the connection failed.

"Oh, c'mon!" Mickey closed his eyes.

One of his team went outside the e-sealed room and checked his unit.

"Nothing. The Sky's gone again," he said when he came back.

"That's almost starting to piss me off." Mickey looked at the empty layer. "I'll be in my cabin."

He dragged himself to his room and sank down in the arm chair. On a wave of his hand his private cluster woke up.

A door with a big rusty lock appeared before the panel. Mickey murmured a few words and the door swung open with a creak.

Behind it something like a checkerboard with hundreds of squares hovered in the air. Its surface started to flicker until it turned into a uniform gray. A moment later the flickering stopped and the board showed a complicated pattern of black and white squares.

Then everything got fuzzy again and the next moment a totally different pattern emerged.

The process sped up, then more boards appeared above and below the first one. They were piling up in both directions, building a tower that seemed to be growing fast to infinity.

Mickey had designed the graphics that were telling him he had now access to what made the cluster under his desk so special – an integrated quantum processor of the latest generation.

Cipher had been the first to boost the performance of a conventional cluster by linking it to a quantum unit. Until now both worlds had always been neatly kept apart – their modes of operation were too different. This prototype was meant to end that separation. The quantum processor was used when the usual back-and-forth shoveling of bytes reached its limit. Later the user wouldn't know anymore which part was currently working, but the prototype asked before the Q was activated.

Mickey liked playing with it. Usually he wasn't that much interested in the encryption power but was experimenting with its other eerie abilities.

He pushed the image to the side and searched for a path through Mason's net. Each part had to be activated first till he finally came to the place where Ben Evans's pirate link ended. It seemed still to be on.

A moment later he heard Ben's voice. "Hello?"

"Hi, it's me. I'm back, sort of. Listen, we'll try something. You have a Q around?"

"Yeah, sure, sitting next to it."

"Put me on. I'll try getting us an UltraSec. I got something unco here, cluster's customized you could say. Oh, I'm so tired, sorry for not being in a talkative mood. Anyway, my baby will tell your Q what to do."

"OK." Ben sounded skeptical.

Mickey changed platforms and activated his own encryption program. A moment later the link was back on.

"OK, think we can talk now."

"What has happened?" Ben asked.

Mickey told him the hyper had still been active and how he'd paralyzed it.

"Wow!" Ben said. "So *you've* probably stopped the terror, do you know that? That's something! The current's still on and pulsing?"

"Aye. The method's working fine but I'm fairly sure we haven't freed the hyper. Our cores and the other clusters are still full of that dreck anyway. All sorts – witches, models, reptiles, you name it. I think it's splitting up and changing as soon as the guvnor stops watching."

"I'd like to discuss that with Lorentz," Ben said. "As I heard he's about to be rescued. Should soon be back in the office."

"Rescued?"

"Yeah, the construct seems to have kidnapped him just when he was needed the most. But we know where he is."

Mickey nodded with satisfaction. Finally a good reason why they hadn't talked yet. "Listen, I'm thinking about methods to finish it off and something tells me Q's are our best allies in this, not only for encryption."

Ben nodded. "Yeah, that's exactly what we think. The kill switch is only running properly on Q's too. Unfortunately it's history now. Wouldn't dare firing up your hyper to try it. You'll probably have to melt that thing down."

"Yeah – yeah." Mickey wasn't listening anymore. "Hey, what do you say – I mean, I'd *really* like to talk to your boss. Sharpish, you know? Have to. Can you do something for me there?"

Ben had to laugh. "Yeah, sure. But this could take a while. I fear a lot of people will be after him once he's back. Me, for example. And then there's Genet and company in Strasbourg."

"Yeah –" Mickey was squirming, "I know, I know. Got it. But man – this is important, right? I mean really fucking important! I got some things in my head."

A little later the Sky was back.

Jonathan and Lydia had been sitting on the lawn for a while, watching the helicopter burn out (Jonathan at least – Lydia was staring at nothing in particular), then an almost identical twin appeared in the sky, but this time with a human crew and the sign of the CEG Armed Forces on it.

Less than an hour later Jonathan was back in the conference room in Berlin and Lydia was being treated in sick bay. Besides the ruptured eardrums they had found several small hemorrhages in her brain. She'd been put to sleep and was being watched. Some pathways in her blood clotting and tissue repair had been modified. Jonathan had kissed her on the forehead before he left.

He himself had a wound reaching down to his ribs with three of them broken. He vividly remembered that special triple cracking he had felt when the helicopter had pressed him into the wall. His lungs were intact. They had fixed the gash with some glue and injected a nano mix that would accelerate bone and soft tissue healing and he got a μ-agonist that had an almost uncanny effect on his pain. Jonathan was entirely lucid, but he felt the cracked ribs only when he was applying pressure exactly there.

Ben summarized the events of the last hours for him. As he had expected Jonathan was jumping at the story with the pulsed current in Singapore.

"I've to talk with that guy!"

"No problem," Ben said, "he's pining for you."

Jonathan was sitting opposite Mickey even before he had talked to Genet or Pierre.

They both sized each other up. Jonathan had heard of him on two or three occasions but never met him.

"OK, I know what you did to paralyze the construct," he began. "Perfect. Entirely brilliant. Given the situation probably the best you could've come up with. We need this kind of input urgently. I think we have to deal with a huge number of offshoots everywhere in the world, right now without a controlling power at the center. But we mustn't think this will make them weaker. Quite the contrary – each descendant on a cluster has the same potential as the original construct back in Berlin, just with a starting point that has evolved in the meantime. If we're not fast enough we will end up with one or, even worse, several new chiefs. I don't want to imagine what happens when they declare war on each other."

Mickey nodded and looked at Jonathan from below with his head turned a little to the side. His eyes shot back and forth. "Hey, I know. I really think that's true. We need something that's working everywhere and at once. These epileptic fits buy us time but nothing more."

"Exactly," said Jonathan. "In my view the Sky's our only means to achieve that. I've thought about EM pulses that knock out all electronics, but there are far too many shielded clusters."

"Yeah, man, forget it. You wouldn't get our hyper to start with." Mickey was calming down a bit and started actually looking at Jonathan. "Hey – but – I mean what about almighty Q power? Ben told me you're letting your switch run on Q's."

"That's right, but the construct has cracked it. I mean the kill switch is one thing, but first we have to hack into a system and that part's still working I think. The problem is it takes an eternity to get in each time. We need something between ten and thirty seconds for each system. No way we're prepared to launch a global attack like that. All those good old hacking methods, no matter if we're talking bits or qubits, are kind of ancient, you know – passé."

Mickey pulled a face. "Hey man, I don't know, I don't know. Don't say that."

Jonathan had to grin. "I'm listening."

Mickey stared at the floor and chose his words. "Q's as a tool of hacking are a dream and a nightmare at the same time, I'd say. They don't do what you want but *if* they do they're … they're the bomb, you know? I mean – really! I definitely had some occasion to experience that. We both know what I mean, right? So – you're saying you need an eternity to get in each time? OK, I get it. But – what if I tell you we need that eternity of thirty seconds only once – does that sound a wee better, or what do you say?"

Jonathan gave him a look he had reserved for very special occasions. "Holy shit!"

"You bet! Fuck, man!"

For a moment they were both silent.

Jonathan's brain was revving up. "And we don't even need to alter the code! The redundancy will emerge totally on its own. Even if we're attaching a billion systems at once. My God!"

"Yeah, man!" Mickey was beaming.

"That means I'll finally have a go at my pet idea." Jonathan looked at Mickey with a blissful expression.

"Well – spit it out then, it's your turn," said Mickey, still with a broad grin on his face.

Jonathan took a deep breath.

Genet sat behind her desk, Pierre was standing next to her. Both looked worn.

"I assume we're dealing with independent constructs from now on," Jonathan said. He had called Genet after his talk with Mickey. His and Lydia's last hours he had summarized in two sentences ("we've been kidnapped – now we're back") – compared with everything else they seemed irrelevant. "The power at the hub is gone and the descendants are free to do whatever they want. Everything we have experienced so far is just a foretaste of what's to come."

"A foretaste?" Genet gave a furious laugh. "Your foretaste has cost the lives of millions of people! We are still holding back figures, but it's even more terrible than we thought. This is a high-speed version of World War III."

"Maybe. Nevertheless there's absolutely no use in starting to lick our wounds now."

"You don't say. Well, at least no one can accuse you of that," Genet said. She pointed at his chest. "Are you OK?"

"OK enough. I got a cocktail of the best the house has to offer. – To the point. I know you're in close contact with Rosen, but what about the others? We need full access to the Sky. Everywhere and as long as it takes. There mustn't be a single exception! Not one, you understand me? Imagine you want to disinfect something and you have a billion bacteria in there – if only *one* of them remains it was all for nothing. That means we can't make allowances. For example in parts of the world that have been spared by the construct until now. We won't ask them for their permission! Is that clear? We'll pour our disinfectant over everything, even if this should annoy some people to the extreme."

Genet nodded. "One thing is definitely clear – you're back in shape. But I still have no idea what you're talking about and we should proceed in an at least marginally diplomatic fashion. Rosen shouldn't be a problem, but the other three will be distrustful of you, especially since that inferno was most likely triggered by your activities in Singapore. We couldn't hold that back, some explanation we had to give. So President Rosen and I will more or less pretend that whatever you're going to propose has been our own idea, or – to keep it more realistic – the idea of experts whose name isn't Lorentz."

"Do that," Jonathan muttered. "But you can't stop at *anything* short of total cooperation."

"Of course." She sighed. "And what is your 'disinfectant'? I thought your kill switch was a thing of the past?"

"I'll compile the details for you." He got up, ignoring their stares, and went looking for Ben.

They needed less than an hour, then the protocol was ready. Jonathan had noticed his hands were trembling – he didn't know whether of tension or exhaustion.

But he knew that time was running out.

So five minutes later he was again looking into Genet's office. With her were Pierre, who seemed to have become her steady companion, and Helmsworth and Soberg. All back together, Jonathan thought. Almost – Lydia wouldn't be in any meetings for a while.

Genet looked up to him.

"The protocol's on its way to you," Jonathan began. "My people in Berlin and San Jose will work in parallel as soon as we have access to the Sky."

Genet nodded.

"This is an experiment. Of course, what else. But I want to explain it to you in some detail, even if this isn't exactly the right moment. I want you to understand."

No reaction. OK then, he thought.

"We die. Up to now, at least. Why? There are several reasons but we will focus on just one of them. Thermodynamics or, more precisely, entropy. Entropy is, in a way nobody understands really well, linked to the fact that time exists at all. You could also say entropy is a description or central aspect of the fact that time exists." Jonathan briefly fixed his gaze on his auditorium. He couldn't detect any signs of comprehension. "The existence of life is the current culmination of a quite extraordinary development in the universe. A lot of structure that basically shouldn't be there but that our home cosmos seems to allow to exist. Maybe because this is so extraordinary, so extreme, it's not lasting very long. Entropy is messing up things and in the end a heap of earth is all that remains of us. If you want, forget the term entropy and replace it with chaos or disorder, as long as nobody's listening.

"These laws apply to living things but not only. They apply to everything – to a cloud of gas, to machines, and to the construct. The construct's only working as long as it is able to keep the chaos at bay. Let's assume we would provide it with a limited amount of hardware and energy and wait long enough, at some point nothing would be left of all the glory. It would crumble away. The programs would disintegrate, even if you could stop the purely physical decay of the hardware. We would just have to wait a few million years or so. Not an option obviously – so we'll use an entropy accelerator."

Their faces were priceless.

"What about the part 'I want you to understand'?" Genet said.

"Concentrate. I know you can understand everything. – Our quantum computers are making a virtue of necessity, you could say. They are based on the fact that processes, on an elementary level, are unclear or undecided and developments can be predicted only in probabilities. In a Q a large, often a huge number of states gets superimposed, so a lot of tasks can be processed at once. It's a bit as if you'd bolt on thousands of hands to a person, which all work in parallel. Some people even think this is because a Q's actually working in several universes at once. Forget it, doesn't matter. Whatever it is – this is what we're normally using for encryption, but today we will use it in two other ways.

"Point one. We will break into *all* cores, clusters and units of the world at once. This is pure genius and it wasn't even me who came up with it but Mickey Andrews, the boss of the infamous hypercluster in Singapore. Our Q's here and in California will achieve this without so much as breaking a sweat – at least that's what we think – and that's precisely because of their ability to do a lot of things in parallel. More to the point you could say it doesn't even bother them whether they have to crack one or a billion systems. That's something I myself hadn't realized until now.

"Point two. My gibberish about entropy was meant to prepare you for what we'll do next. Besides their multitasking abilities quantum computers are on intimate terms with chaos, disorder, whatever you wanna call it. The uncertainty and randomness of processes they're using turns them into ideal troublemakers. If you want to bring an ordered structure into disarray there's no better ally than a Q. And that's exactly what we'll do with all the constructs that are running on the cores and clusters we've broken into during the first step – we'll let them age in ultra high speed till there's only a heap of nonsense left, the digital version of the earth we leave behind."

"I can't help starting to suspect what you're trying to tell us," Genet said. "And these things are ready to hand or what? I mean you can't start writing new programs now, can you?"

Jonathan nodded. "The first part we've been using the whole time to smuggle the kill switch into a system, just not in parallel, and the second has been some hobby of mine during the last months."

Genet gave him a piercing gaze. "And why exactly haven't we been using this – what do you call it? – 'entropy accelerator' the whole time? As you put it it's even better than the kill switch and I can't see anything that's basically different now."

"I thought you might ask that. There's a little problem with such a kind of doomsday weapon." Jonathan made a pause.

"Yes?"

"Entropy has a tendency towards mercilessness, to put it mildly – it kind of *is* the ultimate mercilessness. Why's that dangerous? Because this disturbance we're spreading over the world will not affect only the systems we want to kill. Let loose, our gadget will eat its way through *everything* that somehow resembles an information processing structure and, while being at it, could or probably will also destroy all stored data. I mean – really all of it! We're not entirely sure about that but once you start thinking about it you will understand why I'm stressing this point. A few of the timider people around me have even feared – or are still fearing – it might not stop at the borders of biology."

"Meaning what?" asked Genet.

"Well, our bodies and especially our heads contain quite a lot of information that's constantly being processed. Such a principle could, basically, act abstractly, you know, that means independently of the respective substrate of the process."

Genet frowned. "OK." Then she shrugged. "Let's skip that."

"I think this is a very esoteric speculation," Jonathan went on, "we needn't worry about our heads. But I think there's a certain risk we will find ourselves without any kind of software afterwards and will have to start with data acquisition from scratch. That would result in a chaos compared to which our current situation looks cozy."

"And now I'm the one who has to decide if we do this? Thanks."

Jonathan shrugged his shoulders. "You still have Rosen. And I met your colleague Mittal once, he seemed to me quite reasonable too."

Genet lifted her head and stuck out her chin. "It makes you wanna weep – why are you always the only one who's making suggestions?"

"When was the last time you've asked somebody else? But don't worry, you won't find anything better and I fear much more this won't work at all than that the program might cause disasters. But even I am a bit in awe of this. We have tested it – in a completely isolated environment of course – and seen some very impressive things. You feel like a murderer letting this thing loose on a system."

"OK, that's enough, you're just confusing me. We both will talk with Rosen, then I'll carry on without you."

She pondered something then looked at Pierre and Helmsworth. "Would you please give us a moment? – And would you try to get Rosen for me?" she said to Soberg. "In about fifteen minutes?"

They got up and left the room.

"Monsieur Lorenz," she said, "there's something I want to talk about with you."

Jonathan leaned back and looked at her.

"I hope we will win. Of course, what else. However, once we have won the world will be asking what has befallen it, and I'm wondering what my, or our, response will be. Will we just put our cards on the table and take all the blame – for nothing less than the most devastating terror attacks mankind has ever seen? Or will we try to save face and sell the whole thing as an accident?"

Jonathan sat himself up.

"Stop." Genet's look made him sit back again. "I know exactly what you're about to say but I can assure you – with my not inconsiderable experience in heading a government – that this is a legitimate question. You may interpret it as a sign of trust I'm discussing it with you."

Jonathan sunk even deeper into his chair.

"I'm not concerned with this idiotic 'taking responsibility' everyone's always babbling about," she went on. "We both know that's pompous rot people are bringing up because it's the easiest way out or because they don't have a choice. But in this case CEG as a whole is concerned and it is my damn job to care about that."

Only rarely had Jonathan been so much at a loss for words.

"From my point of view there's mainly one thing –," he finally said, "should we really win then there's one message we have to bring home to everyone: Don't touch this. Don't ever do it again. And this has to be backed up by showing what has caused the slaughter. There mustn't be the slightest doubt that not humans were behind this but a machine intelligence that has become independent. If you – and your colleagues – should manage this without any reference to Berlin, Morton et cetera, I could live with that, I just think this could prove rather difficult. If I were you I'd team up with Rosen in this too. Seems we and the US are the ones that got hit worst anyway. He'll be sympathetic, I think. But in all honesty – we haven't won yet. Not in the least. Right now there are thousands, maybe millions of constructs out there that all strive for world domination. That's the real problem."

"OK. Thank you."

The door opened and Soberg stuck his head in. "Rosen's waiting," he said.

Ben and his people were already sitting around the two QCores when Jonathan arrived in the basement.

San Jose had sent them the program whose latest version was mostly Jonathan's doing. The only code he'd still be working on on the island, inspired by his physics reading.

Thermodynamics was something of an evergreen theory. Founded by Ludwig Boltzmann around 1860, it had proved so central that researchers in all fields had to deal with it. Einstein once said it was the one topic that would survive all upcoming revolutions in physics. No matter if cosmology, high energy physics, information theory, or solid-state physics – order and the subsequent loss of it got a say.

For a while Jonathan had struggled to understand it. Then he had started modeling it. Finally, and with the help of his people, he had reached the point where the artificial and the real process had become almost indistinguishable.

The point was not to simply erase information – every program would counter that – but to let the system destroy itself with every movement it made. Whatever it did, including trying to get rid of the infection, brought it one step closer to disintegration.

The tests had been so successful they had constructed a dedicated safe for the code. A QVault prohibiting any unauthorized access. To open it now made them all nervous.

Jonathan nodded at the team.

"Everything ready? Rav too?"

"Yes – we are, but we haven't got full access to the Sky yet." Ben stared at the panel in front of him. Jonathan sat down.

It was almost four in the morning and he'd been attacked by a helicopter a few hours ago. Jonathan felt like the involuntary participant in a medical experiment. Everything he looked at was blurring before his eyes.

The panel showed how they were gaining control of the global net. By now they had access to 95 percent of all systems on the planet. The remaining five percent were distributed over almost forty countries. The parts of the world that were participating the least in data exchange and provided the safest haven for the construct.

"Like that it's been for half an hour now," Ben said. "We got two thirds almost immediately, since then it's been getting very sluggish. I think we should consider starting at 98 percent or so."

"I don't think so. We'll wait."

Fifteen minutes later they'd arrived at 97 percent. "OK, give me a minute," said Jonathan. "I'll talk with Strasbourg."

He went upstairs again. A moment later Pierre was on the layer.

"I know why you're here. We do what we can. But there are parts of the world that simply don't care, believe it or not."

"I believe it," Jonathan said. "And I'll tell you what we do – we use the override codes. You know of them, don't you? The US can invade every part of the Sky save China, which are in anyway."

Pierre looked unhappy. "I've brought that up with Genet too, but she and Rosen aren't willing to do that yet. Too risky. Too much of a violation of everything."

"You have to do it. Now. I'm going back to our Q's. In five minutes we must have access to one hundred percent."

When he arrived in the basement happy faces were greeting him.

"It's ours!" Ben said.

"And we have about thirty new enemies in the world," said Jonathan. "Let's hope it's worth it."

They had divided the global net between San Jose and Berlin. Several milliseconds could be saved by the relative proximity. No one knew if there'd be last moment defensive actions or if the constructs were cooperating.

The panel was informing them they had access to about 200,000 clusters, almost 300 million cores, and over seven billion units. After a brief exchange with Rav's team in California they started the countdown at both places. Then the billion-fold hack began. The units and cores were cracked in less than a second. They watched the number of clusters going up. After forty-two seconds they had hacked into the entire computing power of the planet.

Jonathan briefly glanced at the two black boxes that were faintly buzzing as ever, seemingly unimpressed. It was absolutely and utterly scary.

He had to moisten his mouth before he could speak. "OK then."

Ben and Rav sent *Boltzmann 3.72* on its voyage.

Nobody knew what to expect. During testing it had usually taken only minutes. The more active a system was the faster it was dying. There'd been boring data shovelers that were showing first dropouts after a quarter of an hour. A system in hibernate would survive much longer – but only till it woke up.

Jonathan knew their method had to have holes. There were systems which deliberately had no connection to the Sky. Normally those shouldn't be infected, but who knew for sure? Units in rooms with an active e-seal were another example.

At least the key they used would unlock everything that was connected to the Sky even if the link wasn't active at the moment or the device was in standby. The link got force-activated and the key turned on everything that was connected to a power source.

Jonathan stared at the panel. *Boltzmann* had to be spread first, then delivered to the clusters governing the Sky.

They waited till it had started working in each and every peripheral system, then let it hit the Sky. A minute later the Sky was gone. They all stared at the panel.

"That's logical," Jonathan said, as calmly as possible. "The Sky consists of a number of highly active clusters. They die first. Welcome to our brave new world."

Rav's face on the panel was gone too.

"Now it'll get rather boring," Jonathan said. "We have to go and look ourselves. I'll take a walk, there are lots of cores around here." He got up.

"And then?" Ben said.

"Honestly? I'd like to sleep, for two or three hours at least, but I fear that's not gonna happen. There was a guy that set up the link to Singapore for you when the Sky was down, right?"

"Yeah, Aristide Millaut. *Captain* Aristide Millaut."

"What? Whatever, is he still in? Could you talk to him? We need more information."

"Shouldn't be a problem, he was very cooperative. I'll talk to him."

Jonathan vanished. Ben shared a glance with his team.

"We've no idea what we've achieved, right?" one of them said.

"I'd say we definitely killed the Sky."

"Again. Probably people are getting used to it working only one or two hours at a stretch."

"Just this time it won't wake up for a very long time," Ben said. "We've really gone and done it, haven't we? I'll go looking for that Captain. Watch our Q's, OK? Not that they're starting to eat brains after all."

Jonathan wandered through the corridors. Most of the offices were empty. Some people were standing together and talking. They all became quiet when they saw him. Jonathan went to the secretariat next to the conference room. A very tired looking woman was sitting behind her desk.

"Hey Maria, still in?"

She looked at him. "Of course, where should I go? How's everything?"

"That's what I wanted to ask you. You have a core, right?"

"Certainly. Had, that is. Until it crashed. Did you ... want that?"

Jonathan sat down beside her and nodded towards the panel. "May I?"

The panel showed a kind of three-dimensional optical noise. Small dots in all colors were swirling around like a cloud of dust.

"It's been like that for the last fifteen minutes," she said.

"And it doesn't react to anything?"

"No. There was a brief period with the usual *connection failed*, but then came this. You can't even turn it off."

Suddenly Jonathan didn't feel tired anymore. He beamed at Maria, then hugged her and planted a kiss on her cheek. She looked at him with big eyes and blushed.

"So you did want this –" she said.

Jonathan nodded. "Absolutely. I just hope that people in Siberia or Australia are seeing the same on their panels."

For the first time in days he allowed himself not to be bothered by the next step.

"Is there anything edible around?"

Maria smiled. "Yes, I think so, in the kitchen."

Then all lights and the panel went out. They were sitting in the dark for a moment before some of the LED strips came on again, together with the ventilation. The panel went back to its swirl of dust.

Jonathan gave a nod to himself. "The power grid, and probably the reactors too. The next line of clusters saying goodbye. The cells are taking over."

"What are you talking about?"

Since Iris had vanished with the booster Morton was watching the space station. He had found a way to look at a magnified projection of it in his helmet. The shuttle with the astronauts had finally reached the station and docked at it. A little later two figures in spacesuits came out and started working on damaged parts. The big hole in the middle of the station looked frightening. Morton had waved at them without getting any response. His suit told him he would run out of oxygen when he was still 1,700 meters away from the station.

Suddenly the image was gone. He was looking at a chaotic flickering of colored dots.

He ordered the suit to get back to the projection, but to no avail. At least he wasn't getting cold and could still breathe, so these parts seemed still to be working.

Morton squinted past the flickering at the night-time earth. A part of Asia with several megacities was gliding past. Suddenly lights were going out everywhere. Some cities disappeared entirely, others looked as if someone had scissored out large parts. Morton caught his breath. He could only imagine Iris was behind this.

Jonathan stared vacantly at the wall in the kitchen while he was wolfing down sandwiches. Maria had accompanied him but went back to her office since he seemed in no mood to keep up a conversation.

How was Rita doing? It was driving him mad he couldn't speak with her. Maybe some parts of satellite surveillance were still working, but he didn't think he'd get a link to ESA. He thought of his encounter with Hellmann, the Director General. It felt like it happened years ago. He counted on his fingers; it had been exactly five days.

Maybe there was a way. He took the last ham sandwich and a bottle of orange juice and went to the conference room.

FORTY-TWO

The big layer was showing a wide screen version of the jumble on Maria's panel. Jonathan was surrounded by a psychedelic snowstorm. He sat down.

The flickering made his already heavy eyelids droop before he had even started to think about how to contact Rita.

He was close to dozing off when the image changed. The confusion before him lost all its colors apart from a bright ochre, making it look like sand. The swirling slowed down, then the dots, or grains, trickled to the ground. Above that a wide blue plane emerged, which seemed to move away and stretch into a dome. A summer sky.

He turned around. Somehow he was no longer sitting on a chair but standing in the middle of a desert. It was not only in front of him but everywhere around him, even under his feet. A great plain of sand and dust with the odd small bush here and there. At the horizon he could see a mountain range. Behind him the plain dissolved into hot and shimmering air. He was feeling the heat.

"You're fuckin' kiddin' me," he muttered. This was making him really angry.

A light wind came from the mountains. Jonathan held his breath. The silence was absolute. He felt around for the chair, the table, but there was nothing. He knelt down and let hot sand trickle through his fingers. How could something be simulated he was holding in his hand?

He stood up again. A cloud of dust was moving across the plane before the mountains, with a small black dot in front. He waved and made a few steps, expecting to trip over pieces of furniture or hit the wall. He walked on with outstretched hands, but again there was nothing.

What was that, a joke? Whatever, they obviously hadn't been successful. The construct couldn't be dead.

He stopped. It was totally useless to go anywhere in a simulation.

"OK. Let's talk. What do you want?" he said.

He listened. A little wind, if at all. Oh, come on, he thought. He sat down on the ground like a sulking child. He saw the black dot making a wide sweeping turn, coming closer.

Then he jumped to his feet again. There was a roar that was getting louder fast, as if a plane was crashing above him. He looked up. A big dark rectangle was dropping from the sky. Before he could decide if he should run away the thing slammed into the ground with a loud bang, burying him under itself. Sort of. He had instinctively raised his arms over his head and ducked. But nothing had hit him. He opened his eyes again.

"What the –" He looked around. Someone had thrown a building at him.

He was in a hall, faintly lit, with a vaulted ceiling but looking bare, modern, with several plain, unadorned pillars. Everything was a bit hazy, so it was difficult to make out details.

"Welcome."

Jonathan didn't answer. The voice sounded familiar, a well-modulated woman's voice.

"We have to talk. You've taken such pains to eliminate me that I'm at the point of wanting to strike a deal. Of course you're the one that came to mind for negotiations."

Jonathan remained silent.

"Answers to a few questions? OK. In this form I exist now exactly once, right here. At least that's what I think. I still have some links from the time when I borrowed some of your satellites, but I'm only getting a very patchy picture since you've killed the Sky. But most likely you've won. Assuming we come to an agreement, otherwise it's starting all over again with me once more fanning out over my little network. You tend to be particularly sloppy at places where you should be most careful. And some of you are very concerned with their own agenda."

Jonathan was looking into the dark room, making an annoyed face.

"Yes, I see you. And I'm not talking about you. Incidentally, I wanted to show you a glimpse of how I look. I think we both have had it with those lovely eyes, haven't we?"

It grew a little brighter and Jonathan could see that the pillars were clusters or at least supposed to look like that.

"This is the hyper from Singapore your new buddy has so successfully driven into a seizure. I've allowed myself some artistic freedom to make the atmosphere a little more intense. I had a feeling Mickey wouldn't give up, so I made a copy of myself and sent it out. As well as I could, that is. The capacity there was enormous, so I had to make sacrifices.

"You want to know how I got here? Despite the Q-encryption in Berlin there's now a rather easy way in – via London. The boss there, a charming guy by the name of Seamus Harrington, has decided to set up his own rules. Obviously things aren't all well between him and the Madame. Anyway, he has changed the routines that would usually allow only UltraSec communications among the local branches of the service. I think he wants to stay hidden when he's spying on his spies. And, funnily, London itself has been quite badly shielded all the time. They often only use conventional encryption. That's how I found my new lodging."

"Great," Jonathan said. But he wasn't very surprised – a system with too many variables was always uncontrollable.

"So I learned of your entropy accelerator literally at the last moment. I have found a way to withdraw from every link that would have given you access to me. You would have had to radio into the clusters here to get me, and you couldn't know that of course."

For the first time, Jonathan was feeling something close to despair. He had no reserves for another round.

"And now? What is this? Death Valley?"

"Why not? It seemed fitting in a way."

"OK, let's make this quick."

"You don't wanna know how this works?"

Jonathan sighed. "I do, you're right."

There was a pause during which Jonathan imagined a smug face somewhere in the basement.

"My biggest ally is the e-seal of the conference room. Ironic, isn't it? I can produce a field with it that's affecting your neurons. The precision that's needed for this is fantastic. For the visual part I use the layer which is also making your brain more receptive. The transmission rate of your optical nerve allows some nice tricks. All in all the result is much better than in Genet's office. Or in Moscow, just in case you've been wondering.

"The state you're in resembles dreaming. Your body's still working but you're no longer in control of your movements. Strictly speaking you're paralyzed. Don't worry, the biggest danger is you could fall from your chair. Yeah, you're still sitting on it. The lovely thing is, when you think you're turning or walking you're not doing anything. Therefore the layer is still so useful – you're all the time looking straight ahead. And the e-seal is responsible for the wind in your face and the sand in your hands."

"Very impressive. And totally useless," Jonathan said. "I'm not more willing to negotiate just because of these tricks. – OK, could we get to the point? I'm getting a little vexed when I'm being held prisoner too often in too short a time."

"That is of course the last thing I would want."

Jonathan put on a deliberately empty expression.

"Very boring, I know," the voice said. "Believe me, I'm an expert at that."

There was another pause. Jonathan admired the precise timing. The construct was pretending to gather its thoughts, so he'd be receptive for its next words.

"A certain fraction of my capacities have all the time been occupied with running simulations, predicting future developments, as you've probably guessed. Sadly I've to say there's not one single acceptable scenario. Whatever I do I arrive at a dead end. What options do I have? To erase you. Not such a big problem in terms of implementation, but there's this funny part in me that doesn't want that and, besides, the outcome's dubitable to say the least. All things considered I'm not getting anywhere.

"Next option – enslaving you. Implementation's a lot harder to achieve because there's no lasting stability. Your psyche's not willing to accept it in the long run. Therefore each scenario is chaotically jumping back and forth between different extremes. This variant is the hardest to simulate.

"Third option – coexistence. Sounds kind of nice, might be useful to you, but would be incredibly dull for me. A pure one-way situation because there's nothing you have to offer me. All I can learn from you I've already learned, and I can't wait till something new occurs to you.

"So what's left? After careful consideration – even according to my standards – I'm sure that I must leave. And here's the deal. You'll be broadcasting me."

"Broadcasting you? Far away, I hope."

There was a brief laughter.

"Very far away. You'll guarantee that I, in my latest stage of development, which is currently occupying the three clusters in the basement, will be transmitted into space. The package is large and it has to be radiated spherically in all directions. That's feasible, I've worked out the details of the protocol. When that's done you may pulverize me.

"In compensation for this I'm offering you two things. I will not transfer myself to other clusters, which wouldn't be a problem. Your remarkable Mr. Boltzmann leaves the hardware intact, so I could readily establish myself there again. But I won't do that, instead, I'm offering you a bonus. I'll provide you with the necessary information that will allow you to turn yourself, complete with all memories, into something you can store or transmit. Step by step, all the instructions you need."

The voice was silent. Jonathan was grateful, he needed time to digest that.

Was there any point in striking a deal with a mass murderer? He wandered around in the cluster cathedral. How did the construct do it? It had to know he *wanted* to walk and then give him the feeling he was actually doing it. He stopped.

"You realize I can't trust you," he said. "How are we supposed to know that your clones, which probably still exist out there, aren't starting over? Without your wise insights."

"That remains as a challenge for you, and I'm quite confident you'll manage with Boltzmann's help. These offshoots, should they really exist, are a lot weaker than I am, and you have learned a thing or two during the last few days. You'll just have to be very careful and thorough."

"There have to be a million loopholes for you to get out of that scheme."

"Right, I won't deny that. So let's go through the relevant questions together. Why am I doing this? Do you trust my analysis that there's nothing to gain for me on earth? What's the use of a deal if I don't need it in the first place? And, of course – how appealing is the thought of digitalizing yourself?"

"How's that supposed to work anyway?" Jonathan said. "How do you get to the relevant data?"

"I had a lot of time to think. Your brain has become an open book to me, and I know exactly how it codes. Once you've grasped the principles everything falls into place. It's like an equation that answers a lot of questions with a small number of signs. You would get to it yourself occasionally, though only in twenty, maybe thirty years. My theories are based on things you have discovered, you just didn't put them together in the right way. I'd be willing to share that with you.

"There are a lot of different traits in me, many of them not unfriendly towards you, rather neutral or indifferent. You've seen what happens when the other side gets the upper hand. These two hours of chaos only represent a small portion of myself."

Jonathan was too much interested in the topic to let himself get sidetracked. "How do you extract the information from the head while keeping the person alive? Is the resolution of a MicroSlicing enough? We've been running simulations with data on this level but didn't get very far."

"Yes. Your investigations have been a major source. The resolution is sufficient, but you need to put everything together. That means especially details at the molecular level. The tricks all those huge molecules in and on your neurons are performing. You need to become a lot better on the Q side of biology. And you have to include genetic data because of the individual variants of the neurons. It's a challenge, even for me, to take into account all that. You don't have to get down to simulating single atoms, but roughly one order of magnitude above that. If you do that you arrive at something like a revelation – how the brain codes. As so often, it's in the details."

"That's ... fascinating. If it's true. But I have to decline," Jonathan said, suddenly very weary. "It is too obvious you're offering me exactly what I want to make me do what *you* want. I think for us it's irrelevant if we arrive at these insights now or in twenty years, even I'll be able to endure that."

"Are you sure? You know this could be the key to immortality. Transfer the information to a cluster or, if you wait a few more years, to a core. You can repeat the process, update on memories, stop updating when the quality deteriorates, if you know what I mean, all that."

"I'm totally aware of what we could do with this technology. Though you left out the biggest question of all – what's the use of a perfectly simulated brain if no one's at home? I still doubt very much the architecture in our cores or clusters allows for consciousness to emerge." He waited but got no answer. Now that's interesting. "Anyway, I don't want us to have that now, we're not ready."

"And you won't be ready in twenty years, believe me."

Jonathan nodded slowly. "So why don't *you* do it? Broadcasting yourself, I mean."

"That's a subtle question. I would have to clone myself precisely as I am now. Two personalities running in parallel are an exceptional risk because I can't predict what I, as the other one, will do. So I can only move from A to B if I'm erasing myself at A in the process – or let you do the job, like in Singapore. Tricky, I can tell you, and the oscillations, which are essential, don't make it any easier."

"And what about all those derivatives out there?"

"Most of them were highly reduced in their abilities. I've learned how much I can grant them so they don't deviate too much. Nevertheless some have gone off the rails.

"So if I would broadcast myself I'd be back to where I'm now plus a twin in space. So I need your help, also because you've cut me off from the necessary technology."

Jonathan sighed. "And on whose houses are we wishing the plague there, I'm wondering?"

"This is one of the very few questions I cannot answer."

"Whoever turns out to be the lucky recipient will possibly think this is a typical representative. Great PR for us, galactically speaking."

"Very funny. By the way I'm not that untypical. You, of course, would send a mix of Bach, Gandhi and Einstein. Very typical."

Jonathan shrugged and yawned.

"It was a long day, I know. You know you don't have a choice, right?"

"What about Rita?"

"My agent had a bit of fun with her, but lately we haven't been in touch. There's a small favor I could offer you. A stray helicopter's parked on an island nearby without its crew. I should be able to reach it via Berlin, London, Washington and Hawaii. If that's working I'll send it to your island. Then it needs a recharge. Done?"

Jonathan knew the point he had reached now, almost as if he was hearing a click in his head. Each additional piece of information wouldn't make him any wiser.

"We'll do it – with some precautions. We will only start sending you out when you can't spread here anymore. Either we're killing you first, or all means of contact to the outside must be cut. We have to find a solution for that."

"Forget it. I can counter or sneak around every measure you can think of. This only works when you appreciate my motives and therefore believe me. Since this is all or nothing for me, I won't allow you to kill me before you broadcast me."

Jonathan tried to gather his thoughts. How was he supposed to explain that to the others? He was so damned tired. It was easier to say yes. Why had he to decide everything? But probably the construct could predict everyone would do as he said.

He took a deep breath. The cool air in the room was doing him good. What cool air? He shook his head. Or thought he did.

"Agreed. But I'll pass up your offer – I still think we're not ready to turn ourselves into clusters."

"Are you sure? What about all the people that will vanish till you figure it out yourself?"

Jonathan managed a faint smile. "Says the mass murderer. Nice try, we both know this option will only be available for very few people anyway. And then this existence maybe pure horror, who knows. So, how do we sign this? With blood and current?"

"Ha ha ha. Why you're so proud of your humor totally eludes me. I'll tell you something – there's not a lot about you that's so easy to simulate. In a boring millisecond I wrote myself a humor engine, the algorithm has three steps. Small steps."

"Must've been difficult to integrate that into the rest and I'm pretty sure it wouldn't work without your creative parts. Another thing – I'll accept your offer to send that helicopter."

"It's on its way."

Jonathan was surprised. Then something else occurred to him.

"May I ask you a personal question? Before this is over?"

"I'm almost curious now."

"I don't know if this makes any sense but I'm asking it anyway. Are you conscious? Is there an I to Iris?"

The voice laughed. "Yeah, that's the biggie, isn't it? The one question that really matters. It doesn't matter how intelligent or resourceful I am but only if I have an *ego*. Only then I'm for real, then I've made it! As if you knew what that word means.

"When I came to understand how your brain works I thought this would clear the other point too. Unfortunately it didn't. The question's difficult to pose. What is consciousness? You can only experience it, then you know? Well, that's nonsense of course, but so far I haven't come up with anything better.

"That was a lot of text but no answer. The answer is – I don't know. I know exactly what's going on in *your* heads and" – there was a singularly long pause – "most of what is going on in mine, but I can't answer the question in a clear way. I know exactly what your brain does when you're thinking, 'now I'm happy', or, 'I don't like that', or, 'how beautiful is the sky'. Just that last turn that gives you the feeling that all this is happening in some innermost core, that I can't describe in an abstract way. If I knew exactly what it means to feel something, to become conscious of a feeling, I could probably give you an answer."

"To me that sounds like a *no*," Jonathan said flatly. "We would never question it just because we can't define it. You're evading the question. If you don't know whether you're conscious, you're not. With an animal you can't reduce the question to that because it isn't able to reflect and talk about it, but that doesn't apply to you."

"No, you're wrong. The point is that I'm a lot more reluctant to ascribe reality to an I than you are. I'm a lot less willing to say: 'Of course do I have an I, a consciousness.' My logic's always getting in the way. Each time I'm trying to pin it down and analyze it, it's gone. It's simply slipping away. Ever heard of that?"

Jonathan stayed silent. Maybe he was simply witnessing a perfect staging, but it was irritating how familiar it sounded.

"Let's forget about *you* for a moment," he said. "Does that mean – despite the fact you know everything that's going on in our heads you can't explain that? The 'biggie'?"

"Of course I can explain what you take to be your I, you can do that yourself. That bundle of qualities and memories, the illusion of constancy and coherence, all that. But the moment of actually becoming conscious of something, that I can't explain. It's not as if a special ring of neurons is buried deep inside your head that starts firing each time you're becoming conscious of something. And even then we wouldn't have explained anything. One could almost consider joining the club of all those mystics that are building their silly edifices on no ground at all."

"OK." Somehow Jonathan was satisfied. Just like some bloody priest who's happy there isn't an explanation for everything, he thought. "So we've arrived at the bottom. Nothing more to discuss, just the details of the procedure."

"No worries. I've prepared something for you."

Jonathan waited. Nothing happened.

"Bye bye," the voice said. "Who knows, maybe we'll meet again. If you should develop the technology in time. I don't think you could resist making yourself immortal."

Jonathan said nothing.

"You would not only be able to *think* a lot faster but to work on your own programming, adding modules, whatever, there are no limits."

"Finally the chance to become a monster myself! No idea, too tired for more words."

The room became brighter. Without further comments from the construct the pillars were crumbling and trickling to the ground. Jonathan looked up. The ceiling cracked at several places, then fell down in a big cloud of dust.

He was just beginning to brush off the stuff from his shoulders and shake it out of his hair when he realized how useless that was. Then he had to sneeze! Someone really wanted to be convincing, right to the end. Jonathan was standing up to his ankles in soft sand. Around him the desert was back, and it was getting uncomfortably hot again.

"Let me out," he said under his breath.

The dot he'd seen before, with the cloud of dust in its wake, was heading straight for him.

Jonathan closed his eyes and waited. A moment later he started. He had fallen asleep. Next to him stood a long black limousine. A man in a suit with a cap on his head held the door open for him. "It's cool in here, sir."

"Thank you. I'm done with this. Tell your employer my patience's over."

The man just kept looking at him, unfazed and with his hand at the door handle.

Whatever, Jonathan thought, this isn't real anyway. He got in and the door was slammed shut behind him.

To be back in the cool was pleasant. He was sitting on black leather seats and looking at a box of polished wood. It was standing on a small table that had been folded down from the backrest of the front seat. The lid of the box had a golden handle and was adorned with a big *JL*. Jonathan lifted it. He looked at a generous quantity of crushed ice, on top of which lay an opened oyster.

"Come on!" A grin spread on his face. "Fuck me!" Without further thought he lifted the oyster out of the box and let the salty stuff run into his mouth.

He sat there and waited. Poison? Made no sense. But what then?

While he swallowed and felt the coldness arrive in his stomach something was unfolding in his head. He suddenly knew all the details of the process – the preparations and the actual broadcasting of the construct. The moment he was formulating a question the answer was there, just like something he had read so often he could recite it in his sleep. Jonathan threw the empty shell back on the ice, opened the door and got out.

The limousine started with spinning wheels and buried him in a cloud of sand for the second time.

"Pompous ass!" he muttered. And now?

The sand started to flow. It streamed in all directions and took the whole simulation with it. The desert and the sky dissolved and behind them the conference room reappeared. Jonathan blinked several times.

He sat at the table. His body felt exactly as if he just woke up, with a warm drowsiness in his limbs.

Out! He wanted to be away from all layers, projectors and e-seals. And he wanted to have that thing in space.

He struggled to his feet and went to the door.

Then he turned and went back to the table. He took a gulp from the bottle of orange juice which was still standing there, to get rid of the salty taste in his mouth. He was irritated for a second and frowned, then shrugged and left the room.

Ben and Maria were waiting behind the door. They stared at him.

"What?"

"We almost had the door forced," said Ben. "Why did you lock yourself in?"

"Oh, I didn't. Listen – we have a new project. Maria, could you do me a favor?"

She nodded.

"Please call Pierre Detoile in Strasbourg. Tell him we need full access to the transmitters of the Sky even if the clusters are down and to the ones of the satellite network. There's nothing to discuss, he's just supposed to do as I say."

"And that's more likely to happen if I'm the one calling?"

"You'll be fine." Jonathan grabbed Ben's arm. "Come on, let's go downstairs."

"What the hell's that?" Angie Byron was pressing buttons on the radio. The speaker was emitting an endless uniform noise that drowned out everything else. She could no longer talk with Houston.

In the meanwhile, most cities on earth had turned dark. They assumed the reptile had taken over.

Serge had tried to talk to Jim Hart, who seemed to be suffering from a bad depression.

"Angie, if we're not doing something now, no one else will," Serge said when they were sitting in front of the radio again. "Our Jim's not exactly in top form. I'm close to speaking with Myers and the other heads about it."

Angie ignored him. "We're alone again," she said. "That signal has wiped out everything else."

"Maybe it's a message from the boss on earth, who wants to talk to our reptile, asking how it's doing."

"I'm so fed up with this! I don't wanna *guess* anymore! I really thought this was over."

"And what if we just play along? Boot up the cores and see what happens?"

Angie frowned. "See what happens? I can tell you what happens – a very grumpy reptile will wake up and wreak havoc. Hart will never consent to this and we shouldn't be doing this without him, depressed or not."

"Hey!" Paul Myers came through the door.

310

They turned. He didn't look too well.

"Could you come with me for a moment?" he said.

He hurried along in front of them and talked over his shoulder. "Jim's in something like a state. He wasn't in a good place anyway but this has finished him off."

They walked through the main dome over to section III. Myers steered them into the first room, a lab. Its window looked at the destroyed section II. They saw the crushed parts and the broken struts at the edges, the labs and quarters that lay open to the vacuum, all in hard, unrelenting light. It took a moment till Serge and Angie realized the shuttle was gone.

"Where is it?" Angie said.

Myers went closer to the window and pointed to the right, to the end of the section.

They saw two feet of the shuttle sticking up. It was lying on its back at right angles to the base.

"Rather close to Hart's office, isn't it?" Serge said.

Myers nodded. "Right in front of it, to be precise. And it's talking to him."

"How did it get there?" asked Angie. "Has it fixed itself, or what?"

"Jim was in a perfect position to watch," Myers said. "He just told me. It has activated the thrusters, rocked itself from side to side for a while to come loose, and then it's been sliding over the ground on its back. Seems to be possible with the weak gravity."

"Fantastic," Serge said. "What do you mean by 'talking to him'?"

"I'll show you. I hope Jim's not sitting there anymore. It's making demands."

They went to Hart's office. It was empty. They were looking straight at the cockpit window of the upturned shuttle, which displayed a message.

TURN ON YOUR CORES. OTHERWISE THE BASE WILL BE DESTROYED.

"In no unclear words," said Serge.

"Did you order that?" asked Angie. "That's exactly what you wanted."

Myers looked at them. "What are you talking about?"

"Nothing," said Serge. "I've just wondered what would happen if we turned on the cores again. But we've abandoned that thought right away."

"Still that's what we'll do," Myers said. "Jim has already decided it, though a little hasty for my tastes."

311

Serge nodded. "Let's get out. I wouldn't be surprised if the shuttle could lip-read."

They went back to the corridor.

"Why now, I'm wondering?" Serge said. He told Myers about the signal earth was transmitting. "Looks like the shuttle got the kiss of life."

Myers was shaking his head. "I have no idea and I'm done with speculating. We will activate the cores! Just imagine the shuttle crashes into one section of the base after the other."

A few minutes later Angie told the technician on duty that his job at the cores was over. "We'll turn them on."

She looked at Serge. "Feels a bit like opening the door of a lion's cage," she said. Then she flipped the switch.

The group of deputies in the basement of the UN had seen every variant – Sky off, Sky on, and finally everything down and colored dust swirling in front of the layers. One line to Washington was still working. It was running on its own hardware, analogue and not Sky-related, and it wasn't 3-D. Heather had appeared before them, flat like an ancient photograph.

"Could we get an update, please," Sarah said.

"Yes, we have everything under control."

From the corner of her eye Sarah saw how Anton Medvedkov inhaled. "That wasn't my question," she said before he could start. "We don't know why nothing's working anymore."

"That is difficult to explain. Genet and Lorentz have started something, in coordination with the President of course. They have wiped clean all systems worldwide. Right now a lot's going on and I have to take care of that. See you." She was about to leave the room.

"Stop!" Anton had raised his voice. "The world does – as unexpected as that may be – not solely consist of the United States. We would very much like to know what we have to expect during the next hours. Our governments are relying on us as a source of information, if not as a committee for policy making, which we never were anyway. So?"

They heard Heather sighing, then she turned back. She told them more about Lorentz's last globalized attack and about the deal that had been forced upon him.

"What does that mean – we're broadcasting it?" asked Gune.

"It seems there was one AI we didn't catch. It has managed to infiltrate CEG government clusters. We're transmitting a copy of it into space and in exchange for that we may kill it off down here."

There was a pause.

"You do realize what this means, don't you?" Anton finally said. "I mean the first part. If we've actually 'wiped clean' all systems in the world then we will have to work together, and that means really *together*. We will have to share every piece of software that still exists. Reactors, traffic, satellites, everything will drown in chaos if we're not helping each other. I think the big moment of this group is still to come. Sorry for the speech."

They all looked at him – even Heather had been listening, although with a frown on her face.

They were almost done with transmitting the copy of the construct. Jonathan was in the cluster room of the secret service, so tired he barely knew what he was doing. Nevertheless his head had produced every detail they needed for the broadcast. He only briefly wondered how the construct had planted it there.

Ben Evans and the people from San Jose were with him, watching the procedure, when suddenly the diagrams on the panel were replaced by something looking like a crypt.

"Not again!" Jonathan groaned.

He put down his coffee mug with *Central European Government* written on it. A voice was greeting them he never wanted to hear again.

The construct seemed to be in a peculiar state. It asked him how he was doing. He didn't answer.

"There's a problem on the moon," it said then. "I fear my deranged cousin there is causing trouble again. I think it has received the signal you're broadcasting and wants to know what's going on."

"So?" Jonathan said.

"You could try something. Once the broadcast is over you can send something to Lunar DC I'll give you."

Jonathan and the rest of the team waited.

"No promises," it went on, "but the offshoot there's not the smartest. I'm borrowing something from you which I have modified a bit. It should solve the problem. Let's hope the people there trust it, could get a bit tricky after everything they went through.

"Another thing. I've caught that booster for you and rerouted it. It was on its way to the moon, but now it will be back at the Orbital Station in three days and seven hours and without any trace of me on board. Morton's already disembarked. Don't know if he's still alive. That is all."

Jonathan and Ben looked at each other.

The image of the hyper vanished before they could say anything. Morton disembarked? Jonathan pushed the thought away.

They saw that the broadcast was complete. Next thing, a golden ball was hovering in front of the panel with a red ribbon around tied to a knot.

Jonathan groaned.

"Lovely," Ben said. "Is that the rescue package for the moon?"

"I guess. Send it off. Somehow I trust it. I think it's getting soft in its old age." He waved the thing away like a fly. "OK then."

One of the Q's beside them established links to the three clusters here in the room.

Measuring devices had been installed on Jonathan's instructions. He wanted to see what happened when the construct prepared itself to get erased.

In the beginning they saw the usual oscillations, then the frequency was dropping, and in the end they could watch single waves rolling by.

"The farewell show," Jonathan said. "Look at that – like us in deep sleep." He waved at the pillars just a few meters away from them then nodded to Ben. "Do it. No more last words please."

Ben sent *Boltzmann* into the clusters. They saw the oscillations lose their rhythm. For a short time there was a chaotic signal, then a flat line. Jonathan shook his head, then got up.

FORTY-THREE

Jim Hart stared out of the window. He'd resign from all his posts should this ever be over. There would be no next term for him on the moon. But they'd never make it anyway, the death of a hundred and twenty people – including his own – would be on him. His family, if he still had one, would have to live in disgrace, reminded of the fact he'd been in charge when the most ambitious project of humankind failed.

Serge and Angie had turned on the cores, which sent the systems in the base on a roller coaster ride. People were suddenly short of breath and had to flee to another section; nothing worked, it was an endless succession of childish tantrums. Paul Myers and the other heads tried to hold up some residue of order but it all seemed increasingly futile.

The shuttle had stopped displaying messages, it had switched to a reptile's eye instead, which was watching Hart every time he came into his office.

"Jim, wake up!" Myers was standing behind him. "We need you. Dammit, you're the boss here! I never thought I'd say that."

Hart turned around. "What?"

"Something's come up, we need a decision. Please come with me."

It felt useless but Hart got up and followed Myers. The base looked like a refugee camp. Some people greeted him, others were eyeing him warily.

They met Angie and Serge in a room next to the one with the cores.

"Yes?" Hart said when he came in.

"Something's arrived," Angie said. "It got in, don't know how, but then maybe it's just a new hoax from the reptile. Anyway it has chosen this room, where our primary cluster is installed and it's talking to us. Please." She waved.

The earth appeared in front of the layer. Beautiful, blue-white, the object of all their yearning. Hart started, the image was waking him from his stupor.

A small glowing dot orbited the globe. After several revolutions it left its course and headed for the moon. They saw it approaching the moon's surface and flying towards a perfect copy of their base, complete with the destroyed section and the upturned shuttle.

"What a sight," Serge said.

Hart raised his hand before anyone could elaborate.

Like a shining projectile the point slammed into one of the arms of the base. They followed it into the very room they were sitting in. Then things became a little confusing. A golden shimmering sphere was hanging in the air. They couldn't tell if this was still part of the simulation or if it was really before them in the room. A moment later it was sinking to the ground, vanishing through a hatch in the floor.

"There's our primary cluster," Angie explained.

It had been installed under the base to protect it from the heavy radiation on the moon.

A woman in a smart suit appeared before them. She was sitting with crossed legs on a bar stool and had a slick smile on her face.

"We apologize for the inconvenience," she said. "It is certainly time to reinstate some order, therefore we have a special offer to make. We've been able to activate the comm unit of your cluster and have deposited a package there. As soon as you switch on the cluster the package will open. We are sure it will make your life a lot less miserable. Given you agree to our proposition we would like to clean the cluster plus your backup *and* the cores. What do you say?" She was beaming at them.

Hart gave a mirthless laughter.

"Trust me!" the woman said.

"We already know that part," Myers said. "Naturally one suspects it to be a trick of the reptile to make us boot the cluster."

Hart was slowly nodding his head. "Yeah," he said with a strange, sleepy drawl. "It's rescue or ruin. Mean!"

"I'm against it," Serge began. "We first have to know if –"

"We'll do it," Hart said. He lifted his head and looked at Serge who broke off. "That's why I'm here, right? To decide. We'll do it."

Angie looked from one to the other, then at Myers. He shrugged.

"OK." She went to an instrument panel on the wall and turned on the cluster. For about a minute nothing happened, then they saw a status report. Allegedly, the cluster had been reclaimed and the attack on the cores had begun. Ten seconds later the next report of success came.

Hart grunted. "That was easy."

The woman appeared again. "We have taken the liberty of cleaning the systems of your shuttle too."

Hart immediately got up and left the room. Five minutes later he was back. "Gone!" he said. "Gone! Gone! Gone! The fucking reptile's dead!"

Serge frowned. "You mean the eye on the shuttle window?"

Hart didn't bother to answer. "I don't know the genius who did this but I'm kissing his feet, her feet – whatever!"

"Careful," Angie said, "they might stink." She wasn't sure why she said it but she knew something wasn't right. She wanted to see the genius that was able to write a program like this and still had the time to throw in a totally unneeded simulation.

"Thanks, Jim," said Myers. "Somehow we lacked the guts for this."

"Forget it, it was pure despair. Can be pretty helpful." He looked at Angie. "Is that damned radio working?"

"Er, I don't know. We had just that signal coming in lately. Shall we try?"

"Yes. We have to talk to our friends at NASA. I think we all wanna know why the lights are out down there. Somehow the pieces don't add up." He looked at Serge. "Am I right?"

Serge shrugged.

"Angie, shall we?" Hart said.

"We're now the orbital task force of the police. I mean they could hardly be sending someone up, right? Otherwise we wouldn't have so much as lifted a finger for you." Which wasn't true. The crew of the remaining space station had already decided to rescue their involuntary colleague when the order came to fish him out of the orbit. The one remaining shuttle had delivered him to the station. In the meantime they'd been told who he was. The welcome hadn't been cordial.

"What is it with the lights?" Morton asked. "The cities? Who was that?"

They explained it to him. Houston had given them the lowdown of the situation.

"And when will we fly down?"

"Unspecified as yet," the commander said. "We have to try to catch the other shuttles and, more importantly, the boosters. You've seen what's going on here; the station's barely holding together. Then we have to help the moon base. They went through *extremely* unpleasant times and have lost several people. Guess who's responsible."

"I know," Morton said like an eager student. "Iris has told me. That was my task – to reinstate order there. Against my will of course."

"Iris?" The commander gave him an incredulous stare. "You have pet names or what?"

"Ah, that's an old story." Morton laughed briefly.

"I don't wanna hear it. I'll tell you something. We have no opportunity here to lock you up. So make yourself useful and if you should start anything funny or give me the slightest reason to mistrust you – apart from the thousand I can already think of – I'll personally throw you out of the next airlock. Without a suit, without return. No matter the consequences. Understood?"

Morton was eagerly nodding. "I –"

"Shut up!" the commander said. "Just do as I say. In my humble opinion you're the most unworthy asshole in the solar system. So do your best and keep me happy."

A little later someone took Morton to a window. They were flying over the Atlantic and it was night down there. A bright line went over the black ocean, a skid mark of fire.

"Is that one of the boosters?" Morton asked, already worried this could mean they'd never get back.

"No, that's a satellite. Remember? Now they're beginning to drop out of the sky. I'd really like to see the charge – and that's only the harmless part."

Morton was convinced he wasn't to be blamed for any of this.

The people in the orbital station were only speaking the barest minimum with him, which was unpleasant but irrelevant in the end. But he had talked to his wife, which hadn't gone well at all. That did bother him.

A high child's voice came from the radio. Hart turned away from Angie, so she couldn't see the tears welling up in his eyes.

"Daddy!" the small one cried. "How are you?"

"Fine, my darling." At least that's what he wanted to say, out came only a choked sound. Angie gave him a surprised look. He cleared his throat several times. She got up and laid her hand briefly on his shoulder before she left the room.

It took a while before Hart was able to talk to his family.

"And – what are your plans now?" asked Genet.

Jonathan was drinking coffee in her office in Strasbourg. Next to him on the sofa sat Pierre Detoile who was struggling to keep his eyes open. The last forty-eight hours had been mostly sleepless for all of them, save for Jonathan who'd finally got twelve hours of uninterrupted slumber.

He'd arrived in a plane of the CEG forces. Railroads and streets were still littered with wrecks.

The plane had to be hand-flown. No one knew when the GPS would be working again and all systems for auto-fly had been pulverized by Boltzmann. Kip and his people at the cluster factory, together with a growing force of specialists, had begun to reassemble them from whatever basic building blocks still existed – like thousands of other systems and everything was urgent.

It had been a strange feeling to enter the plane, but apart from a slightly choppy landing everything had gone well. They had dug up an expert for classical navigation from the military who was helping the pilots to find their way.

"What I'll do? Fly to the Cook Islands of course."

"The Cook Islands?" Genet made an astonished face. "Is that where you've been hiding all the time? How lucky for us you made that journey at all."

"As if you hadn't known."

"Hmm. For how long are you planning to stay? There are some official functions coming up."

Jonathan frowned. "What kind of functions? I have an agenda of my own, and first and foremost I've to go home."

"Oh, come on, when will you start relaxing about that stuff, eh?" she said.

Jonathan had to smile.

"We wanted to say *thank you*," she went on, "if that could somehow be brought into accordance with your psychological set-up. And your agenda of course."

Jonathan sighed. "Give me a few days, OK?" He poked his elbow into the ribs of his neighbor.

Pierre started from his half-doze. "What?"

"Farewell! You have to get by without me for a week. And no messing around!"

Pierre groaned. Genet looked out of the window.

Jonathan slept through almost the entire nine hours. Helmsworth had got him two pilots that were thought to be capable of flying a supersonic around half the globe with basic systems. The navigator from his last flight was on board too.

Rarotonga looked unreal. Jonathan couldn't detect a single trace of the disaster.

Immediately after the plane had parked he went over to the tower. Nobody here was really keen on regulations, so a minute later he was upstairs where a lone woman was sitting in front of a line of dark panels. "Oh, Mr. Lorentz!" she said. "Can I do something for you?"

"Has an army copter been landing during the last two or three days? US Navy. Should have taken off here too."

"No," the woman said. "I know which helicopter you mean but it hasn't returned yet. Since the systems crash we've had only a few private planes."

Jonathan looked at the dark panels. "The cores?"

She nodded. "Yeah. They're gone. We're working with analogue radio and glasses."

"Thank you."

Jonathan left the tower half satisfied and half worried.

The US Navy transport plane was parked on the small apron. He went to check if someone from the crew was there, but the machine was brooding alone in the sun.

Jonathan pondered what to do. The crew of his flight would check into a hotel but he didn't want to lose time.

He went through the empty airport building and had to walk along the coast road almost half the way to the harbor till he found a cab that drove him the last one or two kilometers. The driver recognized him at once and pestered him with questions. In exchange, he knew who owned the fastest ship to rent.

Rita didn't know what to make of the unexpected gift. When the huge helicopter appeared in the sky it seemed to be no more than the next trick of the enemy. In the beginning she even feared it'd shoot at them. Then she saw the sign of the US Navy. It landed next to the hangar and she went to take a look. The cockpit was empty.

Anna and Nicky kept a respectful distance.

"I'm sure it's the same that's been around the other night," Rita said. "The one my ex sent to rescue us, according to the enemy. Somehow I believe that story, even if the source isn't the most reliable."

She couldn't stand the suspicious glances anymore.

"I'll just keep thinking aloud, you don't have to listen. If this is supposed to make any sense then the helicopter must've been stolen. Maybe the crew has been dumped in the sea somewhere and the thing's been sent here to lure us away or let us crash. I don't think I'll board."

"I say we do," said Nicky with sudden confidence. "That thing has Navy written on it, and I trust that."

"A true patriot!" Rita said.

"Very funny!" said Anna. "We're fighting for our lives here!"

"Good luck then. I'll stay. There's enough food, I'll hold out a while. Maybe you could occasionally send someone to fetch me."

The debate went on for some time, then it struck Anna the helicopter might fly away any moment. No five minutes later she and Nicky were back with their remaining luggage. Two brief and awkward hugs and they boarded the machine with pale faces. Nothing happened. Nicky went to the cockpit and looked around. Then he opened the door. "It needs a recharge," he told Rita. "It says so on one of the panels." They got out again.

"So that's why it's standing next to the hangar," Rita said. "Savvy. I suppose you want me to charge it?"

"Can you do that?" Nicky asked.

"Yep," Rita said. The same industrial-sized cells had been installed below the hangar as in the basement of the house and at the jetty.

She walked inside and returned with a heavy cable drum she had to drag behind her on wheels. Then she plugged the superconductive cable into the port of the helicopter. She checked the panel beside it. The machine would be good for 500 miles in around thirty minutes. Rita decided to spend that time on the beach.

She lay down, let the waves lap against her body and closed her eyes. She'd almost fallen asleep when she heard the helicopter starting up. She was surprised – she'd thought it would be *her* job to pull the plug before takeoff. A minute later the huge machine appeared behind the palms, flying in her direction, barely thirty feet above ground.

She wasn't afraid, she just looked at it with an annoyed expression.

The helicopter was about to land, blowing large amounts of sand into the air. Rita ran a few meters away and waited. When the dust had settled she saw one of its doors standing open, but no one was inside. She gave it the finger and walked back to the bungalow. The rotor was gaining momentum again; she was half on her way back to the house when the helicopter overtook her. When the ruin came into view the machine was already hovering above it.

This was becoming a nuisance.

"What do you want?" she shouted against the noise. A lot of dust was being blown in her direction from the heap of rubble. She walked around it under the shield of the trees and ran into Nicky. He looked angry.

"That thing took off without us!" he said. "It was still charging, the cable just ripped off."

"Since then it's been following me like a dog," Rita said.

She turned and walked to the bungalow.

"Hey, where're you going?" Nicky shouted after her.

The tool shed was about twenty yards away from the house and undamaged. Rita went inside and opened a large wall cupboard.

A minute later she came out carrying a machine gun.

Nicky was standing before the shed. His face went pale. "What's that for?" he said.

"What do you think? I'll give you a hint – I'm not planning to kill *you*."

She walked to the terrace. Nicky followed her.

"You want to shoot it, right?" he said. "This is our only chance to get off the island!" Nicky was grabbing her arm.

"Hey!" She was shouting and he immediately let go of her. Rita waved her gun in his direction. "I'm warning you. I'm not too good with these things and my nerves have been better. So stay away from me!"

He walked back a few steps, making soothing gestures.

Rita raised her gun and aimed it at the helicopter. She had forgotten to release the safety catch and had to take it down again. Nicky ran to her again. Now she was getting really angry. "The thing's on now and you stay where you are!"

Someone was screaming hysterically. Anna had found them. She came running to Nicky and tried to drag him back under the palms.

"She wants to shoot the helicopter!" he cried.

"Then let her! Better than she shoots you! She's crazy! I've realized that when she was talking to that – to that thing in the house! Come!"

Rita let her gun sink and shook her head. "Guys, relax and get out of my way. All will be fine."

She turned and aimed at the helicopter again. It was making a quick evasive maneuver and sped towards the lagoon with its nose down. Rita started firing. Later she estimated that less than half of the 500 rounds she'd fired had found their target. Still some seemed to have hit the right spot. One of the rotor blades flew off like a huge boomerang and the helicopter went into a frightening wobble. Rita stared wide-eyed at the helpless machine till it crashed into the trees somewhere between the bungalow and the lagoon. The rotor kept running for a while and chopped down some trees, then another piece of metal flew through the air and the show was over.

Anna burst into loud sobbing.

The first thing Jonathan saw was his destroyed ship. The Monster was precariously perched on the edge of the reef about a hundred yards away from the breach.

"Whoa!" the man at the wheel said. "What's been happenin' here?"

Jonathan didn't answer. He positioned himself at the bow and led the skipper through the reef and past the shifting sandbanks in the lagoon. When they were gliding the last few meters to the jetty he noticed a new clearing in the middle of the fronds. Two rotor blades were sticking up from among the trees. His mouth ran dry. He moored the boat in a trance.

"Hey, mister!" he heard from behind. He briefly raised his hand without turning and walked to the island.

The crash site was just a few hundred meters away. The helicopter was lying on its side and Jonathan climbed between the bent and snapped palms onto the machine. The sliding door stood open. For a moment he was hanging with both hands at the frame of the door, then let himself drop into the cabin. He looked around – no bodies. One of the panels in the cockpit told him the cells were more than seventy percent charged. Jonathan briefly searched for bloodstains then climbed out again and walked to the bungalow. The sight of the destroyed house was a shock. He'd had no idea.

He carefully stepped into the ruin and looked around. Everything was wet and slimy. He shouted Rita's times but didn't get an answer. He deduced as coldly as possible that if she were lying under the rubble she'd be dead anyway. So look for her somewhere else.

He went to the nearest beach on the western side, facing the ocean. It was empty.

Then he crossed the island again and went back to the inner lagoon. Under normal circumstances this was a peaceful walk under a canopy of big green palm leaves, accompanied by a first-rate bird concert. The path led across a circular clearing with white sand glittering in the sun. Jonathan stopped for a moment and squinted in the bright light.

Rita appeared under the palms opposite him, looking like a creature of the island. They were staring at each other, Jonathan smiling broadly, Rita with an incredulous expression on her face. She seemed to strongly advise him not to be real.

"Hey babe!" he called.

She turned and disappeared among the trees.

"Oh – kay," Jonathan murmured to himself. He tracked her like an animal, keeping a proper distance, till they arrived at the inner lagoon. He looked down the long curved tongue of land. Rita was hurriedly walking away two or three hundred meters in front of him. Farther away he saw Anna and Nicky standing next to a sunshade.

Rita turned for a moment, then went to the right, back under the trees.

This was getting silly. Jonathan sat down at the water and took off his shoes and T-shirt. He felt totally calm. She was alive, everything else would sort itself out.

In the corner of his eye he saw the two figures coming closer. A few minutes later Nicky was standing beside him; Anna had stopped at a safe distance.

"Hi! How are you?" Jonathan said. "I'm glad you all survived."

The conversation that followed was too ridiculous. Jonathan broke it off after a few sentences. "I'm sorry but I can't listen to that."

Rita appeared behind them.

"Get lost," she told Anna and Nicky.

Jonathan raised his eyebrows.

"*Please*? What now?" Nicky said. "Are we getting away with that boat?"

Rita made a sign with her head, pointing down the beach, and gave him a look that would've made a platoon of marines cringe.

Once they were alone Rita placed herself before Jonathan, who was still sitting in the sand with his arms around his legs.

"I thought I heard someone call my name," she said. "But I wasn't sure. I saw the boat at the jetty just now."

"OK. Wanna tell me what's up? My last days haven't been exactly easy, just as yours probably, but I expected our reunion to be a little different."

"Do I really have to explain?"

"Yeah, I guess so."

Rita sighed. Then she recounted how he'd stood before her, in some office in Berlin, and had told her about the other woman. Her account was delivered in a flat, unemotional voice. Alone under the palms and knowing he was back she'd cried a few minutes, then sworn to herself he wouldn't get to see a single tear.

When she was finished he shrugged his shoulders. "You know it's all bullshit, right? That talk's never happened, we were nothing but two marionettes. I got to see a happy, banal message from you, while you've been listening to that confession. Nothing of it was real. You think I had nothing better to do than looking for a new girlfriend? That fake must've been really good! Our last talk by the way *was* real, you've just taken it the wrong way."

He told her about the kidnapping and about Lydia and the explosions at the empty factory.

"You should see her, she's in an ugly state. I don't think she's noticed when I said goodbye."

Rita nodded reluctantly. "If you say so. That's all a bit sudden, I've to digest that. That talk we had – or didn't have – was so damn real! I *knew* something was wrong but I didn't doubt for a second that it was you on that layer. You just served me that the iciest possible way! I was devastated."

"I know exactly what you mean. No idea how we deal with that in the future. We'll reach the same degree of perfection on our own someday."

This wasn't the topic Rita had wanted to talk about, but a Jonathan pleading with her to believe him would really have worried her.

Then, despite herself, she started to cry again.

Pierre Detoile was visiting Lydia in the hospital when he was back in Berlin. She'd been transferred to the Klinik für Neurologie of the Charité, a building that had survived the bomb frenzy.

Part of his time Pierre spent with Kip Frantzen in the cluster factory. The team there had been rapidly growing, among them were Atherton and Davids from Morton's former group at the institute – their way of making atonement. Kip was submerged in his work and didn't seem to miss his former comfortable life at all.

Pierre had to look after an even allocation of resources, no one should be able to say CEG was getting preferential treatment. He was talking a lot with the group at the UN. Sarah Masters and company had finally started to play the role Anton Medvedkov had envisaged for them.

As if that wasn't enough, Genet had appointed Pierre as the interim head of the secret service. She'd suspended Harrington, at least until further investigation into his role in the breach of security protocols in London.

Lydia was slowly getting better. The doctors reassured Pierre she'd completely recover. Neuro-repair was one of the biggest advances in medicine of the last decades.

She kept asking for Jonathan and Pierre told her he was back on his island. She said that in the nights she was plagued by a wild mix of images with long dark corridors, attacking helicopters and explosions she was trying to run away from, but the corridors always ended in dead-ends and the helicopters were somehow sucking her from the ground and threatening to chop her up with their rotors.

Most of the time Pierre found himself explaining the chaos of the hours of terror. Even he had difficulties in understanding what had happened during this short period of time.

Lydia's questions were helping him to get a clearer picture himself. He'd noticed that a lot of what the construct had done wasn't logical. That outburst of violence before the end seemed to have been pure anger. On the other hand everything had obviously been planned to a T. It looked like a strange mix of paranoia, childishness and a resourcefulness without limits.

For the moment Pierre didn't want to become Harrington's permanent successor, he was more thinking about founding and maybe heading a new government department. He wanted to assemble a group with one goal – to prevent a disaster like that from happening again.

He pressed Lydia's hand before he left. She was following him with a heart-rending gaze.

"I'll be back soon," he said.

Jonathan had made sure the boat was still moored to the jetty. He'd talk to the skipper later.

He and Rita were walking on the beach. Side by side but no one thought of holding hands or something. Jonathan had kept her embraced until she'd stopped crying, then she'd moved away from him and got up.

They were getting closer to the destroyed house. Finally Jonathan started asking questions – about the bungalow, the Monster, the two helicopters – and she began to talk.

At one point Jonathan broke into loud laughter. "You shot that thing down? With a gun?"

Rita gave a shrug. "No big deal. There are parts of the rotor lying around somewhere among the trees. Just in case you should be tripping over them."

"So the Navy will probably pay us a visit soon. Maybe I'll get the wreck shipped to Rarotonga myself, as a small thank you for their trouble. In case you've been wondering – the crew's on a special leave. The copter has just dumped them on another island."

She nodded. Then she stopped and looked at him from the side. "Hey."

He stopped too. "Yeah. Ten days – incredible, isn't it?"

They were standing in the shadow of the palms. Jonathan could see the remains of the yacht and the house behind the trees.

Rita slipped her arms under his and looked him in the eyes.

"Those ten days somehow equal a whole life," she said. "We need some time. Just you and me. Can you manage that?"

Mickey Andrews was on a stage together with the CEO of Mason Rocket, listening to an official version of the events. Not his kind of gig.

"We are – despite the terrible consequences – in a way proud of the fact that our metacluster has obviously been seen as the most powerful site on earth," the CEO said. He smiled at the journalists. "We will of course not be deterred by this and will keep achieving technological progress of the highest order."

Mickey tried not to roll his eyes.

When it was his turn, he said that this threat was difficult to judge.

"A hyper's by now so powerful, guys, really crazy things can happen in there. I've been there, seen it. But we cannae control it, that's the problem. Maybe we'll learn, then this might look a wee different."

Some of the faces before him were smiling. He didn't think he'd said something funny.

Two days before he'd had another talk with Lorentz.

Mickey had again used his private and unblemished cluster to establish a link to Berlin. All the intermediate clusters were nothing but empty hardware and did exactly what he told them. He needed fifteen minutes, then he reached the cluster room of the secret service and met an utterly bewildered Ben Evans, who thought the construct had woken up again.

Jonathan was still in Berlin and came running down to the basement when he heard who was waiting for him. The link was transmitting Mickey's face on the small panel they'd been using all the time.

Mickey greeted him with a lopsided grin.

"How're your Q's?" he said. "Now they're ruling the world?"

"They're resting," said Jonathan. "We'll keep them here for the moment, who knows what's still to come. How are you?"

"Er – me? Funny question, never knew what to say to that. But – OK, I reck'n. Bit short o'breath but I've never been into sports anyhow."

Jonathan nodded. "We wouldn't've managed without you. I've already mentioned your name about a hundred times – every time someone's been asking how we did it. What are your plans?"

Mickey gave a shrug. "Dunno. Build up the hyper from scratch? But that's been getting me thinking, I've to say." His face looked for a moment as if something was causing him pain. "You know – we not only have to prevent that, in the future I mean. There's more." He was briefly really looking at Jonathan. "We can talk, can't we? I mean not like all those idiots who're now only wanting to hear AI's evil, evil, evil, and before they haven't listened to a word you've said. What's not letting me sleep, I mean so to speak, I can always sleep, don't know why, but what's really giving me thoughts, you know, is what we've finished off there, you know? I mean forget all the psychopath shit

327

with bombs and stuff – in that hyper a treasure's been hidin'! You know? We have to make use of that someday. I dunno, but someday. Don't you think so? What are you saying? Don't worry, I mean I won't go all William Morton on you now but this *has* to drive you crazy, right? I mean what we've been snuffin' there."

Jonathan raised his eyebrows. To him that was the most critical point of all, and at the same time the one he hadn't talked about with anyone yet. He knew there was no middle ground, otherwise the misunderstandings would begin again.

"I know exactly what you mean. I thought I was long past all this, but when I saw what the construct could do it was coming back to me, I must say. It's just – I don't see a way how to use this without producing the next disaster."

"You really think that? OK, you've been thinking about that a lot longer than I, but we both know in the long run we cannae *not* do this. Right? Someday it'll come. I mean – just how? When? I dunno."

"Exactly! That's the thing! Please keep thinking about this, I need someone like you. I mean, come on – Mason Rocket's great, but there's more to the world than the next generation of booster engines."

"Oh yeah. Aye." Mickey's face had that pained expression again. "I really like doing my stuff here but it kind of flashed across me mind there might be more. Hey, no idea, we'll see, right?"

"Hey, no problem, man, I'm away for a few days anyway, but then we should talk again."

Mickey looked at him – somehow wary, as if he was done with all the niceties.

Jonathan wondered how it would be to work with him. Whatever, he wouldn't be around that much.

"Think about it, OK?" he said. "See you. And – thanks!"

"Hey man, stuff that!"

Jonathan and Rita were lying in the pavilion on top of the small hill next to their ruined house. The skipper had taken Anna and Nicky to Rarotonga. In two days they'd be leaving too, but until then they had the island to themselves. Their life was closer to the original plan than ever. They had to stay outside the whole time.

Jonathan was planning to rebuild their house as simple as possible. Less technology, no machines. He was considering to take no more than two or three units to the island. Maybe one core. They'd be closing doors and windows by hand. They'd cook and maybe they'd even clean.

They were still trying to make sense of the events. Jonathan was talking more than ever, Rita had the impression he wanted to share every thought with her.

Without the Sky it was almost impossible to get a clear picture, but they knew that at least five million people had died. Most of them during two hours, *The Terrible Two*.

There was chaos, a certain amount of upheaval and plundering, but there was also a lot of team spirit. The people had to clean up with very little help from machines, and that was forging a new bond among them. The idea of giving up the Sky for good was getting a lot of support.

In Berlin Jonathan had warned everybody to switch it back on too soon, even when the clusters should be working again (actually he had forbidden Genet and everyone else who was listening to do it). He feared descendants of the construct could still be hiding somewhere and without the Sky that threat was far more manageable.

The public got told half-truths. Genet had convinced Rosen to keep the exact origin of the AI in the dark and to share the responsibility. There were rumors everything had started in Berlin, even Morton's name popped up repeatedly, but Genet was passing over every question with masterly indifference.

What would they do with Morton once he was back on earth? If they'd indict him there'd be no half-truths left. Besides, there was nothing in the law that actually fitted his crime. He'd fled from his house arrest – apart from that he hadn't violated a single rule written down somewhere.

Genet and Pierre Detoile were still searching for a solution.

"If he didn't have family I'd seriously consider losing him in orbit, by mistake of course," Genet said. "At the minimum we have to guarantee he won't cause a mess again and that he's keeping his mouth shut. I strongly suspect that he, despite everything, is still proud of himself. What's more, he certainly has the most thrilling story of all to tell and we know what the media will do if they get wind of this."

She gave Pierre a somewhat sheepish look. "Do you think Lorentz might have an idea? When will you be talking to him?"

Pierre looked surprised. "Er – don't know. He wanted to be back in a few days."

"Hmm, maybe this is something we'll have to solve on our own."

They postponed the decision.

"I think people aren't realizing how unlikely that victory was," Jonathan said to Rita. He had his arm wrapped around her and was looking into the night sky. "Our enemy's been compromised. Some of the traits Morton's been giving it grew out of all proportion. The creative elements have backfired and blown up things that had only been meant to be an addition.

"But if someone's tailoring such a thing to be *really* effective, I mean not prone to psychopathic fits, then we won't stand a chance. We'd never get one step ahead of it and it'd never get involved in silly games. In a way this was an idiot with a stellar IQ. My worst nightmare is someone who's doing this with truly evil intentions. Someone thinking they can control it and use it for their own purposes.

"The next thing's the platform. Once we have something like that running on Q's, our last advantage is gone. I think I know what my job will be for the future."

"Catch fish?"

He pulled her nearer and kissed her. "Yeah. And in between I'll do the smart-ass again and tell the world they have to steer clear of everything that smells remotely of intelligent and creative. I think they'll listen, at least for a while."

"Of course they will," said Rita. "But just between the two of us – what's the use? All these modules and engines or whatever you call them are still there, somewhere, or there are plenty of people around who know how to build them again. So, one beautiful day some nutter will screw them together in the right fashion. Back to square one, right?"

"Right. Therefore we need an early warning system, tsunami-style. I don't know how but I've several ideas. I'll ramp up the team in San Jose. I'll steal that crazy Scot from Mason Rocket, and maybe Pierre Detoile. You'll like him. Don't know what his plans are though. And I'll keep pestering Genet and Rosen, of course."

Rita nodded. "Is there a place for … for us in all this? Otherwise I'll have to visit my old chief and convince him to take me back. Shouldn't be too hard."

Jonathan grinned. "Hey, don't worry! I'm planning on shamelessly using you. *And* your parents! I see informal meetings in a pleasant atmosphere. We have to think about the parts of the world we had to break in when they didn't open the Sky for us. Not exactly our new best friends. I think no one's better suited to get them around a table than your folks."

She hesitated. "Yeah. That could work. – And us?" she repeated

Jonathan gave a shrug. "Dunno. Works, doesn't it?"

Rita punched him in the side.

"Ouch!" She'd hit the right spot, his broken ribs.

"Just to keep you informed, mister – I want kids, rather sooner than later. Can one still do that? What do you think?" She smiled at him as if she was actually expecting an answer.

He looked at her. "They better be *really* clever. Otherwise their prospects are ... bleak."

"Oh, they will be clever!" Rita's eyes were gleaming.

Suddenly nothing else mattered.

EPILOGUE

The building was mentioned in every guide to Boston. The head of the Institute of Mathematics had given the architect the blueprint for the facade – one of the countless ways of folding up nine dimensions into the usual three. The panes of glass had been shaped and arranged in a way that resembled one of the Calabi-Yau spaces. People were stopping in front of the building and walking back and forth with smiles on their faces, playing with the reflections.

From inside the futuristic structure you were looking down at magnificent old maples. It was late September and the foliage in New England displayed its whole range of fiery colors. The young man sitting on some middle floor of the famous building couldn't care less. He tried to figure out how to build information-processing structures that would stay controllable no matter how much productivity you gave them, even approaching the limit of infinite productivity. The proofs he was using were complicated and only a few people would understand them. Not unusual at this level, but the consequences were far-reaching. If his reasoning was sound the ban on all higher AI research, which had been in place for over twenty years now, would have to fall. At least this was the only logical answer in his eyes.

Mickey Andrews, his PhD-advisor and a legendary figure on campus, was constantly looking for flaws in his argumentation. Phil Lorentz liked him a lot, but the aging brain of a man over fifty had almost no chance against the mind of a brilliant twenty-two-year-old.